Shameless

USA TODAY BESTSELLING AUTHOR
LEX MARTIN

Copy editing by RJ Locksley

Proofreading by Amanda Maria

Cover by Najla Qamber Designs

Model Photographs by Perrywinkle Photography

February 2018 paperback edition

ISBN 978-0-9975139-1-2

ABOUT THE NOVEL

Brady...

What the hell do I know about raising a baby? Nothing. Not a goddamn thing.

Yet here I am, the sole guardian of my niece. I'd be lost if it weren't for Katherine, the beautiful girl who seems to have all the answers. Katherine, who's slowly finding her way into my cynical heart.

I keep reminding myself that I can't fall for someone when we don't have a future. But telling myself this lie and believing it are two different things.

Katherine...

When Brady shows up on a Harley, looking like an avenging angel—six feet, three inches of chiseled muscle, eyes the color of wild sage, and sun-kissed skin emblazoned with tattoos—I'm not sure if I should fall at his feet or run like hell. Because if I tell him what happened the night his family died, he might hate me.

What I don't count on are the nights we spend together

trying to forget the heartache that brought us here. I promise him it won't mean anything, that I won't fall in love.

I shouldn't make promises I can't keep.

To Matt & my little bears

"In that high place in the darkness the two oddly sensitive human atoms held each other tightly and waited."
- Sherwood Anderson

1

BRADY

HER SLENDER HIPS SWAY TO THE HEAVY BEAT OF THE ARCTIC Monkeys pulsing through the speakers as she glides closer.

"Gonna get naked for you," she purrs, her shirt already hanging off her shoulder.

What?

"You only need to open your top and lower your bra." I suppose I shouldn't discourage her.

She licks her lips and unfastens the clip in her hair, sending blond waves tumbling forward. But when she shakes it loose around her shoulders, a wave of industrial-strength perfume hits my nostrils. I try not to wince, but the scent is nauseating.

Focus, Brady. Hot girl taking off her clothes. Eyes on the prize.

I glance around, wondering how long it will take for the guys to notice she's stripping out of her clothes like a pole dancer on a Saturday night. This girl is hot, so it's not like I'm complaining.

Might as well go out with a bang.

Her fingers start the slow descent as she unbuttons her silky shirt, but then pause between her cleavage. "Kim Kardashian has the same outfit. She wore it the other day when she and Kanye dropped off little North West at..."

LEX MARTIN

Annnd right there, my interest plummets.

Of course, my last night working here and I get Malibu Barbie. I'm half-wondering when she's going to break out her phone for a selfie.

Yanking on my gloves, I watch her unstrap the twins as my irritation builds.

"We can pull the curtain closed." I motion behind her to the partition I should've grabbed on the way in, but she shrugs with a grin and drops her bra.

Okay then.

When she slides into my chair, I lower the back so she's reclining. I have to hold back a laugh when she thrusts her chest out.

I don't know why I think this is funny.

Because you're an asshole.

"So, Chastity—" Yes, her name is Chastity. It's always the ones with the wholesome names. "You want these piercings horizontal, correct?" I make the motion across in case she doesn't know which direction I'm talking about.

She nods and bats her eyelashes at me before she grabs her tits and pinches her nipples. "Do you want me to hold them up for you?"

I almost choke on my gum. "No, that's okay."

A flash of disappointment crosses her face, and I force a smile to counteract my fuck-off vibe. I don't mean to be a jerk. I'm just exhausted. Working seventy hours a week landscaping while I moonlight here at the tattoo parlor will do that. So I try to reassure her. "You have ideal breasts for piercings." Her eyes brighten, and she smiles back.

It's true, though. Her nipples are high and distended. Maybe a tad long if you ask me. Not like *National Geographic* tits or anything. Just a little pouty.

Like someone's been sucking on them.

My dick finally rears up like someone rang a dinner bell.

But then Chastity opens her mouth. "My sorority sisters dared me to do this. I couldn't say no."

That's a terrible reason. I just nod. It's none of my business. But it's enough to make my cock tap out. He should be interested. I haven't been with anyone in a while, not even Gwen. But seeing Gwen takes time, time I don't have.

"Just relax. I'm marking the skin first," I explain.

Chastity takes a deep breath, but when I touch her breast, she lets out a little moan.

I try not to laugh. This girl should *not* be turned on right now. Getting her tits pierced is going to hurt.

After marking a dot on both sides of one nipple, I repeat the process with the other, the whole time ignoring the flush of red down her neck.

I'm a dick for being amused by her obvious state of arousal. But she keeps opening her mouth. "I love that photo. Is she your girlfriend?" She motions toward the front of the tattoo parlor, where a larger-than-life image of me wrapped around a half-naked woman hangs on the wall.

Jesus Christ. I hate that pic. How a favor for a friend in art school last winter became an image plastered all over Boston to advertise the Wicked Tattoo Parlor, I'll never know.

"No, that's not my girlfriend."

The redhead in the photo, Dani, and I were always *just friends*. Someone I definitely hoped would be more than a friend, but things didn't work out that way. In fact, the douchebag she's engaged to was here last week getting a tat of Little Red Riding Hood—for her, no doubt. *Fucker*.

But the experience taught me something important. That unless you find the perfect girl, putting yourself out there is pointless.

My foul mood must be rubbing off, because by the time I

aim the 14-gauge at nipple number two, Chastity is no longer interested in talking. Told you. Nipples and needles are no joke. But I have to admit I'm at a loss when the tears start.

If there's one thing I can't handle, it's a crying woman.

I pat her shoulder. "You took it like a champ."

When I'm done explaining how to care for the piercings, I motion toward her. "Do you have any questions?"

"Yeah, I do." She licks her lower lip that's stopped quivering. "Think you might have time later for a drink?"

Bad idea.

"Wish I could take you up on that, but my schedule's pretty packed." Not a lie. "Maybe some other time." *Or maybe not.*

Be nice, man.

I force myself to smile. "If you decide to get a tattoo, I'll draw something for you." Piercing helps pay the bills. Tats are what I love.

Her eyes brighten, and she nods.

I turn away before I let something rude slip. Because when I'm this exhausted, I have one mode—asshole—and I don't want to treat this girl that way. Or any girl for that matter.

That's why I'm better off alone right now. Flying solo seems to be the only thing I have time for.

In between clients, I text my father an update on the Jackson property. He responds immediately. *Great job, son! Can't thank you enough.*

No thanks needed, my thumbs tap out.

I stare at the screen, hoping we're done and he doesn't launch into another round of apologies, apologies that aren't his to make.

Part of me feels guilty about not wanting to run my father's landscaping company. But this was supposed to be temporary. Just until my brother Cal returned and he took over for my dad, who had a heart attack.

My jaw tightens.

Cal's down in Texas, kicking back with his new wife—the one he eloped with after knowing two weeks—and their baby. Ironically, he was down there taking courses I paid for so he could return to Boston and take over our family's company, but he got sidetracked when some chick tripped over his dick. How else do you have a baby nine months later?

I should be over it by now. Cal's kid is a year old, and the writing is on the wall. He's not coming back. But my parents keep holding out hope. They're afraid he'll get bored down there like he gets bored with everything. And in the time they've held off selling their business and retiring, they lost a great offer on the company and my father's health has gone to shit.

As the night wears on, every time I flip on the ink gun, that staccato buzz heightens my awareness of the clock and builds a slow dread in my chest. It should be a relief to have one less thing to worry about. Except this is the part I love. This is the part that actually feels right when I'm not in such a piss-poor mood.

But I can't keep doing this to myself. Running half a dozen crews on my father's landscaping business and tattooing all night will put me in an early grave.

Chugging down some coffee, I nod toward the dude in my chair. He points to his bicep where I've already transferred a drawing of a pair of oars. "I'm rowing for BU in the fall," he says proudly.

Mustering a smile, I tell him congrats and then focus on the lines I etch into his skin.

We get a lot of college kids in here. I used to enjoy hearing their stories and understanding the meaning behind the symbols I inked on them. Hell, I used to be one of those BU kids.

But now it's tough to stomach the optimism in their voices. It's a reminder that I was a dumb asshole for getting my master's in art. For not going to law school. For not studying something that could've bailed my parents out of their financial crisis.

For thinking like a dreamer.

After my last client, I remove the key from my key ring and hand it to Rudy.

"You always got a place here, man," he says, leaning forward for a bro-hug.

I grumble a thanks and a farewell, knowing full well my spot will be filled by the end of next week, as will the opportunity to partner with him on the new shop.

The whole drive home, it eats at me, missing these opportunities. But there's no one to complain to, and even if there was, there's nothing to say. I've made my decision.

The sound of my keys echoes in the dark apartment. I toe off my work boots, caking the floor in mud, but my roommate is probably over at his girlfriend's, so he's not here to bitch about it.

I'm yawning and so tired, I'm a little nauseous. As I head for my bedroom, I reach for my phone in the back pocket of my jeans to set an alarm. Cal's message flashes on the screen: *I need to talk to you. I have some news. Stop being a cock.*

My temple throbs.

It's two a.m. here, which means it's only one in Texas. He might be up. But can I really deal with talking about this shit right now? I've been up since five this morning when I hauled my ass to the Jackson property.

Scrubbing my face with my palms, I groan.

I'll say something I'll regret if I have that conversation tonight. I'll call him tomorrow or next week or whatever.

With labored movement, I strip out of my jeans and t-shirt, and my muscles scream in protest when I stretch out in bed.

It feels like I've barely fallen asleep when the phone rings. I fumble for it and answer in a daze. The voice sounds a million miles away.

I shake my head and sit up.

"Brady? Did you h... h... hear me?" My mother's voice warbles over the phone in between sobs.

I blink several times. My heart thunders in my chest, tripping over itself in an erratic beat. Rubbing my eyes hard, I try to wake up. She says it again.

What? No, that's just...

A numbness spreads through all of my limbs.

My stomach clenches as she wails the words that gut me. "C... C... Cal is dead. Oh, my God. Cal is dead!"

As I heave into the trash, that conversation with my mom races through my mind. Because when I told her to hang tight, that I was coming to see her, she drop-kicked me with something else. That upon learning the news that my brother, his wife Melissa, and their baby Isabella died in a freak car accident, my father had a heart attack and is in intensive care.

I close my eyes and force myself to breathe through the fear of losing my father. Through the regret and guilt of how I treated Cal. Through the shame.

The moment registers like the event horizon of a black hole, yawning before me like an abyss.

"Sir, are you okay?" a nurse asks me as I heave into the trash for the third time.

I wave her off, shivering when a cold sweat breaks out along my back and neck.

Cal is gone. My baby brother is dead.

Why didn't I call him back? Why couldn't I get my head out of my ass? I don't know the details of the accident, but I can't help but wonder if anything would've been different if I'd just picked up the goddamn phone. Would it have saved them somehow? Could it have kept them home?

A chilling thought grips me. *Was the accident my fault?*

The loss of my brother reverberates through me until dry heaves upend my stomach and make me contemplate curling up on the filthy hospital floor.

By the time I reach the hospital room I'm pretty sure I've puked out my spleen, but the sight of my unconscious father with tubes sticking out of him makes me ignore my own misery.

My mother turns to me. Behind those puffy eyes, I see a flicker of relief. She's hovering over my father, who is pale and hauntingly still. In three long strides I'm by her side, and I tuck her against me where she cries quietly.

"I'm here, Mom," I whisper into her hair.

I inhale her rose perfume, which reminds me of family dinners and laughter and love. Closing my eyes, all I can see is my little brother's face. That grin he'd give me when he broke my stuff. His light blue eyes that crinkled when he laughed. That mess of sandy brown hair he could never tame.

And God, the weight of not being there for him is crushing.

I grip my mom tighter. Her tears soak my shirt, and I hold her until her sobs still to whimpers.

Once she's calmed down, we sit by my father's bed, and she wraps an icy hand around mine. Her lower lip quivers as she smiles sadly toward the bed. "I... I can't leave him. The doctor wants to do the surgery as soon as possible, tomorrow or the day after. I can't leave your father..." She starts to sob again. "But I want to be there for my baby." She always thinks of Cal as her baby even though he's twenty-five.

Was twenty-five.

Goddamn it.

"Mom, what needs to be done in Texas?" I ask gently.

She shudders, and I wrap an arm around her. "I don't even

know," she whispers. The tears start again, and I realize there are funerals to plan. Belongings to pack up. Legal issues to address.

"Did Melissa have any family?"

My mom hiccups. "Probably. They should get the farm. It was... it was her father's before he passed. Or her uncle's or something. Melissa's friend is there now. Kate or Katherine or maybe it's Sandra? But she's watching the property."

Nodding, I rub her shoulder and do what I've always done. "I'll take care of everything in Texas. You just look after Dad. I'll be back as soon as I can."

2

KATHERINE

I'M BOLTING OUT OF BED WHEN I HEAR ISABELLA'S WHIMPERS ON the monitor. She's been doing this every morning, waking up in tears, crying for her parents. *Pobrecita.* I try to console her, but half the time I end up crying too.

I nestle her in a fleece blanket before settling in the rocker by the window. Her little body trembles as she calls out for her momma, and my heart breaks for the millionth time this week. Tilting my head back, I blink quickly and try to hold back my own waterworks.

Keep it together, Katherine. Just a little longer. He'll be here soon.

My eyes are still swollen and itchy from last night. Seriously, how can I cry any more?

Easy. Lose two of your best friends in one night. That's how.

Just like that, my face is wet, and I give in, but this morning they're silent tears as I rock the baby and watch the sunrise on the horizon. At least we celebrated her first birthday a few weeks ago. At least she had that with her parents.

Eventually, the sound of Sampson banging on the barn tells me it's time to get my rear in gear. Sleep or no sleep, I have to get the chores done.

The banging gets louder.

Stupid horse. I'm so freaking furious at him, I want to ship him off to a glue factory.

Yes, the animal lover in me is horrified at the thought, but the rest of me, the part of me seething with rage at how everything happened, isn't surprised such a morbid idea crosses my mind.

I pause to take a few deep breaths, hoping all that yoga-will-center-you crap helps me feel a little less unhinged.

After changing Isabella's diaper and dressing her in a cozy bodysuit, I feed her and strap her to my chest. Together we make the rounds on the property. As I trudge along, I bury my nose in her soft hair, and she nuzzles back, her chest heaving a small sigh.

But when we reach the chicken coop, she lifts her head, and her eyes brighten. She loves these little guys. A moment later, the girls come running, their clucks a musical chorus in an otherwise quiet morning. Isabella claps her pudgy hands, about as ecstatic to see our feathered friends as they are to see us.

"There's my girl," I whisper, relieved to see her smile, however briefly.

A few minutes later, I set her up in a makeshift playpen in the shade just outside the barn so she doesn't breathe the dust when I clean the coop or Sampson's stall.

All day, I find myself looking for them, expecting to see Mel and Cal come around the corner laughing. Or catch them kissing when they think they're alone.

I smile. They were so good together!

When Eric and I broke up, Mel insisted that I come for a visit. "Give yourself a break from the campaign trail. It's simpler here. Uncomplicated," she told me over the phone.

The day I showed up at the farm, at loss for what to do, Mel opened the door, gave me a hug and told me I could crash here as long as I wanted. Mel was always like that, the big sister I never knew I needed.

My chest tightens as the memories underscore the bleak reality that she's gone.

Shaking my head, I ignore the sting of tears as I brush out Sampson's dark mane. I think back to my list and let the chores ground me. I have too much to do to lose it now. Way too much.

By noon, I'm dripping with sweat. I've lost weight since I've been here, but nothing like the last few days. By evening, I'm usually so tired, I'm numb.

But numb is better, because when I'm numb, this doesn't hurt so much.

When the animals are fed and watered and the stable and coop are clean, I lumber into the house and put the baby down for a nap, one I could use myself. But it's no use because I can't sleep.

I'm cleaning the kitchen when my flip phone rings from the back pocket of my jeans. It's Tori, my younger sister.

But when I answer, my dad's gruff voice booms in my ear. "Katherine." Ugh. Not who I want to talk to right now. I love my dad, I really do, but he can be so overprotective. Like right now. "So you're going to stay there with a strange man?"

"Daddy, I can't exactly pack up and leave."

"Look, I loved Melissa too. This accident was a terrible, terrible thing. But this—you living there with a stranger—this isn't right. You don't know him at all. What if he's crazy or some kind of pervert?"

I roll my eyes. "He's Cal's brother. I promise he sounds perfectly sane. Besides, that's all the more reason to stay and watch Bella to be sure she's okay. I owe it to Mel. I don't know if he'll want me around, but I'd like to help get the baby gets settled before I worry about myself. I promise I'll text Tori every day so you can rest assured the guy didn't go all Hannibal Lecter on me."

"*Chingao*. That's not funny, *mija*."

He must be pissed if he's cursing in Spanish. I want to laugh because he's being absurd. Like hell I'm leaving Bella. That's not happening until I'm confident she'll be okay with her uncle. Besides, I heard enough about Brady from Cal to know he's not a lunatic. A little overbearing, perhaps, but not a psycho. *At least I'm used to dealing with overbearing.*

As I listen to my dad list the reasons why staying here is a bad idea, I fight the temptation to ask if he needs money. Usually my sister lets me know if things get bad at home so I can sneak her some funds, but I'm worried she hasn't given me the heads up because I've been so upset about Mel and Cal. My parents work non-stop, but minimum wage jobs don't get bills paid if you're sick or your car breaks down or if there's some other kind of emergency.

But my father is a proud person, and a man deserves to have dignity, so I bite my tongue, which proves difficult when he asks about my ex.

"Maybe you can still work things out," he wonders aloud.

"I know you mean well, but I can't go there, okay?" I realize he sees Eric as a good provider, someone who would look after me. *If only he knew.*

It pains me not to tell my parents why I gave up that prestigious job. As the first person in my family to attend college, I know they had so many hopes pinned on me, and I can't help but feel I've let them down. I wish I could tell them the reason so they'd understand why I've been distant since I came to the farm, but it would crush them. Like it crushed me.

I don't know how long I stand there after the phone call. Finally, I grab a sponge to wipe the kitchen counters and force myself back into action.

Mel's words echo in my head. *It's uncomplicated here. Simpler.*

A hollow laugh escapes me. Uncomplicated? Nothing about this is uncomplicated. Cal and Melissa were the sweetest couple on the planet. They took me in when I had nowhere to go, gave me a home, and now they're gone.

And it's all my fault.

What if I hadn't come? What if I had simply headed home to Corpus with my tail between my legs instead of coming here? They'd still be alive.

Tears stream down my face, and I hold back the sob building in my chest. I scrub the counter harder because that's what I do in a crisis. I clean. Organize. Eric would joke it's the Mexican in me. Like that's even funny.

Worse, though? He said he loved that I didn't *look* Hispanic. WTF, right? It took almost a year and a half of dating him to see his true character. What if I had married that man? I shudder. He might be a senator's son, but I know migrant workers with more class.

A little whimper from the baby monitor reminds me that there are worse things than marrying the wrong guy. *How about marrying the right one and then losing everything?*

The sob I've been holding back breaks from my lips, and I quickly cover my mouth to mask the sounds.

It doesn't take a genius to see I'm in over my head. Way over my head. I keep saying everything will be okay when Brady gets here. I only hope that's true.

3
―――――
BRADY

LOGAN AIRPORT IS BLANKETED IN SEVERAL FEET OF SNOW AND soot after a storm blew in the other night. *Boston in November. It'll get worse before it gets better.*

All around me, the Thanksgiving decorations hanging in the terminal stand garish next to the rage and disbelief churning in my heart. I still can't fully wrap my head around what happened that night.

After playing phone tag with the police department, I finally spoke briefly with a deputy who explained that my brother's truck got caught in a low water crossing during a torrential thunderstorm. His vehicle slid down an embankment and flipped over, trapping him and his family in a flooded creek bed.

My vision blurs as I stare out the massive windows.

"Do those directions make sense?" The Southern drawl in my ear snaps me out of my haze, and I readjust the phone against my shoulder. The woman repeats the words, but I can't process what she's saying. It's like I woke up the other morning and nothing in my life makes sense any more.

Taking a deep breath, I try to pay attention. This is the first phone call Katherine and I have had that hasn't been completely garbled with static. I'm lucky to get one bar of signal on my phone here.

I clear my throat. "Can you do me a favor? Can you text me directions to the farm?"

She sighs. "Sure. No problem. See ya soon."

"Yup. Thanks."

I should be nicer to that woman. Katherine, Melissa's friend, has been keeping an eye on the property since we got the news three days ago. I booked the first flight out, but weather delays have bumped my departure twice. Needless to say, sleeping upright on a hard chair for the last few nights at Logan has put me in a peachy mood.

When I step off the plane in Austin five hours later, I take the used Harley FXR for sale across the street from Hertz as a sign. Granted, it needs *a lot* of work, but I know a good thing when I see it. And since I sold my bike six months ago for twice what I paid after making some repairs, I'm sure I'll be able to get my money back if I need to sell this one. Besides, I'd rather ride this than rent a car for God knows how long.

Forty-five minutes and two grand later, she's mine.

Dropping this kind of money on a bike is the most irresponsible thing I've done in ages. But sitting on the worn leather and gripping the handlebars is the only thing that's made me feel I can keep my shit together. I'm hoping a few long rides will help me clear my head and figure out how the hell to handle everything that needs to be done down here. Fortunately, I packed light, and my belongings fit on the rusty luggage rack that's mounted on the back.

Riding with the sun setting along the horizon, with the smell of cedar thick in the air, helps me feel a little more grounded. That is, until I turn down a dirt road and find myself staring at the little farm house. A dirty sign stands off to the side. *Lovelace Farm.*

The house is modest, a white one-story ranch with a wide front porch. In the dusk, it glows, with warm lights shimmering from one window. But the rest of the house is dark, and it's that darkness that gives me chills.

"I'm sorry, brother. You had a beautiful dream." I idle in the driveway while heat burns my eyes. Rolling hills with row after row of small hedges surround the house. A broken swing sways beneath the branches of a giant oak off to the side.

It's so peaceful here. So different from the chaotic streets of Boston. At the same time, though, it's eerie, almost like I can sense my brother. That's my biggest regret. That I didn't visit him. That I didn't take the time to meet his wife and daughter and see their little farm.

That I didn't call him back that night.

I just was so pissed at him for not returning to Boston and helping our parents. But now, it's painfully obvious how wrong I've been. And somehow, I need to make it right.

Pulling closer to the house, I turn off the engine. I'm taking off my crappy helmet when the front door flies open and a girl stalks out. Her long chestnut hair blows in the wind, barely masking the scowl on her pretty face.

"If you're looking for the Lone Star biker bar, it's about a half mile back that way." Her words are twangy, a little like Reese Witherspoon in *Walk the Line*.

She points to the left before she pushes her black-rimmed glasses up her nose. God, she's cute with these big eyes and quirky frown. What does her t-shirt say? I squint, trying to read the words. *Frack Off* is written in big black letters across her t-shirt that peeks out from her hoodie.

When my eyes reach her face, she looks more pissed. "Do me a favor. When you leave, turn that way down the drive or you'll wake the baby." She nods toward the circular drive I just came down before she freezes and cocks her head. The sound of a baby crying breaks the silence.

"Dang it!" She turns on her heel and is halfway through the door when I call out to her.

"Sorry about waking the baby, but I'm looking for Katherine." She stops mid-stride, and I motion toward the house. "Is she here?"

She turns back to me, her eyes widening. "And you are?"

"Brady." I swing my leg over the bike and step closer. "Cal's brother."

Her eyes widen. "I... You..." She shakes her head. "I'm so sorry! Yes, I've been expecting you." Big hazel eyes stare back from behind her glasses, which she pushes up her pert little nose. Did I mention she's cute? Mentally, I slap myself for ogling somebody's babysitter. Clearly, she's helping out Katherine.

"Give me one sec." She darts into the house but leaves the front door wide open. I stand on the porch and kick off the mud from my boots. When she returns, she's holding a chunky little bundle who has one hell of a set of lungs on him. Or her. I can't tell from this angle.

The girl winces, now clearly going deaf from the little wailer howling in her ear, and holds out her hand. "I'm Katherine."

It's my turn to be shocked. Who the hell put a teenager in charge of the farm? She can't be older than eighteen. I look at her hand a second too long because she starts to frown again.

"Sorry." I reach out, surprised that her grasp is firm. "I don't mean to be rude. I'm Brady Shepherd, Cal's brother."

She nods, still frowning. "You don't look anything like him. It caught me off guard. He was an accountant, and you..." Her eyes dart to the Harley behind me. "You're obviously not."

I want to smile. Cal would be amused someone is finally taking him seriously as a number cruncher.

"No, you're right about that. I'm definitely not an accountant."

We stand, staring at each other. She bites her plump bottom lip, and my eyebrows lift. "Can I come in?"

She blows her bangs out of her face. "Yes, of course. Please." She waves me in behind her.

The living room looks worn in but comfortable with a floral couch and an overstuffed recliner. Knick-knacks dot the bookshelf, and the hardwood floors look well traveled but clean. But what catches my attention is how good everything smells. Fresh, like clean laundry and fruit.

She motions toward the couch. "Have a seat. Can I get you something to drink?"

"No, thanks." I feel bad asking her for anything with that screaming baby in her arms.

I sit on the edge of the couch, not wanting to get it dirty. I should've kicked my boots off, but it feels weird to do that in another person's house.

Katherine sits in the recliner near me and coos in her daughter's ear. Finally the little hellraiser calms down.

She glances up at me, looking relieved, and asks, "Do you want to hold her?"

I stare at her.

This is... weird. Why does this girl want me to hold her baby? Shit, she's young to be a mother. "No, you probably don't want me holding her. I have dirt from about two counties on me." I start to shift uncomfortably when she stills.

"You don't want to hold her?" she asks, incredulous.

That's when she turns the baby toward me, and I get a good look at the child for the first time. Familiar blue eyes blink back... and in that instant, my whole world stops, tilts, and comes barreling off its axis.

What the hell? My mouth goes dry.

"Isabella," she says loudly, like I'm hearing-impaired. "Do you want to hold her?"

"Jesus." I press my palms into my eyes. After a moment, I lower my hands and stare at my brother's baby. I open my mouth, only nothing comes out. Finally, I clear my throat. "That's Isabella?"

She looks at me like I'm an idiot and nods.

"Holy shit." I stare at the child in her arms. At her clear-blue eyes. At those wild tufts of sandy-blond hair. At her rosebud lips. "I thought... I thought she had been with her... with her parents in the accident."

Katherine gasps. "No. God, no." She clutches Isabella closer. "I was watching her that night. I *told* you I was taking care of her." She shakes her head. "Why would you think that?"

Frustration ripples through me. "I could barely hear you when I was at the airport." Rubbing my forehead, I think back to what my mother had said... Fuck. What *did* she say? She was hysterical and crying that she hadn't seen Cal in so long and now he was gone. Crying that she'd never really given Melissa a chance. And then she wailed, *We lost the baby.* Those were her exact words.

I run my hand through my hair, choked up by the memory. "I guess... I guess my mom got confused." *And when you spoke to the police, you just asked for details about how the accident happened, not who was in the truck.*

We sit in silence, and after I've calmed down enough to be rational, one thought hurdles through my mind—it looks like my parents might be inheriting a baby.

4

KATHERINE

BRADY DOESN'T SAY A WORD AS HE POURS HIMSELF ANOTHER SHOT of bourbon. I don't blame him. Thinking Bella was with Cal and Mel that night would send me over the edge too.

I cradle the baby in my arms and smooth down her hair, which probably comforts me more than her, but after that conversation, I need to regroup. After a while, my eyes lift to her uncle.

To say that Brady and Cal are complete opposites is an understatement. Despite his penchant for spreadsheets, Cal was a fair-haired hipster with a carefree laugh. He may have been an accountant, but he acted like a SoCal surfer.

Which is nothing like his brother.

Because Brady's a brewing storm of intensity.

Jet black hair. Piercing green eyes. A few day's worth of stubble covering his strong jaw. And muscular, filling out his leather jacket with broad shoulders that cut a dark swath through my vision.

It's hard not to stare.

He's sitting with his elbows pressed against his wide-spread knees, glaring out the window, looking like a *Sons of Anarchy* character about to kick someone's ass.

He towered over me when he walked in, looking at me like I was some kid he caught trespassing. Yeah, he's intimidating.

And ridiculously hot.

I glance down at my t-shirt, wishing I had put myself together more before he arrived. Closing my hoodie to hide my stupid t-shirt, I suddenly feel self-conscious.

He hasn't said much, but based on his expression a few minutes ago, I know I've just rocked his world. I find myself wanting to comfort him. If we were friends, if I'd known him longer than the ten minutes he's been sitting on the couch, I'd hug him. But obviously, that's weird.

I can't believe he thought Isabella was gone. The thought sends chills through me.

As though she can sense my unease, she snuggles closer. I need to feed her, but it feels wrong to leave Brady right now.

After three shots of Jim Beam, he puts down the glass and sighs, running his hands through his messy hair. How is it that men always look better after doing that?

He looks up and clears his throat. "Let's try this again." He holds out his hand. "Hi, I'm Brady. Sorry it took me so long to get down here. That nor'easter really screwed up my flight."

His accent slides over me and holds me captive. It's intense like the rest of him. Cal had a New England accent too, but for some reason, coming from him, it made me laugh. Brady's sends goose bumps down my arms.

Nothing funny there.

Realizing the man is waiting for me to return the gesture, I extend my hand. "Katherine Duran, family friend and glorified babysitter."

His big paw shakes mine. His skin is calloused and rough, a

little like his exterior. But when those green eyes stare back, butterflies riot in my stomach.

When I let go, I feel a little light-headed. *What the heck is that about?*

"So you're… you're Cal's *younger* brother? You're bigger than Cal." Like *way* bigger. He has to be well over six feet tall.

He chuckles. "Yeah, he hated that I was taller. We're only nine months apart, though. I'm actually older. The bastard likes to tell people he's older."

Just as quickly as it came, that smile fades, and he stares off again. I can tell he's realized his mistake, talking about Cal in the present tense.

The pain in his expression makes my chest constrict. Finally, I can't stand it any longer. Picking up the baby, I scoot over to the couch and place my hand on his broad shoulder. My mind fumbles through a number of things I could say to comfort him, but I'm momentarily distracted by how intimate this seems. By how close we are. By how I can smell his aftershave or shampoo or whatever it is that reminds me of the woods after a thunderstorm.

I'm tempted to yank my hand back, but I've already committed, so I take a deep breath. "Brady, it is an honor to meet you. I loved Cal and Mel like they were my very own brother and sister, and I want you to know I'm here to help however I can."

A little gurgle has us both turning to the baby in my lap who is grinning up at him. *Preciosa.*

I nudge him with my elbow. "Aww, she likes you, and if Isabella likes you, I know you must be a great guy because she is a really good judge of character. She hates Mr. Roosevelt, who cheated on his wife, loves Mrs. MacIntyre, who bakes us the best apple pies, and she's suspicious of Ted Mayfield, which I thought was weird until we found out about his great affection for his sheep."

Brady lets out a choking laugh, and I find myself smiling too. I must be nervous because that was some major word vomit. *Really, Katherine? You've met almost every politician in the state of Texas and this biker boy has your panties in a twist?*

I motion toward him. "Why, uh, why don't you clean up in the kitchen, and then I'll let you hold her. Would... would you like that?"

His eyes well with tears, and damn it, mine do too. He swallows and blinks back the emotion. "Yeah, I would. Thanks."

~

The fleet of butterflies somersaults in my stomach again as Brady and I stare at each other. *Ignore the crazy, Katherine. Get your act together.*

Right now, that means helping the hot biker dude hold his baby niece.

I extend my arms as Isabella squirms between us, and his eyes widen. A laugh escapes me. "Brady Shepherd, this isn't rocket science."

"I've never held a baby before." His voice is deep and scratchy, and for some reason, I wonder what it would sound like whispering in my ear.

I clear my throat. "Ever?"

"Ever."

A small laugh escapes me. "How is that possible?"

Brady runs his hands through his hair and shrugs. Good heaven almighty, he's a sight all flustered like this. Here's this big, strong man intimidated by holding a baby.

He's taken off his leather jacket, so he's just wearing a Boston Red Sox t-shirt that stretches across his muscular chest and tapers snugly at his biceps where tattoos blaze down his arms. If he weren't Cal's brother, there is no way I would be handing

Isabella over to this guy. I mean, he seems harmless enough, but his exterior is just so dang intimidating.

I bounce the baby on my lap while he watches with rapt attention. "You're so good with her," he says. "I don't know how she'll ever take to me like she does you."

"I have a younger sister and ten-thousand little cousins, and while most little girls were out playing with dolls, I was changing diapers and getting spit up on. So don't feel bad. I've had a lifetime of being around kids. You'll get the hang of this."

He looks worried, and my heart melts a little. Without thinking, I grab his shoulder to nudge him farther back on the couch, but the contact sends a jolt through me, and I jerk back.

Fortunately, he doesn't seem to notice my bizarre reaction. Ignoring the pounding of my heart, I motion toward him. "Can you... can you scoot back?" I mumble, placing Isabella in his lap once he's in a better position.

His enormous hands immediately wrap around her pudgy waist.

Ignoring my flustered state, I smile. "Brady, I'd like to introduce you to your niece, Isabella."

Bella stares up at him and grins, showing off her shiny new teeth a second before she grabs his face. He laughs. "Hey, little lady. I'm your Uncle Brady."

She giggles, and I swear to God, her cheeks turn pink.

"Aww. She's totally smitten with you." He tickles Isabella, and she giggles again. I should stop right there, but my mouth can't seem to help itself. "Looks like your uncle is a ladies' man." *What did I just say?* "I mean, you have her in the palm of your hand. Like you're good with women."

I glance at his face, and he looks like he's trying not to laugh. *Great.* Way to welcome the guy. Make him think you're hitting on him.

"I'm just gonna go make her dinner." I motion toward the

kitchen as I get up and try to get away without making a complete fool of myself. "Holler if you guys need anything."

I'm almost out of the room when he calls out, "Katherine." Hearing him say my name in that deep, rumbly voice sends goose bumps down my arms.

I turn back, hoping to God he doesn't think I'm some weirdo. "Yeah?"

"Thank you. For everything. I'm sure I don't even know how much you've helped my family."

My stomach twists. *If only he knew.* "You don't have to thank me. Really." And then I scurry into the kitchen.

5

BRADY

ISABELLA'S SKY-BLUE EYES STARE UP AT ME AS SHE SMILES A toothless grin. Hold up. She has two teeth. I run my hand along the curly patch of hair on her head, mesmerized at how soft it is. And she smells... good. Like baby powder and something floral. I don't know why I thought she'd smell like cheese. I guess I always thought kids were kind of stinky.

She keeps patting my face and smiling, which makes it almost impossible to not grin back.

"Hey, baby." Why am I speaking in a little voice? Honestly, I'm not sure, but it feels right so I'm running with it. "I'm sorry it took so long to get down here, but it looks like you were in good hands with your Aunt Katherine."

And when did Katherine become the baby's aunt? No fucking clue, but the baby doesn't seem to care that I'm talking out my ass. She giggles and coos and squishes my cheeks.

"So, Isabella. Is that what everyone calls you? That's kind of a long name for such a little girl. Do you mind if I call you Izzy?"

She claps and giggles some more, so I take that as a sign. "Great. Izzy it is. Can you say my name? Can you say Bray-dee? Bray-dee."

"Bway-Bway! Bway-Bway!"

Something about her saying my name expands my chest. Holy shit. That's amazing.

I'm immediately overwhelmed by the love I have for Izzy. I've never believed in love at first sight, but that's the only way to describe it. Because I know, without a shadow of a doubt, that I'll do whatever I have to do to protect my niece.

The thought gives me pause. Confounds me, really. Because, in a way, isn't this the very thing I mocked my brother for experiencing? Mocked him for having inexplicable emotions for someone he just met?

I've been a fool.

Izzy calls my name again.

"Atta girl." Holding her up, I blow a raspberry on her tummy and enjoy her bubbly peals of laughter before pulling her in for a hug. She squirms in my lap, kicking her chubby legs as though she's trying to stand. I lean back on the couch and hold her arms while she tries to balance on my lap.

Izzy tilts to the left, and I pretend she's going to fall, saying, "Whoa!" dramatically, before scooping her into my arms. She laughs so hard that her nose scrunches up.

She's wearing sweatpants and a pint-sized Spurs t-shirt. I point at her belly and shake my head. "I need to introduce you to a team called the Celtics, and while we're at it"—I motion to the Red Sox logo emblazoned on my chest—"we need to talk baseball. Every girl needs to know about baseball. And don't let some boy tell you a girl can't play because that's BS."

Izzy nods like she understands and then scoots off my lap. I take her hand and hover over her as she waddles toward the kitchen. Her thick socks slide on the hard wood, so I grip her forearms snugly enough she doesn't take a tumble.

When we enter the kitchen, Katherine is standing at the

sink, leaning one arm on the counter. I'm about to say something when she sniffles.

I'm debating whether to ask if she's okay or give her a few minutes of privacy when Izzy babbles something incoherent. Katherine wipes her eyes and spins around, forcing a smile.

"Perfect timing. I have her dinner ready." Her voice is thick with emotion.

I scoop up the baby and hold her on my hip the way Katherine did earlier.

"You okay?" I ask softly, like she's a wounded animal I'm trying not to frighten. She bites her lip and nods, but her eyes are shiny and her face is splotchy. Before I think better of it, I've wrapped her in a hug with my one free arm, and she starts sobbing into my chest. *Oh, shit.* A crying woman is my kryptonite.

"Hey, it's going to be okay." I gently rub her shoulder, hating that she's this upset.

I try not to notice the way she fits against my side, how delicate she feels beneath my hand, but I can't help it. She shifts, and I catch her light floral scent that somehow reminds me of spring.

Izzy squirms in my other arm, and whatever words of comfort I think to say to Katherine escape me when the baby leans into my neck for her own embrace.

This. I'm not prepared for this.

I let Katherine cry for a few minutes until it sounds like she's done. "So you and Mel were close, huh?"

She nods against me and sniffles.

Izzy jerks in my arms, like she's dying to go to Katherine. "Hey, your number one fan wants you to hold her."

Katherine looks up at me, and even though her face is a little puffy and red, her gorgeous hazel eyes are downright captivating.

Clearing my throat, I step back after she takes the baby, who plants a big, wet kiss on her cheek.

"That's sweet, Izzy. Kisses for Aunt Katherine will make her feel better."

Katherine's eyes dart up to mine, like I've surprised her.

"What?" I rub the back of my neck.

She shakes her head and sniffles again, a small smile playing on her lips. "You're a natural with her. I knew you had nothing to worry about."

But as I watch Katherine with Izzy and how gently she holds her and talks to her, I know *she's* the natural. Thank God because I'm fucking clueless.

When Katherine returns to the kitchen, she turns on a little machine, and the sounds of Izzy babbling in her crib fill the room.

"Baby monitor." She points to the speaker. "We have four or five of these. They reach all the way to the barn and into the adjacent field, which is great because then I can feed the animals while she sleeps in the morning. Well, when she sleeps in."

Katherine looks exhausted, like *she* hasn't slept in days. I'm about to tell her that she should go to bed and we can talk in the morning when I realize what she just said.

"Animals? How many are we talking about?" I knew Cal lived on a farm, but until this moment, I hadn't really thought about what that meant.

"Not that many. This isn't a *farm* farm." Something about that statement starts to put me at ease until she shrugs. "We have about a dozen chickens, a horse named Sampson, and two pygmy goats, Stella and Stanley." Then she mumbles a few more words I can't quite make out.

"I'm sorry. What?"

"I *said* we also have a baby raccoon named Bandit and a box of kittens."

"And *why* do we have a box of kittens, a baby raccoon, and"—I tilt my head—"two goats named after characters in *A Streetcar Named Desire*?"

A breathtaking smile spreads on her face.

"Because Mel took in strays. She could never turn away someone in need." Katherine pulls at a loose thread on her t-shirt. Her voice lowers to a whisper. "Which might explain why I've been living here since the end of May."

"Oh. I don't know why I thought you were a neighbor. Do you work for Mel and Cal?"

"Kind of? I guess you could say I'm their live-in nanny. But I also helped them harvest the crops in August and prune their fields this fall."

"The fields?"

"You really have no idea, do you?" She laughs. "Mel owns one of the largest lavender farms in the Texas Hill Country." Her eyes tighten around the corners. "Well, I guess *you* own one of the largest lavender farms."

I run my hand through my hair for the hundredth time today. "We're getting ahead of ourselves. I still need to talk to their attorney and find out if there's a will. I'm here to plan... all of the arrangements this week." The thought turns my stomach sour. "My mom thought the farm should go to someone in Mel's family."

"Their attorney called this afternoon. Said he's in court tomorrow but he's gonna try to call you afterward. As far as family goes, Mel's dad died a few years ago. She didn't have anyone else."

Why does that make me feel worse? I press the palms of my hands into my eyes.

Her soft voice interrupts my impending panic attack. "I'm sorry I cried all over you earlier." I drop my arms and look over at Katherine, who shifts awkwardly before she twists her long hair into one of those messy bun things girls do. Before I can respond, she darts across the kitchen. "I don't know where my manners are. You traveled all day. You must be starving."

A moment later, she has her head in the fridge, and I'm treated to a full-on view of her tight, round ass. Damn. This girl should never wear anything but yoga pants.

"I could make us *migas*." Her head pops out of the refrigerator, and she looks at me expectantly.

My eyes dart up. Hopefully, she doesn't think I'm checking her out.

"Please don't go to any trouble on my account. Wait. What are *migas*?"

Her eyes widen and she starts waving her hands as she explains. "They're eggs scrambled with fried corn tortillas. I also like to toss in some jalepeños, onion and cilantro. Does that sound good?"

"Jesus, yes. That sounds amazing." I laugh, a little in love with her accent and the way she rolls her R's. Now that I look at her, I realize there's something exotic about the shape of her eyes and her golden-caramel skin.

"I love to cook, so it's no trouble at all. The eggs are really fresh. They're from our chicken coop. But I could make you whatever you'd like."

The earnestness in her expression as she waits for me to tell her what I want for dinner is too sweet. Too tender.

I clear my throat. "Can I ask a question? I know it's rude to ask a woman's age, but you look really young, and..."

Her cheeks flush. "I'm twenty-three."

Those big hazel eyes turn down, and I feel like a jerk for embarrassing her.

"Hey, I'm sorry. It's just that if you're staying here, that's probably something I should know."

"Of course. I understand. I'm not offended." She shifts uncomfortably, and I can tell that might be a little white lie, but then she shrugs. "So... *migas*?"

My stomach growls, and I smile awkwardly. "I guess that's my answer."

She laughs and shakes her head. "Don't worry, big guy. I'll take care of you."

After the last few days I've had, that sounds really good.

6

KATHERINE

BRADY'S HEAVY BOOTS FALL IN STEP BEHIND MINE AS I LEAD HIM down the hallway after dinner. I hold a finger up to my lips and nudge the baby's door open. She's curled up in her crib. It's quiet except for the soft sound of rain coming from the noisemaker in the corner.

I glance up at Brady, and he whispers, "She's precious."

"She's a really good baby. Trust me, I've taken care of a few little monsters, and Bella is a sweetheart."

"Bella?"

We step into the hall, and I nod. "Well, it's Isabella, but we call her Bella."

He frowns. "Maybe I shouldn't call her Izzy. I wasn't even thinking."

The look on his face guts me, and I rub his shoulder. "Mel and Cal would love your nickname for her." Somehow, I'm able to speak despite the now familiar spark that reaches through me when I touch him. His eyes, which look black in the dim light of the hallway, soften. "I promise."

"Yeah?"

"Yeah." I nod and offer him a small smile, which he returns.

"Okay, so follow me." I point to the door across from the baby's room. "This is the bathroom."

I flip on the light, hoping it's clean.

"Towels, shampoo, soap, whatever you need is probably in here," I say, opening the large cabinet, "so please help yourself."

He points toward the claw-foot tub. "Old-school."

"I love that tub, but if you need a shower, I won't take it personally." Pulling back the curtain, I motion toward the wall-mounted shower head. On our way back out, I pause. "Word to the wise—you really need to jam the bathroom door closed. I think the house is shifting after all that rain we've been having, and the dang thing pops open." I give him an apologetic shrug. "The lock broke, so if you use it, you might not be able to get out."

"I'll fix it as soon as I can get my hands on Cal's toolbox."

My eyebrows lift. "I hate to break it to you, but I don't think Cal had a toolbox. He was better balancing the books than doing anything manual. I mean, he harvested one of the fields almost single-handedly, but fixing things wasn't his strength. But Mel was pretty handy herself, so it's not like we were helpless."

His lips flatten, and I feel like I've said something wrong. "Hey, but Mel has a bunch of tools in the shed. I'm sure you'll find what you need in there. We can track them down later."

I motion down the hall, and he follows. My heart beats erratically as I grip the door handle. I haven't stepped into this room since before. "This... this is Mel and Cal's bedroom. I'm not sure what kind of state it's in. But it has a big bed, and I can change the sheets for you."

As I twist the doorknob, his hand comes over mine. "That's okay. I can sleep on the couch."

I breathe a sigh of relief. I don't know why the idea of going in there freaks me out, but given Brady's panicked expression, I'm not alone.

"You can have my bed if you want." I point to the next room and push the door open. "I know it's only a twin, but this is probably your house now, and I'm more than happy to sleep on the couch in the office." My bed is made, and fortunately, I didn't leave anything embarrassing out. Not that I have many belongings here.

"Katherine, don't be silly. I'm not kicking you out of your bed. I'll sleep in the office." His eyes sweep around my room, and he lets out a heavy sigh, furrowing his brows at the sight of his own breath. Intense green eyes snap to mine. "It's cold in here."

"The heat doesn't make it to my room for some reason, so I have to bundle up. You might think Texas is always hot, but at night, here in the hill country, it gets pretty cold sometimes. I should've left the door open so it wouldn't get so chilly, but I have a space heater, so that helps."

"Those things are dangerous. I'll look into fixing the heat for you."

"It's okay. I know you have a lot on your plate. I'm fine. Honestly. But if you see me lookin' like the Stay Puft Marshmallow Man in the morning, that's why. Just don't laugh."

I point an accusing finger at him, and he chuckles. "I would never." His expression gets serious. "But the heat works in the rest of the house?"

I nod half-heartedly. "It gets cold in the living room because it's a drafty, old house, but the baby's room, Mel's bedroom and the office are all okay. It's mostly this room that doesn't get heat for some reason."

Frowning, he nods and follows me to the office. Even though the door is open, it still kinda smells like Cal, like coffee and the faintest hint of the clove cigarettes he'd sneak at night. Swallowing down an unexpected rush of emotion, I turn on the floor lamp, which casts a warm light.

On one end of the room a rustic-looking desk overflows with mail and manila folders. Cal was good with numbers. Not so good with organization.

"Somewhere underneath that mess, you'll find Cal's laptop." Brady glances around, and I point to the flat screen TV that's mounted above the book shelf. "The PlayStation is hooked up if you want to chill." He raises an eyebrow, and I smile. "I know how guys are. Wanting to sit around in your underwear and scratch yourselves while you play *Call of Duty*."

He laughs, looking a little sheepish.

I head into the hall to grab a few blankets and pillows out of the closet and return to find Brady studying a framed photo on the wall. After a minute I allow myself to look too, but the second I do, I wish I hadn't.

My arms tighten around the bedding as I take in Mel and Cal, who are grinning at the camera like two fools while they hold Bella. Something deep in my heart aches at the sight.

He clears his throat. "So they were happy?"

The words rush out of me. "Yes. Very. They were so in love. Sometimes, when they looked at each other, it was like no one else existed. Which was great for them." I wrinkle my nose. "Awkward for everyone else."

When I look up, he's smiling, but then he rubs the back of his neck and his lips press tight. "I hate to bring this up again, but do you have any idea why my mom thought Izzy was with her parents that night? I distinctly remember her saying 'we lost the baby too,' and I just don't know how she got so confused."

I think about that night, *really* think about it, and all at once, I realize my mistake. Heat stings my eyes, and I blink it back. "I... It's my fault. I'm so sorry. I can see how she misunderstood what I was saying." I pause, trying to find the words. "Mel was... Mel was pregnant."

His eyes clench shut, and I fight to keep my emotions under control.

His silence unravels me more, and I rush to explain. "I was so upset that night. I just... I wasn't thinking. Sheriff Tate called your mom for consent for Bella to stay here. Then he told me to call too. Honestly, it probably wasn't the best time for me to talk to anyone." I take a deep breath, remembering flashes from that night.

"You did the best you could." His voice is soft and surprisingly gentle. "She must have been in shock." He lets out a weary sigh. "You know, after those calls, my dad had a heart attack, and she rushed him to the hospital."

"Oh, God."

"I mean, she told me she spoke to the sheriff, but clearly she couldn't grasp everything."

"I'm sorry, though. I shouldn't have unloaded so much on her. I swear I didn't mean to traumatize her."

His eyes pass over me. "Don't blame yourself. It was a fucked-up night. I know none of this is your fault."

Hearing those words is like a punch to my chest, and suddenly I can't breathe. God, am I hyperventilating? Dropping the bedding, I cover my eyes with my hands, too horrified to tell him the truth. *He's going to hate you.*

A strangled sound breaks from my lips. It sounds foreign, like it's coming from someone else, but my shoulders are shaking, and I can't catch my breath.

Before I know what's happening, he's wrapped me in a hug, and for the second time tonight, I melt into his arms. They're strong and warm and so comforting.

All at once my lungs fill. I take long pulls of air against his t-shirt. His smells faintly of cologne and detergent and warm male, and when I shudder, his hold tightens.

He whispers into my hair, "It'll be okay, Katherine. I got you."

Closing my eyes, I ignore that inner voice that's screaming at me to stop being such a wuss, to man up and tell him the rest, but I can't get anything past the boulder in my throat.

A few moments go by, and I can't let this poor guy deal with my pathetic ass any longer. I put my hands on his waist to push away, but...

Holy six-pack.

I should pull my hands back, but I can't. Maybe the oxygen deprivation warped my brain because my head is screaming to let go, but my fingers have a mind of their own... and they start to squeeze the taut muscle. He stills and then inches away. *Oh, God. What am I doing?* I'm about to run and hide under the front porch when he laughs.

I tilt my head up, way up because he towers over me. He looks embarrassed. And then I laugh.

"Are you... are you ticklish?"

He schools his features. "Nah." Shrugging, he glances away.

"Haha. *Sons of Anarchy* is ticklish."

His head rears back. "What'd you call me?"

I let out a weak laugh, hoping he's not offended, and I mumble it again.

"Katherine," he deadpans.

"What? You rode in here today looking like you wanted to shank someone. I think the nickname is fitting."

He shakes his head, but he can't hide the smile on his lips. I realize I'm still all up in his business, and I start to move away. "Okay, well, I'm gonna get out of your hair before I freak out again. Thanks, you know, for letting me cry on your shoulder or —" I wave wildly at him "—or whatever that was. I swear I'm not usually a basket case. I just haven't slept in days, and I get a little loopy when I can't sleep. I mean, really loopy. Like in college, during finals, I really—"

"Katherine."

My mouth snaps shut, and those butterflies riot in my stomach again. Why do I love the way he says my name?

He squeezes my arm gently. "You've been amazing. Thank you for that incredible dinner and for being so welcoming. You can cry on my shoulder anytime." He smiles, and a dimple pops out on his left cheek. "But maybe I'll grab us some life preservers just in case."

Forcing a frown, I grumble, "Hardee har har." Stepping back, I pick up his bedding that I dropped a few minutes ago and drape them on the couch. "Make yourself at home. Holler if you need anything."

"I'll set my alarm early. I have to check in with my dad and call the funeral home and Cal's attorney, but I'll shovel hay or milk your goats or whatever you need. Just point me in the right direction."

I snort. "I don't think you can milk our goats. I mean, they have nipples, but..." What on God's green earth am I saying right now?

His eyebrows lift to his hairline, and then we're both laughing. He shrugs. "Then I'll keep my hands off their nipples. Making a mental note of that now. Do not touch the goats' nipples. Done."

Pretty sure I'm blushing all the way down to my toes. I start toward the door before I can say anything else idiotic. "Look, get settled tomorrow. Make your calls. I have everything under control. Honestly, I feel a hundred times better now that you're here. And I'll get you if I need something."

I wish him goodnight, yank the door closed behind me, and sag against it with a deep sigh. Seriously, what the hell is wrong with me? He must think I'm a lunatic.

Where is the girl who always had her act together? I wish I knew. That was the whole point of coming to Mel's farm. But right now, I'm nowhere closer to figuring it out.

7

BRADY

Holy motherfu—

No, I am not imagining it. Something is definitely gnawing on my ankle right now. I pry one eye open as I roll over and come face to face with a furry nose.

"Meow."

Shit. A kitten.

I scrub my face, forcing myself to wake up.

Kittens. That's right. Katherine said something about kittens... and two pygmy goats. *Christ.*

My head drops back to the pillow, and I take a deep breath. Every muscle in my back aches from sleeping at the airport for two nights and then traveling all day yesterday. Pair that with trying to sleep on this awful couch, and it'll be a week before I feel like myself again.

The sun is blasting through the window, so it must be late. *Five more minutes.*

When I reach for the covers around my waist, I realize that the kitten who's now purring and kneading my neck is not the same little vampire who's chewing on my ankle.

I sit up quickly and yank back the blanket.

Two black, beady eyes stare back between my feet.

"What the fuck?"

The masked little face sneers back at me.

As I leap off the couch, my legs get tangled in the bedding, and I end up on the hardwood floor.

"Meow! Meow! Meow!"

Furry bodies come charging over me like I've set off an alarm.

"Brady? Hey, sorry to bother you, but I need to get in there."

A knock comes at the door, and I'm scrambling to get up, but the sheet is still wrapped around my legs, and I land on my ass again.

Collapsing back, I resign myself to being eaten by a damn raccoon.

Someone snickers behind me. "Are you okay?"

I look over my shoulder and see Katherine, who's bouncing Izzy on her hip.

"Yeah, I think I just met your friends from *Animal Planet*."

Her laughter is airy and light, but it subsides when her eyes travel over me.

I look down and realize I'm only wearing black boxers, and my morning wood is threatening to make an escape. Shit.

Quickly, I roll over and grab the sheet on my way to cover my junk.

"Sorry. I should have given you a minute before I barged in. I just need—" She races by, half covering her face until she reaches the desk. "Just need Mel's address book." Using the book to hide her eyes again and the other one to hang on to Izzy, she darts back across, and I marvel at the little cyclone. I can't decide if she's the cutest thing I've ever seen or a complete disaster.

I expect her to run out the door, but she pauses to make this little clicking sound with her tongue and say, "C'mon, babies. It's time to eat. *¡Venga!*"

Before meeting Katherine, I never thought Southern accents were very appealing, but hers is charming. *And the Spanish? Yeah, that's sexy.*

She clicks again, and three kittens and that fucking raccoon go scrambling over me and follow Katherine like she's the Pied Piper. My eyes lift a little higher, in time to catch her curvy ass waltz away in a pair of form-fitting jeans, which does nothing to help my boner.

I lie back on the floor and rub my face again.

No, you cannot lust after the babysitter, asshole.

One ice-cold shower later—no, not because I need to get a handle on my dick, because I would've gladly jerked one out in the shower, but because the hot water was out—and I'm throwing on a pair of jeans and a t-shirt. How I've gotten this far today without coffee is an outright miracle, but I'm not particularly excited about talking to Katherine this morning after nearly flashing her my goods.

I really don't want to make this more awkward than it is. I don't know why I kept hugging her last night. She just wouldn't stop crying and the last thing I'm prepared to deal with right now is a distraught woman. And I definitely don't want her to think I'm some giant creep.

Fortunately, the kitchen is empty when I walk in. Except there's a plate in the middle of the table with foil and a note with my name on it. *Make yourself at home. Here's breakfast. If you're a vegan or a vegetarian, don't tell me. It'll ruin my impression that you barbecue roadkill. Just kidding! Kinda.*

I laugh. She's a riot, that one.

Something about her message relaxes me. She seems like a cool girl, the kind who wouldn't get the wrong idea about a couple of hugs.

Girl? Sure, Katherine looks young, but nothing about her

body says she's a girl. She's about five-five and slender but with curves a guy would want to travel.

Yeah, no more hugging Katherine.

This whole thing—the trip, my brother, not sleeping in days —is messing with my head. I've never been one of those douchebags who can't hug girls because he wants to hump their leg.

Last year when Dani was bawling her eyes out on my shoulder because that asshole treated her like crap, I could hug her and not want to strip her naked. And I definitely had a thing for Dani.

But here's what really gets under my skin about Katherine. She smells good. Really good. When she nestled into my arms last night, her floral scent—light and sweet and innocent—overwhelmed me.

And then afterward, I noticed how her scent was everywhere. The sheets. The pillowcase. The shower. Oh, God. The shower. She must use some fancy bath gel because when I walked in there, all I could think about was her. Wet and sudsy and silky soft.

Fuck me.

Maybe I'll just stock the bathroom with Dial and Head & Shoulders and hope she lays off the Victoria's Secret Hot Bod 3000 products.

A guy can hope.

8

———

KATHERINE

AS I CLEAN OUT SAMPSON'S STALL, I KEEP ONE EYE ON BELLA, who's playing with a few toys in a playpen under the shade of an oak tree. Even though it's almost the end of November, it's warm today. That's the thing about Texas winters. One day you're shivering and the next you're running around in shorts.

A quick glance to my ratty watch tells me I have forty minutes before the funeral home calls me back with a cost estimate, so I need to hurry.

Grunting as I lift a bale of hay, I scoot it deeper into the barn. Brady told me he wanted to help today, but his phone has been ringing all morning. I've only popped in the office to bring him a sandwich. That's when I offered to help with the funeral arrangements because he looked stressed out trying to juggle calls from the funeral home and his father's cardiologist.

Otherwise, I've left him alone. Truthfully, I've barely been able to make eye contact with him since I barged in on him this morning.

Him sprawled on the floor with the kittens and Bandit attacking his legs was the funniest thing I'd ever seen. But then I got a look at him. A *good* look. And holy mother of all hotness.

The ink is what got my attention first. Tattoos swirled across his hard chest in colorful streaks. I couldn't help but ogle his sleek muscles that stretched down his ridged stomach.

I wish I could say my wandering eyes stopped there because, if they had, I wouldn't be a nervous wreck right now. But no, the little traitors slipped farther down to the bulge in his boxers.

And let me just say that Brady is *fully* loaded.

I fan myself, not sure if I'm sweating because the afternoon sun has finally popped out or if Brady has fried my brain.

Glancing at the feed bins, I remember I need to get some scratch grain for the chickens. It's pretty dang satisfying to gather your own home-grown eggs. My friends and family can think I'm a whack job for leaving the senator's campaign, but I love it here. I've always loved it here. It's honestly the only place that's ever felt like home.

"Momm, momma, moom, mom, mom," Bella calls out from her playpen.

My heart plummets. "I know, *mija*. I miss your momma too."

Scooping her up, I hug her to me and nuzzle my face against her downy-soft hair, and I realize I can't keep falling apart. It doesn't matter how poorly I sleep. Mel would want me to be strong for her daughter. Which means I need to put her needs first.

And definitely no more lusting for Brady. He's a lovely man, a beautiful man, but I know I have no business with a guy like him. He's all sharp edges and intense stares, and I'm a bookworm who prefers to stay home on a Saturday night and watch old rom-coms. How in the world would we ever be compatible? Besides, if I brought home a guy who looked like Brady, my father would probably disown me.

No, what I need to do is be a good friend to the family. That's what I owe Mel and Cal.

You need to figure out a plan for when Brady kicks you out, you little fool, my head screams. *You can't just hang out here forever.*

Ignoring that ugly voice, I vow to tell Brady the truth. I'm not looking forward to finding a place to live or getting another job, but he deserves to hear what happened that night, no matter how much it pains me to tell him.

9

———

BRADY

I clear my throat and reposition the phone. "I love you too, Dad. Everything will be okay. All I want you to worry about is getting through surgery."

I can't lose you too, I think, wishing I could say it to him, to someone, and unburden myself for once.

I've been talking to my parents on and off all morning. I was afraid to tell them about Izzy, afraid how my dad would take the news given that he had a heart attack when he learned about my brother's car accident. When I told him, he was relieved and choked up, but he held it together so my mom could fall apart. She was happy, of course, but emotional.

Dad says he's not surprised she got so confused about Izzy. "Your mom went home to change yesterday and came back with her shirt inside out." He sighs. "And then she locked the keys in her car. She's just... overwhelmed."

I rub the stubble on my chin. "Yeah. I get that."

"She wishes she had been more welcoming to Melissa."

It's not that my parents were ever rude, but they were frustrated with Cal, and I'm sure that came across to his new wife.

"I know, Dad. I have regrets too."

The silence on the phone makes the heavy feeling in my chest more palpable.

"Brady, you've grown into such a good man. Son, I'll never be able to repay you for doing this."

Between Cal's car accident and my dad's surgery, which got re-scheduled for the day after tomorrow—the morning before the funerals—he and my mom can't stop gushing about how awesome I am.

For the record, I'm not. I'm really fucking not. *Because only an asshole abandons his brother the night he's killed.*

Emotion overwhelms me.

I'm so sorry I let you down, Cal. So fucking sorry.

I clear my throat. "We're family. You don't have to repay me." I get that they need to feel like they're encouraging me or appreciating me. I'm sure this has everything to do with Cal's death and not my virtue.

Trying to switch gears before my dad gets any heavier, I tell him that Jose has all of the properties under control. Thank God for Jose. Since I hired him last spring, he's been one of my best workers, and now he's a kickass manager. "We'll be talking every day to plan out the logistics of the workload, but Dad, we have to give him a raise. I'll pay him out of my own pocket if I have to, but we've doubled his workload, and he needs to be compensated. I have a little in savings—"

"Son, no. Let me cash out those IRAs and see if—"

"You're not touching your retirement. At least not now." I offer that concession, knowing full well I'll never let him use that money. "I just need a little time to get things straightened out over here."

A knock comes at the door, and I've never been more grateful for an interruption. "Sorry, Dad, I gotta go. I'll call you tomorrow."

"Okay. Thanks for the call. Love you, son."

"Love you too, old man. Rest up."

He chuckles, and I end the call.

"I'm so sorry to interrupt," Katherine says from the hallway. Now that she's seen me half naked, she's not as eager to come traipsing in, huh? Not sure why that bothers me. "I need a credit card."

I slide one out of my wallet and wave her in. "Thanks so much for coordinating this." I haven't known her for a full twenty-four hours, but she's been a lifesaver already.

When she leans over to grab my card, her hazel eyes meet mine for the first time since our awkward interaction this morning.

"It's no problem." A frown cuts across her pretty face. "But Brady"—she lowers her voice—"it's *really* expensive. I tried to cut costs with flowers, which I thought I could do myself, but the two funerals are going to cost a total of... thirteen."

"Thirteen hundred?" That's not so bad. I've heard horror stories of how much funerals run.

She shakes her head and swallows. "Thirteen *thousand*."

I drop my head into my hands. "Fuck."

"And that doesn't include the cemetery plot or headstones. Unless you wanted, um, cremation."

Pressing my forehead into my palm, I try to relieve the pounding behind my eyes. "Shit." What would my brother want? I have no goddamn idea.

"Has his attorney called back yet? I'm wondering if Cal left any clues in his will."

"No, he hasn't called."

I glance up to find her worrying her bottom lip. "Do you have any suggestions? My brother and I haven't been close for a while..." My voice trails off.

"Sorry, we never talked about this sort of thing."

Would my mom want the ashes? My stomach churns at the thought of having to ask her, and I swallow back the bile.

As though sensing my distress, Katherine says, "Brady, they weren't religious. Mel went to Mass on Christmas and Easter, but that was pretty much it. I think she'd be fine without having any kind of service in a church."

"I hadn't even thought about whether we needed a priest or some kind of religious officiant. Cal and I weren't raised religious."

Silence lingers between us for a moment, and then Katherine pulls a chair up next to the desk.

"The funeral home has a nondenominational minister who can say a few words if you want. They're emailing me an invoice tomorrow that has all of the costs itemized, so if there's something you don't want or something you think we should add, I can still make changes."

I nod, feeling like I'm fucking up my brother's funeral. The guilt of that bullshit argument we had weighs on me, and the question I keep asking myself plays on repeat in my head: Why didn't I call him back that night?

My throat is tight when I tell her to get the flowers. I don't see how she'll have time to do them herself anyway, and trying to save a few hundred dollars on the funerals makes me feel like a bigger dick.

"Hey," she says softly. "Cal and Mel were really low maintenance. Whatever you decide is fine. I'm sure of it. They wouldn't want you to stress out over details."

I close my eyes and take a deep breath. "Thanks for that. I'm one crisis away from losing my shit."

Katherine's quiet a moment, and when I look up, she's biting that lower lip again. "Would dinner help? You must be starving. You've been in here brooding since you tried to flash me your palm tree this morning."

And then I do the last thing I expect at a time like this. I laugh. *Jesus. This girl.*

"I most definitely did not try to flash you. Had you not unleashed the *Wild Kingdom* in my room, I would've had the goods locked away."

She chuckles, and I can't help but smile back. "Sorry about that. I left the porch unlocked, and Bandit snuck in here, and wherever Bandit goes, the kittens follow."

I sigh. "Tell me again why we have a pet raccoon?"

She shrugs. "Because he needed a home." Then she winks like that's the most obvious answer in the world and waltzes out the door.

10

KATHERINE

I HAD DECIDED TO ACT LIKE THIS MORNING NEVER HAPPENED, BUT Brady looked so stressed out this afternoon that I wanted to say something to lighten his mood. So yes, I called attention to his enormous erection.

My mother would be mortified.

A smile tilts my lips. I've always been a good girl. Not the naughty one. *Never* the naughty one. No, that honor goes to my younger sister Tori. So teasing Brady is not my style, but I won't deny I enjoyed it.

After stirring the casserole and returning it to the oven, I turn around in time to get a huge spoonful of sweet potato puree tossed at me.

"Oh, Isabella, you're lucky you're so cute."

She laughs, delighted with herself. *At least she's smiling.* She could paint me from head to toe in sweet potatoes if it meant the kid would be happy.

I unbutton my flannel shirt and peel it off so I can wash it out under the faucet. Fortunately, my white tank top escaped the attack.

Goose bumps break out on my arms as I dip my hands under the water.

"It's chilly in here, baby," I call out to Bella.

A deep male voice replies, "It is."

Brady strides in and bends down to kiss Bella on her head before dropping into a chair at the kitchen table. "You're a mess, little girl."

Then he turns to me and stares, not saying a word.

My eyes widen. "What?"

He smirks like I'm missing something, and I glance down to see my nipples poking through my sheer bra and thin tank.

My cheeks burn. "No, this isn't the same thing as your boner." I pull the front of my shirt away from my chest so I don't look indecent. I'm only a C cup, but this white tank top makes the girls look enormous. "I'm cold." I wave at my chest. "This has nothing to do with being turned on. Right now, I bet your nipples are hard too."

He laughs, a wicked smile spreading on his face, and says, "You might be right, but I doubt it's from the temperature."

Oh, sweet mother.

I clear my throat. "You're trouble, mister."

He laughs again, and the sound is rich and deep and makes me shiver. "I was going to say the same thing about you, Tex."

"Tex, huh?" I try to glare, but his grin only deepens.

Wow. That smile.

A cooking timer blares over the stove, making me jump, and I grab an oven mitt to pull out our dinner. My mouth starts running because I'm suddenly nervous. "You're gonna have to live with Mrs. Bergenmeyer's chicken casserole tonight because I was too busy to chop up the vegetables for the stew. And I really need to give Bella a bath in a bit and get her to bed, but I'm gonna plate this up for you first."

Grabbing a bowl, I scoop in a big serving. When I place it in front of Brady, he's frowning. "You're not joining me?"

Those mesmerizing green eyes stare up at me, and my heart beats double-time. "I can. If you don't mind waiting for me to bathe Bella and get her to bed."

"I'll wait." He breaks out another heart-stopping smile, and I grin back like a fool. "But can I ask a favor?"

Anything. Anything at all. "Of course."

"Can I help you with Bella? I'm thinking I need to figure out this baby thing." He runs his hands through his thick, black hair, sending messy strands every which way. "The attorney didn't happen to return my call yet, did he?"

I shake my head. "It's late. He probably won't get back to you until tomorrow. You worried about getting custody?"

"Honestly? I'm worried about my parents. Cal would've given them Izzy. Not me." His forehead pinches in worry. "My dad is having heart surgery the day after tomorrow to replace a valve. I don't see how they can handle a toddler running around their house."

Hearing this reminds me that I'll be losing Bella soon. Because of course she's moving to Boston to be with Brady's family.

I swallow the lump in my throat and blink back the sting in my eyes. *Don't freaking cry.* Not again. When I can finally talk, I whisper, "If you guys lived closer, I'd be happy to help out."

"You've done so much for us. I'm not sure I'd survive this week without you."

Yeah, that doesn't help the urge to cry, but I bite the inside of my cheek and try to keep my act together. "I'm glad I can be here." I keep my eyes down because there is no way I can look at him or Isabella, or I'll start bawling.

After an awkward silence, Brady clears his throat. "Katherine, I've been meaning to ask..." Ugh. My stomach tightens. *Don't ask me anything else about that night. I'm not ready to talk about it.* "How much was my brother paying you to help out around here? I'm trying to figure out my finances, and you mentioned you got room and board, but I've also seen you busting your ass all day. You're like a hummingbird around here, buzzing around, doing everything, really. So Cal had to be paying you something too, right?"

I shrug, trying not to look too relieved. "Yeah, but you don't have to worry about that right now. I know how much the funerals are costing you, and I feel bad making you pay me anything. Melissa was one of my best friends and—"

"Katherine. How much?" When our eyes meet, he cants his head forward and raises his brows. "How much?"

Finally, I tell him. "A hundred."

"A day?" He looks like he's doing calculations in his head.

Dios mío. I laugh. "Sweet heavens, no. A week."

I'm met with silence. Finally, he lets out an exasperated sigh. "That's all?" His jaw tightens. "What the fuck?"

Bella squeals, "Whadda buck? Whadda buck?"

He and I look at each other, and his cheeks turn pink. Beneath his breath he says, "Aw, hell." He leans over and kisses her head. "Sorry, Izzy. Can we pretend I didn't say that?"

"Whadda buck?" she yells again, this time with an eager clap.

Shrugging, I grin. "Whoops."

He taps the table. "Okay, really. A hundred. A week?"

My smile falters. Because Brady is in scary, wants-to-shank-someone mode again. "Yes."

"Unbelievable."

I'm afraid to say anything and upset him more, so I grab a clean washcloth and wipe down the baby's face.

"How often were you paid? Every week? Tell me what I need to know here."

This is embarrassing. I hate telling him any more, but I have to because he's... he's my employer now? Ugh. How did the hot biker guy become my boss?

"Cal paid me in cash every Friday." It's my turn to blush because I'm sure the implication is clear that he paid me under the table.

Brady sighs, sounding exasperated. "Are you okay if I write you a check? Because I need to be able to write off all of my expenses."

I nod, because what else am I going to say? "Whatever you want is fine."

"When was the last time you were paid?"

I might as well tell him. "Three weeks ago."

A thick silence fills the kitchen as I wipe Bella's hands, and I can feel Brady's anger without even looking at him. But then he grabs my wrist, and I turn to face him. "I need you to know I'm not mad at you. I'm frustrated with the situation. And I'm frustrated with Cal and feeling guilty as hell about it."

He lets go of my arm and stares out the window. The urge to hug him is overwhelming, but I know we have to have some boundaries.

"Don't be upset with Cal on my account. He treated me really well. Like a sister. And I love living here." The tension in his face starts to wane, so I continue. "You don't owe me anything. In fact, if it's a burden to have me here, I can... I can go." Oh, God. What am I saying? My heart pounds at the thought of leaving, but I don't want Brady to feel like I'm some squatter or feel obligated to keep me on if he can't afford it.

His head jerks back. "Jesus. That's what you're getting from this conversation?" He rubs the back of his neck. "I'm sorry, Katherine. That's not what I mean at all. Fuck, I feel like an asshole."

"Ash-hoo. Ash-hoo." Bella grins up at us, and I smack Brady in the shoulder.

"Stop, or she's going to sound worse than your biker bar friends."

He rubs his arm, chuckling. "I don't hang out at biker bars."

I huff out a breath and deadpan, "Fine. Your strip club friends."

He laughs. *Thank God.* "Try art-school friends."

Realizing I'd better take advantage of the smiling guy in front of me before he turns into Mr. Moody Pants again, I motion toward the hallway. "All right, Picasso. Get your biker butt into the bathroom. And don't forget the bubbles."

He raises an eyebrow. "So you like bubbles."

I mock punch him in the arm. "For the baby, perv."

That grin widens. "Sure." That dimple winks at me. "For the baby."

11

BRADY

I survey the mess in the bathroom. As I shift on the cold, wet tile, my knees protest. "Is this a *nightly* routine?" Please say no.

A gleam of humor flickers in Katherine's eyes. "C'mon, tough guy. It's just a little water." But then she realizes she's soaked from head to toe and she sighs. "Okay, it's a lot of water. Can you watch her a sec while I change?" She shakes her head.

"Yup. I've got her." I reach over to scoot the baby away from the faucet as Katherine's footsteps fall away.

The tub is full of floating characters I've never heard of until now. Guess I'd better learn.

Katherine returns a minute later as I hold up a rather phallic-looking, bumpy pink guy with one eye. I glance back at her with a questioning look. "Really? This is what kids are playing with these days? It looks like a di—"

She covers my mouth with a finger and laughs. "Let's not teach Bella any more new words tonight." Her hand falls away. "That's Dippy from *Dippy and His Magical Kingdom*, which I assure you is a family-friendly show. The music will make you insane, but kids love it."

"He looks like a cock," I mouth.

She shakes her head at me and does her best to hold back a laugh. She's changed into a pair of yoga pants and a dark, long-sleeved Henley that hugs her slender curves. She's not wearing any makeup, just those ridiculously sexy glasses that slip down her nose.

Employee. I repeat that to myself. *You do not check out your employees.*

Which reminds me. She needs to fill out a 1099.

As I blow bath bubbles at Izzy, the phone rings in the other room, and after making sure I've got the baby, Katherine trots off to answer it.

Izzy tips forward. "Whoa there," I say, trying to reposition her. "You're a slick little bugger when you're wet." She laughs, babbling away as she splashes around.

No lie, I'm going to have a goddamn heart attack. What if she topples over? What if she bangs her head on the tub? What if she knocks out one of those little teeth on the faucet? What if she inhales some water?

Wiping my forehead on my arm, I take a deep breath.

I don't know how my parents can care for a one-year-old. Izzy is a great baby, but she's constantly moving. I have no idea how Katherine keeps up with her, much less how my parents will be able to handle her.

A splash catches me in the eyes. "Nice aim, doll."

Izzy giggles, and I smile even though I'm momentarily blind. Feeling around for a towel, I manage to knock over some bath soaps. Eventually, I give up and reach for the hem of my t-shirt and yank it up to dry my face.

Someone clears her throat, and I drop my shirt to catch Katherine standing there, lips parted, cheeks slightly flushed. Her eyes dip away, and she nods toward the other room. "That was one of our neighbors calling to check on us. Make sure we were okay. They do that around here. It's kinda nice."

"In Boston, you're lucky if you don't get run over. We're called Massholes for a reason."

She chuckles, placing a hand on me to scoot around and get the baby out of the tub. I try not to notice the warmth of her touch or how good she smells. I shouldn't notice these things. But I do.

Moving out of the way, I study her smile. The soft pink hue of her full lips. The way she tilts her head like she's embarrassed. How gentle she is with Izzy when she dries her off.

It's been a long day. The girl must be exhausted—she was up long before I was—but she's yet to complain. I have no idea how I'm going to afford her and her back wages, what she really should've gotten and not some measly hundred dollars a week, but I'll figure out a way, even if it means selling the Harley.

As we head into the hall, she pauses. "I'll write down Bella's schedule for you and create a list of all of her favorite things, so you'll have a cheat sheet."

I nod, grateful. Because I am so not fucking prepared here.

In the nursery, she shows me how to put on the baby's diaper, and after a little wrestling match, I finally get Izzy into her PJs.

I'm learning everything has a name in babyspeak. Onesie. Blankie. Binkie.

Binkie?

Yeah, that's basically a portable nipple. Kids get all the cool stuff.

I kiss my niece's chubby cheek and tug the zipper up on her Party In My Crib onesie. "This is nice, sweetheart, but I have a really cute onesie at home too." Izzy laughs like she understands I'm being a goof.

Katherine smiles, looking like she's ready to pass out.

"I can put Izzy to bed. Just tell me what I should do and you can knock out. I know you're wiped."

We were supposed to eat dinner together, but the girl looks like she's barely standing.

She nibbles her plump bottom lip. "You don't mind?"

"Not at all. I need to take over Izzy's schedule, and it's good of you to give me some time to get situated, but I can do more. Soon, I'll have to handle baby duty without your help anyway."

Those big hazel eyes widen. She nods, not looking excited like I thought she would. She looks... upset. Like she did in the kitchen when she offered to leave so she wouldn't be a financial burden.

"Hey, that doesn't mean Izzy doesn't need you."

Her eyes well with tears that she blinks away. Damn. I didn't mean to upset her more. Clearing her throat, she nods again. "Sorry. I'm not usually so emotional. Of course you want to be able to take care of your niece on your own. For when you guys move home."

I open my mouth, to say what, I don't know, but she starts backing out of the room. "I'll put her bottle to warm in the kitchen. Give it five minutes, shake it, test it on your wrist and then you can give it to her."

I take a step toward her, but she shakes her head. "That Elmo blanket in the crib is her favorite. Wrap her in it as you rock her. She'll be asleep in about fifteen minutes. Help yourself to the casserole."

"Katherine..."

She offers me a sad smile. "I'll be in my room if you need anything."

Then she walks out, and I feel like an ass. Again.

12

KATHERINE

You're so stupid. So, so stupid.

Objectively, I know Brady and Isabella are moving back to Boston. No one needs to tell me this. He said as much in the kitchen this evening. And I can't even begin to consider what that means for Mel's farm.

But you'd think I was one hundred percent clueless because when he said he wanted to take care of the baby himself, a little piece of my heart died.

This is good, I tell myself, trying to keep a stiff upper lip. I need a reminder that I'm not family. I'm no one. *Not everyone will treat you like Mel.*

Shaking my head, I decide I won't go down this road. I won't feel sorry for myself. This is about Mel and Cal and the baby. Not me.

I'll help Brady as much as I can while I figure out what to do next. I need a plan. A real one. I applied to a few positions a few weeks ago, but I honestly don't care about them. Right now, it's hard to care about anything but Isabella and getting through the funerals.

I can hear what my parents will say. *Wasn't that the whole point of going to Melissa's months ago? You still haven't figured out what you're doing with your life?*

It hurts to think I'm a disappointment to them. I was supposed to be a lawyer or doctor. You'd think I'd stabbed someone in the aorta when I told them I was majoring in marketing and PR. But they made so many sacrifices to send me to college so I wouldn't have to struggle like they did. We were dirt poor when I was little, and when I say dirt, I mean we literally had dirt floors because the places we stayed at weren't exactly built by code.

A part of me realizes it's all in my head, that my parents would welcome me with open arms, but going home feels like defeat. Because I've crashed and burned hard, and I just don't know how to get back up again.

Closing my eyes, I curl up under the covers on my twin bed. My legs ache from standing all day. I'd kill to be able to afford a massage right now. Living in Austin spoiled me. Working on the senator's campaign spoiled me. Company cars and smartphones. Travel accounts and hotels. Thousand-thread count sheets and down pillows at the best hotels. Yes, people actually live like that. I wouldn't have believed it if I hadn't seen it firsthand.

I never would've gotten that job without Eric. The thought burns me a little. He bought me the clothes and showed me how to act around the muckety-mucks.

But I left all of that behind. I'm back to my t-shirts from Target, and I'm okay with that. Because this feels honest. Everything here is real—Isabella, the farm, the animals. They don't play games, and they won't hurt me.

After a few minutes, sleep overpowers me, and I drift off.

In the middle of the night, I get up for a drink of water and peek into Bella's room to check on her only to find the crib empty. Shivering as I head to the office, I'm relieved when I find her fast asleep on her uncle's chest where she's sprawled out with one hand gripping a fistful of his black hair and another one smack dab in the middle of his face. And they're both snoring.

Big, brooding tattooed biker snuggling his baby niece...

Well, that did the trick. I'm warm. *All over.*

It's no contest. If Isabella was his, he'd be the hottest dad ever.

Once I finish cleaning the barn, I take a deep breath and head for the house.

My cheeks warm at the thought of facing Brady this morning. If I'm lucky, he and Bella are still sleeping.

A loud squeal from the kitchen squashes that thought. As I pass the box of kittens on the enclosed back porch, I peek in and find them snuggled against Bandit. A sleepy furry face peers up at me.

"I'll grab your breakfast," I whisper and pat his little head.

After washing my hands in the bathroom, I walk hesitantly into the kitchen. Isabella is seated in her high chair and is busy smashing slices of banana all over herself. I chuckle... until I look up and find Brady standing shirtless at the sink.

He's only wearing some black track pants. Some *thin* track pants. I may have already seen him in his boxers, but seriously, this never gets old.

The ability to speak leaves me as my eyes travel up. A dark treasure trail. That v-cut leading to a six pack. More muscles. Tattoos. A knowing grin.

Shit.

"See something you like?" He smirks.

I force a bland expression despite the flush in my cheeks. "I usually wait until after breakfast to throw money at strippers, but if you can't help but rip your clothes off around me, I can go look for some singles."

He laughs so loudly, Isabella jumps in her seat.

Shaking his head, he turns back to the sink where I realize he's washing off his shirt, likely another casualty from trying to feed the baby.

Calling over his shoulder, he says, "I didn't know what you fed her in the morning, but I thought bananas and a handful of that baby mush stuff were a safe place to start." He lifts a bottle from a container of water and turns toward me. "I assume she also gets one of these like she did at bedtime?" He shakes it, drips a few drops on his wrist and then licks it off. He definitely listened to my directions last night, except...

It's my turn to laugh. "How'd that taste?"

"Not bad. I don't know why I had the impression that formula tasted rank."

"That's not formula, Brady. That's breast milk."

He stiffens, his eyes wide with horror, before he leans over the sink and spits. After swishing some water in his mouth and spitting it out, he turns to me. "What the hell? Why didn't you tell me?"

I snort. "I didn't think you were gonna taste it."

He runs his hands through his thick hair, which points in a million different directions. "Jesus Christ, Kat. You should warn a guy."

"Sorry." I grab my stomach, which hurts at this point because I'm still laughing.

"So it's not..." He points at my chest. "This doesn't belong to..." He starts waving the milk at me.

"No, weirdo. I'm not lactating." I laugh harder.

Swear to God, his face turns red. "No, of course not. I just... I just... I don't know what I'm thinking."

I pat his hard bicep.

Focus, Katherine.

Peering up at him, I smile. "C'mon, muscles. Go put on some clothes so a girl can concentrate."

Nudging him over, I pour two cups of coffee. His footsteps fall away as he heads back to the office. When he returns a minute later, he's wearing a black t-shirt that molds to his body and makes those tattoos stand out even more.

Motioning toward the bottle, I explain. "That's frozen breast milk I thawed yesterday. We have a few more days' worth, but I've already started transitioning her to whole milk." My voice falls to a whisper.

He nods solemnly, and I know he understands where the milk came from now. At first I feel guilty for laughing about it, but before I can fully freak out, I realize Mel would've thought it was hysterical too. She'd probably remind him about it for the next twenty years.

Realizing I have two coffees in my hand, I pour some cream into one and hand him his cup. He takes it gratefully. As he lifts it to his mouth, he pauses, looks in his mug and then back at me. "You made it for me."

"Well, yeah. You take it with cream, right? Why would I hand you a cup of black coffee?" I tilt my head and look up at him. He has the strangest expression. "Are you feeling okay?" I reach up and place my hand on his forehead.

Mistake. *Big* mistake.

This close, I can smell his body wash or cologne or whatever it is that's making my pulse riot. This close, I realize I come up to his chin, which is chiseled and scruffy and ridiculously rugged. This close, I realize just how lethally good-looking he is.

I yank my hand back, but before I can take a step away, my eyes lift to his mouth. His lips are parted, and he sucks in a breath. The urge to kiss him is so strong, my whole body throbs.

His green eyes darken as he stares at my lips, and just when I think I'm going to spontaneously combust, the sound of a falling bowl makes us both jump. I turn to find that Isabella has tossed her baby food all over the floor.

Thank God for small mercies. I was two seconds from embarrassing myself. *Seriously, what's wrong with me?*

I grab some washcloths and wipe down the mess. "Sorry about last night," I blurt before I chicken out.

"For what? You don't have anything to apologize for," he says gruffly. "I'm sorry I upset you. Here you are, working your ass off, and I hurt your feelings."

I peek at him over my shoulder. He's standing in front of the sink, bracing himself on the counter. His head is bent.

"Really. I'm fine. I got a good night's sleep and feel better this morning." Not true, but he doesn't need to know that. I stand up to face him. "We're cool. I promise."

He turns around, his eyes soft.

Reaching for the baby, I brush her bangs out of her face. "I'll do what I can to set you guys up so when you're flying solo you don't crash and burn."

He gives me a sad smile.

I motion toward Izzy's bottle with a grin. "And I promise not to let you drink breast milk again."

He grimaces but then a genuine smile breaks through. "That would be much appreciated."

Desperate for something mundane to talk about to lighten the mood, my eyes land on the three bins along the opposite wall.

"Mm, before I forget, we recycle." I point to the back of the kitchen. "I've color-coded and labeled everything, so even a Neanderthal can figure it out. I drop off the blue one at the recycling center every week. And we also have more green bins outside for leaves and tree limbs. But really, I'd love to learn how to compost." Those last words come out slowly as I notice the expression on Brady's face that's etched in hard lines.

He arches a brow. "Are you calling me a Neanderthal? You know, just because I ride a motorcycle and sport some ink doesn't mean I'm missing a frontal lobe." His deep voice rumbles through me.

"What?" My eyes bulge. "No. God, no. I just... I mean... I'm so sorry if that's what you thought I was saying. I would never think that. Ever."

His deadly-serious expression suddenly morphs into a smile. "I'm kidding. But that was for letting me drink breast milk."

I stare at him, my jaw slack. "Not. Funny."

He laughs, pointing at me. "You should've seen your face."

Pressing my hand to my chest, I will my heart to slow down. *Calmate.* "Okay, haha. Hysterical."

That's when I study his beaming smile. The way his eyes crinkle with amusement. That unfiltered laugh.

Holy smokes. That dimple.

Trapped by his gaze, I smile back like an idiot until the awkward silence is noticeable. *Speak, Katherine. Say something.* "So, um, I need to head to the grocery store to get a few things for Bella. My car is out of commission, and Mel always let me borrow her truck. Would it be okay if I use it?"

His expression turns serious again. "Why wouldn't it be?"

"I don't know, but I thought I should ask."

"Kat, you've lived here longer than I have. You don't need my permission to borrow Melissa's car." He rubs his neck. "What's wrong with yours?"

I grab my coffee and take a sip. "Not sure. I hadn't driven it in a while, and it barely got me to the farm when it died. I've been saving up to get it repaired." I cringe, hating how it makes me feel like a kid when we had two cars but neither of them worked.

"Where are your keys?" I stare back at him, and he tilts his head forward. "So I can take a look at it."

Oh. "That would be really awesome. If you can fix it, I will totally pay you."

He frowns. "Don't be ridiculous. Keep your money, Kat."

His cell phone rings down the hall, and he strides out of the room. *Kat.* He's been calling me Kat this morning.

No one calls me that. Before this biker boy drove up, I've always been a very prim Katherine, the girl who stays in on Friday nights and does homework. The girl who always does what she's told. The girl who's... boring.

Kat sounds like she has a social life and throws caution to the wind. Like she dances on bars and tosses back shots. Like she lets hot guys work on her car.

I think I like Kat.

13

KATHERINE

THE NEXT MORNING, I DRAG MYSELF TO MY LAPTOP. WHILE I KNOW what to expect when I open my email, it doesn't make finalizing the funeral arrangements any easier. Brady reviews the print out with a stoic expression and signs off on everything, even the ridiculously expensive flowers.

I want to cheer him up, but I haven't a clue what to do besides make sure he eats and hand him an occasional cup of coffee. He sounds worried sick about his father. I can't imagine what he must be going through right now, so I try to be as upbeat as possible.

And maybe, wanting to cheer him up is a little selfish on my part because I love seeing him laugh. His green eyes warm, and his shoulders relax. Sometimes, if I'm lucky, that one dimple comes out and taunts me.

Needing a distraction from thinking too much about my new housemate, I return to my laptop to finish the logo for Mel's new honey-lavender lotion. I have no idea if Brady will continue making Mel's bath and body products, but it seems wrong to stop the design now. I'll finish, and he can do with it what he will. I'm no graphic designer, but I had to do so many graphics for the senator's campaign that I got pretty decent.

Besides, I need it for the farmers' fair.

Oh, dear Lord. *The farmers' fair.*

Mel and Cal were planning to host this big event next month. Since the winter is slow around here, everyone thought it'd be fun to do something to promote all of the nearby farms. The neighbors are bringing some of their goods to sell, and Mel wanted to set up a little petting zoo for the kids.

I rub the throb in my temple. *Like Brady needs one more thing to deal with.*

Worst-case scenario, he can cancel. Or maybe one of the other farms can host.

Clicking over to my other email account, I check to see if I have any more responses from the newspapers about the event.

I can still hear Mel's voice, teasing me that I'd spend hours on her press releases when I wouldn't take the time to apply to the opening on Congressman Mitchell's staff. But I'm not sure I want to return to the lion's den.

Is it wrong that I love working on the farm? I enjoy everything, from harvesting the crops and distilling the essential oil to perfecting Mel's products and finding the best way to sell them. But if I tell my parents I love doing the very thing they loathe—farming—would they understand? They've always wanted something different for me, a better life, because farming represents a lifestyle that just beat them down.

I know they want me to give Austin another shot, but I don't think I can deal with seeing my ex around every corner, which is bound to happen because those political circles aren't that big.

Glancing at my worn jeans and flannel shirt, I can't imagine what Eric would say if he saw me "slumming it" again.

When I hightailed it out of Austin, I left everything behind that came from him—my clothes, my phone, my job. He can keep it all. Because when the going got tough, he bailed.

That's not what I need. Who wants a man who doesn't fight for what he wants? For the woman he supposedly loves? No, Eric got cold feet at the worst possible time. When I was alone and scared. Who can respect a man like that? Look at Brady. He's obviously knee deep in family responsibilities and you don't see him running for the hills.

I barely know the man but already I respect him so much. He might be kind of grumpy sometimes, but who wouldn't be with this much stress? He's busting his butt to take care of his parents and his niece.

You need to tell him.

My stomach nosedives. God, I need to get this over with.

After the funerals. Maybe on Sunday once we've gotten through the worst of it.

But I vow to tell him soon. Although I hate keeping secrets, I think if I told him now, it would be more to ease my guilty conscience than anything. I can handle the nightmares if it means he has less to deal with this week. I just hope he understands.

14

BRADY

"You're kidding me." This isn't right.

Davis DeGregory, my brother's attorney, clears his throat. "I can assure you this is correct. You're the beneficiary of the farm, all businesses relating to the farm, and all of the family's assets, assuming you take custody of Isabella."

I press my palm into one eye and then the other before I mumble into the phone, "So the will doesn't list my parents or maybe one of Melissa's relatives? I just don't see why they'd consider me." Cal and I weren't talking. He knew I was pissed. "Is it possible the forms are outdated?"

"No, we spoke last month. Your brother found out Melissa was pregnant again, and he wanted to make sure she'd be cared for in the event something happened to him, so he executed a will. Had he been the only one who passed, his wife would have been the beneficiary. But in the event something happened to both of them, everything defaults to you. Both signed the documents."

My head is reeling. "He didn't think our parents would be a better choice?"

"He said your father had health issues."

"And Melissa didn't have any relatives?"

The sound of papers shuffling in the background comes through the line. "Not that I'm aware of. Except…"

"Except what?"

"They mentioned a friend. Someone who lives on the farm. I think they considered her as a potential legal guardian should you decline custody." He pauses. "Here it is. Katherine Duran. She's the woman who cared for Isabella in your absence, correct?"

"Yes."

"You're lucky she was there to care for the child. Dealing with Social Services is a nightmare, and that's where Isabella would've gone without a family friend to intervene. In any event, Cal and Melissa decided you were more appropriate since you're related, but they thought Katherine was a strong candidate to get custody of their daughter, which is why I didn't object to her caring for Isabella until you arrived. However, if you decide to decline conservatorship, the state then looks toward a child's grandparents as the next suitable option."

Why the fuck would I decline custody? And they considered giving Izzy to Katherine over our parents?

"You're saying the state of Texas is just going to hand me a child?"

"You're a blood relative, and you're listed on the will. So, basically, yes."

"And Child Protective Services doesn't need to make sure I'm not a bank robber or anything?"

He chuckles. "With no history of abuse here, CPS doesn't get involved. But I will need you to sign off on a full background check to ensure you don't have a criminal history." He pauses briefly. "You don't have a criminal background, do you?"

"Surprisingly, no."

He laughs again. "That's good. You'll need to hire a social

worker—I have a few you can call. He or she will need to come to your house for an interview, but that's pretty much the extent of the state's inquiry into your suitability."

"How many visits does the social worker make?" If I had to guess, I'd say a dozen. We're talking about handing the welfare of a child to someone named in a will. If Izzy were my baby, I'd want at least that many visits to make sure the person wasn't some closet drunk or dope fiend. *Fuck me sideways.* How will I deal with a dozen visits?

Sweat beads my brow, and I grip the phone and await his answer.

"Just once. The person will conduct an interview and walk through the house to make sure it's inhabitable. The rest of the process is pretty simple. I file a few documents. You come before the court and swear to take care of Isabella. You pay the fee—about seven hundred dollars—and that's it." He lowers his voice. "We'll also need death certificates, but I'll handle that. Can you get me a copy of the baby's birth certificate?"

I mumble *yes* even though I have no clue. Maybe Katherine knows where Cal kept those records.

Closing my eyes, I wade through a dark tide of emotion. "How long does this process take?"

"Two to three months typically."

Two to three months. Did I really expect to head home sooner with a child and a farm to look after?

When I get off the phone, I'm nauseous.

All this time I'd been thinking Cal was a delinquent for not coming back to Boston, but here he was, making out a will and taking care of his family.

A deep ache in my gut starts to spread as the realization of what all of this means.

My brother gave me Izzy. The farm. His life insurance policy. Everything.

He thinks I'd be a good parent? A single, twenty-six-year-old tattoo artist who rides a Harley and hasn't a clue what the fuck he's doing with his life? What the hell was he thinking? Before this week, I'd never even held a baby.

I may have changed a diaper or two in the last twenty-four hours, but that doesn't qualify me to be a parent or guardian or whatever this is.

A dozen scenarios race through my head. What am I supposed to do when Izzy gets sick and wants her mom to comfort her? Or when she wants her real parents to come to the open house at her school? Or when... Oh, Jesus. Someday she'll date, and I'll have to kill the poor asshole who thinks he's getting his hands on that little angel.

I am not equipped for this.

All this time, I assumed I'd be bringing Izzy home to my parents after my dad got better. That was the only thing that gave me the confidence to think I could care for her while we were in Texas. Because I was handing her off to my parents who had already raised kids.

How do I tell them? Will this come as a relief or crush them?

Of course, I agreed to adopt her. How could I not?

The office door creeps open, and Izzy comes cruising in on some kind of baby walker on wheels.

"Hey, Bella, we need to let Uncle Brady work." Katherine runs in behind my niece. "Sorry about that. She's getting faster in this thing." Katherine's smiling until she gets a good look at me. "Are you... Are you okay?"

I shake my head, not even knowing where to begin.

Typically, this is something I'd discuss with my parents, but given that my father is heading into surgery tomorrow, I can't.

Katherine frowns. "Wanna talk about it?" Hesitantly, she sits next to me on the couch.

There's something about those big hazel eyes that makes me

want to confide in her. *She knew Cal and Melissa better than anyone.*

So I unload on her. When I'm done, her eyes are wide. "Okay. Well, I know this isn't what you were expecting, but I can't say I'm surprised you're getting custody of Bella."

"What?" I rub my neck. "I don't know how much my brother told you about me, but we'd been arguing over him being in Texas. For a while."

"Sure, but he loved you, and even though you guys were pissed at each other, you're the kinda guy who puts his family first. It's why you're here right now. It's why you were upset with him in the first place. Because of your parents. So, see, deep down he knew there was no one better to take care of his baby girl than you."

My eyes sting, and I blink several times, feeling overwhelmed. Dropping my head, I brace my elbows on my thighs.

We sit in silence, the only sound coming from Izzy as she scurries back and forth across the room in her walker.

"Did... Did he ever talk about me?" I hate how needy that sounds, but Kat gives me a warm smile.

"Of course he did." She places her hand on my arm. "He said you were his hero. That there was no one he respected more."

Fuck.

That's when it hits me. How angry I've been at him. Not just for refusing to come back to Boston, but for dying. For leaving when everything was unresolved between us. For not giving me a chance to tell him how much I loved him and appreciated him as my brother.

He called you that night. He called. This is on you.

I lower my head again and clench my eyes. All that time I wasted being upset with him.

"He loved you, Brady," she whispers. "He'd want you to make peace with this."

I nod, not able to look up yet.

We sit side by side, shoulder to shoulder, with the sound of Izzy's chatter in the background. Then I realize Kat's rested her head on my shoulder. And for a quiet moment, we share the loss. Together.

Closing my eyes, I breathe in her spring scent of flowers and citrus. It makes my heart knock against my chest and wish for something simpler in my life. Something different than this endless treadmill I've been running. Is that what my brother found here? Is that why he left everything behind to be with Melissa?

With an easy squeeze on my arm, Katherine pulls away. "If it makes you feel any better, Cal once told me there were two things I needed to know about you. One, that he was better-looking, and two, that you were a stubborn son of a bitch."

She giggles, and suddenly we're both laughing. How am I laughing right now?

"Yeah, maybe I am stubborn," I admit. I laugh again. "Fucker, he wasn't better-looking."

"And hey, don't worry. I won't tell the social worker about your porn addiction or your inclination to flash innocent bystanders."

I snort. "Ha. Funny."

She grins again and stands up. "Okay, big guy, I need to change the baby." She nibbles on her lip a second. "I haven't shown you all of the property yet. Wanna come along? Bella and I can give you the grand tour. It's kinda nice outside today, and since this place is yours now, you probably need to get the big picture and see what you're dealing with. Maybe take your mind off all this deep stuff for a little while."

I heave a sigh of relief. "That would be great."

Her lips lift a little higher, and I have to admit it feels pretty good to have that smile aimed at me. I start to wonder what a girl like her is doing on a farm in the middle of nowhere.

On her way out of the office, I call her name, and she stops in the doorway.

"Thanks again. For everything."

She glances down and smiles shyly before walking out.

I can see why Cal and Melissa adored her. It's a little hard not to.

15

KATHERINE

I thought it'd be good to get Brady out of the house for a little while, to distract him from the heavy conversations he had this morning, but based on his frown and the tightness of his shoulders, mentioning the farmers' fair wasn't the way to do it. And now that we're touring the property, he looks even more tense.

He's wearing a faded Red Sox baseball cap curved tight and pulled low over his handsome face while he scribbles in his notepad.

"Explain that again," he mumbles.

"We prune in the spring and again in the fall. We grow English lavender, which is the type that most people think of, along with Provence and Grosso."

"Three different kinds of the same flower."

"They're not all 'the same flower' exactly. One is good for cooking." I point to the adjacent field. "The other is great for potpourri and other crafts." I motion toward the rows behind us. "And the third—the plants just over that hill—is what we use for essential oil and hydrasol, or linen spray."

"Potpourri?" he deadpans as he scribbles more notes.

I ignore the derision in his voice. He doesn't get it. *What do you expect? He's a guy.* Most guys don't get it. That's why Mel loved Cal so much. He understood. In fact, he encouraged her. He loved that she made lotions and bath salts and linen sprays.

It's hard not to marvel at how different Brady is from his brother, and I wonder what it would've been like to hang out with both of them back when they weren't at odds.

Hearing Brady ask about Cal, wondering if his brother ever talked about him, nearly broke my heart. Every part of me wishes I could go back in time and force the brothers to work things out.

Izzy tugs on my leg, and I reach down to pick her up. "You're such a big girl." I bounce her on my hip, and she giggles.

We trudge along for a while as I point out the different fields of lavender and the issues they're having, like pH balance and drainage. Finally, Brady sighs and turns to me.

"What?"

"Give me the baby."

I stare back. "Why? What's wrong?"

"I'm not going to let you lug her all over the farm. She weighs half as much as you do."

I snort laugh. "Hmm. I doubt that." Squinting in the bright sun, I tilt my head up at him. "I should've brought the baby carrier, but I got excited to show you the farm."

"Baby carrier?"

"Yeah, it's this fabric contraption I use to strap her to my chest."

Those intense green eyes dip down my body, and I briefly wonder if he's as attracted to me as I am to him, but just as quickly they dart away. He clears his throat. "Next time, let's get the baby carrier, and I'll use it." He rubs his palm against his stubbled chin. "For now, though, let me do the heavy lifting."

Brady reaches over, and Bella eagerly goes to her uncle. His eyes light up when he holds his niece.

"Hey, little muffin," he teases. "Let's give your Aunt Kat a break."

My heart does a strange little trippy thing when he calls me Kat. It's so familiar. Like we're the oldest of friends. And I want us to be friends. I suspect any girl in her right mind would want to be friends with Brady.

Which makes me wonder what his life is like in Boston. If he has a girlfriend. Or girlfriends. Or hookups.

Ignoring the irrational bolt of jealousy that streaks through me, I kick at a large rock and watch it skitter across the ground. When I glance up, Brady brushes a wisp of hair out of the baby's eyes and kisses her forehead, and I swear my ovaries throb. On one hand, Brady is gruff and rough around the edges, and on the other, there's a tenderness about him that screams husband material.

Not for me. *Obviously.* But for some lucky girl in Boston.

I'm trying not to swoon at the sight of this spectacularly hot guy holding a baby when he hands me his pad of paper and asks me to take notes. I'm finding he *really* likes to take notes. Every phone call he's taken this morning is scribbled down in his notepad. The man likes a record of everything. Cal was never that organized. Which makes me wonder what Brady does for a living. I know he's helping with his father's company, but I get the impression there's a lot more to him.

I shouldn't be nosy, but I really want to know what's underneath that tough exterior.

Not to mention under those faded jeans.

16

BRADY

WE'VE BEEN WALKING AROUND THE PROPERTY FOR FORTY-FIVE minutes. It's hot as hell for November. I'm wearing jeans and a t-shirt and sweating my balls off. And Jesus Christ, Izzy is getting heavy—my arm went numb twenty minutes ago.

I brush a kiss over her forehead and pull the wide-brimmed hat a little lower over her face so she doesn't get too much sun. When I glance over at Katherine, she's giving me the strangest look. It's one of those tender expressions she's been shooting my way whenever I hold my niece. If I'm being honest, it makes me uncomfortable.

I can see it in her sweet expression. It's that oh-he's-such-a-good-guy look. Which I'm not. I would've resolved that shit with my brother long ago if I were.

Averting my eyes, I push ahead on our trek. Kat explains which parts of the farm need what. The chicken coop needs re-roofing and re-wiring. The area of the barn where the lavender is hung to dry is too damp. The back field floods.

Jesus. Fucking. Christ.

I damn near hyperventilated when she mentioned that farmers' fair.

But everything gets worse when we turn along a creek that runs adjacent to the property. Katherine comes to an abrupt halt and stares down the riverbed, a haunted expression on her face.

Mud covers all of the tree trunks along the banks to a height of about four feet. Watermarks from a flood.

My mouth goes dry.

It must have happened here.

As I stare down the nearly dry creek bed, I can't swallow.

"Katherine," I mutter. "Let's go."

Her head snaps toward me, and for a half second, I almost reach out a hand to steady her. She's white as a sheet. She blinks once, twice, and then, like she's on autopilot, reaches for the baby and tucks Izzy to her chest before she treks back to the house.

I think about it the rest of the day. The flooded creek bed, deserted like a tornado swept through and sucked out all the water.

Katherine and I are quiet all evening, only saying the most essential things to feed Izzy and get her to bed. If I feel tortured by what I saw today, I can only imagine what she's feeling. But I can't bring myself to say anything to comfort her, because as much as I want to, she'd reciprocate. She'd try to make me feel better—it's what she's done since I arrived—and I don't fucking deserve it. Because deep down, I feel like I abandoned my brother, and that realization, that awareness, guts me.

So I do what I can to make things right. I accept the grief. Welcome it with open arms.

But I feel bad that I can't be there for Katherine.

At night, she and I bump around each other in our own private little hell, like two stars that orbit a black hole, both afraid to move in the wrong direction.

At one point, Izzy stirs, but when I peek into her room, Katherine is already there. For hours, I hear the rocking chair creek on the hard wood floor. I wonder if she's obsessing about her last interactions with Cal the way I am. Even the smallest things seem momentous now. Death does that. Sticks everything under a magnifying glass and makes each scratch or cut feel like a gaping wound.

The next morning, it's obvious neither of us slept, but we don't discuss it.

Instead, I talk to my dad before surgery. I shovel out shit from the barn and chicken coop. I finish two landscaping estimates via email. I stare at the itemized funeral arrangements, resigned to the fact that I'll be broke soon.

The best laid plans...

Around noon, a soft knock on the office door interrupts me, and I look up to see those golden eyes.

Katherine drops off a sandwich, and when she's almost out the door, I blurt it out. "Did Cal or Melissa ever discuss selling the farm?"

She freezes, her arm on the door frame. She shakes her head no, with obvious disappointment in her expression. When she doesn't say anything, just walks out, I have the irrational desire to yell after her and ask her what the hell my options are. I want her to understand the fucked-up position I'm in. Jose has my dad's business under control for now, but I'm hemorrhaging cash like a broken ATM.

I can't handle this mortgage, my parents' mortgage, *and* the rent for my apartment in Boston. Never mind my school loans and the payments my parents still owe on their trucks and equipment. Cal's modest life insurance policy will take at least six weeks to process. That will bring a small reprieve, but it won't get me through the long haul.

What the fuck do I even know about farming? Sure, I have experience landscaping, but that's short-term work. It takes a shovel and a little elbow grease to plant things. But actually nurturing something to grow month after month, year after year? That requires dedication. Fortitude. Hell, even love.

I stew in these thoughts as I busy myself with an estimate for Jose. I even call a realtor, curious if anyone would even buy a goddamn lavender farm. I'm surprised when he tells me they're growing in popularity.

"But it's a niche market," Kent, the realtor, explains, "so I'm not sure if I have any clients who are looking at the moment, but it can't hurt for you to make cosmetic improvements in case someone turns up."

He says he'll do a little research and get back to me.

Selling the farm has to be the answer, but it's one that makes me feel like shit for wanting to dismantle something my brother loved.

Several hours later, after I've bathed my niece who was covered from head to toe in spaghetti sauce, my mother calls to tell me my dad is out of surgery. Mom says he's being a "grumpy pain in her tushie" but sounds relieved. The moment the call ends, I make sure Kat doesn't mind watching the baby, and I head for the only thing that can offer me relief. The Harley.

It's dark when I return, and all of the lights are out. I stare at the humble farm house, wishing I could drown my sorrows in bourbon. But I don't. Because the least I can do is show up to my brother's funeral sober.

Afterward, all bets are off. I don't plan on stopping until I see the bottom of the bottle. I'm not a drinker, but I need something to relieve the pressure. Anything.

17

BRADY

THE BLACK SUIT HANGS ON THE DOOR OF THE CLOSET. IT'S THE
one decent thing I brought to wear.

At nine-thirty, after I knot my tie, I open the office door just
as Katherine strides out of the bathroom.

For a second, all I do is stare. And then my heart kicks into
high gear.

Gone is the messy bun. Gone are the work boots and jeans.
Gone is the mud from under her nails. The woman in front of
me is stunning. Sophisticated.

Her chestnut hair hangs in thick waves along her shoulders.
For the first time since I've been here, she's wearing makeup.
Those amber eyes are smoky and intense, and her lips are
slicked in pale gloss.

I study the slant of her neck and how it dips beneath a fitted
black dress that buttons down her body, starting just above her
breasts and leading down her slender thighs.

The fabric clings to her curves, and even though everything
is covered, I can't help but wonder what's underneath.

I blink. Once. Twice. Then I notice sleek four-inch heels, and
my lips part.

"You look nice," I rasp as I move around her.

Eager to get some distance, I turn toward the kitchen and pour us two cups of coffee. *She must be wearing contacts today. That's why she looks so different.*

When I hand her one mug, she glances down at the cup and then reaches for the cream and a packet of sweetener.

Shit. She's been making my coffee all week, and I have no clue how she takes hers.

Way to be considerate, dickhead.

After a few half-hearted sips, she sets her mug down. "I'll get the baby's things, and we can leave," she whispers.

She returns with a giant green bag that I can only assume houses an entire Babies 'R Us store and reaches for Izzy, who's sitting in her playpen.

I bundle the girls in their coats, because it's actually cold outside today. Which I figured out when I froze my balls off this morning feeding all of the animals.

After we load Izzy into her car seat in the extended cab of Melissa's truck, I offer Katherine a hand and help her up.

The drive is quiet. Even Izzy is silent, like some part of her realizes what she's lost.

When we pull into the parking lot of the funeral home, I fight the overwhelming tide of sadness that pulls at my gut.

You're not supposed to bury your younger brothers. You're supposed to grow old together. Get houses in the same neighborhoods. Take your kids to Little League and debate how far the Red Sox will go at the end of the season.

Not this.

As soon as we enter the building, people rush to greet Kat and offer their condolences. Izzy clings to me, and I gently bounce her in my arms as we wade through the crowd and head for the front of the room.

Suddenly, she lunges forward and starts wailing, "Mommm!

Mommmm! Dadadada!" I turn to find several blown-up photographs of Melissa and Cal staring back, leaving me speechless. But when Izzy's bottom lip quivers and tears stream down her face, a gaping hole breaks open in the center of my body.

My heart clenches, and my vision blurs.

When a soft hand reaches for mine, I clasp it. Katherine's voice warbles, barely above a whisper. "I thought it would be nice to have photos since it was closed casket, but... I'm sorry. I wasn't thinking." Her eyes are just about to spill over with tears.

"It's okay." I swallow and struggle to clear my throat. "It's okay. This... was very thoughtful. Thank you." Wrapping my arm around her shoulders, I pull her in close and kiss her fore-head. We stay like that for a moment. Just the three of us. Until I can breathe again.

We settle into the front row seats reserved for family, and Izzy reaches for Kat, who snuggles her close. A minister says a few words, but all I can see are my brother's blue eyes staring back at me. He looks so happy. *And I begrudged him this happiness.*

I try to listen to the minister, but I can't concentrate on anything but the two caskets on the dais. I study the mahogany finish. The polished handrails. The delicate carvings along the lids. It's all so permanent.

I'm finally jarred when Izzy crawls into my lap, and Kat and I end up passing the baby back and forth.

An odd sensation comes over me when I watch Kat kiss Izzy. In different circumstances, she'd totally be the kind of girl I'd go for. She's sweet and thoughtful. Funny and outgoing. The girl-next-door but also incredibly sexy without even trying.

I shake the thought from my head. *Never gonna happen, man. You're headed back to Boston.*

The hollowness in my chest swells.

The minister talks, about what, I'm not sure. Finally, he

motions toward me, and I realize he wants me to come up to the podium. I vaguely remember Katherine asking if I wanted to say something today. I thought I declined, but clearly, that's not what the minister thinks.

Straightening my suit, I walk up.

Grateful the audience can't see my white knuckles gripping the podium, I take a deep breath. My attention lands on Katherine. When our eyes meet and she nods slightly, the words spill out of me.

"I want to thank everyone for coming. My parents can't be here today because of my father's medical condition, but they extend their gratitude. They'll be having a memorial service in Boston once my father has recovered, and I'll be sure our friends and family back home know how many of you came to extend your condolences."

I glance over at the photos. "Melissa, thank you for being a wonderful wife and mother. It's clear from everything I've seen at your farm how dedicated you were to my brother and niece. I'm honored you were my sister and hope you know how loved you are. Half of South Texas showed up here today to honor your memory." Heads nod in the audience. "I wish things had been different. I wish we had gotten to know each other, and you could explain why we have two pygmy goats and a baby raccoon."

Everyone chuckles, and a sad smile tilts my lips as I loosen my grip on the podium.

"I also need to thank you all for welcoming my brother. He loved this place. Loved living here with Melissa and Isabella. I don't know if you know this, but he basically dropped everything in Boston to move here and be with Mel." I shrug, not sure if people will understand what I have to say but needing to say it anyway. "He and I didn't see eye to eye on this, but the great thing about Cal is he didn't need people's approval to do what was right for him and his family, which is something I've come to admire about my brother."

I rub my jaw, realizing I didn't shave. "I, um, I let him down. For so many reasons. So I need to apologize to you, Cal, for being an ass"—I glance back toward his casket —"and not trying to see things from your perspective." A sniffle in the front row catches my attention as Katherine wipes away tears. "What I didn't understand is that when you find your own little slice of heaven on Earth, you do everything you can to preserve it. To protect it. To nurture it. The way you would your lavender fields." Katherine's eyes meet mine, and I swallow back the lump in my throat and look away.

"Brother, I hope you'll forgive me. Please know that I'll spend the rest of my days trying to make it up to you and caring for Isabella. She and I have agreed that she's not dating before she's thirty, so that should please you. And in case anyone has other ideas, I found your shotgun, so we're all good."

The audience laughs, and I try to get past the ache in my sternum so I can finish. "I'll miss you, brother. Forever. And as long as I have breath in my lungs, I'll love and care for your daughter."

When I get back to my seat, Katherine is crying softly, and before I know what I'm doing, I'm pulling her and Izzy into my chest where Kat openly begins to sob. The baby crawls into my lap, and I hook my arm around her and hug her closer, vowing to do my best to take care of her. Her chubby little cheek drops to my shoulder, and it's all I can do to keep from breaking down myself.

18

KATHERINE

When the service is over, Brady grabs my hand and tugs me alongside him. People hug us and cry, and I'm barely putting one foot in front of another. The cemetery is worse. So much worse. Brady holds Izzy and keeps a comforting arm around me the whole time, and even though my heart aches for the loss of my friends, a strange warmth comes over me when he grips me tighter.

I stare up at him as we walk to the truck, and when our eyes connect, the pain of today ebbs away just a little bit, making me wish I knew him in different circumstances. Because in another lifetime, in a parallel world—one where he doesn't live on the other side of the country—I think he's the kind of man I could love.

The realization is so strong, so jarring, I trip, but he hangs on to my arm and keeps me from wiping out.

"Careful, Grace," he mumbles, and even though I'm embarrassed, I smile.

As I'm regaining my bearings, Mrs. MacIntyre stops in front of us. "Give me the baby. Y'all need a night to recuperate, and if I know you"—she points at me—"you're working yourself to the bone. You can pick her up in the morning."

Brady looks to me, and I introduce them. "This is our neighbor, Mrs. MacIntyre. She watches Isabella sometimes when I work at the diner. She's been out of town, or I'm sure you would've met her by now."

He frowns and stares at me a moment. "You work at a diner?"

"Yes, but I took this week off. I go back on Monday."

His frown turns into more of a scowl, and I feel like I just poked a bear.

Mrs. Mac ignores our conversation and takes Bella, who grins up at her. "Hey, little miss." She turns to Brady. "Call me if you two need anything. Is there milk in here?" She points to the diaper bag.

I nod, but before I can say anything, she pats my arm, turns on her heel and waltzes off.

As we watch our neighbor cross the parking lot, Brady whispers, "Please tell me we didn't just send her off with a lunatic."

And then I laugh for the first time today, and it feels surprisingly good.

"Mrs. Mac babysits for us a lot. She loves Izzy." *Izzy.* I've never called her that before.

As though Brady recognizes that, his eyes warm. "C'mon. I'm going to pass out if we don't eat something soon. Aren't you hungry? We didn't eat breakfast, and it's almost two."

That's true. I fed the baby and spent the rest of the morning packing her diaper bag and getting both of us dressed.

Once we're in the truck, I lean my head against the window.

"You're shivering."

I hadn't noticed, but he's right. I wrap my arms around my waist.

Brady turns up the heat as I stare at the dark clouds blanketing the sky. A low rumble of thunder echoes in the distance, and goose bumps spread down my arms. It's going to rain. I used to love the rain.

Not any more.

Both of us are wiped out, so he says he'll order a pizza when we get home.

Without Izzy's chatter, it's eerily quiet when we walk in the house. Neither of us bothers to turn on the lights, and with a storm rolling in, it's dark in here. My heels break the silence, clacking along the hard wood floor.

I head toward my room, certain that Brady wants to be alone like he did yesterday, but then he calls out my name. Pausing in the doorway of my bedroom, I turn to look at him.

He's loosened his tie and looks utterly beautiful in his suit. Scruffy and tired, hands shoved into his pockets, like he's been at the office all afternoon. Someday, one lucky girl will get to come home to this. Inwardly, I sigh.

His lips flatten. "You okay?"

I shrug. I don't have words to describe what I'm feeling right now.

His head cants to the side as he studies me, his green eyes magnetic. I get the impression he wants to say something, but then he looks away.

It's funny how he could wrap his arms around me and kiss my forehead while we were surrounded by a hundred people, but get us alone, and I get the distinct impression I make him uncomfortable.

He clears his throat. "Thanks for setting everything up today. You did a great job."

"You paid for it. I just made a few phone calls."

"Kat, c'mon. You keep this place running, and the way you jumped in and took care of the details for today means a lot to me."

"No problem. I'm happy to help."

We stare at each other, and I can't stop thinking about how good it felt when he hugged me today. I want to thank him for being so sweet, but the words get lodged in my throat because the vibe between us right now is so painfully awkward.

Probably because you cried hysterically. What was he supposed to do?

But then he shifts and rubs the back of his neck, a cute smile on his face as he motions toward the office. "Wanna hang out? The pizza should be here soon, and we could watch a movie or something."

Part of me feels like we shouldn't spend more time together. Like we're crossing some kind of boundary after everything we shared today. But do I really want to be alone in my room right now? Besides, we're talking about pizza, which is harmless.

That dimple peeks out, making my heart skitter and weakening my resistance.

"Sure. Give me a few minutes, and I'll meet you in the office."

Tonight. You should tell him about Cal's accident. He needs to know what really happened.

I take a deep breath. *Yes, tonight.* Because telling him is the right thing to do.

When I join him, he's changed out of his suit and is wearing some worn jeans and a black t-shirt that stretches across his hard chest. I glance down at my dress. I should've changed too, but all I could manage was kicking off my heels and pulling on some fuzzy slippers.

Brady motions toward my feet. "Cute." He gives me a goofy grin that somehow dispels whatever weirdness we've had brewing since yesterday.

Maybe it's because I've been crying all day. Or maybe it's

because I haven't slept in a week, but I'm so grateful that we survived this afternoon and are gonna hang out, I'm practically lightheaded.

"They're all the rage," I joke as I pose in my hot pink poofy house slippers. They're made out of a furry material Izzy likes to pet. "You're just jealous. You know you want a pair."

He laughs. "Is it that obvious?"

"Big, tough guys always want hot pink house slippers." I sit next to him, nudging him with my shoulder. "Don't worry. Your secret's safe with me."

It feels good to be talking to him again.

He nudges me back. "I was about to have a drink, but now I'm worried you'll get me to confess all of my deep, dark secrets." That's when I notice the bottle of tequila on the coffee table and two shot glasses. He pours one and looks at me. "It's been a fucked-up day, and I was planning to get blasted. But not so tanked that I end up in my underwear on the neighbor's lawn."

"Meh, I've already seen you in your underwear." I wave at him nonchalantly. "Nothing special going on there." He barks out a laugh, and I giggle. "Okay, I'm lying. There's *a lot* there." I bulge my eyes meaningfully, and he looks down, still laughing, his cheeks turning the slightest tinge of pink.

I don't know where my bravado is coming from, but for once, I don't feel so dang uptight. I'm sure I'll be embarrassed as hell tomorrow, but today has been so stressful, and I'm too tired to care. He'll just have to deal with crazy Katherine.

"We're back to boner jokes, I see." He snickers.

"I can get a lot of mileage out of a good boner." We look at each other and then crack up. "Okay, that sounded *really* bad. I'm shutting up now."

"You're a goof." He pours two shots and holds one out to me.

After we toss them back, I slouch down on the couch. I close my eyes and let the alcohol seep through my veins.

He pours another round, and as I start to bring it to my lips, he nudges me again. "Sorry if I was kind of a dick this week. I know we don't know each other well, but I swear I'm not always so moody."

I can feel his eyes rake over me, but I can't quite bring myself to look at him. "You weren't a dick at all. You're a really good guy. The best." For some reason, those last few words sound breathy. I take a sip of my tequila, knowing I need to slow down or he'll have to peel me off the floor in a little while. Kicking off my slippers, I tuck my legs underneath me.

"Are you cold?" He leans over the couch, giving me a whiff of his sexy woodsy scent, and tosses a fleece blanket over my shoulders.

"Thank you. I don't know why I keep shivering."

He sits back down on the couch and stares at the blank flat screen TV. "Today was a little traumatic. This is your body's way of dealing with it."

My mind feels fuzzy, like an empty chalkboard after all the words have been erased and there's just a blur of white powder left.

I feel like I should try to come up with something to talk about, but honestly, just sitting here with him feels nice when my head has that post-hysteria throb behind my eyes.

Brady leans forward to pour another shot, and I take a moment to admire the way his shoulder muscles tug at his t-shirt, showcasing those sexy tattoos that decorate his arms.

I've never particularly liked tattoos, but I'd have to be blind to not see the appeal here. They scream of confidence. Of not giving a damn about what other people think. Of wanting to carve your own path in life. And I get that. I *so* get that.

He glances at me over his shoulder. "Can I ask you something?"

"Yup." My whole body feels like I'm melting into the couch. *Mmm. Tequila.*

"Cal left me a message the night of the accident." That statement hangs in the air, and my insides clench as I wait for him to continue. "I was exhausted. It had been a long day, and I didn't want to argue with him, so I didn't return his call. But now, not knowing what he wanted to tell me is agonizing."

I struggle to swallow. "I'm so sorry." I think about what he's asking me. "Cal probably called to tell you about Mel's pregnancy. He felt bad because he knew you were waiting for him to come home. He thought he'd be able to go to Boston for a few months to help your parents, but then Mel found out she was pregnant, and he couldn't leave her. I offered to stay with her, but I don't think he was comfortable not being here in case anything went wrong."

"That's understandable. I would never leave my pregnant wife either."

See, there are good guys out there. "Exactly. So my guess is he probably wanted to give you an update."

He takes a shot of the tequila, hissing afterward. "I was such a dick to Cal. I helped him pay for these business courses in Austin. I thought it would help him get focused. He was always a little flighty. Always had his head in the clouds. I was worried about him. That he'd wander through life without a plan. But when he didn't come home, when he and Melissa eloped, I was so pissed. I just assumed everything he was doing here was a joke."

I'm not sure what to say, so I don't say anything. Finally, he shakes his head. "The irony is that I was telling a friend of mine to go for her dreams. To take chances. To do what she loved. And the whole time, I was being an asshole to Cal, pressuring him to figure out his shit." A sad laugh leaves him. "I can think of a hundred other things he should have studied instead of business."

I have to admit I'm wildly curious about her, the *friend*, but I ignore it to focus on what he's saying about his brother. "If it's any consolation, Cal really did help Mel organize her finances. The farm is still struggling because we had a lot of rain last winter, which affected the crops, but he helped her create a budget and set up her accounting system so her bill payments wouldn't be late any more. And he helped me get her bath products online."

He rolls his lips between his teeth and stares into his glass of tequila like it holds all the answers. "And he made a will. Only someone who's thinking long term makes a will."

I nod as I think about what I need to tell Brady. The idea suffocates me, like it's a physical entity tightening around my neck. But he looks so heartbroken, and I can't bring myself to say the words, because all I want to do is make him feel better.

Before I can second guess myself, I touch his arm. "Brady, I swear to God, Cal was happy. No matter what you had going on between the two of you, he had what he wanted. He was excited about the new baby. That's one thing that gives me solace. Knowing that Mel and Cal had what they wanted—each other and Bella with another one on the way. Most men would be so lucky."

After a moment, his shoulders relax. "Thanks. I needed to hear that."

He leans back against the sofa, and we sit there in silence, each of us lost in our own thoughts for a while.

I motion toward him. "My little sister drives me crazy too. Tori's seventeen and thinks she knows everything and doesn't want my input unless there's a crisis she can't handle. But when she needs money, she heads straight to me like I'm her personal ATM." My lips twist. "I can handle the thankless role of big sister, but she's going through this wild phase right now that worries me."

"So I'm not the only one who struggles with this stuff?"

"Not at all. Tor definitely tests my patience. But I love her, and she knows it. The same way Cal knew you loved him." I bump his knee with mine. "If it makes you feel any better, Cal said you were a 'well-intentioned asshole.'"

I'm trying not to snicker when Brady rolls his eyes, but when he starts to laugh, I pour us both shots and raise my glass. "To being a well-intentioned asshole."

Grinning, Brady shakes his head and clinks his glass against mine. "To being a well-intentioned asshole."

We toss back the shots. Shivering, I place my glass on the coffee table and slouch back on the couch.

My eyes are getting heavy, and I'm thinking I should take a power nap when Brady breaks the silence. "Can I ask you something else?"

It's funny how he prefaces every question with a question. Rolling my head against the couch, I turn to look at him. "Anything."

"How does the whole town know you? Not just know you, but downright adore you. Not that you're not awesome. You are. But you said you've only been here a few months and yet you seemed to know everyone who came out today."

I try to focus on what he's asking instead of the way my heart flutters at his compliment. The answer is something that would've embarrassed my ex. Shamed him, really. And that plain sucks. Nobody should have the right to make me feel that way.

Pointing to my shot glass, I motion for another drink. *Here's to me embracing where I came from.* Brady obliges, and in a matter of seconds I'm tossing back more tequila. The sharp taste burns my throat and I wince, covering my mouth with my hand.

"I grew up here," I blurt. Lowering my hand, I place it in my lap, wishing I had something better to do with it. Like touch Brady. *I'd like to touch Brady.* I smile to myself, making a mental note to cut myself off from the booze.

His eyebrows lift, and I shake my head. "Not *here* here exactly." I lick my lips, which are numb.

Suddenly, I want to tell him and see his reaction. I tense, hoping like hell his response doesn't ruin what I've already come to admire about him.

"My parents were migrant workers, and when I was little, we traveled all over South Texas. This was one of the farms we worked at." And then I hiccup.

19

BRADY

I'm not sure what I was expecting Kat to say, but this isn't it. But everything about this girl screams resilience, so I shouldn't be surprised that she's the daughter of migrant workers.

When those beautiful hazel eyes look up at me, they're guarded, but she continues. "One day, we ended up here. Mel's dad Bob ran it at the time. I don't know what happened to her mom. I got the impression she hightailed it when Mel was little. My parents helped harvest and did odd jobs for a while." She reaches for her hair and braids it as she talks. "Mel's dad offered to let us stay on, but my father didn't feel right accepting when there wasn't much to do, so my family moved to another farm near Dallas. We eventually settled down in Corpus."

I smile as I tug on her braid. "Okay, Anne of Green Gables, so how did you and Melissa end up being best buds?"

She laughs. "How do you know who Anne of Green Gables is?"

"I might be a momma's boy. She likes those books."

Toying with a button on her dress, which I notice is now

open along her toned thigh, she grins back, and Jesus, that smile. It's luminous. "Well, your momma has good taste. Those are great books." Smiling, she adds, "Mel and I got close after I wrote her a postcard telling her how much fun I had here that summer and thanking her for being so nice to me."

She shrugs, looking a little shy. "I didn't have a lot of friends growing up. It was tough when we moved so often. People don't always treat migrant workers well. And it's hard to find common ground with the other kids at school. They return from summer break talking about vacations and Disneyland, and I spent most of that time picking cotton. Anyway, Mel wrote me back, and we stayed in touch from then on."

God, I can only imagine a young Kat, all big eyes and beaming smiles, her lush, dark hair twisted in a braid, and I have the sudden urge to hurt the assholes who were cruel to her and her family when she was a kid.

"Did you guys live here in the house back then too?"

Kat shakes her head, her face reddening before she whispers, "We slept in our van at a rest stop just off the highway."

It takes a full minute to process what she says.

What the holy fuck?

I try to school my features because I don't want to offend her. But Jesus. It makes me realize how easy I've had it my whole life.

A declaration like that requires a drink. I pour us shots and hold up my glass. "To being a badass."

Her eyes linger on the shot glass as though she's warring with herself about taking another. Ultimately, she grabs it and shoots me one of her killer smiles. "Says the pot."

My grin widens. This girl. I'm busy staring at her, seeing her with new eyes, when she clears her throat.

"So, um, is your girlfriend back home gonna be freaked out that you're bringing home a baby?"

Cute. She's so damn cute. I can't lie—her fishing for details about me feels pretty good.

Blowing out a breath, I think about how to answer that question. "No girlfriend. No wife. Poor Izzy is going to have to accept that her uncle can't coordinate her outfits for shit." I laugh and run my hands through my hair. "Been flying solo for a while, I guess."

Her eyebrows lift. "You guess?"

How exactly do I explain Gwen and I were only fucking? Yeah, I don't.

"Maybe I should say the last girl I saw wasn't serious. For either of us." She nods, and I can't help but ask the obvious question. "And you?"

"I broke up with my boyfriend just before coming here."

I wait for her to tell me more, but she doesn't. "Was it serious?"

She rolls her lips between her teeth. "Serious enough."

I want to know what that means, but deep down, I realize I shouldn't be delving too deep. It's not like anything can happen here. I live in Boston. She lives in Texas. End of story. Fortunately, the doorbell stops me from asking anything I'll regret tomorrow.

When I return a few minutes later with a pizza and dessert, she makes this little sound.

I pause as I balance boxes of food in my arms. "Did you just purr?"

A giggle escapes her. "Maybe. I'm just really excited about the pizza."

"Clearly."

We chow down for a bit, barely pausing to breathe. I'm feeling so much lighter since we talked about Cal. I didn't realize how much that was weighing on me.

I find myself watching Kat as she munches on a slice of

hand-tossed. There's something so disarming about her. Maybe it's her laugh or that easy smile. Maybe it's the way her eyes brighten when she's amused. Whatever it is, I like that I can talk to her. But even more, I like that she opens up to me.

After our second piece, she licks her lips and sighs. "How is it that Pizza Hut is this good? If I were on a deserted island and could only pick one food for all of eternity, it would be this mushroom pepperoni pizza."

"Hey, there's an idea. Maybe I can pay you in pizza." I chuckle as I shovel in another bite, but when I glance at Kat, she's frowning.

"Brady, I feel bad taking your money. I love Izzy like she's my own, and I'm happy to help as long as you need me. Please don't feel like—"

"Katherine, stop. I'm paying you. In fact, I just transferred over some money yesterday so I can write you a check." I wipe my hand on a napkin and do my best to glare, but her pouty lips are making it difficult. "I'm serious. You can't go around doing everything for free."

She nods like I've scolded her, and now I feel like an ass.

I soften my voice, wanting her to know I'm in her corner. "I just don't want anyone to take advantage of your kindness, so please tell me that diner pays you."

Her cheeks, which are already flushed from the alcohol, turn a deeper shade of red. "Yes, they do."

Obviously, this girl needs the money or she wouldn't be waiting tables. Not that there's anything wrong with waiting tables, but she's capable of so much more. Which makes me realize how little I know about her.

"So, your family is in Corpus? Is that where you went to school?"

"Yeah, I went to high school in Corpus. Was more or less

homeschooled before that because we moved so much. Ended up at Texas A&M for my undergrad."

"So you're an Aggie?" I shake my head at her like I'm disappointed.

She smacks my shoulder playfully. "Hey, don't make fun. I know UT is cooler, but my dad would rather get dipped in hot tar than let his daughter go to a liberal school in Austin."

"Are you conservative too?"

Her eyebrows knit together and she shakes her head. "God, no. I'm sure I would've preferred attending UT. I got a full ride to both schools, but I went to A&M because I didn't want to let my dad down." She sighs. "I know that sounds lame."

"Full ride, huh?" I'm not surprised with the way she runs things around here. She's a powerhouse. She reminds me of a little hummingbird, the way she never stops working.

"Yes, that's how my nerdiness through high school was rewarded."

"You? A nerd? I find that hard to believe." *Especially in that dress.* I fight to not glance down at her bare thigh that's peeking through the slit in the front.

"I'm sure this is gonna sound strange, but it was tough to finally settle down and go to an actual school. I was so used to studying when we were on the road. Reading under a big oak tree or in a field of cotton with the wind blowing in my face."

I smile at her Southern accent and the way *studying and reading* sound like *studyin' and readin'*.

"A lot of kids in situations like mine miss school and end up dropping out later, but my dad was on my butt every day. He'd get assignments from my aunt. She's a teacher. So yeah, when I finally went to high school, I was a bona fide nerd, complete with glasses and a mouth full of metal."

I chuckle as I pour another shot. "Braces aren't so bad. I had a retainer in high school. Great for my teeth. Bad for making out with cheerleaders."

"Cheerleaders, huh? You and I ran in different stratospheres then. But I'm not surprised you dated cheerleaders. You probably still do."

I wait until she looks up at me. "Cheerleaders are overrated."

She stares at me a moment before a smile spreads on her face. And then she laughs. "I have a t-shirt that says, *Nerds Do It Better.*"

"I bet." And maybe it's the alcohol that's letting me take a few liberties, but I give in to the urge I've had all day and let my eyes wander over her body. "I'd like to test that theory sometime," I mumble under my breath.

The blanket has fallen off her shoulders, and she's sitting with her legs tucked under her while she sports that little nine-teen fifties-style dress that makes my pulse kick up. Which is surprising because it's modest. Demure even. But fuck, all I can think about is the way those buttons lead between those lush breasts, and I can't help but wonder how she'd feel in my hands.

When my eyes lift to hers, I see the same longing reflected back at me.

We're sitting side by side on this huge couch. It would be so easy to lean forward and delve between those luscious pink lips.

Warning bells go off in my head.

This is wrong. I'm leaving soon. I have a shitload of responsibility that makes having a relationship right now impossible. Izzy. My parents. A farm house. A failing business in Boston. And I doubt Kat is the kind of girl to hook up.

But between the emotional day we've had and the alcohol numbing my brain, I can't deny how much I want to strip her of that dress and lose myself in her body.

We stare at each other, and it's all I can do to not reach for her. But then a thunderbolt shatters the silence, and we both jerk back.

I'm not one for believing in signs, but if ever there was one that screamed, *Don't be a fucking idiot,* that was it.

I laugh nervously and find a reason to take a breather. "Be back in a sec. Nature's calling."

20

KATHERINE

My heart is racing the whole time he's gone. The way Brady was looking at me, like he wanted nothing more than to yank me into his lap and have his way with me, made my body spark to life. Even now that he's stepped away, I want to chase after him.

Ugh. Pathetic.

I take a deep breath and my eyes drop down to the half-empty bottle of tequila.

Not good. We're both buzzed, really buzzed, and strung out from today. A flash of skin catches my attention, and I realize my thigh is on full display.

Oh, for heaven's sakes. No wonder he wants to jump your bones. You're half-naked.

I pull the fabric over my legs and yank the blanket over me as he strolls back in. He glances at the TV and then back at me.

"What should we watch?"

He flips through the channels, and we debate different movies. I want a John Hughes film, and he wants *Die Hard* or *Terminator.* I shake my head. Men.

He tosses the remote next to the half-eaten box of pizza, and

Steve Carell's voice fills the room. We settle on *40-Year-Old Virgin* without ever saying anything. It just happens to be on TV.

I don't miss the way he sits on the other side of the couch this time or how he leans away like he's deliberately putting distance between us.

For some reason, this makes me like him more. So many men would use today as an excuse to get in a girl's panties. But not Brady. He totally could have had me ten ways to Sunday a few minutes ago.

But then a nagging thought starts looping in my brain.

Maybe he doesn't want me. Maybe he realizes that a short fling with a farm girl is more trouble than it's worth. Maybe he's not attracted to me like I am to him.

Ignoring the heat in my cheeks, I pour another shot of tequila. I'm gonna regret the alcohol tomorrow, but this might numb the sting of rejection.

It's late. We've been downing one Steve Carell comedy after another. The pizza is gone and so is half a casserole I microwaved. My buzz has worn off, and I suspect Brady's has too. We stopped drinking a while ago.

I turn to Brady as I stand up and stretch. "Want some Advil? I'm gonna grab a couple before I go to bed."

He nods and mutters thanks.

When I return, I hold out his glass of water and two orange tablets, which he takes with a small smile. "Wake me up tomorrow so I can help feed all the little beasts."

Oh, crap.

How being around Brady could make me forget the obvious things I should be doing right now frustrates me. "I should check on everyone. It's been raining pretty hard."

I bolt out of the room before he can answer. I know he doesn't understand why we have so many animals, but Mel loved them, and Izzy does too, and despite how much work they are, I'd rather lose a limb than let anything happen to them.

In my bedroom, I throw on my work boots and shrug into a coat. As I'm heading out the back door, Brady grips my arm. I turn and find him inches away, so close that I can feel his breath on my skin.

"You shouldn't go out there in the storm. Let me go."

His words send a panic through me. *That night. The way my friends left in the thunderstorm. How they never came back.*

My heart races, and I grip his shirt with both hands. "No fucking way."

His eyebrows lift in surprise. But there's no way in hell I'm letting him go out there.

I shake my head, my hands trembling. I can't breathe, and I start gasping for air.

He closes his eyes briefly. I see the moment he realizes why I'm freaking out, because he reaches for me and presses me against his chest.

His chin rests on top of my head, and I want to melt into him, but the secret I've been keeping is too much to bear. I've been trying to put it out of my head all week just to get through the funerals, but I can't let this go any longer. He deserves to know. He might kick me out, but I *have* to tell him.

"Brady." My voice is muffled against his chest. *Inhale. Exhale.*

"Shh. It's okay. Calm down. Nothing bad is going to happen tonight."

Guilt floods me. I can't let him comfort me. It's not right.

"I have to tell you something." I push against him until he lets me go. "It's about the accident."

We stand in the dark hallway, and I hear little meows

coming from the back porch. I ignore the kittens and prepare myself for what needs to be said. "It was my fault." My face tilts down. "What happened. Why Sampson got out. The reason Cal and Mel drove out into the storm."

He stills, and even in the dark, I can feel his piercing eyes. "What do you mean?"

"I was supposed to lock up Sampson. I had gone to the barn to check on him. He was restless." I blink back the familiar sting of tears in my eyes. "That horse hates thunder and was kicking against his stall. I walked in there to brush his mane and talk to him until he settled down. But I must have left the stall unlatched because later it was banging in the wind."

I can tell Brady doesn't get what I'm saying, so I continue. "It's why Mel and Cal went out that night. Because Sampson got out. It's why they took their truck and went down to the back creek. He always wanders down there when he breaks loose."

My throat stings, and I close my eyes, waiting for Brady to yell at me, but he never does.

When I get the courage to look at him, his head is lowered, and he's rubbing the back of his neck. A minute passes, and finally he whispers, "Accidents happen, Kat."

I wait for him to say more, but he doesn't. He just nudges me to the door with a sigh. "Let's check and make sure everyone's locked down for the night. C'mon. We'll go together."

Nodding, I follow him out to the porch where the kittens start mewling. I kneel down and pet their damp fur. The wind is so strong, the rain is pelting through the back porch screen.

Glancing around, I worry when I don't see Bandit lurking. Even though the porch is enclosed, that little rascal knows how to work the latch on the flimsy door that leads outside. Hopefully, he's nice and warm under the house.

"Why don't you put the kittens in Izzy's room tonight?"

"Great idea." I scoop them up and put them in their little box. As I'm heading into the house, I look back at Brady. "Wait for me. I'll just be a minute."

His eyes warm. "I'm not going anywhere without you. I promise."

21

———

BRADY

Something happened while I watched Kat race around the property with ice-cold water pelting her skin and soaking her clothes. My admiration for her grew. As did the weight of what she told me earlier. I can't believe she holds herself responsible.

But I straight-up don't know any woman who would willingly head out in a thunderstorm to do this.

She dragged me across the farm to check on the chickens and goats and that horse. Everyone was locked away and dry. But that didn't stop her from cooing at them sweetly.

As we stand on the porch, drenched, she laughs. "So maybe I was overreacting. Maybe they didn't need us to check on them."

Our breaths come out like little puffs of smoke in the cold air.

I smile as I wipe water out of my eyes. "Better to be safe than sorry. But we should get out of these wet clothes before we catch pneumonia. Why don't you hit the shower first? It's too late for coffee, right?" It has to be after midnight.

She thinks a long, hard minute as she shivers. "Probably. But dang, coffee sounds good."

"How about some tea? Or hot chocolate?"

Her eyes brighten. "I'd love some hot chocolate! Check above the coffee maker. I think we have those little marsh-mallows."

She smiles, and I grin back like an idiot. I just ran around in some cold-ass rain for an hour, but one look from this girl, and I'd do it all over again.

Her small hands start to unbutton her coat. She's still wearing that dress. Only now she's sporting work boots.

I help her take off her coat, which is about fifteen pounds heavier since it's drenched. I drape it over a chair so it can dry on the porch as she kicks off her boots. Motioning for her to get in the house, I follow behind. She turns to me as she reaches for the light in the bathroom. It backlights her so she glows, and it stops me in my tracks.

She's so fucking beautiful. Her cheeks are flushed and her skin is damp. Wet tendrils of hair stick to her neck.

And that dress. Goddamn. The fabric is glued to her like a second skin, and even though the dress is black, it's hard to miss her nipples standing at attention. Especially since her chest is heaving from the cold.

Fuck me.

I had a hell of a time not kissing her earlier, and seeing her like this is not helping.

"I'm going to grab us those drinks," I mumble, stalking away before I beg her to let me join her in the shower. Because the thought of her naked body, soapy and slick, has me hard enough to pound nails.

By the time we swap places, I've barely managed to get the milk microwaved, but at least the boner crisis has subsided.

Until I step into the shower that smells just like her.

My resistance, which has been hanging by a very fine thread, finally snaps.

There's only so much shit I can deal with in one day. I may

not be able to act on my attraction to her, but at least I can take the edge off so I don't strip her bare and fuck her against a wall.

For the first time since I've met her, I really let myself think about Kat, the gorgeous woman who's been here for me since the moment I walked through that front door. Have I really only known her five days? Jesus. I feel like I've been here weeks, not days. Everything about our situation is intense. I shouldn't be surprised that the vibe between us is too.

I ignore the strange emotion darting around in my chest. This, thinking about her while I rub one out, has to be purely physical. It can't be more. Nothing about our relationship can mean more.

Leaning against the shower wall with one hand, I close my eyes as the hot water beats against my skin. My dick bounces against my stomach, and I grip it hard as I give into the fantasy.

She fills my vision with her honey-colored eyes and pouty lips. With that taut body and round ass. With those toned legs and full breasts.

I think about what it would feel like to have that sexy mouth on me. How she'd writhe when I bite her pretty pink nipples.

My cock swells as I imagine her wet curves fitting against me. The sounds she'd make as I lick up her sweet center.

The way she'd moan before chanting my name.

The rush of making her come hard.

And that's all it takes.

The kitchen is dark when I get done with my shower, so I head to the office. Two cups of hot chocolate sit on the coffee table, but Kat is sound asleep. She's curled up on half of the couch while her damp hair drips down her arms. I close my eyes so I don't stare at her like a creep.

Reaching over, I take off her glasses and set them on the coffee table.

Damn. I don't want to wake her up, but where am I supposed to sleep? I'm sure as shit not using Cal's bed, and I think it would be a little weird if Kat woke up tomorrow morning and found me passed out in her room.

I grab a blanket and drape it over her. If the goose bumps on her arms are any indication, she's freezing. It's chilly in here, and she's just wearing thin sweat pants and a t-shirt.

Which reminds me that I need to figure out the problem with the heating vents so she doesn't catch pneumonia in her bedroom.

But first, where do I sleep tonight?

My brain feels like mush, especially after the tequila, that shower, and my impromptu jerk-off session. I'm ready to pass out. When my eyes land on the hot chocolate, though, I can't resist taking a sip. *Goddamn. It's good.*

After a minute, I set down the mug and debate what to do. Briefly, I consider the couch in the living room but dismiss it when I remember the broken springs that would probably poke a hole in my ass.

Deciding I need to sit, I park myself on the far end of the couch, opposite Kat. When I lean back, I'm surprised when it gives more than I expect.

It only took you five days to figure out that it's a lounger, dumbass.

After grabbing another blanket, I settle in.

The rain beats against the windows, creating an hypnotic sound. I'm pretty sure I pass out a minute after my head hits the cushion. I'm hoping I can sleep into next week.

But I bolt upright when a scream cuts through the silence.

I look over to find Kat huddled on the couch. She's trembling, whispering, "No, no!"

She's still asleep.

I crouch down in front of her. "Kat. Wake up, babe. You're dreaming."

Her face contorts, and she cries out again. I can't stand seeing her this way, so I grab her arms and try to shake her awake gently.

Her eyes fly open, and she gasps.

I don't have time to apologize for waking her because she launches herself into my arms, and I land on my ass, but the trembling girl I'm holding doesn't seem to care. Her heart is racing, and she's ice cold.

"Hey," I whisper. "It's okay." I stroke her back, and she takes a shuddering breath. Damn. That must've been one hell of a dream.

Is this why she always looks exhausted? "Babe, how long has this been going on? Do you have a lot of nightmares?"

She nods against me.

"Since the accident," she whimpers.

Damn.

Does she always scream in her sleep, and I've just never heard her?

I hold her until her breaths begin to even out. "You okay?"

She laughs, but it sounds hollow. "Trying to be."

"C'mon. Let's tuck you in bed." I get up slowly, keeping my arm around her shoulders as we head to her room. I don't bother turning on the light. Her window blinds are cracked open, and there's enough moonlight to see her twin bed. Immediately, I see my breath.

"It's fucking freezing. You can't sleep here."

"It's okay. I'm used to it."

"But your hair is wet. You're going to get sick." We were already running around in the ice-cold rain tonight.

All of a sudden, I'm pissed. This girl busts her ass around here, and this is where she sleeps?

"Fuck this." I grab her hand and drag her back to the office. "Sit." Pointing at the couch, I don't wait for her response as I jack up the thermostat as high as it'll go and then duck into the bathroom for a hair dyer.

When I stalk back, she motions toward me. "Why are you so pissed off right now?"

"This. You freezing." Growling, I plug the hair dryer into the wall. "I'm going to fix the fucking temperature in your room, but for right now, let's dry your hair. Turn around." Her eyebrows lift, and we stare at each other. "Kat. I'm not joking. Turn around."

She huffs out a breath. "*¿Seriament?* I can do it myself you know. I'm not five."

"Sure you can. But you didn't. C'mon." I flip on the dryer and put my hand up to my ear, shrugging like I can't hear her protests. She rolls her eyes but finally turns so that her back is to me.

Reaching for her thick, damp locks, I thread my fingers through her dark hair as I wave the dryer. The scent of lavender and mandarin reach my nose. I know this because I read all the damn labels in the bathroom earlier tonight when I was trying not to get her naked.

I've never done this for a woman before. It's surprisingly intimate. How close we are. How much I have to touch her.

The strands are silky soft and flutter around her shoulders as I weave my fingers in and out of her hair. Rhythmically, I repeat the motion. After a few minutes, she drops her head to the side.

I study her graceful neck and the long line of her shoulder, and I have the sudden urge to kiss her there. Is she ticklish. Would she giggle? Or would she moan and beg for more?

When the blood in my body starts heading south, I realize I have to stop this shit before it gets out of hand.

Ten minutes later, after I've recounted Red Sox stats instead of studying the soft curves of the woman in front of me, I click off the dryer, and she turns around. Her eyes are sleepy. "Thank you," she whispers as she gets up.

"Nuh-uh. You're not going anywhere." Reaching into the closet, I grab a few more blankets and another pillow. "Lie down." I motion toward the couch.

She looks at me, bewildered. "Where are you gonna sleep?"

"The floor."

Her mouth drops open. "Brady, no. This is silly. I sleep in that room every night. I'll be fine."

"I insist."

She sighs. "Let me sleep on the floor. You take the couch."

"Kat, I realize we haven't known each other that long, but what part of me do you think is asshole enough to let a woman sleep on the floor?"

She stares up at me while she nibbles her bottom lip. "How about we share it? It's a pretty big couch. I could sleep on one end or in the lounger. Whichever you wanted."

I tuck a strand of hair behind her ear. "Fine."

She sits slowly and pulls up the blanket.

Settling back into the lounger does nothing to ease the nervous energy that pounded through me when I heard her scream. Jesus Christ. That scared the hell out of me. But when I think about how she leapt into my arms, I can't deny how good she felt.

She keeps shifting, so I know she's still awake. And I can't fucking sleep.

"Want to see what's on TV?" I ask her in the darkness.

"Yeah, that'd be great."

The Steve Carell marathon is still going strong, so we settle in with *Anchorman*. It's barely audible, but neither of us seems to care.

I glance at her, and she's curled up, looking like she's afraid whatever happened in her dream is going to bust through the front door.

This is probably the worst idea in the history of bad ideas, but I can't stop myself. I have a crazy need to make sure she's okay. And right now, I know she's not.

"Hey."

She turns to look at me, her eyes tinged with fear.

I hold out my arm. "Come here."

There's no hesitation. She just scoots closer and curls into me like she belongs pasted along my side. Her body's still trembling, from the cold or her dream, I'm not sure.

"Want to talk about it?" I ask softly.

She shakes her head no, and I drop it. For now.

I reach over and spread the blanket over both of us. I'm sure I'll regret this in the morning, but for now, at least I feel like I'm doing what I can to make her feel better.

Ignoring how good she feels against me, I close my eyes and try to sleep. Kat must be relaxing finally because she sighs and melts deeper against me. Her arm wraps around my waist, and her head slides to my chest. I glance down, and I realize how small she is. My arm tightens around her.

"Everything will be okay," I whisper. "I got you."

22

KATHERINE

I'm warm. So deliciously warm.

Usually, I wake up freezing, but right now, I'm in a cocoon of warmth that reminds me of a long summer afternoon. I could sleep like this into the new year.

Except for the pounding in my head. *Whoa.*

Then I remember the tequila.

Geesh. How many shots did I have? My mouth feels like I drank a pint of Pine Sol.

I squint through pasty eyes, hating the harsh light that filters through the blinds. Funny, I never realized how bright my bedroom gets in the morning.

But then something squeezes me, and I look down to see an arm draped over my hip.

One very tattooed and muscular arm.

The reason for the warmth squeezes me again, and I try not to squeak.

Then it comes rushing back to me. My nightmare. Curling up to Brady afterward. How he held me until I calmed down.

He's such a sweetheart.

Wait.

We're spooning.

My heart thrashes against my ribs. One of his arms is nestled under my head while the other anchors me firmly to his chest. A muscular thigh rests between my legs, and... and... his long, thick erection presses against my bottom.

I hold my breath. *Do not arch your back. Do not arch your back.*

I really want to arch my back.

My ex was not a snuggler. I never thought much about it since he was the first guy I had regular sleepovers with, so I guess I didn't realize what I was missing because this feels heavenly.

Brady sighs and then, dear Lord, presses his length against my ass.

He's thick and hard and feels so good.

Instinctively, I push back, and a deep, raspy groan sounds in my ear, making my neck and everything south of it tingle. Then the hand that's wrapped around my waist slides up over my breast and squeezes.

Gah!

My eyes flutter closed, and I try to breathe.

A deep throb starts at my core, and it's so very tempting to grind into his thigh to relieve the pressure.

I don't know what this means, what we're doing, but I'm filled with so much need, rational thought has escaped my brain.

He nuzzles against my neck while that hand rubs slowly across my nipple, back and forth, and warmth floods my panties. My skin is on fire, and I'm two seconds from turning around and launching myself at him when he mutters something I can't quite make out.

I debate whether or not to say anything when he mumbles it again.

"Scale down the art."

Wait. What?

Then he says something about an artichoke.

Um.

Yeah, he's asleep.

Curse words I never say bounce around in my head. For the first time since he arrived, I admit how much I want him. I've never lusted over any guy, but there's something about Brady that has me wanting to do all of the dirty things to him that I've only read about in books.

Disappointment washes over me at the realization that this comatose man will have no recollection of feeling me up once he wakes.

That hand squeezes my aching breast again, and I let out a gasp. Is it wrong that I'm enjoying this?

A lot.

Dang. If Brady is this good at foreplay when he's sleeping, I can't even imagine how good he is when he's awake.

I start to wonder how far I'll let this go. I usually pride myself on being an ethical person. I don't cheat. I don't steal. I don't lie.

And I don't usually fool around with guys I only met a week ago. *Not even a week. Six days ago.*

That's not right, is it?

Closing my eyes, I count back to when he arrived. Internally, I shake my head. Here I am thinking I would totally drop my panties for a guy I haven't even known a full week.

My mother's voice rings loud and clear. *Sinvergüenza.* She'd say I was shameless, all tangled up, half naked with a man I barely know.

But that's not totally true.

The way he held me yesterday. The sweet words he whispered to me, trying to calm me down after my nightmare. How he ran around in the frigid downpour to help me. My ex never would've done any of that even after all that time we were together.

Mel always said she had an immediate connection to Cal, like they'd known each other for years. That's why they eloped after only knowing each other two weeks.

Not that I plan to elope with Brady.

He sighs, and that big chest rubs against my back. Actually, everything rubs against my back.

More. More, I think, embarrassed to be this turned on by a guy who isn't even conscious.

If I press back, can I chalk it up to my hangover?

The erection slowly grinding between my ass cheeks is obviously short-circuiting my brain.

This is such a colossally bad idea.

"You feel so good, babe," he mumbles as his hand slides under the thin fabric of my shirt and back up to my breast.

Oh, God, is he awake? Please, please let this happen.

And that's when I realized what he said. *Babe.* He called me that last night after the nightmare too.

My stupid heart goes all aflutter.

His big, calloused hand slides over my sensitive skin, dragging over my tortured nipple, and I moan. My heart is racing, my panties are having a meltdown, and I'm panting.

When I don't think I can stand it any more, I take a deep breath, preparing to turn around and slide on top of him when he... he... snores.

Really?

Goddamn it.

23

BRADY

I wake with an erection so hard, it's fucking painful. Thankfully, I'm alone, so Kat isn't here to witness the wood. And if I'm being honest, it's a distraction from the rest of my life. From yesterday. From the conversation I need to have with my parents about Izzy's custody. From the woman I'm lusting over but can't have.

My head throbs, from stress or last night's alcohol perhaps. I'm wound. Tight. Tension pulls at my shoulders and neck, and as I twist on the couch, every muscle groans.

Jerking off last night to thoughts of Kat was probably stupid, but I haven't been with anyone in months, and the last thing I need to do is let myself be tempted.

I laugh humorously. *She doesn't even know how tempting she is.*

I'm halfway to convincing myself that I need to cut Kat from my mental porn reel when I catch a whiff of her shampoo. I pull my t-shirt to my nose, and sure enough, it's her sexy-as-fuck scent, which makes the throbbing worse. Everywhere.

Thoughts of last night flicker in my head. The way she looked so vulnerable when she told me she needed to check on the animals. *Like I was going to let her go out alone in a torrential rainstorm.*

A powerful urge to protect her fills me when I think about it.

But fuck, seeing her tremble on the couch after her nightmare? I don't know if anything will ever wipe that memory out of my head. Holding her felt right somehow. I'm sure that's what planted the dirty dream in my head.

And Jesus, what a dream.

We were tangled here on the couch when she slid on top of me, tore off her little t-shirt and thrust her tits in my face. I took one perky, pink nipple between my lips and sucked until she ground herself against me.

My dick throbs harder, and I realize I'd better deal with this somewhere a little more private. I glance over at the closed door and then to the wall-mounted clock. It's still early. She's probably out feeding the animals. I vow to get my ass out there to help her as soon as I'm done dealing with my dick.

I grab a change of clothes and head to the bathroom for a quick shower and a slow-motion replay of that dream. When I'm done and can walk upright again, I get dressed and head for the fresh pot of coffee.

Is it wrong to love a girl for making the coffee every morning? I pour in a little cream and take a sip. Perfection. Strong but not burn-your-esophagus strength.

My eyes land on a familiar Dunkin' Donuts travel mug on the dish rack, and part of me wants to fill my brother's coffee cup. He drank it with extra cream, extra sugar.

A deep sadness wells over in my chest. "I miss you, brother." I hold up my mug, wishing like hell he were here to give me shit about something. Anything.

The back door slams shut, and I turn to find Kat holding the baby, who's wrapped in a blanket.

Clearing my throat, I ask, "When did you go get Izzy from the MacIntyres'?"

Her eyes dart down with a shy smile. "I didn't." She laughs and tilts her arms. A little masked face leers at me.

It's the fucking raccoon.

I jerk back, and she laughs harder. "Relax. He's a baby and he doesn't have rabies or anything." *So she says.* "I found him asleep in the shed. The little rascal found a way in there last night, which is good because we got record rain, which is great for the aquifers but bad for the fields."

"The aquifers?"

She pushes her glasses up her nose. "Texas gets its water from nine major and twenty-one minor aquifers. Around here, the most important ones are Edwards and Trinity." She nibbles on her plump lip. "That's why fracking is such a bad idea. If we contaminate our water supply, we're screwed. I mean, obviously. But that means even more for farmers than the average person."

"Fracking? Is that why you were wearing that *Frack Off* t-shirt when I first met you?"

Kat smiles while snuggling that giant rodent to her chest. He wraps his creepy arms around her neck and makes this weird little snick, snick, snick noise. "Not everyone loves that t-shirt as much as I do." She strokes the mongrel. "Fracking stands for hydraulic fracturing," she says slowly, like she's testing whether or not I want to hear what she has to say.

I nod, prompting her to continue. I know about the issue. It's not like I live under a rock, but I'm surprised to see her so interested in the topic.

She continues. "It's a process that uses millions of gallons of water—aquifer water, I should add—to blast out oil and gas from shale deposits." Her frown deepens. "You can smell the fumes for miles, and those tanker trucks drip chemicals all along their routes."

The sun filters through the kitchen blinds and highlights the soft tendril of hair that's escaped her messy bun. Honestly? She's a vision. Even in sweats. I've never met a girl who looks so goddamn hot without makeup. The fact that she's all riled up is even hotter.

Kat stares up at me, her eyes bright. "We have twelve *thousand* gas wells here, and that number is only going up. Never mind that many experts suspect that's why we're having earthquakes for the first time ever. Mining the five-thousand-mile shale formation that runs along the eastern side of the state sounds feasible until you realize how much of that sits over our water supply."

The one hand that's not holding the raccoon starts waving wildly, and I hold back a grin. "Fracking is great for gas prices and oil companies and tax revenues, but terrible for Texans, who eventually will be ingesting God knows what in our water. Some ranchers are trying to fight it, but unless politicians have a major change of heart soon—good luck with that—it's a done deal."

She's so serious—her brow is furrowed, her jaw tight. I'm smiling at her like a dumbass, strangely more attracted to her now that she's unleashed that little rant.

"Sorry," she laughs, flushing. "I'm getting carried away, aren't I?"

"A little, but it's cute." I like this spitfire version of Katherine. I chuckle at her embarrassed grin. "How do you know so much about this? Did you study environmental issues in college?"

She sighs and shakes her head. "Not exactly."

Before I can ask another question, the phone rings, and she runs off to answer. When she returns, she looks a little panicked.

"That was the diner. Would you mind if I take a shift this afternoon? Someone called in sick, and they're short-handed."

"Not at all. Do what you need to do." I hate that she has to work on a Sunday.

You do it all the time.

It's true. I do, but it seems wrong that this girl is running herself ragged. I make a mental note to figure out how much I owe her so I can write that check tonight.

She pours a cup of coffee and calls over her shoulder, "I bet Mrs. Mac won't mind watching Izzy until this evening. I can call her after I take a shower."

"It's okay. Give me her number, and I'll see what they're up to over there. You said they're nearby?"

"Yup. Just down the road about a half mile." She heads into the office and pulls out a list of important phone numbers. Everything is on here—neighbors, vets, you name it. I smile knowing that Kat made this because it's color-coded in her handwriting, the same writing I found on a Post-It in the fridge the other day when she wrapped me a sandwich and labeled it, "Brady, bite me."

She disappears to take a shower, and I grab the phone. Mrs. Mac says she'd be happy to watch the baby until dinner time, and then she asks if her husband can borrow our truck to haul some firewood.

"Absolutely. Any time you need it, just let me know."

"You're a doll. Just like your brother."

I rub my forehead, feeling a sudden burn of shame. "Thank you, ma'am."

She tells me he'll walk down to pick up the truck. Ten minutes later, there's a knock on the door.

Mr. Mac is a slender man with a friendly face and gray hair. We chat for a bit about the weather and his constipated pig Gerald. Then he tells me he likes my tattoos and pulls up his sleeve to show me an American eagle on his forearm.

I have to say I like all of this neighborly stuff. I think Massholes would rather have their kidneys punctured than have to talk to neighbors like this, but I'm warming up to it.

When Kat walks into the office a few minutes later, she's looking panicked again. "Did... did Mel's truck just drive off?"

"Yeah, the MacIntyres need it to haul some wood. I said they could borrow it this afternoon."

"Oh." She bites her nail.

"Why?"

She looks up at me sheepishly. "I need a ride to work, and I assumed I could take the truck. I'm so sorry. That was presumptuous of me."

"Shit. Sorry. No, that wasn't presumptuous." I rub my neck, ignoring how cute she looks in her simple white t-shirt and jeans. "I could take you to work if you don't mind hopping on the back of the bike."

She stills. "You mean the Harley?"

"Yeah. You up for that?"

A huge smile lifts her lips. "If it's not too much trouble. That sounds kinda fun."

She's bouncing on her toes as we head toward the motorcycle. I strap my helmet on her, and she flashes one of those killer grins that makes my heart beat faster.

"Button up." I tap on the lapel of her coat and hop on the bike. When she jumps on behind me, I show her where to put her feet before adjusting my rear view mirror. "Hang on tight. Don't want you sliding off."

She whacks my arm. "That's not nice, Brady."

I chuckle. "Don't worry, sweetheart. I'd never let anything happen to you."

As I rev the engine, her arms slide around my waist and her thighs tighten against mine.

Fuck. Okay, maybe I thought it was a good idea, but clearly it isn't if my dick thinks it's playtime. *Down, dude.* I reach down to adjust myself. Jesus. It's like I'm in middle school, sporting spontaneous wood.

Kat gives me directions, and we take off down the country road. It's a gorgeous day, bright and sunny with a chill in the air. The roads are muddy, so we take it easy until we get to the main drag where I can go a little faster.

Every time we turn, she squeals a little and tightens herself around me.

If I thought riding around by myself was awesome, having her on the back of my bike is exhilarating. The heat of her body and the press of her curves to mine make me want to forget all of the reasons starting anything with her would be a bad idea. She's a cool girl. Sweet and unassuming. Beautiful inside and out. And she likes to ride.

A guy could get used to this.

I ignore the voice telling me this is a bad idea. Right now, I don't give a shit. After how upset she was last night, after how emotional yesterday was, I'm guessing we could both use a fun ride. Even if it ends the minute she gets off.

The minute she gets off.

For a second I stop breathing. Because the idea of Kat getting off has me hard all over again.

Thankfully, the diner comes into view. It looks like an old-fashioned rail car with retro, fifties-style neon lettering on the front that says The Lone Star Station. I pull into a spot close to the door.

Turning off the engine, I hold out my hand to help Kat dismount. Her small hand fits in mine, and I grip her tightly until she's on the ground. When she pulls off my helmet, her hair cascades everywhere. It's like one of those shampoo commercials in slow motion. The sun catching her highlights. Strands tumbling around her beautiful face. I catch a whiff of her scent and resist the urge to reach out and touch a soft tendril.

"Thanks for bringing me to work. I can probably catch a ride home later." Her cheeks are pink from the cold.

When I motion for my helmet, she hands it to me. "What time do you get off?"

She gathers her thick hair and twists it back. "Probably around five or six. I just need to help through the lunch-hour rush and prep for dinner."

"Call me when you're ready, and I'll come get you. What's your number? I should have it anyway." Grabbing my cell, I call her, and once she has my info on her phone, she worries that plump bottom lip, one I'm dying to taste.

"Thanks for everything last night. Sorry about freaking out. Again."

"It's been a rough week. Probably par for the course."

"Maybe, but I wanted you to know I appreciate it."

I motion toward the diner. "Sorry you have to work this week."

"They needed the help. Plus, I kinda need the job."

She pulls her jacket around her tighter, and I tell her with a wink, "I should pay you more."

Her whole face lights up when she smiles again. "You don't pay me anything."

"Exactly. I should pay you more." I tap her nose and she laughs.

When our eyes connect, I feel it, this energy that snaps and crackles between us, making me want to fist her hair and drag her mouth to mine.

"That was fun." She motions toward my bike. "How about we go for a long ride some time?"

My whole body burns. "Kat, I'd love to give you a long ride."

More than you know.

24

BRADY

THE DINER IS STILL BUSY WHEN I RETURN SEVERAL HOURS LATER. Parking myself on a stool at the counter, I grab a menu and wait for Kat. My eyes scan the images on the shiny pages. Burgers. Fries. Shakes. Typical American fare.

Kat's bubbly laughter catches my attention. Turning, I see her in the back, taking the orders for several baseball players at a booth. Her hair is up in one of those crazy ponytails that makes her look young and free-spirited, and the guys are staring at her like she's an entree.

When she sets down their drinks and one guy openly stares at her breasts, my jaw clenches.

Chill, man.

Returning my attention to the menu, I try to focus on the words in front of me.

You're thinking crazy. I should not be feeling so possessive of her. Nothing can happen between us. *Nothing.* I remind myself of all of the reasons why, the biggest of which is we live half a continent away from each other.

But what if one of those assholes asks her out? Am I going to be okay with that?

Fuck, no.

I turn back quickly to check out the situation again. She's laughing with them but not being overly flirty. Just in that sweet Katherine way that makes you want to smack her on the ass for being so damn cute.

But when one touches her wrist to get her attention, I have half a mind to break his hand.

"What can I get you, handsome?"

I look up to see a waitress leaning so far over the counter that her double D's greet me before I get a chance to see her face. Blinking, I jerk my head back.

The redhead chuckles, like she knows full well what she's doing.

Clearing my throat, I motion behind me. "If you don't mind, ma'am, I'd like to wait for Kat." *When did I start calling every female ma'am?*

The smile on her face falls. "Suit yourself." She saunters off, swaying her ass a little more than necessary.

"Hey." Katherine's breathy little voice at my side has me smiling before I even see her. Now that I'm sitting on a stool, she's almost eye level with me.

"Is it okay if I wait here until you're done?"

She breaks out one of those killer smiles. One, I might add, she didn't flash at those assholes in the booth.

"Absolutely. Do you want something to eat?" She touches my arm. "You're probably starving. Did you grab lunch at home?"

The way she calls the farm home fills me with a stupid warmth that has me grinning like a moron. Never mind that she's worried about whether or not I ate. Come to think of it, I haven't.

"Nope. Haven't had a chance. Wanted to cut up that fallen tree and dry out the firewood in the barn before it rains again." It helped get my mind off my brother, off yesterday, and off Katherine. The only thing it didn't help with was the raging headache I had all afternoon, but the four Advil I took eventually kicked in.

Her eyes widen. "You did all of that this afternoon?"

"Yeah. I still need to deal with the stump, but at least we'll have some firewood instead of a rotting tree."

"That sounds great." She moves in closer and points out a few dishes on the menu she thinks I'd like. I fight like hell not to stare at her breasts, which aren't the double D's the other waitress flashed at me, but the redhead's tits didn't have me wondering how her skin would taste. Kat has a great rack, though. High and pert with a little bounce that I'm guessing would be the perfect handful.

I have no clue what the hell Kat just said but I nod, she smiles, and a few minutes later, she brings me a giant plate of chicken fried steak that makes my mouth water. "Eat up, buttercup. When you're done, I'll bring you some pie." And just like that, she trots off to wait on another table.

By the time we leave, it's dark outside, and I'm so full, I wish I could crawl into bed. "Let's head to the MacIntyres' house to pick up Izzy. You can drive her back in Melissa's truck." I rev the engine of the Harley as Kat's slender arms wrap around me. "Sorry if I stink." I chuckle. "Haven't had a chance to take another shower."

I'm surprised when she pulls me tighter and buries her nose in my neck, instantly making my blood rush south. "You don't stink. You actually smell kinda good," she says in this throaty little voice as her lips whisper over my skin.

I hold in a groan. This girl is seriously giving me the worst case of blue balls known to man.

Once we pick up the baby and pull up to the farm, I help Kat get my niece out of the truck.

"I've missed you, squirt," I tell Izzy as I lift her up to blow a raspberry on her tummy.

She squeals and claps. I smile back until I remember I still need to tell my parents I'm getting custody.

It's nice heading into the house with Kat, though. I don't know why, but it takes the edge off. Somehow, being here with her and Izzy makes this house a home. It's... comforting.

I'm about to get Izzy ready for bed when Kat calls my name. With one arm around the baby, I head into the kitchen to find her holding up the envelope I left her.

"What's this?" she asks.

"Since it has your name on it, I'm guessing it's for you." I don't know why I'm teasing her, but she gets a flirty glint in her eye that makes me want to tease her more. I motion toward it. "Open it and find out, Sherlock."

She tears into it and gasps. "Holy shit, Brady," she whispers. I nearly gasp myself because the girl never curses. "This is too much."

"Sorry, it's non-negotiable. Although I still need you to fill out a 1099. And if it's not too much trouble, I'd like to photocopy your ID so I can add you to the car insurance."

Her eyes glisten, and she blinks rapid fire. Then she comes crashing into me for a hug.

"You work hard around here. You deserve it," I mumble into her hair.

Her soft body melts against mine, and that buzz I get around her kicks in to overdrive.

She gives me another squeeze and then reaches for the baby with a sigh.

"Seriously, Brady, two grand is way too much. Cal only owed me for the last few weeks. That's like three hundred max."

I frown and ignore the inclination to criticize my brother.

"You bust your ass. Hell, I don't think two grand is enough, but that's all I can afford right now. I wish I could pay you more."

She bites her lower lip. After a moment, she whispers, "Thank you. So much. You have no idea how much I appreciate it."

I nod, truly wishing I could give her more, wishing I could give her everything. And as terrifying as that idea should be, for some reason, it isn't.

25

KATHERINE

My pen pauses on the grocery list. I turn toward the baby monitor and listen to Brady get Izzy ready for bed.

"Oh, baby! No, no, no. We're licensed for *residential* poops. This is an *industrial-sized* poop."

Izzy squeals with delight, and I choke on a laugh. Good Lord, he's adorable with her.

Being with him tonight, having him pick me up from work was freaking awesome. I'm not the bragging type, but seeing him brush off Darla's advances at the diner made me want to do a victory dance.

Not that I blame her for hitting on him. From the moment he strode in on those long, muscular legs, every female turned her head toward Brady. It's hard to ignore his dark, brooding vibe. When he took off his jacket, I swear the girls in the diner let out a collective sigh because those tattoos are sexy as all get-out.

Yeah, Brady looks like a badass with that swagger and ink.

For some reason, I think of my dad and how much he'd probably hate Brady on the spot. I can just hear him now. *What kind of man rides a motorcycle? One who isn't family-minded. Why does he need tattoos? Only gang bangers have tattoos.*

I roll my eyes, hating how conservative my dad can be. I think he experienced such hardships growing up that he went overboard trying to protect me and my sister. So sometimes, he makes snap judgments and they're wrong. So wrong.

Like with Eric. My father loved my ex. Thought he'd be the kind of man to watch out for his daughter. Thought he'd protect me. Love me through the bad times and not just the good. My dad couldn't have been more off the mark.

"The munchkin's in bed." Brady's voice makes me snap my head up. "Sorry," he says. "Didn't mean to startle you."

I place my hand over my chest and laugh. My heart is racing because he did kinda scare the crap outta me. "It's okay. I was just making a grocery list. Oh, before I forget—" I reach into my purse and pull out my driver's license. "You said you needed this."

He takes a long look at it, and for some reason, it makes me nervous. "What?"

Shrugging, he says with a chuckle, "Nothing. Just making sure you're legal."

I roll my eyes. "I know I look young, but I'm not *that* young." I already told him my age.

"No, twenty-three is old enough."

"Old enough for what?" I ask innocently as I stare up at him. *Old enough for you?*

He clears his throat. "Old enough to vote."

I hold in the laughter that's dying to burst out of me. "You're kind of a nerd. A hot, tatted nerd."

Wait. What?

"Hot, huh?" Now it's his turn to smirk.

"Shut up. You know you're attractive." I roll my eyes again and return to my grocery list.

The chair scrapes the floor as he sits at the table behind me. Mentally, I go through the items we'll need for the week before I add them to the list, but after a moment, I get the distinct feeling Brady's watching me.

When I turn around suddenly, his eyes lift to my face. Busted!

"Were you staring at my bottom?"

His chest shakes with laughter. "Bottom?"

"Yeah, bottom. Booty. Butt."

He holds out his hand like he's being helpful. "Ass?"

"Sure."

His face is expressionless. "No, I was not staring at your *ass*. It was in my line of vision."

I give him a deadpan look and return to my grocery list, not missing the way his lips tug up.

He rasps, "I fixed your vent problem. Your room should be warmer tonight."

I'm glad he can't see my face right now because I'm a little disappointed. I was sorta hoping for a repeat of last night... and this morning. Well, minus the snoring. "That's great. Thanks. How did you fix it?" I turn around and try to muster a genuine smile.

"Can't say I fixed it exactly. But I closed off the other vents. Everything except for the baby's room, which sends all the warm air to your room."

"But what about you? Won't you be cold?"

"No, it's pretty comfortable back there. Unless the temperature really dips like it did last night. Whatever. I'll grab more blankets."

Damn. He's sweet.

I give him a crooked grin and stick my head into the fridge to see if we have enough milk. Several casseroles are piled up, one on top of another. Gifts from thoughtful neighbors. See, that's why Mel and Cal were so right for this little town. People here take care of each other. I take a deep breath to quell the sudden rush of emotions at the thought that my best friends are gone.

As though Brady senses my pensive attitude, he doesn't say anything else for a while as I duck in and out of cabinets to inventory what we need.

Finally, as he's getting up, he motions toward me. "You still owe me some hot chocolate, you know."

"What?" I pause mid-stride.

"Hot chocolate. You fell asleep before we had a chance to drink it. And since I was about to watch a movie, you can join me. If you bring the hot chocolate, that is."

He says this so casually. I bite the inside of my cheek to keep from grinning like a *tontita*. "You're bargaining for hot chocolate?"

"Yours tastes different. Spicier or something." He shoves his hands in his pockets. "I like it."

"It's the cinnamon." My stupid little heart backflips. I stare up at him, hoping I don't look like a lovesick fool. I mean, not that I love him. That would be ridiculous. But him wanting to spend time with me has to mean something, right?

"I guess I could make you some hot chocolate." My voice sounds low and breathy. I try to swallow, but my mouth is dry.

"With those little marshmallows?"

I laugh. "Yes, Brady, with those little marshmallows." I motion toward the back office. "Go queue up a movie. Your pick. But no *Terminator* or *Die Hard*."

His face tightens with mock indignation. "You drive a hard bargain, Kit Kat."

Yes, I'll happily be his Kit Kat. *Especially if that means you'd bite me tonight.*

LEX MARTIN

He points behind him. "Let me grab a quick shower, and I'll meet you back there in ten."

"Sounds good."

Brady in the shower. Everything in me tingles. *No, that sounds amazing.*

26

BRADY

THE BLUISH LIGHT OF THE FLAT SCREEN GLOWS IN THE DARK ROOM. We're sitting a respectable distance apart on the couch, watching *Comedy Central*, when the baby stirs. Kat leaps off the couch before I can stop her, and when she returns ten minutes later, I motion toward the hall. "I'll get her the next time she wakes."

She gives me a big smile and agrees.

It's nice sitting with her like this. If I'm being honest, I think I like not being alone the most. The fact that it's Kat next to me is just a bonus.

That's probably a shitty reason to enjoy someone's company, but everywhere I look, I see my brother and how I failed him.

Were my parents really that much worse off when Cal didn't return home? I was so pissed to be inconvenienced that I never stopped to wonder if maybe things would've been the same if he had returned to Boston. Maybe I still would've needed to quit my job at the tattoo parlor to help Mom and Dad.

The bottle of tequila tempts me from the coffee table, but I know I can't take that route again. It would be too easy to keep reaching for it. But as I sit here in the dark watching TV, I can't quell the despair that settles in my bones. Because the thought of spending the next several weeks here dismantling everything my brother loved ravages my conscience.

Absentmindedly, I stretch my arms, and everything tightens and pulls. *Holy shit.* I let out a groan.

"Are you okay?" Kat asks as she curls up on the couch.

"Yeah, just a little sore from chopping up that tree." I had hoped that hot shower I took when I got home would help, but I'm still sore as fuck.

"Aww." She motions in front of her. "Come here, Paul Bunyan. I'll give you a massage."

I look at her warily. She's changed out of her jeans and t-shirt into a pair of dark pajama bottoms and a cranberry-colored Henley that buttons up the front and swells around her full breasts. Her black-framed glasses sit perched on that cute little nose.

Katherine. Sweet, sexy Katherine.

Don't do this.

Internally, I war with myself. Because when I look at her, all of the darkness from the last week seems to ebb away.

She pats the couch in front of her and gives me a look, questioning whether I'm really going to turn down a massage.

Ignoring the voice in my head that's calling me a dumbass, I get up and sit in front of her. She spreads her legs, and I lean back between them until I'm resting up against the couch. "Be gentle."

She snickers and starts kneading my shoulders.

"Damn, that feels good." I let my head hang down as her grip tightens. She's a strong little thing.

Up and down my neck and across my shoulders she goes in a rhythmic motion that would put me to sleep if I weren't so fucking aware of how close she is right now. The insides of her warm thighs press against my arms, and all I can think about is how much I'd rather be facing the other way.

Every once in a while, her breath fans my neck, making all the nerve endings in my body stand at attention, especially when her fingers dip beneath the thin fabric of my t-shirt.

After about ten minutes, she stops, and my eyes crack open. "That was awesome." I haul my ass up onto the couch and spread my legs. "Your turn." Because, hell yes, I want to touch her.

She bites her lower lip, and I pat the couch in front of me. I can see the wheels turning in her head, and internally, I'm agreeing with her. *Yes, this is a terrible idea. No, I can't help it either.*

After a moment, she takes off her glasses and lowers herself to the floor. Scooting back, she nestles between my legs.

I can do this without getting turned on. I can.

I'm ready to be an upstanding guy when she whips her hair up into one of her crazy buns and I stare down at her bare neck. It's sexy the way her shirt drifts off her shoulder, giving me a hint of her black bra.

Yeah, I'm officially a dumbass. She's this tempting dessert I'm not supposed to eat, but I really fucking want to. You know, maybe lick the frosting off the top.

The moment my hands touch her small shoulders, goose bumps break out on her skin.

"Are you cold?" My voice comes out rougher than I expect.

She shakes her head as I smooth my hands over her back. I wish I could whip off her shirt and do this properly. A back massage with clothes is a waste of friction.

She's tight, and I actually have to dig into her shoulders for a while until the tension starts to dissipate.

See, I can do this.

But then she lets out a breathy moan. "God, so good."

My mind instantly pictures her moaning these words as I pound into her, which puts my cock on full alert.

I pause, like I've stepped on some kind of landmine, not sure which motion will set off the bomb.

I'm already in trouble because her head dips back into my lap. Her eyes are closed, and I'm altogether enchanted by her slender neck and shoulders. By her thick hair that smells so good, I can't think straight. By her mouth that screams to be kissed. And by the neckline in her t-shirt that pulls low, displaying the crests of her breasts.

Without thinking, I tangle my fingers in her hair and massage her scalp.

"Holy crap," she whispers. "That's amazing."

Slowly, I loosen her hair and let my fingers drift in and out of the silky soft tendrils. She looks like a dreamy mirage, and I half wonder if I'm asleep and I'm going to wake up and find myself alone in Boston.

Her eyes flutter open, and she stares up at me. My hand cradles her cheek. I don't remember moving my hand to her face, but there it is. Her mouth parts on a sigh, and then she leans, just the slightest bit, into my hand.

"You're beautiful, Kat," I rasp.

She blinks back at me, sweet and so fucking sexy, everything in me aches.

Those big amber eyes are dilated and dark, and her chest rises and falls with quick breaths.

My hand drifts down her neck where her skin is soft, so soft and smooth and pale. *Like a canvas.*

For the first time in I don't know how long, I long to draw something, anything. And I really want to draw it on her.

I drag one finger slowly back and forth along the slope of her neck and shoulder, envisioning the lines I'd paint on her skin. The rich colors I'd blend. The gentle touch I'd use.

She shivers, and with her back arched this way, I can see her nipples poking through her top. On a sigh, her eyes close, but her tongue darts out to lick those full lips. Everything in me tightens as I resist the urge to drag her whole body on to my lap.

Those lips glisten in the low light, and when my fingers drag along her cheek, they part more. My heart is pounding in my chest. *Fuck, I want this girl.*

When she opens her eyes again, I slide my thumb against her bottom lip. It's slick and pouty, and I'm dying for a taste. She's watching me, her expression intense. Is it my imagination or did she just arch her back more?

Suddenly, her mouth opens, and she sucks my thumb before biting the pad gently.

I stare, a little dumbstruck by my finger that's caught between her teeth. But it's the wet slide of her tongue across my skin that sets me in motion.

"Get up here."

I'm not sure if I yank her up or if she moves on her own accord because my hands are on her and she's crawling into my lap.

The moment our mouths crash into each other, the only thing I can think is, *Thank fucking God.*

27

KATHERINE

He tastes like hot chocolate. Sweet. Rich. Addicting.

My hands are on his muscular shoulders. I'm straddling his thighs, and he has one big hand on my hip and one in my hair as he covers my mouth with his. He's so dang hot, I might combust.

But when that hand on my hip tightens and scoots me closer until our hips align, I'm sure I'm about to die because he feels so good. *And heaven help me, he's huge.*

Brady pauses to look up at me. My hair cascades around us, casting a shadow over him. I want to freeze-frame this moment. Softly, he licks my bottom lip like he's tasting me, and I groan and grind down on him.

That gets me a low grunt, which makes me smile and do it again. When I angle my mouth over his, that hand grips my hair to hold me still, making my heart beat faster.

I pant against his lips, frozen. *Touch me. God, touch me.*

As though he can hear my pleas, his hand slides up my side as he leans in to nip my neck.

"Is this okay?" he asks, his voice low and gruff.

I almost want to laugh. Hell yes, this is okay. But I don't say anything. I just strip off my shirt, which leaves me in a sheer, black lacy bra.

Yes, I wore it for him. When he invited me to watch a movie, I couldn't help but hope something would happen. I would've been mortified if we had gotten horizontal and I was wearing plain old cotton. Hello, not sexy. Comfortable, yes. Seductive, no.

The black lace was a good choice because he's riveted to my breasts, so I know he can see how hard my nipples are through the thin lace. In an instant, his mouth descends on one, and the second his tongue lashes out through the fabric, my hands tangle in his hair to hold him to me.

More. I want more.

I want him hard and thick and pulsing between my thighs. I want to ride him until he shouts my name. I want him to remember this, *me*, when he's back in Boston.

The fact that he's leaving doesn't even give me pause. Yes, it'll hurt like hell when he's gone. In fact, I have a sinking suspicion it'll break my heart because I can't dance this close to the fire and not get burned. And he's all flame, a raging inferno that makes my skin heat and heart race.

But I can't walk away. Even though I probably should.

That sinful mouth reaches my other aching nipple, but this time, he bites gently, just a little, sending a zap straight to my core.

"Brady." A breathy sigh leaves me, and I can feel him smile against me.

But when I reach back and undo my bra, he stills.

I lower it slowly, so just the peaks of my breasts show over the fabric. He looks up, his eyes burning into me as he swipes his tongue under the material. My head falls back as he plumps my breast with one hand and sucks me into his mouth.

"So beautiful," he murmurs against my skin.

My heart skitters, euphoria rushing through me at the realization that this is really happening with Brady.

That he's here. Under me. Touching me. Wanting me.

It's almost too much to bear.

I grind on him, my hips moving on their own, and I'm so wet I'm sure he can feel me through my thin pajama bottoms. I want him so badly my entire body pulses.

In one swift motion, I'm on my back and he's hovering over me. He pauses, just a second, just enough for me to reach out and yank him closer. Because I'm desperate to have him, and tonight, I don't want to let anything get in the way of what I want.

Sinvergüenza. Yes. That's me. Shameless.

His muscular thighs nestle between mine. I have to spread my legs wide to make room for his large frame. I thread my fingers through his thick, black hair, still damp from his shower, as his whole body aligns with mine.

Moaning into his mouth, I revel in how good he feels. All muscle, thick and hard against my sensitive skin.

But I realize what would feel even better.

I tug his shirt. "Off."

He doesn't hesitate. Just leans back and reaches behind his head with one hand to pull it off.

My hands find his hard pecs, and his eyes hood as I slide back and forth over his smooth skin. He has a smattering of dark hair on his chest but is otherwise pretty bare. And then there's that treasure trail that promises pleasures yet to come.

Leaning up, I press a kiss to his shoulder. *It's my turn to taste.* Then I bite him and revel in the hiss that escapes his lips before I lick the offended skin and do it again.

He must like this because he groans and thrusts harder against me, his hands tightening on my breasts in a way that makes me breathless. But the next time I nip him, he grabs my wrists and pins them with one big hand above my head before he dips down for a kiss.

Our tongues tangle as I struggle against him so I can get closer. So I can grab and touch and soothe and feel.

Being held down by his muscular body heats me in a way I've never experienced before. Because I'm at his mercy. *And I like it.*

His hold on my wrists is tight, like I'm his little plaything. His possession. All I can do is moan against his mouth and hope he doesn't stop.

Then he angles his mouth over mine to kiss me more deeply while his erection grinds against me. *Thrust. Thrust. Thrust.* I can almost hear our rhythm as we move to the steady beat of my heart.

And when I think it can't get better, when I can't get any more turned on, he releases my wrists and slides down my body.

Down my neck with hot, open-mouthed kisses. Over my breasts with sucks and licks and bites. Over my stomach, rasping against my sensitive skin with his five o'clock shadow. All the while playing to that steady beat between my legs.

His fingers hook into my pajama bottoms, and then they're off, leaving me in my black lace underwear. Slowly, he pulls down the fabric until nothing stands in his way.

He stares, his eyes molten. I let him stare and see how wet I am for him. I watch how his green eyes darken until all I'm left with is his black hunger that threatens to drown me.

Everything in me trembles as I spread my legs a little more.

An invitation.

He sucks in a breath, but rather than go to the source of my ache, he drags a calloused finger between my thighs and rubs in the crease of my leg. First one side, then the other.

I arch my back, needing him to touch me *there*. He's close, so close, but I know he's toying with me.

He settles between my legs, his hands spreading my thighs wide.

But again, he teases and rubs along the crease of my legs, pushing my swollen lips together.

"Brady," I gasp. "Please."

"Please, what, Katherine?"

Oh, Jesus. Now he chooses to use my full name. Why that's so hot right now, I have no clue. But his voice, thick and raspy, sends chills down my back. And the way he says it. Like I'm sexy and seductive.

"Touch me," I beg.

"I am."

Then he does it again, pushes my lips together, sliding me against myself, making the ache worse, not better.

His hot breath on my tender skin sends another shiver through me, but when his lips whisper over my clit, just barely grazing me, a whimper escapes me.

I'm writhing, gasping, and just when I think I might die, his thumbs spread me apart—wide—and he slowly swipes his hot tongue against me.

"Holy shit." Wow. Something else unintelligible falls from my lips.

I'm panting and writhing when he does it again. And again. Soft, so soft, I have half a mind to yank his hair and make him do it harder. But then he flattens his tongue for a long, steady lick, and I arch off the couch.

"God, yes. More."

My eyes are rolling back in my head, my hands grasping at the fabric of the couch as Brady pins me down and works me over.

He groans against me. "You taste so fucking good."

Then he delves again, this time pushing one rough finger into me. Licking and sucking and pressing into me, over and over. Deep, so deep, it has me thinking about what he'll feel like when he sinks into me for real.

"Oh, God. I'm gonna come," I pant.

Everything hurts and feels so good at the same time. But when he pushes a second finger into me, we both groan.

"Jesus, you're tight," he whispers against my wet skin.

My whole body throbs and constricts, like strings pulled taut on an instrument.

And then I'm falling... falling... falling. Coming apart and somehow being pulled back together.

I quake and shiver, my legs slamming against his body as I writhe with my release. I've never felt this good, and I never want it to stop.

It goes on and on as he softens his touch until I can't take it any longer.

When I crack open my eyes a few minutes later, I realize I'm gripping his hair. He's resting against my legs, his mouth wet from me, a sly grin on his lips.

"Come here," I whisper, my voice hoarse. I'm sleepy, so sleepy, but I still want the main event. You don't drive all the way to the circus and not check out the Big Top.

He crawls up my body, and as he's about to settle down over me, it happens.

No, no, no!

I squeeze my eyes shut as the baby wails through the monitor.

28

BRADY

"ARE YOU FUCKING KIDDING ME?" I HANG MY HEAD, TOO frustrated to move.

My mouth is still wet from going down on Kat, my dick so hard it hurts, and I'm being cockblocked by my niece.

This cannot be happening.

And yet it is.

Katherine scoots out from under me and reaches for some clothes. I turn my head in time to see her naked body disappear under my t-shirt. But before she runs out of the room, she ducks down to give me a kiss.

"I'll be right back," she whispers against my cheek. "Don't move."

I don't think I could even if I wanted. You want to kill your enemy? Want to take him down? Shoot him ten seconds before he thinks he's about to get laid.

Christ.

Collapsing on the couch, I try to catch my breath. Kat's voice comes over the baby monitor. "*Mamacita*, what's wrong?"

Izzy babbles something incoherent, and Kat coos back at her sweetly.

Reaching for the damn thing, I turn it off. Because you know what kills an erection? Baby talk. To a real baby.

How the fuck did my brother get his wife pregnant *again* with another child in the house?

I give my cock a tug to relieve the pressure before I reach for the remote and turn on *SportsCenter*.

My eyes glaze over as NBA game results flicker across the screen.

I'm pissed. I shouldn't be. It's not Izzy's fault she's a one-year-old and probably shit her pants. But for once, I want something to be easy. Just one goddamn thing in my life. And clearly this isn't it.

Because the longer I sit here in the dark, the more I realize how fucking wrong this is. Number one, Kat is my *employee*. I pay her to help me on the farm, to take care of my niece, and I just tongued her up like a melting ice cream on a hot summer's day.

Number two, she just lost her best friend. This has been an emotionally-charged week. Am I taking advantage of her? I think she wanted us to hook up as much as I did, but grief makes you do stupid shit.

Number three—and this one is the motherfucker of all reasons—we live together. Here. In close quarters. What if she ends up regretting this? What if I regret this? I'm moving back to Boston soon. Will she want more? Will she expect it? We're constantly around each other, so if this goes south, we'll have to face this awkwardness every day.

My temple throbs, and I press my palms into my eyes.

I toss the remote on the coffee table, and it hits with a bang. I reach for another t-shirt and slip it over my head. It's cold in here now, but at least I know Kat's room is warm.

Ignoring the urge to reach for the tequila, I check my phone instead. It's late, but I have an email from Jose about two jobs. I head to the desk and open Cal's laptop to pull up an estimate. I don't know how long I work when the soft pad of bare feet sound in the hall.

"Hey." Kat hovers in the doorway. "You're working?" I can hear the hesitancy in her voice. And if I'm not imagining it, hurt.

You're a dick, man.

"Yeah. Something came up. The guy who's running my parents' landscaping business needs some help on this estimate."

She blinks, canting her head. "At midnight?"

I'm an asshole for doing this, but it gives me an excuse. Because do I want to tell her all of the reasons what we just did was a mistake? Fuck, no. I'm usually straight up with women, but I don't want to hurt her feelings, and if I take the honest route, I know I will.

Not that I don't want to get naked with her. God, I do. My cock is still throbbing. But the cost is so damn high. Too high. I can't risk this going to hell.

I swallow and nod. "He needs it early tomorrow. I missed a text he sent me earlier." Not a total lie. He needs it, but I could've gotten up in the morning and finished the estimate.

She nods slowly, but the expression on her face tells me she knows what I'm doing. She knows this is bullshit. Because I see it in her eyes. The disappointment. In me. And I feel like crap for it.

"Well, then," she says with a sigh. "Good luck with that. Here ya go."

And then she shucks off my t-shirt, tossing it in my direction, before she stalks out of the room stark naked.

I should be happy that she took the hint, but I'm not. I call out her name, but she doesn't return, and I don't go after her.

By morning, I'm pretty sure I'm the biggest douchewad on the planet. This beautiful, amazing girl lets me go down on her and I repay her with some bullshit excuse. I almost want to punch myself in the face.

I get up early because I can't sleep and grab Izzy when she wakes up so we can let Kat sleep in. And I'm thinking my level of douchebaggery requires more than an apology. So I start by making her breakfast.

But Izzy and I aren't very good at keeping down the noise because I've only scrambled the eggs when Izzy drops her bowl of Cheerios. It goes clattering over the hard wood floor.

A few seconds later, Kat comes sliding into the kitchen wearing her glasses and an oversized t-shirt, looking rumpled as hell and cute as fuck. Her hair is wild around her shoulders and her bare legs have me swelling in my track pants.

I want to toss her over my shoulder and finish what we started last night, but the look on her face when we make eye contact tells me I have some groveling to do first. I'm ready to own my own bullshit. I hope she understands.

"Kat, I'm sorry about last ni—"

"Don't." She tosses her hair into a ponytail and grabs a broom to sweep up the cereal on the floor. Her face is flushed like she's embarrassed to be around me. Awesome.

"Katherine. Come on. I need to talk to you."

When she stands, her expression is icy. "Do you really want to do this? Add insult to injury?" Her voice is raspy with sleep. She lifts her chin. "I got your message loud and clear, Casanova. We're good. Let me do my *job* and get Izzy fed."

Ouch.

"Okay, I deserved that. But let me explain."

When she finishes cleaning the cereal, she pours herself a cup of coffee and glares at me over the lip of her mug. "I'm not sure anything you could say would excuse the hard diss you gave me last night, so maybe we should just spare ourselves this conversation altogether. I have shit I need to do anyway."

Wow. She's really pissed.

I blow out a breath. All right. I should man up and give it to her straight.

Stalking closer, I grab her shoulders. She gasps, but doesn't move. "Stop being so damn stubborn and listen." That glare intensifies, and I seriously think I might be in danger of losing a nut right now, but I take a fortifying breath and continue. "I like you. A lot. And I don't want to hurt you. Izzy and I are moving back to Boston in a few weeks or maybe months. Hell, I don't know. That's the point. And the last thing I should be doing is getting involved with you."

Her lips thin into a straight line. Yeah, I'm not helping my case here.

"What I'm trying to say—and not doing a very good job of it —is that I'd love nothing more than to spend whatever time I have here with you doing any assortment of dirty, naked things. But you work for me. I don't want you to feel some weird kind of obligation or feel like I'm perving on you."

I sigh and release her shoulders to run my hands through my hair. "Look, last week was rough, and I know you're vulnerable. I don't want to take advantage of you. You're an awesome girl. If we were in Boston, you're absolutely the kind of woman I'd go for. And not just for a fling. I might be a dick for how I handled last night, but you have to know I have your best interest at heart. Because the very last thing I want to do is hurt you when I leave."

Her lips flatten more. "Are you done?"

Um. That's not very promising. "Yeah."

"Great. Thanks for the pep talk. This was fun. I'm glad you think so highly of my own ability to care for myself and make good decisions." She huffs a breath. "Why am I not surprised?

No one else seems to think I can take care of myself." Then she tosses up her hands. *"Por qué todo el mundo me trata de esta manera? Mi padre, mi madre, toda mi familia, y ahora tú?"*

I have no idea what she's saying, but just when I don't think she could get any more attractive, she yells at me in Spanish. I shouldn't be turned on right now.

Her eyes are wild, her hair in complete disarray, and her mouth is moving a million miles an hour. I want her. Right the fuck now.

My restraint is hanging by a thread, and when she pokes me in the shoulder, I snap.

I grab her and crush her lips to mine. She pushes me once and then yanks on my hair and pulls me closer. I crowd her against the pantry, away from the kitchen table where Izzy is probably playing with her breakfast.

Kat whimpers into my mouth.

"Shut up," I tell her between kisses. "I never want you to think I don't believe in you." And then I pick her up, and she crosses her ankles behind my back as I press her to the wall.

One very deep kiss later, I pause and rest my forehead against her. We're both panting. "I'm sorry. I know I was an ass. I panicked. I'm under a lot of pressure, and I wasn't thinking clearly." I close my eyes for a second and then tell her the God's honest truth. "I just—I have so much responsibility right now. If we were to do this, it couldn't mean more than a good distraction for both of us. And I don't know if I feel right about that. I meant what I said—the last thing I want to do is hurt you."

She slides down my body, and I wrap my arms around her as I push my nose into her hair. We stand there in an embrace, and I feel her nod. "I'm sorry I overreacted. You didn't deserve my tirade."

"No, I'm pretty sure I did."

When she leans back to stare up at me, I'm surprised by the

emotion I have for her. Then she places her small hand on my chest and gives me a sad smile. "Brady, I know you're leaving. And I don't expect anything from you. If you really don't want this, I'll understand."

I start to protest, and she puts a finger over my lips. "Why don't you think about it? If you want this"—she motions between us—"for the time you're here, I'm a willing participant. If you don't, that's okay too. But know that I'm under no delusion. You don't have to worry—I'm not going to fall in love with you. You won't break my heart. I get that this is no more than just two friends comforting each other before you leave."

Then she steps up on her tiptoes to kiss my cheek and walks away.

But maybe her heart isn't the only one I'm worried about.

29

KATHERINE

I CAN SEE THE INDECISION ON BRADY'S FACE EVERY TIME HE LOOKS at me. You'd think this would be a good thing, but it's not. It's torture. I laid it out there for him, friends with benefits—something I've never done before—and he still keeps a good three feet between us whenever we talk.

Hi, I'm Katherine Duran, and I'm a charter member of the Shameless Club.

But I see him watching me. Looking at my mouth, mostly. And sometimes, he winces like he's in actual pain.

I don't want to do this to him. I'm dying myself, but I'm not gonna beg. Hell, no. I said my piece. Told him to think about it, and clearly he is.

Apparently, shamelessness has its limits.

If there's any bright lining, it's that I went after what I wanted. I told him how I felt, and now the ball is in his court. Coming here to Mel's farm has always been about figuring out what I want in life. Brady is one of those things, even if it's just short term.

For the last two nights, we didn't watch TV together after I put the baby down. He went to his room, and I went to mine where I tossed and turned. Eventually, I ended up in Izzy's room on the couch. I don't like sleeping alone, not since Mel's accident, and at least in the baby's room I have some company, even if she's asleep.

Tonight, Brady and I are doing the same awkward dance around each other, and it's so painful, I have half a mind to go home to Corpus. But Thanksgiving is tomorrow. I don't think he even realizes it. And while I'm not enjoying the tension, I don't want him and Izzy to be alone during the holiday. Besides, the social worker is coming next week, and I know he needs help preparing for her visit.

From the other side of the kitchen, I watch him work at the table, my skin heating when I remember what it was like to be together. What it was like to have his lips on my skin.

I clear my throat. "I was planning to make a roasted chicken tomorrow with a cornbread stuffing and mashed potatoes. I thought I could pick up a pie from work in the morning. Is that okay?"

He looks up from an impressive spread of invoices and bills. "Sure," he says hesitantly, confusion written all over his scruffy face.

"Since tomorrow is Thanksgiving." I answer the question he doesn't know how to ask.

He closes his eyes and nods, running a hand through his thick hair. "Well, that makes sense."

My eyebrows lift, and he continues. "Jose said something on the phone this morning about not working tomorrow, and I thought he was sick or had an appointment or something, but now I'm feeling pretty stupid."

I chuckle and head into the pantry to get the ingredients for the cornbread. "I would make a turkey, but big birds kinda scare me. I'm always afraid of undercooking them, and I'm sure the last thing you want is salmonella."

When I put down the armload of seasonings and cornmeal on the kitchen counter, I feel him staring again. Ignoring his presence, I get out a bowl and butter a pan.

"Kat."

"Hmm?" I resist the urge to turn around. I know this recipe by heart. It was my grandmother's. Cornmeal, raisins, cranberries, nuts...

He says my name again, and I glance over my shoulder.

His voice is gruff. "You don't need to do this. You don't have to make anything special. I could pick up some dinner so you don't have to cook." He groans. "You do too much as it is."

Why this makes me want to tear up, I'm not sure, but I return to my bowl and start measuring and pouring. It's hard not to wonder who takes care of Brady when he's back home. Who makes sure he gets a home-cooked dinner? Who brews his coffee in the morning? Who makes sure he doesn't work too hard?

I know I sound like some nineteen-fifties woman, but my family is very traditional, and if I'm being honest, I like taking care of Brady. Which is a little shocking. Because I didn't feel this way with my ex.

But with Brady, every female instinct is dialed up. I want to take care of him. Feed him. Love him. Even if it's only physical. And even if it has an expiration date.

This should scare me to hell and beyond, but for some reason it doesn't.

I'm learning a lot about myself here. I used to think I didn't want children. Ironically, it's an argument Eric and I had more than once. But now that I've been around Mel and Cal and Izzy, I'd be hard pressed to say that again.

I decide to put Brady out of his misery. "I'd be knee deep in *masa* right now if I were home. I'd be slinging that stuff all over the kitchen forced-labor style while I made two hundred and fifty tamales so every family member could take home a dozen when they left our Thanksgiving table. So trust me when I say it's no hardship to make dinner for the two of us."

He's quiet for a long time, and then finally asks, "So you have a big family?"

"Yup. My mother is the oldest of eight, my father is the oldest of five. I already told you about my sister, who's obnoxious as hell, and I have too many cousins to count."

Then he surprises me. "That must be nice."

I turn back to look at him, to see if he's joking. He's not. "Tell me about your family. Is it just you and your parents?"

"My mom has a sister, but she's in New York. Otherwise, it's just me and my parents." He doesn't have to say the rest—it's just him and his parents *now*—but I hear it in his voice.

I bite my lip, trying to think of something to cheer him up. "Want some hot chocolate? I was gonna make some for myself." I wasn't, but I know he likes it, and if it helps take his mind off Mel and Cal, then it's an easy thing to do. Maybe it's lame, but it's the first thing I think of.

"Sure. I'd love it. But, Kat, you don't have to do this. You don't have to wait on me."

I turn, and what I see breaks my heart. Because I know he feels alone. It's etched in his expression and in the slump of his shoulders. I feel it too. Acutely. And because I meant what I said about us being friends, I do what I would with any friend right now.

Wiping my hands on a towel, I tell him, "Get up."

He stares at me, looking like he doesn't understand. I repeat the words and he stands hesitantly. And then I band my arms around him in a hug. A second later, he's hugging me back. We stand there for a minute, and I whisper, "Don't make more of this than it is, but I kinda like taking care of you. It's not a big deal, though, okay?"

He doesn't say anything, just squeezes me tighter before he plants a kiss on the top of my head.

When I step away, I ask, "So marshmallows?"

His responding smile makes me grin too. "Please."

30

BRADY

THE SMELLS COMING FROM THE KITCHEN MAKE MY STOMACH growl. I bounce Izzy on my lap and kiss her strawberry-scented hair before I hoist her into my arms. "Let's go see what Aunt Kat is cooking up, hmm?"

She nods, her beautiful eyes playful. *My brother's eyes,* I think sadly.

I stop in the doorway and watch Katherine scurry back and forth across the kitchen, checking the pots and pans on the stove.

"You do realize you're only feeding two point five people, right?" I ask.

"Point five?" She glances at me over her shoulder. Her hair is tied up, which emphasizes her graceful neck.

Jesus Christ. Since when are necks graceful?

I try to focus on her question. "I believe Little Miss Sunshine here qualifies as the point five."

Kat chuckles. "I suppose so." She holds up a spoon of home-made stuffing. "Wanna bite, baby?"

"Uh, *yeaaah.*" *Is it weird that she just called me baby?* It doesn't stop me from charging toward the food.

Kat gives me a deadpan look. "I meant the *actual* baby."

"Oh." My lips twist as I scratch the back of my neck. "That makes sense."

She barely keeps in a laugh as she holds the spoon to my mouth. "Here, goofball."

I give her a cheesy grin as I gobble it down. "Damn, this is good." The beaming smile I get from Kat makes my chest hurt just a little bit.

And that hug she gave me last night? Yeah, that killed me too.

I meant what I said the other day. If we had met in Boston, I'd be pursing her like a fly ball at Fenway. But we're not in Boston.

As tempted as I am to take her up on her offer, she's a sweet girl. A good girl. I'm pretty sure she doesn't sleep around, not that I have a problem with that, but I know enough to see she's not a casual sex kind of woman even if she seems to be willing to try it for me.

None of this stops me from wishing things were different. I can't stop thinking about her. How I could feel her heat when she straddled my lap. How she writhed beneath me when I pinned her down. How she moaned and gasped my name when she came against my mouth.

The truth, though? I'm going to be thinking about her long after I'm back home. And not because we never had sex.

Boston seems like a different world, and for a fleeting instant, I wonder what it would be like to stay here.

My eyes travel to Kat, where she makes our Thanksgiving dinner, and a strange, raw emotion cuts through me. I hoist Izzy higher, trying to shake off this absurd idea of remaining in Texas because there's no way I can afford it.

Kat waves that wooden spoon at me. "Dinner won't be ready for another half hour. You know, there's a camera on Cal's laptop if you wanted to Skype with your parents. Is your dad still in the hospital?"

She has this little apron wrapped around her tiny waist and that gorgeous hair all tied up on top of her head. Her glasses are perched at the end of her nose.

Looking over her shoulder at me, she lifts an eyebrow, and I realize I still haven't spoken. "Um, yeah, he's still there, but I think my mom has her laptop. She likes to play Candy Crush." I place the baby on the counter, keeping my hands on her waist so she doesn't take a tumble. "That's a good idea. They'd probably like to see the baby."

"And you too, silly. I'm sure they miss you."

Yeah, they probably do. Inwardly, I groan.

As if sensing my reluctance, she asks, "You haven't talked to them about adopting Izzy yet, huh?"

"No, I've pussied out the last few times we've spoken."

"Brady," she says sternly, shooting me a look. "Let's not use *that* word around the baby."

"Oh, shit. You're right."

She sighs and shakes her head.

Okay, so I have a little ways to go when it comes to using age-appropriate language around Izzy.

"Go call them if you'd like. You don't have to talk about anything serious. Just say hi. And oh! Be sure to tell them that Bandit nearly ate you for breakfast this morning."

She laughs. Like it's funny that little raccoon fucker tried to bite me. Again.

"He's a menace."

"He's a baby." She turns to look at me so I can see that she's rolling her eyes.

I swing Izzy into my arms, and she giggles and grabs my face. "Bray, Bray, Bray!" I don't think hearing her say my name will ever get old.

"What do you say, kid? Wanna call Granny and Gramps?"

"Gwamps!"

"Okay. Let's go."

As we head for the hall, I catch the smile on Katherine's face as she stirs that giant wooden spoon into a pan. "Hey." I wait for her to turn to me. "Have you had a chance to call your parents yet? We can hold off on dinner if you want to do that first."

Her smile falters, but she pastes it back on. "Um, yeah. Maybe."

It strikes me then that she could have gone home for Thanksgiving, but she chose to stay here instead. *And make you dinner.*

I rub the stubble on my chin. "Everything okay back home?" She half nods, half shrugs. "I know you said your dad is pretty conservative. Is he okay with you living alone here with me?"

Her chest heaves with a sigh. "He is definitely *not* okay with me living here with you, but it's really not any of his business."

Shit. That doesn't sound good.

Her shoulders slump. "Don't worry about it. My dad is never happy with any of my decisions. Or at least that's how it feels." Another deep sigh leaves her. "Go Skype. I'll call you when dinner is ready."

I squeeze her arm, feeling somehow responsible for whatever is going on with her parents.

After a quick phone call home, Izzy and I return to the kitchen. I hear Katherine's voice. She sounds tense.

Her back is to me while she faces the sink. "Tori, seriously, tell Dad I'm fine. Brady is completely normal. He's not a serial killer or anything."

I pause at the mention of my name. Izzy squirms in my arms, and I tighten my hold on the little ninja.

Kat shakes her head. "No, and for the millionth time, I am not going back to that job in Austin. I don't care if that makes me the biggest loser on the planet, it's not happening. And if Eric calls again, tell him—" Her whole body stiffens. "Ugh. He's such an asshole. Just hang up on him next time. I'm serious. You cannot give him my number." She sighs. "Yeah? You think he's such a great catch? Fine. You date him."

Who the fuck is Eric?

Realizing I'm eavesdropping like a dick, I back out of the kitchen and return to the office to give Kat some privacy. The baby and I emerge once I think that phone conversation is over.

"That was fast," Kat says as she reaches into the cabinet for some dishes.

I want to ask about that guy Eric. *It's none of your business, man. Don't make things weird.*

Leaning over to strap my niece into the high chair, I motion toward the office. "My parents couldn't really Skype right now. The doctor came in and needed to go over the plan for my dad. He might go home soon."

Kat's face lights up. "That's fantastic! I'm so happy to hear that. I bet you're relieved."

"I am so fuck—" I pause and look down at my niece who's watching me with that toothy grin. "I am so *freaking* relieved." When my eyes lift to Kat, she winks at me in encouragement for not totally corrupting my niece before she goes back to serving dinner.

Despite our failed hookup the other night and the fact that I've been terrified things would be weird between us, they're not, at least not any more. Kat and I enjoy watching the baby blow bubbles in her apple juice, and for one brief moment, everything seems right in the world. I love her laugh. It's light and airy, and when I tell her a stupid joke, I feel like a lucky asshole whenever she smiles.

If I'm being honest, I thought sharing all of this domestic stuff with a woman I barely know would be awkward as hell, but with Kat, it's surprisingly normal. When I'm not overrun with sexual frustration, I really like being around her. There's something calming about her.

She feeds Izzy a bite of mashed potatoes, and I have a brief flash of her doing that for our own baby.

What in the ever-loving hell?

Not the kind of fantasy I need right now. I have to cut this shit out. A week and a half with this girl, and I need to book a one-way ticket to an insane asylum.

Gritting my teeth, I try to focus on the hard-and-fast truth—I have to sell the farm. Even with my brother's modest life insurance, I can't deal with this place while I dig my parents out of their financial pit back home. So staying here to play house with Kat isn't really an option.

So much for everything seeming right in the world.

"Are you working tomorrow?" I ask, hoping she's free.

"No, thank God. Working on Black Friday is a fate I wouldn't wish on my worst enemies." She pushes her glasses up her nose. "Why? What's up?"

"I'd like to check out that nursery by the highway and talk to them about our fields. That's where Melissa got all of her supplies, right?" I've seen a few receipts, but I should make sure first.

"Yeah, ask for Hank. He knows everything. He'll help you."

I push some cornbread around on my plate. "Would you mind coming with me? In case I have any questions?"

"Sure, although I'm by no means an expert."

"Trust me when I say you know a helluva lot more than I do."

She shifts in her seat and clears her throat. "I wanted to ask you about that farmers' event we were supposed to host. Do you want to cancel it? I have to tell our neighbors if you do. And if we're having it, I need to whip up some soaps and a few other products we sell."

She's trying to be nonchalant, but I can tell she wants to do this.

I rub my forehead, hating how much I want to bail, but the least I can do is follow through on the last plans my brother made.

"Okay. Let's do it."

"I'd need some help creating a pen for the animals for the petting zoo," she says hesitantly.

Reaching over to the counter, I grab a spiral and start jotting down notes so I don't forget this shit. I blow out a breath. "You're not going to make me pet the raccoon or anything, are you?"

She laughs. "No. I promise."

"Fine. Write out a list of what you need me to do. When is it again?"

"Two and a half weeks."

"Does this mean you'll make me more hot chocolate?"

Her grin kicks up. "Any time you want."

Returning my focus to dinner, I shovel down the rest of my meal before I remember one more question. "Can I ask another favor?"

"Of course."

"You can say no. I mean it."

She motions for me to lay it on her, so I continue. "I'd like to check out a tattoo parlor in Austin."

Her eyes travel over my arms in a way that heats my skin. The girl likes my tats. Duly noted.

"You're getting more ink?"

"No, it's owned by a friend of a friend, and I hear there's an opening for an artist. My roommate is shipping all of my gear to me. Should be here in a few days. My portfolio is online, so I don't need it for an interview, but I'd like to check out the vibe. They know my situation and are cool if it's only temporary." I could certainly use the cash.

Her head tilts, making her crazy ponytail flop to the side. "How did I not know you were a tattoo artist?"

I shrug. "Maybe because we've only known each other for ten days."

She nods, biting her bottom lip. Something about her expression tells me this hurts her feelings for some reason. It's not like I know that much about her. Like the real reason she's hiding out here on a farm in the middle of Bumblefuck.

But I don't like that this is creating distance between us, so I quickly add, "I really haven't inked much lately. I was pretty busy with my parents' landscaping business for the last several months."

She releases that bottom lip and her expression brightens. "I'd love to see your work."

"Sure." I smile back reassuringly. "If this hammers out, though, I'll be working a few nights a week, and I'd need you to babysit. With pay, of course. If we work around your schedule at the diner, do you think this could happen? I'm just hoping to make a little money to keep things afloat around here until the insurance pays or until I sell this place."

Her eyes dip and she stares at the table. "Whatever you need, Brady."

"Hey." I wait for her to look up. "I don't have a choice." My voice comes out harsher than I intend.

She stares back, looking just as devastated as the first time I told her I'd be selling the farm. But she nods slowly. "I know. I'm not judging you for needing to do this." She sighs, and the sound settles around my heart and squeezes. "I just wish things were different."

Me too, sweetheart. My gaze settles on her lips. *Me too.*

31
———

KATHERINE

THE KNOCK ON MY BEDROOM DOOR BARELY REGISTERS UNTIL I HEAR Brady's voice. "What are you doing?"

I scoot closer to my tiny TV. "Shh. The Lone Stars are kicking for a field goal." When they make it, I jump off my bed and do a little dance.

I'm mid hip-thrust when I turn to him and stop my celebration. Because seeing Brady watch me gets my attention. His heated eyes wander slowly down my bare legs and back up again. Which makes me realize I'm only wearing a tiny white t-shirt and undies. But I didn't expect to see him again tonight.

After he helped me put away our Thanksgiving leftovers, he headed to his room, and I went to mine. And now that he's fixed the temperature in here, it's almost too warm, which is why I'm wearing the thinnest t-shirt I own.

I pull at the hem of my top before I realize it's ridiculous. The man had his mouth between my thighs the other day and licked me to an orgasm, for Pete's sake. *Shrug it off, Kat.*

Kat sounds like the girl who can walk around in her underwear and not care.

I motion toward him. "What's up?"

His jaw works back and forth. "Why are you watching the game in here in the dark on that thirty-year-old box? I'm watching it in the office. On the flat screen."

Turning, I look at the small TV. It belonged to Mel's father and flickers on and off sometimes, but no matter. Right now, it's doing its job, so I like it just fine.

I consider his question a moment. "I didn't think you wanted me there."

He curses under his breath and presses his palms into his eyes. "Why would you think that?"

Oh, I don't know. Kicking me out the other night? Not taking me up on my offer to hook up?

Yes, I get that he likes me, maybe even wants me, but I'm not going to throw myself at him while we watch TV. Been there, done that. And something tells me that if I'm in there with him, all alone in the dark, I'm gonna try again, and I just don't have it in me to get shot down twice. *Gracias, pero no.* A girl has to have some pride.

Besides, I get the distinct impression he's firmly placed me in the friend zone, and hearing him talk about me babysitting for Izzy and getting paid only serves as a reminder that I'm his employee. *I'm the babysitter.* Awesome.

"Brady, honestly?" I blow out a frustrated breath and remind myself that he's a guy who clearly still has his head up his rear. I decide I can be as obtuse as him. "I'm watching the Lone Stars beat your precious Boston Rebels all up and down the field. Is this really the best you guys can do?"

Placing my hand on my hip, I cock it out. My tiny t-shirt slides up, and I don't miss his quick intake of breath. I suppose little black lace boy shorts do the trick. Score one for Kat and her slutty underwear. Internally, I laugh. My mother considers anything that doesn't look like a cotton granny panty slutty.

I stand stock still, my nipples pebbling under his stare, and I fight the urge to cross my arms over my chest because I know he can probably see them through the thin material of my t-shirt.

His laughter fills my room as he mumbles something I can't quite make out.

"Excuse me?" I ask with mock irritation.

His lips curl into a smirk. "I said I'm this close to spanking your ass."

My mouth drops open. Why those words turn me on, I'm not totally sure. No one has ever spanked me, and I've never really understood the appeal. Until now. His big, calloused hand on my ass. Yes, please.

And then I do something very un-Katherine-like. I lift my t-shirt off my backside, making sure he can get a peek as I peer back at the area like I'm considering it. Then I return my attention to him and lift my eyebrow. "Interesting. But you'd have to catch me first."

We stare at each other a beat before he lunges, and I jerk away, laughing, until we're both tumbling toward my bed that groans under our weight. And then the big jerk tickles me.

"Not fair! No, Brady!" I squeal.

He pauses, his breath hot on my neck as he holds me down. "Shh. You're going to wake the baby." He rears back slightly to look into my eyes and I'm drowning in the depths of his stare.

The conversation we had this week mocks me. *No-strings sex? Bullshit. It's all bullshit,* a little voice inside me screams.

His lips are closing in. Close, so close. And holy mother, does he smell good. I'm pulsing, my whole body throbbing from how he holds me down. He's big and hard, his weight pressing deliciously along my soft ridges.

And just as I think he's going to kiss me, the sexy bastard continues his assault and tickles me.

I gulp down a laugh, and his hand rests over my mouth. Mirth and fire and lust all swirl in his eyes as he challenges me to do something about this. So I buck up and push, still laughing, laughing so hard my side hurts.

He's a big guy and all my bucking does is wedge his strong thigh between my legs. I'm gasping, still wiggling and fighting him, which only makes him yank my arms up and pin them together with one hand.

Oh, God. The throb grows. My panties flood with warmth, my hips lifting on their own accord.

My t-shirt has slid up and rests just below my breasts, which comes to his attention as he tickles my side.

He pauses, his green eyes traveling down my body.

If I thought his expression was intense before, it's a volcanic eruption now. And there's no doubt how much he wants me as his thick bulge presses against my hip.

"You excited to see me?" I ask, out of breath.

He slides his other leg over and wedges himself fully between my thighs and rasps, "You have no fucking idea."

Here I am, stretched out beneath him, completely at his mercy. I'm panting, from being tickled or wrestling with him or being so turned on, I think I might die. And I need relief. Now.

So I undulate my hips beneath him to feel that bulge and smile when he groans and drops his head to my neck. I'm rewarded with a hot, open-mouthed kiss along my jaw.

I close my eyes and arch my back, needing more friction. His hand slides under my t-shirt and pinches my nipple before he tugs it.

"Yes," I gasp, wrapping my ankles behind his back. Those strong hips move against mine in a dirty rhythm that makes me see stars. Through his thin track pants, I can feel *everything.* His thickness. His length. The ridge of his cock.

I feel myself blushing all the way down to my roots. *Cock.* Because that is certainly what's pulsing against me. My skin burns as I wonder what it would feel like in my hand. How he'd feel against my tongue. How he'd taste.

A moan escapes my lips as he kneads my breast. I want to tell him how wet I am right now, how he's the only one to make me this way—a wanton little sex maniac who's willing to give it up without a promise for anything in return. But I don't because I'm not quite that brave.

He rises up so we're nose to nose. His lips are close, so close to mine, but he makes no move to kiss me as he grinds his length between my thighs and flicks his thumb over my taut nipple.

Freaking tease - he wants to play this game? I can dish it out too.

I smirk as I lick my lips. Slowly. Arching into him, I work one wrist out of his hold and tangle my fingers through his hair. His eyes darken as I lower my hand to hold his jaw and brush my mouth against him. Once, twice, and then I lick the seam of his lips.

The groan he releases is music to my ears. And then his mouth crashes down to mine.

We kiss, and it's frantic, all gasps and lips and tongues. After a moment, I yank on his shirt, and we part to strip out of our clothes until I'm left in my boy shorts and he's in his track pants. And then he's back on me.

But before his lips descend on mine, he pauses and looks me over. I half think he's changed his mind again, which means I might have to strangle him, but he levels me with a stare. "Are you sure you want to do this?"

I hate the indecision in his eyes. Hate that he isn't as consumed by the moment as I am and has the presence of mind to ask that question.

Damn him for not being more wound up. Because I want him to give in to this attraction that's been building between us from the moment he stepped into this house.

So I go for broke, whispering words that I've never before uttered. "Yes, Brady, I'm pretty sure I want you to fuck me."

His nostrils flare, and then his hand winds into my hair, yanking until I feel a bite of pain, to hold me still as he presses his mouth to mine like he's finally claiming me.

32

BRADY

She tastes like sugar and spice and my own wicked fantasy.

I could hear her reacting to the game I was watching through our shared wall. What I couldn't figure out was why she'd rather watch it alone than with me.

It's been hard to resist her this week—telling her no all the while wanting to make her scream yes.

My resistance was hanging by a thread. Especially once it looked like she accepted the fact I wasn't going to make a move.

Because, yeah, I want her to want me. And yeah, I get that this makes me an asshole.

But coming in here and finding her sweet ass on display in those hotter-than-hell booty shorts had me instantly hard. And when she decided to unleash that smart mouth on me? Game over.

And goddamn. She feels good.

I'm nestled between her legs, mulling over the genius of these thin track pants I'm wearing. Because right now, my cock feels like a heat-seeking missile homed in on the warmth of her pussy.

One that I know is bare except for a small triangular strip.

She arches, her soft curves fitting to my hard lines, and I wish the lights were on and not just her ancient TV set so I could see her beautiful body. Her breasts are pebbled against my chest, and with every thrust, they bounce.

I tug her hair so her head tilts over, and I bury my nose against her skin. This scent will forever remind me of this girl. Clean, floral, sweet.

Reaching behind her, I run my hand down one of her legs, dipping underneath the crease of her thigh until it gets close to where I know she needs me. Back and forth I stroke, under the gorgeous globe of her ass until she gasps, and I grip her hair tighter.

Her panting breaths are the only thing I focus on as I gently bite her neck. I'm rewarded with an unintelligible sound from her mouth.

"Feel good, baby?"

She groans her response, and I run my finger against the hem of her boy shorts. Her legs drop open beneath me, and I hold in a chuckle. My girl wants it. But Jesus Christ, so do I.

I pause.

My girl?

Fuck.

I shake my head.

I shouldn't be thinking this way. I shouldn't be thinking about her so possessively.

This is wrong. *We* are wrong. Deep in my heart, I know I shouldn't let this happen, but I want her too fucking badly to stop.

She arches beneath me, and that's all it takes for my brain to shut down.

I let go of her hair to caress her breast that fills my hand so exquisitely my cock throbs.

Dipping down, I lick and suck and tease her dusky pink

nipple, and her hands dig into my hair. And then I move my hips back so I can reach between us where I find her soaked underwear. I slide them down, pulling up on my knees so I can tug her panties off her leg.

At that moment, the TV brightens the room and I take in her arched back. Those beautiful plump breasts. Her trim waist and lean thighs. Those glistening lips between her legs.

"You're beautiful, Katherine."

Her hazy eyes open, and she gives me a shy smile.

Fucking hell. This girl. Equal parts vixen and virgin. Though I know she's not really a virgin, I can't escape the vulnerability in her expression.

It's a look I've seen on her face all week.

And then I say something I probably shouldn't. "You know I want you, right?" Because the last thing I want is her thinking my resistance had anything to do with her or her beauty or intelligence. She's grade-A girlfriend material. I'd be a lucky asshole to be dating her back home.

Her eyes close briefly while her smile widens.

I fight the urge to kiss her because while she should know how much I want her, I know I need to minimize any tenderness. We agreed that this is fucking. Fucking I can do. Making love, though, is off the table, and if I kiss her right now and give in to the way I want to hold her, I think we'd both walk away confused.

Ignoring the twinge of guilt in my chest for taking something that can never ultimately be mine, I lower myself to her warm body. Fucking will have to do.

33

KATHERINE

SOMETHING CHANGES IN BRADY. IT'S LIKE THE MOMENT HE realizes he's being vulnerable with me, the shutters come down.

I want to analyze it and deconstruct everything that's just happened, but when he takes a long, slow lick between my legs, all rational thought dissipates because...

It.

Feels.

So.

Good.

He grips my thighs, pressing me wider and into my bed while his wicked tongue strokes and soothes the painful pulse.

All I can hear are my panting breaths and the sound of him licking. It sounds so dirty. So illicit.

When I glance down and see his dark head of hair between my thighs and those powerful arms, colored and swirled in ink, wrapped around my legs, I want to sing a hallelujah chorus.

Because I need to drown out the negative thoughts about how this will never work. How he's leaving. How we're too different to be together.

I'm a pale canvas next to his tattoos. Something about our

juxtaposition makes me feel bland. Like I'm whatever nameless piece of art that's mounted next to the Mona Lisa. I'm a little girl from Texas, and he's this beautiful tattoo artist from Boston. He's edgy and biting and brisk, and I'm all Southern hospitality and polite welcomes.

Except nothing about my legs dangling open on either side of his face is polite.

My breath catches in my chest. God, I love the fact that he gave in to this.

That's what I need to do. Give in. Live in the moment for once and enjoy this fling.

Because that's all we'll ever be. A fling.

And when he pushes two thick fingers into me, that's exactly what I do. Give in.

His tongue swipes at the pulse between my legs, and it's all I can do to hold in a scream. I toss my arm over my mouth and writhe on my bed. His hand grips my thigh tighter while he works me over. Until I'm gasping and tightening and pulsing against him.

"Oh, my God," I gasp, turning my face into my pillow. "Fuck. Fuck. It feels too good. Stop."

But I don't want him to stop. And he doesn't. Just softens his touch as I come down.

I'm basking in the warm glow of the best orgasm of my life when he collapses next to me and pulls me to him.

I expect him to throw on a condom and start pounding into me, but he doesn't. Instead, he lazily strokes my hair.

Closing my eyes, I toss my leg over his and snuggle against him. In the background, behind the gentle hum of the rain coming from the baby monitor, the football game ends, but I couldn't care less who won.

His arms wrap around me and he rests his cheek against my forehead.

My heart squeezes, wanting to let myself feel for him. It's easy to feel for Brady.

But I remind myself that's not what he wants. Or needs, not with everything he has going on right now.

So I do my best to stamp out my emotions. And then I pull myself up over him.

His eyes open as his hands lift to my hips. I want to squirm with the way he watches me. I'm stark naked and he's still wearing track pants, but the slow sweep of his attention over my body makes my tummy flutter.

I drop down to kiss him, and as my tongue slips between his lips, he moans. I can taste myself on him, which makes me wonder how he'll taste.

"Can I reciprocate this time?" I whisper against his mouth.

A laugh escapes him. "You'd better. My dick has been pissed at me all week."

I snicker as I nuzzle against his neck. "Hmm. Well, we can't have that." I mark a path down his body with kisses and licks, stopping to appreciate his deliciously cut abs that lead to the promised land.

When I press my lips to his lower stomach, I pause to stare at the wall of tattoos in front of me, wishing there was more light so I could appreciate his ink. Later. I'll *definitely* have to look later.

An appreciative grunt rumbles in his chest when I rub him through his thin track pants.

I look up and pause when I realize he's watching me, which makes me feel the urge to put on a show. Because I want this to be the best hookup of his life.

So rather than pull down his pants, I lean down and stretch the fabric taut over his erection and run my tongue slowly across his length.

His thighs tense beneath me, and I glance up in time to see him clench his jaw and groan, "Fuck, that was hot."

I smile as I hook my thumbs in his pants and tug them down. His length surges upward and bobs between us.

Whoa, he's hung. I mean, I knew he was packing something serious, but it's different to be up close and personal.

That pulse starts again between my legs as I take him in my hand and squeeze. My fingers barely make it around and at the base don't even touch.

That's gonna hurt.

A sick part of me gets excited.

With both hands tight at his root, I lick up that vein, shuddering at the thought of having him in me. When I make it to the tip, I swipe my lips across his flared head. Once. Twice.

His big hand tangles through my hair and grips me tight, and I pause, my mouth resting at his tip. I can't move, so I part my lips and swipe my tongue across him. I can feel him watching me as I lick slowly before running my lips across his swollen crown.

He's the tiniest bit salty on my tongue and smells like his bath gel and clean male.

I glance up and feel a heated rush from how Brady's eyes are lasered in on what I'm doing. As if he realizes how tightly he's holding my hair, he lets go and presses his palm to my cheek.

I lean in, all the while, letting my mouth rub against his sensitive skin.

"Jesus Christ, Katherine," he grunts as he juts his hips forward slightly.

My breath is a faint flutter in my chest to see him this turned on. And I want to feed the fire. So I whisper against his cock, "Go ahead. Pull my hair," just before I take him in my mouth.

Those fingers tangle in my tresses again, but he doesn't hold me down, just lets me bob up and down in his lap, at times tensing and groaning.

After a few minutes, I let him slide out with a pop.

I work my jaw back and forth and grin. "You're, um, more than a mouthful."

His chest rumbles with a laugh.

Rising up on my knees, I rest my hands on his broad shoulders. His hands immediately fall to my thighs and pull me against him.

"Condom?" I ask, feeling a little out of breath.

Please, dear baby Jesus, let him have a condom.

He scrubs his face and groans. "The other room. Hang tight." He scoots out from under me and I watch his muscular ass saunter out of the room.

I stare at the baby monitor and send up another prayer to let Izzy sleep. Which feels all kinds of sacrilegious. Here I am, praying for condoms and uninterrupted sex.

When he strides in, my eyes eat him up. His lean, cut muscles. That beautiful canvas of color on his arms and chest. His manhood jutting proudly between muscular legs.

If you were to ask what my definition of male perfection is, I would point to Brady Shepherd because he is downright breathtaking.

I know it seems stupid to feel so wrapped up in this cloud of lust—which clearly this is—but when I combine it with what I know about him, how great he is with his niece and how much he loves his family, something else blooms in my chest, an emotion I'm too afraid to label.

He stands in front of me, and I tilt my head up to smile. As he stares down, half of his hair falls over his face, and the other half sits at right angles from me yanking on it.

I fight to hold in my grin. *Be sexy, Kat. Don't laugh at the man's hair.*

When I hold out my hand, he grins and steps closer until his big, proud dick bobs in my palm. "Hi, I'm Brady. It's nice to meet you."

Laughter spills from my lips. "Oh, my God. I was asking for the condom."

His lips pull up higher. "Ask and ye shall receive." He drops the foil package next to me.

I tear it open and roll the latex over his velvety hard muscle. Doing this feels so personal. Like this, whatever this is between us, is so much more than we're both saying.

Brady motions for me to scoot up the bed, and I shake my head. I get up and motion for him to lie down.

His eyebrow lifts. "Wanna ride me, huh?"

"Like a bronco." I lick my lips. "This is Texas after all."

He laughs and collapses on the bed before folding his arms behind his head.

My eyes slide slowly over him. I want to remember the way his hair falls over his right temple. The way his lips ghost a smile. How his beautiful body, cast in shadows, reclines on my bed.

I straddle his lap, enjoying how that hint of a smile disappears when I slide my wet core across him. Those strong hands move down to grab my rear and pull me closer.

Tilting my hips, I rub harder, loving the grunt of approval that escapes him.

And then I open my mouth because I can't help it. "So you're sure you're not gonna bail on me this time?"

I watch for his response as I glide up and down.

"Fuck no." His grip on my thighs tightens.

Thank God. Because if he leaves this time, I might actually die.

Biting my lip, I angle him toward my entrance. And then I'm sinking, down, down, down.

My head falls back because I can't breathe as he stretches me.

Wow.

I'm too full, but it's so good.

He's thick and hard and hitting all the right spots when I begin to slide up and back down again, taking a little bit more of him each time.

"You feel amazing," he groans.

I arch my back as I take him all the way. His calloused hands grip my breasts and knead me as I begin to bounce up and down on his lap.

Oh, my God. Yes.

Faster and faster and harder and harder I go, loving how his hands are everywhere—my breasts, my ass, my hips. Tangled in my hair. Toying with my nipples.

But when his hand dips down between us, the contact jolts me. I lean back and grip his thighs to give him more room to touch me. And let's be honest, to give him a better show.

If I'm basing anything on the feral look in his eyes, I'm doing a darn good job.

His attention is trained between my legs, and I undulate my hips, lifting up just enough so he can see what he's doing to me. It doesn't take long before that pressure builds.

"I'm about to come all over you," I gasp, too far gone to care how wanton that sounds.

He lets out a choked laugh. "Jesus, you're hot when you talk like that."

My breath catches as he swirls tight circles against that throb between my legs.

All of a sudden, I'm falling apart. Everything tightens as I squeeze my eyes shut and groan. And just when I think it's too much, he sits up and wraps his arms around me, sending his cock deeper.

I scream. I can't help it. He pulses his release in me as he fuses our mouths together to muffle my sounds.

After a moment, he collapses back and pulls me with him.

I'm panting and out of breath. "That was..."

"Oh, yeah...."

"Wow..."

We're gasping and sweaty, and I'm so awash in euphoria, all I can do is mumble, "Thank you," against his chest.

He laughs. "Did you just thank me for sex?"

I nod, glad he can't see my embarrassed grin.

He smacks my ass, and the shock of it makes me squeeze my thighs together, sending a groan through both of us as I tighten around him.

Slowly, I slide off and stretch out next to him. Hello, empty spot between my legs.

With a groan, he gets up. His footsteps pad across the room, and my heart sputters as I wonder if he'll come back. If he'll sleep in here with me tonight. If he'll stay.

Which is stupid. So, so stupid.

Of course he's not going to sleep with me. I may not have any experience with casual sex, but I know you're not supposed to actually *sleep* together after the act.

A sudden sting in my eyes has me blinking back the heat.

You can't cry, Katherine. He told you what he wanted.

I swallow the lump in my throat and slide under the covers, hating how empty my bed feels. I turn toward the wall, bracing myself for the disappointment, but a few minutes later, his footsteps return, and the blanket lifts as he slides in behind me.

One warm hand grips my hip and pulls me to his hard chest as his bare thigh slips between my legs. I let out a breath I didn't realize I was holding.

Just when I think this can't get any better, he presses a soft kiss on my neck and whispers, "Get some sleep, babe."

I close my eyes with a contented sigh. Whatever this is, I want it. For however long I can keep it.

I'll worry about what will happen to us when he leaves later. For now, I'm going to live in the moment.

Because I don't think I'll forget about this one for a long, long time to come.

34

BRADY

The nursery guy, Hank, walks us over to the counter where he pulls out a giant binder of seeds and plants he can order for me. Katherine glances at me and gives me a shy smile.

That look she gives me. It's enough to make my skin burn with an awareness of her.

I want to touch her.

Leaning over the counter, I try to focus on what Hank's saying, but I'm distracted after what happened last night. And again this morning.

Fuck, this morning.

I can still smell her sweet perfume. Feel her soft skin on mine. Feel how she moved under me. Over me. Around me.

Taking a deep, steady breath, I focus on Hank's unwieldy ear hair to get control of my growing erection.

But Kat's presence is too much. I can still taste her on my tongue and remember how she moaned against me when I sucked on her pretty pink nipples.

Finally, I give in and drift my hand over her wrist. Her breath catches, and I let my fingers travel down to her palm where I squeeze her gently. We're hidden behind the counter, so Hank can't see what I just did.

It feels wrong to touch her in public. I'm not sure why. Neither of us said anything about hiding what's going on between us, but I know I should be cautious. This is a small town where everyone knows everyone else's business, and when I leave, I don't want her having to deal with anyone's small-minded ideas about what we've been up to.

For the first time, the thought of leaving seems truly bitter-sweet. I can't deny how good it felt to wake up with this girl wrapped around me. And I'm not a sleepover kind of guy. Gwen and I hooked up for months, and I never felt the urge to stay in her bed when we were done. Or God forbid, hold her when we were done. But when I got up last night to clean up, I couldn't fathom *not* crawling back into bed with Kat.

Sleeping with her felt amazing, almost as good as waking up with my morning wood pressed firmly against her curvy ass. And when she arched into me with a sleepy moan, I couldn't help but go for round two.

God bless my baby niece for sleeping through the night. And bless Mrs. Mac for dropping by and offering to babysit for two hours so we could hit up the nursery.

"Which is it?" Hank asks, breaking me from my thoughts.

"I'm sorry. Can you repeat the question?" I should be paying closer attention. It was my idea to come here after all.

Kat tries to hide a grin. Is she replaying last night in her head too?

Hank points at the picture of the plant. "Is it four from center or five?"

I frown, feeling like I should know this shit after working for my dad these last several months. Thankfully, Katherine responds. "Five feet from center." Then she whispers to me,

"The distance between the rows, starting at the center of the plant."

He nods and scratches his bald head. His eyebrows lift. "How's your pH balance?"

Again, I have no fucking clue, but Kat answers again. "Seven point five." She glances at me. "I just checked last week. The back field is six, but I think we have a little lime we can put down."

Hank nods his approval. "You should be all set for the spring."

He ambles off to gather a few supplies, and I stare at this beautiful girl in front of me. "How do you do that?"

Her head tilts. "Do what?"

"Save my ass. Every time."

She laughs. "Just doing my job. Don't be melodramatic."

"Bullshit. You're amazing at everything—knowing the plants, taking care of Izzy, caring for the animals. Seriously."

She shrugs. "You know I love the farm. It's easy to care of the things you love."

Those hazel eyes dart away, and I don't miss the deepening hue in her cheeks. I nod and ignore the tightness in my chest at those words. And then I kiss her forehead. "You're too good for me. Just so we're clear."

"Don't I know it." She laughs, sounding relieved I didn't make more of what she just said. But I know the sincerity behind those words, and I'm not a dick enough to think they're directed at me.

Hank returns with a few different pairs of shears, and I let Kat pick out the ones we buy because she obviously knows more about this shit than I do.

We order a few supplies for the farmers' event, and as we're checking out, I watch her chat with Hank and enjoy their easy banter. She asks about his wife and listens as he complains about his herniated disc. She tells him about Izzy walking and wanting to get into everything. He tells her his wife loved her lemon-lavender bar recipe.

I'm watching them with a smile... until I remember why we're at the nursery in the first place—so I can prep the farm to sell it.

Getting my realtor's message the other day that he's had several people express interest in the farm had me both leaping for joy and dreading the day I sell. Because while nothing about the lifestyle is easy, I see why my brother loved it so much. Everywhere I look, I see his life and what he was trying to build with his new family.

And I feel like a rotten bastard for wanting to hand it over to the highest bidder. To a perfect stranger.

But the reason my stomach is in knots is because I loathe the day I have to tell Katherine it's over. Because that day is coming.

We're not officially on the market yet, but Kent says he wants me to carry on with my plan to make any cosmetic changes the farm needs. Then he noted I should prep the fields for the upcoming harvest in the event this process takes longer than expected.

"It could take a few weeks or months or longer," Kent said, not wanting to get my hopes up.

Weeks. The word made my heart sink. Which is fucking insane. I spent one night with Kat, and already it's muddling what I know I need to do. What I have to do. Because I don't have a choice.

35

KATHERINE

T<small>HE SOUND OF AN ENGINE STARTING AND SPUTTERING ACROSS THE</small> dinner table makes my lips quirk up.

Brady has a spoon full of mashed potatoes he's been trying to get Izzy to eat for the last five minutes, but every time he gets it near her mouth, she tightens her lips with an impish grin. So he's gone to full-out airplane mode, pretending to fly her food like a little Cessna coming in for a landing.

When she finally relents and gobbles it down, he cheers her on.

"All right, baby! Fist jab!" He holds out his clenched hand, and his niece thwacks her hand into his with a giggle.

Oh, Lord. I hold in a laugh.

Brady might not have held a baby before he arrived here, but you'd never know that now. To look at him, you'd think he was a pro. Well, except for the occasional toxic poop that gets him crying to me for help.

After dinner, he swabs her little face with a warm washcloth and starts loading the dishes into the dishwasher.

"I can do that," I offer as I sip my coffee.

"Nah, I got it." When he finishes with the last dish, he heads down the hall where I hear him run the water in the tub. A few minutes later, he strides in, scoops up the baby and leans her over to me. "Give your hot Aunt Kat kisses so we can get you ready for bed."

I chuckle as Izzy slobbers on my cheek.

"You want some help with her bath?"

"Nope. I think I can handle it."

I'm smiling up at him like a big fool when he leans down and kisses me. Aside from that quick PDA at Hank's nursery, Brady has been pretty hands-off all day. I haven't known what to think. Whether we're done or if we're headed for another dirty sleepover.

This kiss, though, this kiss blooms the seed in my chest, the one that I've been trying to stamp out—the seed of hope.

Of hope for more than just one night. For more than a sexy fling. For more than something casual and meaningless.

Even though that's what I promised him.

Brilliant, Katherine. Really freaking brilliant. Summa cum laude and this is where you end up.

He saunters off with the baby, and my smile fades as the truth settles in.

My heart skitters around in my chest as I tell myself not to hold out hope. Sex between friends. That's what this is. I'll never be his girlfriend. We'll never be more.

It's what you promised him, dimwit.

I crumple my napkin, my heart already protesting our arrangement.

The irony couldn't be any more glaring. My ex pushed for us to be more, to speed things up, and I bucked every step of the way. I didn't want to move too fast. Didn't want to rush things. But with Brady, I feel sucked in, like he's the tidal wave, and I'm the sand.

I should look on the bright side—he stayed in my bed last

night. I fully expected him to bolt. Isn't that what guys do after sex? But Brady is a good guy and held me tightly after. I haven't slept that well since before Mel and Cal died.

Trudging to my room, I feel a heaviness settle in my stomach as I hear him playing with Izzy in the tub.

Some day soon, this will end. Brady is taking Izzy to Boston. Get used to the idea. Don't get attached.

I don't bother to turn on the lights as I strip out of my jeans and slide off my bra and collapse in bed. I can't bring myself to see if Brady wants to hang out tonight or to debate what it means if he doesn't. Vowing to get my shit together and start looking for a job tomorrow, I pull the covers over me and curl up against my pillow.

My eyes flutter closed. In the background, the baby monitor hums the quiet sounds of Izzy getting tucked in.

I'm going to miss this. Being here. Playing with the baby and seeing Brady every morning as we wait for the coffee to percolate. Having them both all to myself.

Finally, I start to drift off despite the raw restlessness that aches in my bones.

The creak of the door breaks through my dreamless sleep.

"Hey," Brady whispers. "Sorry, I didn't know you were going to sleep. Are you okay?"

I automatically reach for him, and he scoots me over and tugs me to his chest where I snuggle against him. He's cozy and warm, his heat radiating through his t-shirt and sweatpants.

"Hmm." I don't want to tell him more. I don't want to voice my fears.

His hand runs up and down my back, and I shiver closer.

"You cold, baby?"

I nod, and he pulls the blankets higher. We're resting chest to chest, and he's hard against my thigh.

"Did you come in for a booty call?" I murmur sleepily.

He chuckles. "No, not really. But my dick has a mind of its own when you're around." He strokes my hair, and I'm so relaxed, I could purr. "I actually just wanted to see if you'd like to hang out and watch *The Walking Dead,* but you're all sleepy and warm and sexy as fuck."

I laugh and snuggle closer, tossing my leg over his muscular thigh. "Mmm. That actually sounds really good. I love zombies."

We might have just agreed to watch TV, but neither of us attempts to get up.

His hand travels under the back of my shirt and my skin tingles under his warm touch. We're just lying here against each other, but already I can feel every cell in my body awaken.

I arch my hips, needing friction for the sudden throb between my legs. He does that. Makes me ache. Getting the hint, he grabs my hips and pulls me fully on top of him where I stretch out like a lazy cat.

My hands dip under his t-shirt to glide over his smooth muscles. I lean down and run my nose along his neck. He smells like soap and warm man.

Reaching up, he pulls out my ponytail, and my hair cascades around us. He's watching me, his dark green eyes hooded, his lips slightly parted.

I don't know where my bravado comes from, but I have to ask... "Did you think about me today, about this?" It's a shameless question but an easy one to ask in the dark.

"Only every fucking minute." He threads his fingers through my hair and pulls me close so his lips brush against my ear, giving me chills. "I can't stop thinking about you riding me," he whispers as I press my weight down on his erection. "All day. Half thought about pulling the truck over behind Hank's nursery to test out the suspension."

Smiling, I try to calm the beating of my heart. "Why didn't you pull over?"

He stills. "Babe, you deserve better than a quick fuck in the enclosed cab."

I hold my breath, afraid to give in to the hope blooming in my chest. *Brady, we could be amazing together,* I think, wishing I could say the words.

But then he flexes his hips, and the contact against my core feels so good, I moan. His grip tightens on my skin. "I swear I didn't wake you up to get laid."

I laugh, sitting up to strip off my shirt. "Sure you did," I joke.

He reaches up and strokes my cheek with his thumb, the calloused pad of his finger trailing against my skin. "Kat, I'm serious. We can stop right now. I just came in to spend time with you. We don't have to have sex."

The fear I've carried around me all day begins to uncoil. He wants me for more than one night. I swallow. *Maybe this isn't meaningless for him.* Only a guy who respects you, a friend, would say something like that.

And that right there makes me want to give him my heart. As stupid as that may be.

I don't say anything in fear of uttering the wrong words. Instead, I lean down and brush my lips against his.

We kiss, and it's gentle. He tastes minty, and I want to breathe him in. Fill myself with his scent and warmth.

When his lips part, I slip in and run the tip of my tongue against his. He doesn't rush me, doesn't push for more.

I tangle my fingers through his thick hair and whisper, "How about we get naked and then watch TV?"

His whole body rumbles beneath me as he laughs. "I like the way you think."

He strokes my shoulders and breasts, and I arch into him, wanting to feel him everywhere.

What happened to the good girl who made a guy take her on several dates before she even considered going to first base?

Yeah, she took a hike the moment Brady blazed into my life like a wildfire.

He fists my hair, making me tilt my head over as he holds me still. Arching up, he rubs his nose against my neck, sending goose bumps down my arms. "You always smell so good." He breathes against me, the heat scorching my skin.

I close my eyes as he opens his mouth and nibbles the curve of my shoulder. That tender spot behind my ear. The slope of my jaw.

Mentally, I take a snapshot so I can remember this. I want to remember everything. So when this is over, when he's gone, I'll still have a little piece of our time together.

He makes an appreciative noise in the back of his throat as he squeezes my breast and slides me higher so he can bring me to his mouth. "You have a beautiful body." The sound of him sucking my nipple sends a bolt of lust through me. "I can't lie. I really enjoyed waking up with you this morning."

Yo tambien.

"Well, if you play your cards right, maybe you'll get another naked wake-up call tomorrow," I rasp as I rotate my hips over him.

"I like the sound of that. Maybe then I won't have to jerk off in the shower while I think about you."

I laugh at his admission. Closing my eyes, I can picture him in the shower. The way the water travels over his beautiful tattoos, how his thighs flex, the way every atom in my body lights on fire as I watch.

Clearing my throat, I run my hands down his hard chest. "I have a confession." His eyes meet mine. "I may have accidentally walked in on one of your private bathroom sessions the other day."

I'm not sure what I expect him to say, but his mouth tilts up in a devilish grin. "Really?"

I nod, feeling suddenly shy, so I glance down. He grabs my chin so I have to look at him. "And?"

"And what?" I lick my lips.

"Did it turn you on?"

A smile creeps on my mouth. "Yeah. A lot." I thrust against him. "You were big and hard. Your tattoos were so beautiful under the water. And the way your hand moved over your body…" I can't say any more.

His nostrils flare. "Did it make you wet?" he whispers.

He still has my chin in his big hand, so I can't look away. "Yes."

"Are you wet now?"

I turn my head so his fingers travel over my lips. They dip into my mouth, and I suck one deeper, enjoying the way his jaw tightens, like he's wrestling with his control. When he slides out, I ask, "Why don't you find out?"

His hand snakes its way between our bodies, and he slides my thong over and rubs my wetness up and down my swollen skin.

"Fuck, yes, you're wet."

"Brady," I gasp as he strokes that spot.

"Let go. Let me make you feel good."

My head falls to his shoulder where I breathe him in. Already I'm so close. I want to let go. But I want him to come with me.

I reach down to tug down his track pants, and he springs out. I pull my undies over more and trap him between our bodies to slide across his hot length. Sitting up, I grind against him slowly, the throbbing in my clit grows. He watches our connection with a fevered look before he groans. That deep, guttural sound urges me on. I thrust faster because having his hard cock rub against my sensitive skin is too much, and I can't wait.

"I'm gonna come," I pant.

He grips my hips, holding me in place as he flexes and moves against me, beneath me, stroking me in all the right spots.

I look down. A pale moonlight illuminates enough for me to see the erotic act, and the sight of us fitting together sends me over the edge. I tighten and pulse, collapsing on him when I can't hold myself up any longer. "Oh, God."

He threads his fingers through my hair. "I love watching you fall apart."

Those strong arms wrap around me, and he kisses my forehead and relaxes back into the bed.

After a moment, I crack my eyes open. "Honey, what about you?"

A sigh. "Condom's in the other room." He chuckles. "See, told you I wasn't coming for a booty call."

Threading my fingers through his thick, black hair, I whisper, "You can either go get one... or I can take care of you another way."

I slide down him and take his hard length in my hand. When I lick his skin, I taste him. I taste me. I feel like I should be embarrassed to be doing this, to be tasting us like this, but I'm not.

His head falls back as I hollow my cheeks and take him in my mouth. He groans. "Goddamn, that's good."

I want to smile but I can't because my mouth is full. Instead, I pump and stroke and suck until he grunts out a warning. I let him slide out of my mouth and lean back slightly. Because I've been taking mental snapshots all night, and I want him to take one now too.

He's watching me, jaw tight as he tenses and spills out across my breasts.

"Oh, fuck," he grunts, still throbbing in my slick hands as I repeat the motions, just slower. "That was so goddamn hot."

He pulls me to him, and even though I'm damp and we're

sticky, I love that he wants to hold me. He whispers how beautiful I am and how much he loves hanging out with me.

I commit those words to memory. My mental scrapbook fills with his warm gaze and husky laugh. With his tender touches and whispered words.

When we stumble into the shower, I want to tell him I've changed my mind about our arrangement. I want to tell him I want more. That I want us to be together. That I want him to stay.

But I don't because I promised.

No expectations. No demands.

And I'll keep that promise.

Even if it ends up breaking my heart.

36

BRADY

I can't sleep, not with everything I need to do in the next few days, so I stroke Katherine's back and listen to her breathe while I mentally go through my to-do list. *Help Jose with an estimate. Rewire the chicken coop. Reattach the tire swing.*

I'm starting with the fastest cosmetic changes I can make, hoping I won't have to do anything major like paint the damn house. Although, really, I should. If this were my house, I'd do that this spring. And it could use some sanding and priming.

Kat said a few neighbors were coming by to adopt the kittens in a few weeks, and I didn't miss how bummed she looked. That girl loves those kittens. I feel bad getting rid of them, but they're the most easily adopted animals we have. Not sure what I'm going to do with that mammoth-sized "baby" raccoon, but one problem at a time.

I'm hoping I can talk to the neighbors about adopting some of our animals when we host that farmers' event in two weeks. Shit. If getting rid of some kittens upsets Katherine, I can only imagine how she'll look when I sell the chickens.

My hand threads through her hair. It's silky soft. I breathe in her scent, wishing I could wake up to this in Boston.

Around midnight, her eyes flutter open. She leans up to kiss me, and we fuck like it's our last day on the planet. At least she had the foresight to grab the condoms last night after our shower where we enjoyed another round of orgasms.

I can't get over how I actually like cramming into a twin bed with her. I've become notoriously anti-snuggle over the years. An old girlfriend may have broken up with me over this issue, but whatever. A man likes what a man likes, and even though I enjoy hugging women, I could never stand to have them all up in my space at night. Not that I ever treated them disrespectfully, but I don't think it's weird that once we were done with whatever bedtime activities we had, I appreciated sleeping on *my* side of the bed.

For some reason, Kat's different.

Her head rests on my shoulder, her soft curves pressed to me, and her hair is everywhere—on my chest and shoulder, hell, a little is in my mouth—and I love it.

Not gonna lie. The sex is phenomenal. It might have something to do with how buttoned-up she seems, with her prim little glasses and polite Southern attitude.

But get Katherine naked, and there's a dirty girl lurking with dirty moves, a dirty mouth and a sinfully hot body.

I kiss her forehead and relish how her arm tightens around me. *My filthy girl.*

If I were a good guy, I wouldn't have given in. Or at least not more than once to scratch the itch, but I can't be around her twenty-four seven and not want this. And if she's willing to be together while I'm living here, I can't bring myself to walk away. Yeah, I guess that makes me a selfish prick.

This shit is on my mind the rest of the night until the beautiful girl lifts her sleepy head and smiles at me.

"Can't sleep?" she asks, her voice raspy and low and sexy as hell.

"Too much on my mind." I can't see the clock from here, but I'm guessing it's early morning.

As if she's just noticing that she's half sleeping on me, she smiles shyly and starts to peel herself off me. "Sorry, I didn't mean to use you as a body pillow."

I tuck a strand of her wild hair behind her ear. "It's okay. Kinda liked it."

Izzy starts chatting on the monitor, and Kat mutters something in Spanish and ducks down, yanking the covers over her head. I laugh and pull her up over me. She whispers, "If we're quiet, she might go back to sleep."

She nuzzles against my neck in a full-body hug, and I trail my fingers up and down her smooth back.

"Not likely. I appreciate your optimism, though. But I'll get Izzy. I kept you up late last night. You can go back to sleep."

"Mmm. Who says chivalry is dead?" she murmurs against my lips before she collapses back on top of me. I laugh and stroke her back.

In the low morning light beginning to filter through the window, I see a row of blue vials lining her small bureau.

"What are those?"

She lifts her head to see what I'm looking at. "Essential oils." Her raspy voice sounds so damn sexy. She blinks, her eyes heavy with sleep. "I used to help Mel mix the scents for her lotions. We came up with five of our favorites. We sell them on the farm's website right now." Her brow furrows. "Actually, I need to catch up on those orders. I have to make them for the farmers' fair anyway, so I should motivate."

"Is that why you always smell so good?" I brush my nose against the slender column of her neck and inhale. "I swear, I smell your perfume, and I get hard."

She laughs, edging away because I know she's ticklish there. "You like this scent?"

"Baby, it smells so good, I'd gobble you up if I could."

The smile on her face—Jesus, it's stunning.

"It's a new scent I came up with—a little lavender, a few drops of mandarin, and a hint of sandalwood."

She holds her wrist to my nose, and I breathe her in. "Delicious. I always notice it in the shower."

"I made a bath gel. That's probably what you're smelling."

I kiss her cheek. "You have too many talents for your own good." Swinging my legs over the edge of the bed, I groan at the day ahead. Kat rubs my back, and I turn back to look at her. The sheets have bunched at her hips, and her hair is wild around her shoulders and her beautiful round breasts.

Leaning down, I press another kiss to her lips. "I can't look at you right now if I need to go get Izzy. I'll make us some coffee and feed the kittens before they scale the back door."

"Sounds good. I'll help in a sec."

"It's okay. I got it. Go back to sleep."

She sighs contently and nods.

I reach for my track pants and a t-shirt. I feel her eyes on me as I dress. "Stop looking at me like that." I'm two seconds away from ignoring everything but my angry erection. I turn so she can see how she's affecting me.

She chuckles. "Just enjoying the show."

The two white puffs of fluff bounce back and forth like they're excited to see us. Admittedly, Stella and Stanley, our pygmy goats, are cute.

Pet goats.

I shake my head as I run my hand through my hair. *Seriously, what the hell am I going to do with two pet goats?*

I've been ignoring this issue for the last few weeks, but my realtor is right. If I want to sell this farm, I need to get serious about prepping it for new owners, who probably don't need pet goats. It's not like you can even milk these two.

Gross. The thought of drinking goat milk makes me gag a little.

I have half a mind to put an ad in the newspaper to get rid of them. But then Katherine motions toward Izzy, who has her arm wrapped around Stanley's neck and is whispering, "Moochie smoochie."

I can't help but laugh. Isabella is puckering her lips and trying to get the animal to face her. "No, baby. We don't kiss the goats."

Izzy frowns at me before making another grab for Stanley. "Moochie smoochies!"

Swooping down until I'm nose to nose with her, I shake my head. "Those are just for me and Kat, okay?" I point to my cheek. "Lay one on me, cutie."

She giggles and plants a wet kiss on my cheek. I lift her up and hoist her onto my shoulders where she squeals and wraps her arms around my head like an octopus.

Kat laughs as I peel a little finger out of my eye socket.

"Don't encourage her eye-poking skills."

She laughs harder.

Squinting through a maze of pointy fingers that have reappeared in my face, I have to ask the obvious. "Seriously, babe, why do we have goats?"

"Because they're cute."

"I'm serious."

"I am being serious." She sighs and leans down to pet Stella, who makes these little sounds of contentment as she nuzzles against Katherine's leg. "These two were abandoned on this old farm just outside of Austin. When Mel heard, she got down there as fast as she could. She adopted these little guys because no one else wanted them."

Well, fuck.

I kinda hate myself for wanting to leave the animals on someone's porch.

Blowing out a breath, I put Izzy down. "Now I feel like a jerk."

She laughs at me. "Don't be so hard on yourself. Not everyone shares Mel's affinity for saving the lost."

Her voice conveys a reverence that I feel all the way down to my bones.

I think back to that conversation we had when I first arrived, when she told me Mel took in strays and that's why Katherine has been here since May.

It's on the tip of my tongue to ask why she's hiding out on a farm.

I've almost asked her a million times what really brought her here. I get that she and Melissa were great friends, and I know she was getting over a breakup, but she's never told me the details of why she left her job in Austin. When it came up the other night, she mumbled that she worked for a politician. That sure as hell got my attention, but she quickly changed the subject.

I didn't pry, even though I wanted to. Maybe it was the expression on her face that stopped me because I got the impression she has a lot of ghosts wrapped up behind door number one. So I didn't push. God knows the shit going on here has been tough enough. I don't need to cross any more boundaries with her. Not if I want to keep things casual.

Nothing about this is casual.

Warring emotions rage in my chest as I watch her baby-talk to Stella and Stanley, who bounce around, excited by her attention.

She motions toward them. "Adopting these two is what gave me the idea for the farmers' event. I thought we could do a petting zoo, and use it to promote our products. Business around here dies in the winter, but since the temperature is often so mild, it seemed silly that no one hosts any events to maintain interest in the local farming."

"That was your idea?"

"Yeah. Why? Do you hate it?"

"Not at all. I think it's a great idea. I just wish prepping for it wasn't such a time suck." I still have to finish making that pen for the animals.

She bites that bottom lip. "Sorry. I thought I was helping."

Lifting my hand to her chin, I tilt her face up. "Hey, I didn't mean anything by that. In fact, getting people to see our farm might kind of serve as an open house. If people like what they see, then maybe someone will want to buy it."

A flash of emotion crosses her face, but just like that, it's gone.

"Right." She pulls away, and immediately, I know I've said the wrong thing. But then she gives me an understanding smile, almost like she's trying to make me feel better. She clears her throat. "I, uh, finished the new labels for Mel's bath products. Would you like to see them?"

I reach over and pull her to me, needing that connection. "Definitely," I mumble as I kiss her forehead.

Once we're in the house, I put Izzy in her walker as Kat lays out several glossy prints on her small desk.

"Kat, these are great." I pick them up one by one to study. I run my fingers over the logo. The words *Lovelace Lavender* wrap around the image of a small farm house. It's rustic but romantic. She has labels for different lotions and perfumes, each sporting the same beautiful design. "You did this?"

"Yup."

"What did this stuff look like before?"

Her lips twist as she looks around her room. She reaches for a little white bottle with a handwritten label.

I stare at her, completely confused how this talented girl is working for me on a farm. "Katherine." Her back straightens, and she looks at me questioningly. "Did you come up with the name too? Lovelace Lavender?"

She nods slowly, looking confused. "It's the name of the farm."

I laugh. "The name of the farm is Lovelace Farm."

"So?"

"So you took the name of the farm and rebranded the products."

She still looks confused. "Okay?"

"You took handwritten labels, developed a branding identity, designed the logo, and basically came up with a commercially viable product line."

She shrugs. "I guess."

Why does she not appreciate how much she's done here? "Can I ask how much Mel paid you for this?"

Her eyebrows knot. "Nothing. I did it for fun. I wanted to help her keep the farm from going bankrupt."

My MFA taught me one thing. Design—good design—isn't cheap. And I have no idea how to compensate this girl for her efforts.

I rub my chin as I consider how I can show her my gratitude. "What else do we need to do for the farmers' event?"

Her eyes brighten. "I have to finish packaging the soaps and lotions. And we need to finish the animal pen. Mr. Mac is bringing over some tables so the different farms can set up their products."

I nod and tuck a strand of hair behind her ear before I lean down to bite her earlobe. She shivers when I whisper in her ear, "You're so talented."

Her slender arms wrap around me before she nestles her body to mine and sighs against my chest. And an ache in the deepest part of me makes me wish I didn't have to let her go.

37

KATHERINE

THE DINER IS FULL, MY ORDERS ARE UP, BUT ALL I CAN FOCUS ON IS that ruggedly beautiful man in my booth who's snuggling a baby to his chest.

And I'm not the only one staring. My boss Carol stands next to me fanning herself. "Honey," she whispers, "if I were twenty years younger…"

"What about George?" I laugh.

"Eh." She waves her hand. "Technicalities."

All of the waitresses stop by the table to hold Izzy, but I know Brady is part of the lure. He's almost too handsome to escape the attention.

When I swing by with a fresh cup of coffee, that dimple peeks out, and he gives me one of those dangerous smiles that makes my heart race.

The word that comes to mind is lovesick. Like, if I could forego food and just wrap myself in Brady Shepherd, I totally would.

God, help me.

Because I have never in my life felt like this. Never wanted to throw caution to the wind to see what happens. But Brady makes me want to put everything on the line. Even my heart.

I try to focus on my tables, but I'm having a hard time concentrating. Finally, I give up and pour myself a cold glass of water to regroup.

"You guys bumping nasties?" someone whispers over my shoulder.

I nearly drop my drink. "What?" I whirl around to see my smirking co-worker Jaycee.

"You don't have to answer that. I can tell by your expression that you know that man in a Biblical sense, and I am completely green with envy."

Jaycee is my favorite person to work with. She grabs a few shifts a week whenever her college schedule allows it.

A nervous laugh escapes me. "I'm that obvious?"

She shakes her head. "I'd be concerned if you weren't having naked playtimes with that hottie." She sighs, and we both turn to stare at Brady who's doing a little food airplane into Izzy's mouth.

"Is everyone talking about us?" I whisper, almost afraid of the answer. But this is a small town where gossip reigns supreme.

She shrugs. "People know you two have been through a lot. Let me put it this way. I don't think anyone is surprised you two are an item."

When Carol rings up my order, I start to reach for the food when Jaycee motions toward Brady. "I don't mean to be a Nervous Nellie, but are you gonna be okay when he leaves?"

I freeze, mid-motion. She nods toward his table. "He's moving back to Boston, right? I mean, I assumed when I heard the farm was for sale."

Swallowing the lump in my throat requires a Herculean

effort. "Yes." He may not realize it, but as soon as he started talking to that realtor, word about the farm spread like wildfire.

Jaycee frowns before she gives me a sad smile and squeezes my hand. "Then you and I will have a date with some Bacardi."

38

BRADY

THE EARLY EVENING SUN MAKES THE HORIZON GLOW AS WE DRIVE home from Kat's shift at the diner.

I study the rolling hills and the contrast of shadow against the dimming light. It's beautiful here. Lush and tranquil. I finally understand why you'd want a hammock in the backyard or a swing on the porch. There's something about the cedar in the air that makes you want to sit back and breathe. Or draw.

In fact, my fingers are itching to pick up my sketch pad at home. I'm about to mention this when we cross over the creek, and I steal a glance at Kat.

Those big hazel eyes are pinch closed as she tilts her head forward to rest against the window.

I reach over and grab her hand.

"Wanna talk about it?" I ask softly when I pull the truck into the driveway a few minutes later. I know it has something to do with my brother's accident. She got that same anguished expression when we first toured the property a few weeks ago.

She turns to me, her eyes haunted. "Not really."

I want to prod, but I don't. She looks traumatized by the memory of what happened.

Guilt washes over me. Here I've been banging the hell out of Kat, using her to forget about everything else.

That sounds so epically fucked up.

The truth is I really like her, and I know the attraction is mutual, so I don't feel like a total asshole for trying to lose myself in sex.

But a part of me knows I don't deserve this. I don't deserve the comfort of this beautiful woman. I don't deserve to wake up in her arms or kiss her lips or taste her skin. Why should I find solace amid my brother's suffering?

We unload the groceries in silence as Izzy chatters contentedly.

Tonight I have to work on a few estimates for Jose, but I feel bad not being there for Kat when she's obviously still upset. But I blew this off all day, and now I need to get it done. I stare at the laptop, wishing I could push it off until morning and go curl up with Kat. I need to take advantage of our time together before I start working at the tattoo parlor in a few days.

I got the job with one phone call and a quick visit to the shop, which surprised me, but my old job gave me a great reference. Although I definitely could use the money, I'm not looking forward to leaving Kat and the baby alone at night.

Kat says she's tired, kisses me on the cheek as I work in the office, and heads off to bed. I'm tempted to grab her and hug her and tell her everything will be all right, but I know that's not true. Because soon, I won't be here for her, and that's killing me.

It's almost midnight when I finally email the last estimate. I'm about to turn off the lights and take a quick shower when her scream pierces the silence.

My heart is pounding when I round the hallway and burst into her bedroom. She's sitting up in bed, sobbing.

I sit and pull her into my lap. Kat's arms wrap around my neck and her whole body quakes.

"I got you, baby. It's okay." I stroke her hair and take a deep breath, trying to calm my racing heart.

I don't know how long we sit in the dark when she finally whispers, "I was there, Brady. I was there that night."

My hand stills on her back. *That night.* She told me she was babysitting Izzy.

She scoots off my lap and leans against the wall, pulling her knees to her chest, as she wipes tears from her damp cheeks. "When they were gone so long, I called a neighbor to watch Izzy so I could look for Cal and Melissa. I knew something was wrong. Even in the rain, it shouldn't have taken so long. That horse always ran down to the creek. They knew where to look." Tears stream down her face. "It shouldn't have taken so long."

I sit, barely breathing, and wait for her to continue.

She glances up, a look of utter devastation on her face. "I ran down to the creek bed. I knew it was faster than driving all the way around the property, especially in that weather." Her chest fills with a deep breath. "That's when it hit me. I didn't want to drive because I was afraid of the flash floods we get down here and the low water crossing by the creek. My dad always warned me about that. He lost a friend that way. The kid was just washed away."

All of the hair on my arms stands up as I wait for her to finish. I get an image of Kat running to the other side of the property in the middle of the night while being pelted with cold rain.

Her eyes close, and she starts to cry again. "By the time I got there, I could hear the sirens, but it was too late. The sheriff thought a sudden rush of water had pushed the truck past the small landing off to the side. When the truck hit this concrete ledge, it flipped and got dragged deeper. The water was so fast. We couldn't reach them until the next morning. I stood there for hours and waited. I felt so helpless. I couldn't do a goddamn thing."

I reach for her, and she shakes her head. "I know what you said about the barn door, that accidents happen, but as long as I live, I'll never forgive myself for that night."

I'm about to say something—what, I'm not sure—when she levels me with a heartbroken stare. "I watched them get pulled from the water, Brady. I had to identify their bodies," she whimpers.

It takes a moment to fully process what she's saying. Then I can see it all. A rain-soaked Katherine standing along the banks as Cal and Mel get dredged from the river.

"Jesus Christ." I grab her and hold her close as she cries into my shoulder.

No wonder she has nightmares. No wonder she screams in her sleep.

I can't breathe. I don't know that she can either, but we sit together in the darkness and grieve.

When Kat falls asleep, I lay her down in bed and crawl in behind her. I hold her until morning, desperate to keep her safe the only way I know how.

39

KATHERINE

I GET UP EARLY AND MAKE BREAKFAST. A PART OF ME FEELS relieved to have gotten all of that off my chest, but I hate that I had to burden Brady with what happened. I'm sure he wanted to know, but that doesn't make living with those images any easier.

When he wanders into the kitchen, I half wonder if he'll be upset that I didn't tell him everything until last night. But I'm certainly not expecting the warm smile and hug or the kiss to my forehead. He does it with such tenderness, I could cry all over again.

"I'm sorry I unloaded all of that on you last night," I whisper against his chest.

"Why? I'm not." He kisses my cheek. "You needed to talk about it. I can't believe you hadn't. No wonder you've been having nightmares."

It feels so good to let him hold me. I close my eyes and breathe in his woodsy scent.

I'm going to miss you so much when you leave. Don't go.

I blink back the heat in my eyes as I turn back to the stove, needing some distance. "I made you something to eat. Farm-fresh eggs." Once I've regained my composure, I glance back at him.

He rubs his face and yawns. "Those chickens scare me. Their beady little eyes freak me out."

I laugh, and it surprises me. That after everything I told him about last night, he can make me laugh.

"The chickens are harmless."

He frowns and leans back against the counter. "Doubtful. I'm pretty sure they could peck your eyes out if they got hungry enough. Didn't you ever see that Alfred Hitchcock movie, *The Birds*?"

"Those were mostly blackbirds. I don't think there were any chickens in that film." I snicker.

"Well, if someone made a movie about killer chickens, it would be terrifying. All of that clucking and those icy little stares." He kisses the back of my neck as I serve his breakfast. Goose bumps break out on my arms, and I drop my head to the side as he nibbles his way to my ear. "But I'd protect you from those scary-ass birds."

I want to laugh again, but it's hard when his mouth is on my skin, so all I do is mumble something unintelligible.

"How much longer before the baby wakes up?" he growls in my ear before he pushes me against the counter and presses himself to my rear.

"Hmm." I can't think. I just tilt my head back until it rests on his chest. His hand slides under my shirt and palms my breast. I arch against his erection and contemplate stripping naked in the kitchen when the baby starts babbling on the monitor.

"Seriously?"

I laugh again. "Get used to it, big guy." Turning in his arms, I lean up to kiss him. Wrapping my arms around his neck, I snuggle close and let his mouth ravish mine.

I feel it too. The urgency to be closer. To forget all of the heartache that's hung over this farm for the last several weeks and just be together before he goes back to Boston.

Finally, I break away, a little out of breath. "Good morning to you too." I straighten my shirt and glance down at his tented sweat pants.

He groans and drops his head to my shoulder. I thread my fingers through his hair, loving that he wants me like this. "How about we grab a quickie when she goes down for her nap?"

His laughter rumbles in my ear. "I like how you think."

Unfortunately, we don't get time for a quickie.

When Izzy goes down for her nap, Brady has to take a conference call from one of his contractors in Boston. When he gets off the call, I'm making dinner. In between all of that we're cleaning the house for the social worker's visit tomorrow, which forces us to brave going into Cal and Mel's bedroom to figure out how to organize their belongings. It's rough, but with Brady by my side, we somehow get through it.

And when I collapse in bed at night, exhausted and emotionally drained, he's right there to hold me tight. Almost like he needs the contact as much as I do.

40

BRADY

IT FEELS WRONG TO HAVE THIS MEETING BEFORE I'VE BROKEN THE news to my parents that I'm adopting Izzy, but today is the only opening the social worker has for five weeks, and I don't think I should wait. Kat keeps telling me to relax, that it's not official until the late January court date, but I know I need to have that conversation as soon as possible.

But my father's heart surgeon warned me privately that I shouldn't drop any bombs on my dad until his next doctor's appointment, so I've just assured my parents that I've spoken to our attorney about adoption and gotten the paperwork rolling. I need to tell them soon, though. For my own sanity.

My nerves are shot. Between going through Cal's bedroom last night and worrying about the adoption process and my family's finances, I could use a time out.

Wiping my sweaty palms on my jeans, I watch Mrs. Gonzalez, the social worker, as she scribbles on her form.

Kat places a cup of coffee next to the woman and returns to her seat next to me at the kitchen table. I hold Izzy, who munches on a banana.

The older woman waves her pen toward us. "So you and the baby live here by yourself with Ms. Duran?"

I'm suddenly worried about how to explain our situation. Do I say Kat's my employee or do I explain that we're... We're what? Dating? After I gave Kat that whole song and dance about how this has to stay casual, it seems wrong to use that term now. Even though, yeah, I'm enjoying the time we spend together. Way more than any other woman I've dated.

But Kat once again comes to the rescue. "I'm the nanny. I knew Brady's brother and sister-in-law so I've come to help until Brady can get on his feet."

Mrs. Gonzalez nods and begins writing again. "That's kind of you."

"What are friends for?" She catches my eye and winks, and just like that, the worry in my gut starts to wane.

I smile back, so grateful for this girl. She looks completely relaxed as she helps me field the questions, and within ten minutes, she and Mrs. Gonzalez are chatting in Spanish. I have no clue what they're saying, but judging by how the social worker turns to me several times to smile, I'm guessing it's going well.

A few minutes later, she asks to take a tour of the house that ends up taking all of three minutes, and then she's out the door.

Kat, Izzy and I stand on the porch and watch the Honda Civic tear down the driveway.

"That was fast," I mumble as I peek at the clock on my phone. "She was here, what, forty minutes? What if I was a psycho? What if I collected my nail clippings in a little jar or made voodoo dolls out of hair? Shouldn't she suss that out?"

Kat snorts. "You can be really weird sometimes." She rolls her eyes. "Mrs. Gonzalez liked you and how you were with Izzy. Said you seemed like a hard worker."

I scoff. "How would she know?" When I think about it, she didn't really ask many probing questions.

"I told her, silly. About how you take care of the baby and feed her and bathe her. How you tell her bedtime stories and brush her hair. How you've been fixing up the property and learned how to care for all of the animals." She shrugs. "She was impressed. Said Izzy was lucky to have you, and I agreed."

Jesus. That was one hell of a conversation they had in Spanish.

"You said all that?"

"Yeah. Do I get a bonus?" She giggles and nudges me in the ribs, and I laugh.

"Can I pay you with pizza?"

"Absolutely. But only if it's Pizza Hut."

I wrap her in a hug and kiss her forehead. "It's a deal."

Once we get Izzy to bed and order pizza, we curl up on the couch. Kat's head is in my lap, and I'm threading my fingers through her hair as we watch the *SportsCenter* highlight reel. When a clip from the Celtics game comes on, she turns back toward me.

"Do you miss home? Do you miss Boston?"

My hand drifts in and out of the soft waves as I think about it. "Yeah. I miss my parents and my sports teams." She smiles, and I run a finger along her neck until she shivers. "But I have to admit I like the pace of life down here."

"What do you mean?"

"Everything in Boston is intense. The traffic. The people. The weather." I take a strand of hair and push it behind her ear. "Life is slower here."

"You mean boring?"

"No, not at all. I mean, okay, I can see how it could be. We have a lot of entertainment in Boston that you don't have in the Texas Hill Country. But here people don't rush. They look you in the eye when they talk to you. They seem to genuinely care what your response is when they ask how you're doing. I like that."

She smiles like she's proud. "So what you're saying is you like it here?"

Huh. "Yeah, I guess I do. Now if I could get Bandit to stop peeing on my stuff, we'd be golden."

Kat chuckles and reaches up to run her hand across the back of my neck. She stares at me in a way that I feel all the way down to my knees. That playful grin spreads on her lips. "Wanna snuggle?"

"Abso-fucking-lutely." I slide down next to her and spoon her from behind. "Thank you for your help today," I murmur against her hair as I reach down to pull her closer.

She turns in my arms and kisses me gently. "Any time, honey. Any time."

41

KATHERINE

THE NEXT MORNING IS SURPRISINGLY CHILLY. WRAPPING MY hoodie around me, I smile as I stare out the back porch. Brady is wearing a pair of jeans and a long-sleeved black Henley, his usual attire, but what has me chuckling to myself is the look of absolute horror on his face.

"Oh, fuck," Brady yells as three hungry kittens scale up his jeans.

"Hurry and put the tuna down before they eat you alive," I warn as I peel them off one by one. I stop to give little Valentine a kiss on his pink nose. He's the runt of the litter and my favorite.

Brady places the bowl of food on the floor and rubs his thighs. "Don't consort with the enemy. They have sharp claws."

I pat his shoulder sympathetically. "Poor baby. I'll kiss it later and make it feel better."

Before I know what's happening, I'm in the air, hanging upside down over his shoulder. "You'd better," he says with a smack to my ass.

I'm laughing and swatting at his rear end in retaliation, trying to keep my glasses on my face, when we reach the kitchen and he slides me down his hard body onto the counter. I shiver and spread my legs to make room for him.

It's good to see him smiling. I kiss him and enjoy his hard, warm body press against mine as he tangles his hand through my hair.

I know he's relieved the social worker's visit went well yesterday. He was paranoid she didn't stay long enough, but a quick phone call to his attorney put him at ease. Everything is on track to adopt his niece, and it looks like a weight has been lifted from his shoulders.

But I can't help but wonder if there's more to his mood change. Since my nightmare earlier this week, he's been more affectionate. Sweeter. More tender. Almost like... almost like I'm his girlfriend. Almost like he's finally given in to whatever this is.

When he leans back, I run my palm down his stubbled chin. "You look hot like this." He's beautiful clean-shaven, but there's something about his grizzled lumberjack vibe that makes me want to rip off all of his clothes with my teeth.

That little dimple peeks out. "You always look hot. Even when you were telling me off the first time I met you."

I gasp. "I did not tell you off," I say indignantly.

He laughs and kisses me. "Yeah, I seem to recall you telling me to get the hell off the driveway."

"Oh, my God. You're right." I drop my head to his shoulder, embarrassed. "I'm so sorry."

His lips graze my ear. "You were so sexy with that stern look on your face and your fuck-me librarian glasses. And then I thought you were the hot high-school babysitter, and I felt like a deviant for wanting to fuck you senseless."

My face burns and I shake my head against him. "Stop, I know I look young."

He laughs. "See, you've unleashed the real me, raw and unedited."

"And all it took was a little naked time and a couple of blow jobs," I joke, loving how his arm snakes around me.

"Do not diminish the importance of those blow jobs, babe." He rubs his nose against mine. "Hey, are you gonna be okay watching Izzy tonight? I hate leaving you guys alone."

"Yeah. We'll be fine. Just be careful driving to Austin." He's starting at that tattoo parlor tonight.

"I will. I promise." He kisses me before he strides off to unload the dishwasher. I watch, entranced by the way those jeans hug his rear. When he finishes, he pours two cups of coffee and adds some milk and sweetener to one and hands it to me.

I smile. "You remember how I take my coffee."

"I'd be a dick if I didn't by now." My heart does stupid things in my chest. But before I can say anything about his comment, he pushes the sleeves of his Henley up his arms and asks, "Have you seen Izzy's pink binkie? I couldn't find it last night."

He wanders out of the room and comes back with the baby, who looks adorably rumpled. She actually slept in this morning, which is a miracle of all miracles. Then his voice lightens. "Izzy Pizzy needs her binkie, right, cutie pie?"

She giggles. "Izzy Pizzy!"

He kisses her chubby cheek and glances over at me.

I'm pretty sure little hearts are popping out of my eyes right now. Here is this hot man, tattoos decorating his rugged arms, muscles tugging at the fabric, asking me about the baby's binkie while he holds her close to his chest. Hello, ovary explosion.

God, I have it bad for him.

"What?" he asks, noticing me staring.

"You're getting good at this baby stuff."

He leans over to kiss me. "Only because this awesome girl I know taught me everything there is to know about babies."

Inwardly, I sigh, feeling like a sappy teenager. If I were a cartoon character right now, little birds would be singing over my shoulder.

Even though everything inside of me warns that I should proceed with caution, I can't put any conviction behind the idea. I like Brady too much to keep my emotions in reserve.

In fact, the other L-word comes to mind.

42

KATHERINE

WE SPEND THE NEXT SEVERAL DAYS PREPPING FOR THE FARMERS' event we're hosting this weekend. I package lotions and soaps and body scrubs while Brady finishes the animal pen for our petting zoo. On the night before the event, by the time we're done and the baby is tucked in bed, we're too tired to function.

Brady's in great shape and can usually handle the physical labor around here, but since he started working nights in Austin, he's totally wiped out. I feel bad that I didn't cancel the event. He's running himself ragged. In fact, we've been too tired to do more than wrap ourselves around each other at night and fall asleep, but I've loved every moment together. Even if we're just sleeping.

Once again, my head is in his lap as we watch *SportsCenter*. He runs his hand through my hair, and it's so soothing, I'm pretty sure I'm about to pass out.

I love how he touches me. I want to tell him this. I want to tell him so many things, but I don't. *If you were mine, I'd take such good care of you, Brady. I would tell you how your touch lights me on fire. How your scent makes me wild. How your sarcastic mouth makes my heart hum.*

"I mean this in all seriousness," he says, sounding exhausted. "How the hell did Cal get Melissa pregnant again? When did they have time to have sex?"

I laugh, opening my mouth to answer, but think better of it and shake my head.

"No, really," he continues. "Between the animals, and pruning every bush and shrub this side of Austin, and the baby waking at the *worst* times, I don't see how it was even possible. I don't think I could get my dick up now if I tried."

I smile at his honesty. "Is that a challenge?"

"Okay, well, maybe he'd come out to play for you. I guess what I mean is sustainable fucking."

I nearly choke on my spit. "Sustainable fucking?"

"Yeah, the day-to-day sex I'm assuming a happily married couple enjoys. Sustainable fucking."

"You mean you don't buy the concept that sex flies out the window when you're married?"

"Clearly it didn't with Cal and Melissa."

I'm pretty sure Brady would high-five his brother for the amount of sex he had if he only knew. Finally, I let it out. "I may have, ya know, run interference."

He leans over me to make eye contact, and I try to hold in my embarrassed grin. "And that means what exactly?"

I stare up at him and laugh. "I told Mel I'd get up with the baby at night. To make, uh, *things* easier for them."

His brows lift higher. "You watched Izzy so they could..."

"Have sexy times."

He snorts. "Seriously?"

My face must be ten shades of red right now. "Yes, seriously."

"You weren't kidding when you said you and Melissa were close."

"It's not like we sat around and talked about sex. Not really." He stares at me like he doesn't believe a word I'm saying. I blow out a breath. "Fine. We talked about sex, but in general terms because it's not like I wanted details about her and Cal. Eww. Besides, I knew everything was good in the hood."

"Good in the hood?" His lips lift up in a smirk.

"Yes, they got along *muy bien*." My eyes widen meaningfully.

"But you guys didn't talk about it?"

"We didn't have to. Because when they went to pound town, the neighbors a mile away knew exactly how well they got along."

Brady shakes his head, looking a little grossed out and... dare I say proud of his bro? I sit up, still laughing.

"I'm totally mortified that I'm telling you these things, but think of it this way. I was usually already up because of the dirty noises coming from their room. With my bedroom right next to theirs, it was dang near impossible to sleep through it. So I'd go to Izzy's room, turn up the sound machine and catnap on the couch in there. If the baby woke up, she and I would snuggle. So therein lies the mystery of how Mel got pregnant again. I admit I aided and abetted."

He leans over and kisses me. "You should have charged them more for your services."

I laugh and play with the buttons on his Henley. "No way. I'm a hopeless romantic, and those two were definitely in love. Even after they had Izzy." It's how I want to be some day with my husband.

Glancing up, I see Brady's dark green eyes searching mine.

He clears his throat. "In case I haven't told you lately, I'm really grateful for everything you do around here."

I reach up and push my hand into his thick, black hair. "Staring at you these last several weeks has been a real hardship. I'm not sure how I've survived."

He laughs and snakes his hand into my shirt, and I hold back a giggle because I'm pretty sure he's trying to tickle me. But then his rough fingers stroke the side of my breast, and my breathing quickens.

As he brushes his lips against mine, he rasps, "Remember what I said earlier about being too tired to have sex?"

"But can you handle sustainable fucking?" I blush when I say the words, but I don't look away.

His eyes darken. "We should probably test that theory. You know, for the sake of science."

"As long as it's for scientific research," I whisper as I pull him down to me, "challenge accepted."

43

BRADY

I'M NOT SURE WHAT I WAS EXPECTING TODAY AT THE FARMERS' fair. Maybe something akin to a garage sale where people stop by to nose around half-heartedly in your belongings before they head off to do what they'd really planned for the day.

But that's not what's happening here. Because the whole town has shown up.

A line of cars is parked up and down our driveway, all the way from the house to the main road over the hill. People meander from table to table, sampling food from The Lone Star Station and other snacks the neighboring farms have set out. Kat invited a local band from Austin to play today, and their country covers of holiday songs are making this feel like a county fair, especially since Mr. Mac strung holiday lights around the stands.

I rub the stubble on my chin, realizing I'd damn near forgotten it's almost Christmas. The Scrooge in me is tallying up how much larger our electrical bill is going to be with all of those holiday lights, but it's hard to be thinking about finances when everyone is so cheery.

Rubbing my eyes, I try to wake up while I balance Izzy on my hip. It's been a long week, and as much as I love tattooing, I'm glad I have a break this weekend to hang out with the girls.

I can't help but smile as Kat corrals a half dozen kids to pet Stella and Stanley, who hop around excitedly.

She's been running back and forth between the animals and our table where she has all of our products set up. Even with dozens of people everywhere, my eyes follow Kat.

"She's one of a kind, isn't she?"

I turn to find Mrs. Mac.

"Yes, ma'am."

"I've known that girl since she was seven. Hardest little worker I've ever seen. Never complains. Always smiling."

"I never would've been able to handle things without her help."

"Katherine is the kind of woman who puts her whole heart and soul into whatever she does. Just look at your table over there."

I know what it looks like, but I turn anyway. About a dozen farms in the area have little stands with products and produce, but our table is the busiest. Kat's sold most of the lotions and soaps she'd made, and that's saying something as the table was overflowing this morning.

"She's been busting her ass to prep everything." Pride surges in my chest.

Mrs. Mac motions toward her. "Did you know she sent press releases to every newspaper in South Texas? She got our event in those weekend calendars in the San Antonio and Austin papers. The smarty pants advertised it as a Christmas event, so that probably doubled our attendance." She chuckles. "We thought we were just putting up a few little fruit stands."

I'm not surprised Katherine went all out, but I wonder why she never mentioned all of the publicity she's done.

"She didn't even tell you about that, did she?" Mrs. Mac

doesn't wait for me to answer. "No, of course not. Because that's her way. She just does what needs to be done."

My attention drifts back to Kat, who is standing behind our stand, talking to customers. Her hair is braided and hangs down her shoulder. Her flannel red shirt fits snug to her slender body, hugging all of her curves in a way that makes my mouth water.

Those bright eyes cut across to mine, and Kat shoots me one of those smiles I feel all the way down to my boots.

Mrs. Mac clears her throat, and I remember we're in the middle of a conversation. I return my attention to her, and she gives me a wink.

"You'll never do better than Katherine Duran. And even though her father is gonna give you hell, just remember that she is one hundred percent worth it."

My mouth drops open. I don't know what to say. Telling her this isn't permanent enough to meet her father feels like the biggest dickhead thing to bring up. Never mind that the idea of not being with Kat is damn near soul-crushing.

Mrs. Mac pats my shoulder like she knows the extent of my confusion. "Son, you're a good man. Worlds better than that fiancé of hers. Don't let her get away."

What the fuck?

Fiancé?

She chuckles. "Ex-fiancé, I should say. Good riddance." She waves her hand like she didn't just drop a bomb on me. "Spoiled senator's son. Oh, he said all of the right things, but I knew he was a cad. I'm glad Kat figured it out. Besides, you're a much better catch."

And with that, she strolls off, leaving me in more turmoil than I should be feeling for a relationship that doesn't technically exist.

Fiancé.

All afternoon it bothers me.

That word clangs around in my head until I have half a mind to sit Kat down and make her tell me what happened.

But I don't.

Because we don't have that kind of relationship, I remind myself. She never asks about my exes because she understands our boundaries.

Not that we ever drew a line in the sand and said, hey, no discussing former relationships, but we've both avoided the subject. I get that that's only something you do when you're moving forward, and as much as it bugs the fuck out of me, Kat and I are in a holding pattern as we wait for me to leave.

But it's not like I can give up my life in Boston for a woman I've known for a month. That would be crazy. Right up there with my brother eloping with a girl he'd known for, what? Two weeks? Insanity.

Vowing to keep my big, fat mouth shut, I finish folding the last table as Kat closes up the barn.

I stand on the porch watching the last truck roll down the driveway as she trudges up the stairs. When the Macs offered to take Izzy for the night, I jumped at the chance to veg out with Kat. She put Pizza Hut on speed dial so I'd have it handy for such an occasion. I've already phoned in our order.

"You did a great job, killer." I pull her in for a hug. Her arms wrap around me, and she sighs. "You sold out of everything, didn't you?"

She nods, a little smile pulling at her lips. "Before I forget, you need to call this guy Frank." She pulls a business card out of her back pocket. "He runs some fragrance company, and he likes our stuff."

"Your stuff."

"What?" Her nose scrunches, and those black-rimmed glasses slide down her nose.

"He liked your stuff." When she doesn't say anything, I laugh. "It's okay. I know you're not going to take credit for all of those products you sold, but between us, I've figured out that those were all your creations." I let that sink in before I prod. "Right?" When she doesn't respond, I squeeze her tighter. "You don't diminish anything Cal and Melissa built by taking credit. But I know enough about this place to realize the only reason Melissa started making those soaps is because of you."

After a moment, she asks, "How do you know?"

I let go of her and lean back against the porch railing. "This place has been in the red for years. I've spent the last few weeks digging through bank statements and sales receipts. I know Mel got some life insurance from her father, and maybe that helped keep this place afloat for a while, but it wasn't until she rolled out a line of bath products that she had any hope of being financially stable. And I'm guessing that had everything to do with you."

"She needed help," Kat says softly. "I brainstormed with her. Sent her some recipes. Nothing major."

I laugh. "Okay." I step closer until we're nose to nose, and I tilt her head up to kiss her cheek. "I'm calling bullshit, but okay." Besides, I've seen Melissa's notes. Pages and pages of emails from Kat with recipes and ideas. She even went out and bought supplies to test out ideas before she forwarded them to her best friend. And from what I've gathered, one of Kat's emails is what sent Mel to that business class in Austin where she met my brother, who was there to learn how to run things for our parents.

Dropping my arms to her shoulders, I turn her around to head inside, but I pause when I realize how tense she is.

"You sore, babe?" I ask as I knead her taut muscles.

A little moan escapes her. "Hmm. Maybe."

Placing a kiss on her neck, I mumble against her skin, "I have a great way to alleviate this tension."

Because if I'm leaving, I plan to make the most of every moment possible with her.

Starting now.

44

KATHERINE

Brady strokes over my naked body with confident hands, kneading each and every one of my sore muscles.

"Holy smokes, you give great massages."

"I thought we'd already established that." His sexy voice sends goose bumps down my arms.

"Mmm," I moan when he hits that spot between my shoulder blades.

His jeans scratch my thighs, but I'm enjoying his attention too much to mention it. Besides, I know he'll be naked soon too.

Smiling into the pillow, it's hard not to feel carried away when Brady ordered my favorite pizza, fed me, and is now giving me the world's best massage.

When he kisses my shoulder, my heart flutters in my chest.

"Katherine, can I ask you something?"

I still, wondering why he's using my full name, which is something he really only says when we're having sex.

"Sure."

"The promotion you did for today..." He doesn't need to finish that statement because I know where this is headed. "Where did you learn that? In your last job?"

I nod, hating that my dream job has become such a source of embarrassment.

He clears his throat. "You don't want to talk about it."

I tap his thigh for him to move, and he slides down next to me and props his head up on one arm before he threads his fingers through my hair. I stare at his tattoos, knowing that sharing about myself will make the end of us that much harder. "I don't mean to be mysterious. It's just that it's tied into a lot of things I'm not really proud of."

He nods, but I can see he's curious.

Taking a deep sigh, I pull up the covers so I'm not so naked and return my attention to him. "It's nothing terrible, really. I'm probably being a drama queen. But I've always been a really private person. You get used to being at the center of people's ire when you're the kid of migrant workers, so I've learned it's better to keep my mouth shut." I don't say the rest. What's on the tip of my tongue. *So no one can hurt me.*

His lips form a straight line, and I trace the outline of the ouroboros on his chest. "I worked as a public relations specialist for Senator Harrington." I nibble my bottom lip, hating that I have to say more.

"That's a big job right out of college," he observes.

"It helped that I was dating his son, who also worked on the senator's re-election campaign." I shake my head. "I mean, that's not why I was dating him. Eric and I met in college. He asked me out a few times, but I always declined. I finally agreed to go out with him near the end of our senior year. I knew the guy was driven, and he talked about going into politics. I liked that he seemed passionate about making a difference. He introduced me to his father at graduation. Next thing I knew, Senator Harrington was offering me a job."

His lips twitch, and I say it before he gets the chance to. "Yeah, totally suspicious, right? But what the hell did I know? I was a poor college grad who needed a job, and here was one of the most respected men in the state giving me a great opportunity. Never mind that I'm not even a Republican."

Brady chuckles, and that hand comes down to rest on my hip as I continue. "But I did follow politics, and I knew at the heart of his campaign was fracking reform. And as you know, I'm passionate about the issue. Which is why, at Eric's graduation dinner, I might have told the senator his platform was a little flimsy and that if he really wanted to make a difference, he needed to restrict the number of fracking wells in the state."

A smile creeps out on Brady's lips as he watches me rant. "It's not what I would want, mind you, but I thought it would be a big step in the right direction. If it were up to me, it would be banned, plain and simple, but I'm not fool enough to think that will ever happen. But when the senator told me I had impressed him and that he'd love for me to help him craft that very message on his campaign, I thought it was a dream come true. I mean, what PR grad gets offered an amazing job within hours of getting her diploma?"

I fidget with a loose thread hanging from my sheet, hating the rest of this story. "Working for the senator was surreal. His team decided I couldn't very well traipse across the state representing the esteemed Walter Harrington in my Target-brand threads, so they bought me clothes."

Clearing my throat, I continue. "And then it somehow became Eric who bought me clothes and gave me a company car and expensive phone. And then it became about me needing to talk a certain way when I spoke to the press, so we practiced getting rid of my twang so I wouldn't come across as a hick." Another reason why I love living on the farm. Nobody here gives a damn how I talk.

My face burns with that admission. Brady must sense my

humiliation because he tugs me closer until I'm fully wrapped in his arms. "They sound like assholes."

I laugh. "Yeah. Well, it got worse." Biting my lip, I wonder how much Brady wants to hear.

He leans down and kisses my forehead. "Babe, you don't have to tell me if you really don't want to."

That's just it. I want to tell him. I want him to know what happened, but I'm worried it's too much. That we're crossing a line.

Swallowing past the lump in my throat, I whisper, "It's not that I don't want to tell you. It's that you're leaving... and I'm worried this is more personal than you really want to hear. Most guys don't want to hear about ex-boyfriends."

A deep sigh leaves him. "Truth?" He studies my face, and I nod. "I want to know everything about you, Kat. I know we should have some boundaries, but I'm having a hard time pulling back."

My heart thumps wildly in my chest. There it is again. Hope.

And the million-dollar question raises its ugly head. *Would he stay if he loved me?*

I decide to throw caution to the wind. Because yes, Brady makes me want to take risks. And I'll share this with him if it means even the slightest chance of changing things between us and making us more permanent somehow.

But I don't get the chance because Brady squeezes his eyes shut. "I'm sorry," he grits out. "You're right. Let's not do this."

The sharp inhale of my breath tells us both that I'm more than a little surprised. His lips brush mine. "Come on. I have a better idea."

He grabs my hand and leads me away from the bed before I can analyze the small cracks in my heart.

45

BRADY

As Katherine lowers her body into the hot, sudsy water and presses her ass between my thighs, I'm thinking this is the best damn idea I've ever had. Better than me unearthing her past and making her feel vulnerable.

"Mmm," she moans as the water rises around us. "I don't know why I don't take more baths."

I kiss her neck and she drops her head back to my shoulder. "I think I was eight the last time I took one, but now it's my new favorite thing."

The steam rises around us, and I wrap my arms around Kat, enjoying how well her wet body fits against mine.

"Better?" I ask as my lips skim her temple.

"Mmm."

"Hand me your shampoo." I motion toward the bottle, and she looks at me over her shoulder.

"You're gonna wash my hair?"

"Yeah. Turn back around."

She stares at me, eyes wide. I lean down and run my nose against hers. "Hurry up. The sooner I'm done washing your hair, the sooner I can wash the rest of your naked parts."

She makes a noise of approval in the back of her throat before leaning forward so I can do my thing. I'm sure she's fully aware her hair is the last thing on my radar right now as my dick is firmly pressed against her back.

I've never washed a woman's hair before, and I'm surprised by how much I enjoy doing this. I like taking care of Katherine, I'm finding. *More than you should.*

Little moans escape her as I massage her scalp. She's leaning against her knee, bent forward so that her wet curls trail over her slender back.

At this angle, I can see her profile. The gentle curve of her neck. Her flushed cheeks. Those luscious pink lips.

It's at this moment I realize how much she trusts me. How much she must want this, knowing full well that I'm leaving soon, and yet here she is.

She turns back to offer a sleepy smile, those hazel eyes more naked than the rest of her, and emotion overpowers me.

I want to offer her so much more than I can.

Does she know how much I want her, how my thoughts are becoming more and more consumed by her? Does she realize that I reach for her at night and dread the day when she's no longer by my side?

All the more reasons for us to not discuss our exes.

When I'm done washing and conditioning her hair, she collapses with her back against my chest and stretches her arms up around my neck. I drizzle body wash over her and skate my hands over every inch of her as her breath quickens. Leaning down, I lick and suck her shoulder as I caress her body. She's slick and sudsy, and so goddamn beautiful.

Her nipples are beaded tight, her skin a flushed pink from the hot water and steam. I massage and pinch her nipples between my fingers, thrusting slowly against her body, which is a beautiful torture.

When I bite her neck, she sighs, sounding both delighted and in pain. "I'll make it better, baby," I whisper into her ear before I suck on her lobe.

Reaching around her trim waist, I pull her higher until she's nestled on top of my thighs, and she stretches out over me. I grab her hips and slide her ass over my aching cock.

"Fuck, you feel so good."

I lick her skin, loving the breathy moan that escapes her as I squeeze her breasts. Her hips begin to move of their own accord, the sloshing water the soundtrack to the slide of our bodies.

"Brady," she groans. "Touch me."

"Put your legs up." I spread her thighs wide. "Brace your feet on the ledge of the tub." She leans back against me, and I tuck my knees between her legs to keep her pinned open.

She's panting above me as I trail my hands over the soft curves of her hips and the slope of her thighs. She's tortured, moaning because I haven't eased her pain, but perhaps that's only fair play as every part of me is throbbing too.

"Oh, God," she whimpers as I tease her slick opening with a gentle touch.

Her head leans back, arching against my shoulder. I breathe into her skin and whisper things I've only ever said to this woman.

"Do you know how much I want you?" I slowly sink a finger into her wet heat. "Why can't I get enough of you? Why do you feel so fucking good?"

Her hips roll, sliding the crease of her ass against my erection.

I grip her hair with my other hand and turn her to face me. She gasps but immediately fuses her mouth to mine as she writhes above me. I pump my finger in and out of her, circling her tight clit with my thumb, wishing I could fuck her bare.

Suddenly, a bath seems idiotic because I know condoms

aren't really effective in a hot bath, and even though she's on the pill, we agreed to use both. So I resign myself to letting this be about her, to making her feel good.

But then she pulls her legs down and slides my dick between her thighs, squeezing me as she rolls her hips.

Jesus Christ.

She arches and twists toward me, and I swear, for as long as I live, I'll never forget this sight. Her hungry hazel eyes. That pouty mouth. Her glistening skin.

Water sloshes over the side of the tub as we move against each other, our breaths hot on one another's lips. My hands move to her breasts, which shimmer in the soapy water. I'm thinking this can't get any better when she reaches between us to press my cock tighter against her swollen pussy.

"Katherine." It's all I can say before she sucks on my tongue, whimpering into my mouth as she glides against my cock.

And then she arches up and positions me at her entrance.

I still her hips. "Babe, we don't have to—"

She kisses me, her eyes urgent with emotion as she whispers, "It's okay. I want to do this with you."

Her tongue darts out to lick across the seam of my lips, and my thread of control snaps.

I sink into her, all of my nerves straining to get closer to this woman. I squeeze her breasts as delirium washes over me.

"Oh, fuck," I grunt against her neck.

Swear to God, sex has never felt this good before.

Her hips jerk, and she lets out a moan that makes me swell harder inside her tight body. I take a deep breath and try to keep myself from going over the edge.

After a moment, I grip her hips and move her faster. "Touch yourself, baby." I know she's shy in this weird way, not about giving me pleasure, but about giving herself what she needs.

Her hand disappears under the water, and I feel her fingers between her legs, dipping low to stroke where we join.

I thrust harder.

"Brady," she gasps.

"Let go, baby."

My hand joins hers, and I rub her swollen clit in quick circles.

Her eyes squeeze shut as her whole body rocks against me. She thrashes, sending water everywhere when she comes, her sharp moans echoing in the small bathroom. And I follow right behind, spilling my release into her.

I'm sure we're going to regret tonight's fuckfest tomorrow when we have to get up at the crack of dawn, but once we broke the seal and went without a condom, we couldn't get enough of each other.

I know it's stupid, not using protection, because the last thing either of us needs is a pregnancy, and as much as I want to spend every night losing myself in her body, this can't happen again. She and I already had the birth control talk. She'd gotten tested after she broke up with her ex, and I got tested a few months ago. I don't think you can ever be too careful when you work with needles, so I make it a priority to make sure I'm safe.

I've never gone bare. Never been tempted to. Until now.

It's well past two in the morning, and we've collapsed in her small bed. She's draped across me, one naked thigh over mine, as her fingers drift across the lines on my chest. Most girls ask what they mean, but she never has, though I see her interest. She always studies me, her eyes drifting across my skin like she's trying to memorize my ink.

"They're beautiful," she whispers, her lips swollen from our activities.

"They're just lines."

"No, I mean it. Your tattoos are stunning." Her finger traces the lines of the dragon on my bicep.

"That one is for my grandfather. He died when I was little, but we were close." I point to my chest where two figures dot the sky. "This is the constellation Gemini. It's the first one I ever got."

"The twins."

I nod. "I was a twin, but my brother Scotty died when we were five."

"Oh, my God, I'm so sorry." She rubs the image like she's trying to soothe me.

"What happened?"

"He got sick. Caught pneumonia." I lick my dry lips. "Scotty and Cal both caught a really bad flu that winter, but Scotty never recovered." I'm quiet as I think about those old memories. "I always felt guilty that I was the stronger brother. I never got sick. Never broke a bone. Everyone always told me I was the lucky one. Except I never felt lucky."

I close my eyes as her finger traces under my collarbone. "That's the ouroboros. It came next."

"It's intense, like you."

I laugh. "I'm not that intense."

She pokes my ribs. "Yeah, you kind of are." She folds her arms on my chest and peers down at me, her bottom lip caught between her teeth.

I study the slant of her nose. How her face is outlined in shadow. "Have you ever wanted a tat?"

Her head tilts to the side. "No. Not really." She nibbles that lip. "Well, not until now, I should say."

That piques my interest. "What would you get?"

"That's just it. How do you mark your skin forever?" She

shakes her head. "I'd hate regretting it. What if I changed my mind?"

I reach over to her desk where I saw a marker the other day. "Let's do a trial run. Tell me what you want, and I'll draw it on you. It'll wash off in a day or two."

"Really?" She smiles.

"Yeah." I kiss her jaw and work my way down to her neck where I take a bite.

"Um." She laughs. "I can't concentrate when you're biting me."

I lick the faint indentation of my teeth marks and settle back against the pillow with a sly grin. "Tell me or I'll come up with something random and weird."

She pushes me. "You would not."

I laugh. "You're right, sunshine. I'd draw something beautiful for you."

Her lips meet mine as she pushes her hand into my hair. Her mouth is soft. Sweet. It makes my chest ache.

"Okay," she says and rolls over onto her stomach. "I want something across my shoulders."

Glancing down at the pen, I realize I can't use it. "Shit. This one's a Sharpie." Not sure she wants me to use a permanent marker. This stuff will wash off in a week or two, but still.

She shrugs. "Go ahead. If you screw up, at least I won't have to stare at it all day."

I smack her bare ass. "The fuck I'll screw up." Her laughter makes me smile as I uncap the pen and start marking her smooth skin. "I'll tell you, though, my MFA in painting never taught me how to concentrate when I'm doing this to a beautiful, naked woman in her bed."

"Oh, you sweet talker. And I can't believe you didn't tell me you have an MFA. That's incredible," she murmurs into her pillow. "Where'd you go to school?"

"Boston University for my undergrad and grad school."

"That sounds amazing. And expensive."

"Trust me when I say you don't want to see my school loans."

Ignoring the tight coil of anxiety that always flares when I think about my finances, I try to concentrate on Kat. On the way she's smiling even though she's drowsy. On the way her hair is a wild mess but so incredibly beautiful. On her gentle sigh when I caress her skin.

When I'm done, she's asleep, her soft breaths deep and even.

I kiss her shoulder. "You can see it in the morning, sweetheart."

I love the idea that she let me mark her. Reaching behind me, I touch the scratches on my back and chuckle. I guess we're even.

46

KATHERINE

I LEAN AGAINST THE FORMICA COUNTER AS *BITTERSWEET SYMPHONY* by the Verve plays in the background chaos of the diner.

My mom has always loved this song. One day I looked it up online and read that the Verve used a sample, that famous string intro, from a Rolling Stones song, and had to cough up all of their royalties to the Stones after it became a hit. So they had a huge international hit and became a household name, but they could never make any money from the song that got them there.

Yes, bittersweet indeed.

Sort of how I'm feeling this morning. Because beneath the artwork Brady sketched on my skin and the night we spent tangled together whispering dirty things to one another, I'm still lanced by how he shut me down. I was right. He doesn't want to hear what happened with my ex-boyfriend. Which means my crazy hope that he'd fall in love with me is just that. Crazy.

My mother always says that when you love someone, you want to know everything about the other person, the good, the bad, and the ugly. So if I was looking for an answer for where Brady and I are headed, I have it now.

I guess I'd hoped that after all these weeks, things would be different.

Worse, though? I'm sick over the fact that I basically begged him to fuck me without a condom. *Who does that?* Especially after what happened with Eric.

Stupid, stupid, stupid.

Sinvergüenza. My cheeks burn at the thought.

Taking a deep breath, I try to calm down. I'm not the same girl I was last spring.

A small ball of panic coils in my stomach. I think back to how I've taken those pills religiously in the months since that fiasco.

No, I'm good. There will be no little Brady Shepherds rolling around nine months from now.

My throat tightens.

In the moment, I just wanted to show Brady that I loved him. Because I had never gone without a condom before, and I wanted that connection with him.

I shake my head and try to focus on the positive, to focus on everything that happened after that ill-advised conversation last night.

Touching my lips that are still slightly swollen, I finally let myself smile as I think about all the ways he touched me in the tub. How he couldn't seem to get enough of me once we'd gone bare. And finally, the beautiful images still branding my shoulders.

I want to cling to that. Cling to the hope that what happened after that conversation means more. That it means enough.

Besides, how many guys *really* want to hear about ex-boyfriends? And anyway, I'm the one who hesitated. I'm the one who suggested that it might not be a good idea to talk about it.

A small semblance of calm washes over me. I fill my lungs with another deep breath.

Everything will be okay. Stop reading into this.

Enjoy the now, I remind myself. If I subtract that conversation, last night was perfect. The way he talked to me and loved my body. How he moved over me and in me. How he filled me so completely, I wanted to cry from the pleasure of it all.

Squeezing my thighs together, I relish the soreness that runs through all of my limbs.

Images of him sliding into me flicker in my mind, and I feel my cheeks flush. I smile, I can't help it, and I let myself relish those moments.

"Someone got laid last night," my co-worker Darla drawls as she struts by me with a tray full of food.

My smile falters.

Carol nudges me as she reaches for the coffee. "Ignore her. She got her panties in a twist because someone didn't tip her." Her knowing eyes pass over me. "It's okay to be happy, Katherine. And if it involves doing the horizontal mambo with that handsome biker boy you've been living with, even better."

She winks and walks off before I can say anything.

Ugh. I hate people knowing my business, but I don't have time to worry about it because my phone buzzes in my apron. It's my sister.

"Tori, what's wrong?" I say under my breath as I turn down the hall toward the bathrooms.

"Why do you always assume something's wrong?"

"Because the only time you call me is in an emergency. Or if you need money." Mentally, I start calculating how much I have in my bank account in case this phone call comes with a big price tag.

Tori attends a small Catholic school that's expensive as hell, but she's on an academic scholarship that covers her tuition. Except my family can't afford what the scholarship doesn't cover —books, supplies and uniforms—so I try to bridge the gap. As

LEX MARTIN

painful as it is to foot the bill sometimes, she's safer there than at our nearby public school, which is overrun with gangs.

"Relax, Katherine. Mom wants to know if you're coming home for Christmas. You know, since you blew us off for Thanksgiving."

Pressing the bridge of my nose, I sigh. "I don't know. Maybe I can drive down for a day or two." Brady is working on my car today, so if it's up and running, I might be able to head to Corpus.

Little butterflies ripple in my stomach when I think about how I woke up this morning with that beautiful art on my back. He drew a hummingbird fluttering out of a starburst. He said it's because I remind him of the sunrise.

My stomach does a crazy flipflop when I think about how he rasped those words in my ear before I left for work.

"Hello?" Tori squawks on the phone.

"I'm here."

"Are you sure?" Tori asks. "I've had to repeat myself three times. *I said* that Dad really wants you to come home. And just so you know, you should call Eric back already. He's been blowing up our phone this last week."

God, he just does not give it a rest.

"Do not give him my number, Tori. I'm serious." If nothing else, my time with Brady has shown me how much I don't want to be with Eric. Why is he still calling?

"Are you positive? He's rich and really hot. Maybe you should give him another chance. Unless he has a little weenie. Does he have a little weenie?"

I nearly choke. "Victoria, I'm paying a shitload of money to help you attend that private school. Don't they teach you any manners?"

"Whoa. Look who curses now, Little Miss Stick Up Her Ass."

Seriously? All I've done is help my little sister, and this is the thanks I get?

"Whatever. I gotta go. But next time you need clothes or money for some dumb formal dance, don't call me."

"C'mon, Katherine, you know I'm joking. I'm sorry!"

I shake my head. Tori and I haven't been close in a while. I'm seven years older, and I get a little irritated because she gets away with murder. My parents had me on a tight leash, and she gets to stay out to all hours because she looks angelic. But I know my parents are always comparing us. She's not the student I was, so she gets the "why can't you study harder like Katherine" speeches.

That's what I loved about Mel. She was the big sister I should have had. Not that I don't love Tori, but I just wish we could be close like Mel and I were.

When I get off the phone, I wish more than anything that I could talk to Mel about Brady. I wish I could pour out my heart to her because she would know what to do.

After spazzing out all day at the diner, I'm relieved to come home and find Brady just as warm and sweet as he was last night. Part of me was afraid that he'd be different after so much intimacy, but no. He's affectionate, kissing me on the mouth when I walk through the door, hugging me once I tug off my coat.

He tells me he's going to Skype with his parents. "Wish me luck."

"You don't need it." Well, he might. I lean up and kiss his cheek. "Watch. It'll be fine. They'll be relieved."

"God, I hope so."

He strides down the hall, and I try to busy myself in cleaning the kitchen. After a quiet ten minutes, I hear laughter coming from the office, so I know the hard part must be over.

I'm about to check Izzy's diaper when Brady calls my name. I pick her up, and when we peek into the office, he's all smiles.

"My parents want to see the baby," he says, motioning for me to come over. I walk over to hand her to him when he scoots a chair next to his.

Oh, God. I'm not even wearing makeup. Lovely.

I push up my glasses and sit in front of the screen.

"Izzy is getting so big!" his mom squeals when she sees the baby. His mother is a beautiful woman with light brown hair and big blue eyes. She looks so much like Cal, it's almost painful. "Hi, baby!" she coos.

Izzy claps and says, "Hi, hi, hi," and grins as I bounce her on my lap.

Then his mom notices me, and her smile widens.

"Hi, Mr. and Mrs. Shepherd." I wave at them, hoping I don't look as stupid as I feel right now. *Maybe* Brady could have given me a little warning that he wanted me to video conference with his parents.

"Well, aren't you the prettiest thing! And please call me Rebecca," his mom says. She nudges her husband. "Jonathan, isn't Katherine beautiful?"

Her husband's dark green eyes are intense like Brady's as he stares through the screen, but then they crinkle in the corners when he offers me a warm smile. "You're the poor girl who has to put up with my son? I hope he hasn't been too much of a handful. He can get a little pissy sometimes."

I laugh and turn to Brady, who's frowning. "Really, Dad?"

The baby crawls out of my lap into his, and he gives her a sweet kiss and turns her to face the computer.

Nodding, I motion toward him. "He can be a little prickly sometimes, but I find that feeding him helps."

Brady rolls his eyes, and I nudge him. He doesn't say anything. Instead, he reaches down and grips my thigh, and I laugh and try to get him to stop. It's not fair for him to tickle me in front of his parents.

They obviously can't see anything but me writhing around like a crazy person while Brady sits there pretending to be innocent.

I grab his arm and in my firmest voice say, "If you don't stop, I'm not making you dinner."

He immediately pulls his hand away and shakes his head, the whole time keeping a straight face. "We can't have that."

When I turn back to his parents, they're watching us with rapt attention. I cough, feeling uncomfortable.

His mom offers me a warm smile. "We're so grateful you've been there to help. Brady says he wouldn't know what to do without you."

My face heats, and I laugh nervously. "I'm sure he'd manage."

"Well, we're relieved, especially now since he gets the honor of adopting this sweet little darling. Hopefully, she'll raise hell just like he did as a child, so he can get a taste of his own medicine."

"Really, Mom?" Brady laughs.

"What? You were a handful!" She turns to me. "When he was five, he loved to moon the neighbors. And sometimes, if he couldn't get into the house fast enough, he'd tinkle on the bushes outside."

"Jesus Christ," he mumbles.

I cover my mouth to muffle my laughter. As Izzy crawls into my lap, I pat him on the shoulder. "I'm happy to report, he's fully potty trained now. Good job!" His deadpan stare makes me grin. "Haha. Brady tinkled on the bushes," I taunt.

His parents howl with laughter, and I have to wipe my eyes from laughing so hard.

When I turn back to the laptop, Rebecca tilts her head. "Who does she remind me of? Jonathan, doesn't Katherine remind you of one of Brady's old girlfriends?" Brady stills next to me. Then she snaps her fingers. "The one you took that photo with. Oh, my goodness. You should see that picture, Katherine. It was all over Boston on these billboards. They used it to advertise the tattoo parlor where he worked, and the girls lined up to get him to do their tattoos." She laughs and shades her face. "I blushed every time I drove by it."

God, I look like one of his ex-girlfriends? And what is this photo all about?

"Mother," Brady warns. "It was a photo I took for an art class. My friend got lucky and sold it to my shop."

Ignoring his obvious discomfort, she asks, "What *was* her name?"

I finally turn to look at him, and his hard expression as he shoots lasers at the laptop does nothing to assuage my anxiety.

He clears his throat. "Dani, and we never dated."

"Right. Well." His mother shakes her head and turns to me. "You should have seen him. He moped for months after they broke up."

"Mother, I just said we never dated."

"What's she doing these days?"

He hoists Izzy higher on his lap. "Marrying a professional soccer player."

Rebecca sighs. "Her loss, I suppose. I shouldn't be in his business, but Brady was a sad panda for a while." Her lips twist like she's studying me. "Actually, you don't look like her exactly. But there's something about you that reminds me of her."

I nod, wishing I could rewind the last five minutes of this conversation and start over.

"It was nice meeting you guys," I say softly. "I need to go start dinner. I'm so glad to see you're feeling better, Mr. Shepherd."

Brady's dad offers me an apologetic smile, and I beeline it out of there, fighting emotions I wish I didn't have.

47

BRADY

I'M REALLY NOT IN THE MOOD FOR THIS SHIT.

The half-naked chick in front of me giggles at her friend, another blonde, and I frown as a cold sweat breaks out on my neck.

As I stare down at the woman's bare breasts, warning bells go off in my head. *You should tell Kat,* I think, feeling confused as fuck about why I feel guilty I'm piercing another girl's nipples when all I'm just doing my job.

Just like the three tattoos I did tonight on drunk frat boys, this is no different.

Except the way the blonde thrusts her chest out at me is definitely not the way the frat boys sat in my chair.

Running my hand through my hair, I wince. I've never thought twice about how my girlfriends felt about this. Which I'm realizing was insensitive, but am I really supposed to feel bad now? Kat and I agreed that we end when I head back to Boston.

Jesus. That makes me ill. I don't want to leave her. And that's what it feels like. Abandoning her.

Maybe we've been through too much traumatic shit together for this to be anything less than a serious relationship.

I sigh, wondering how the hell I ended up in this position.

The woman giggles again as I pull her nipple taut between the steel forceps. With a breathy little moan, she asks, "Is this going to hurt?"

"Yes." Usually, I try to talk people off the ledge and focus on the positives, but tonight, I don't give a fuck. It's late, I'm tired, and I'd rather be in bed with Katherine than piercing some sorority girl, who looks like she's one bad decision away from offering me a blow job. Between working here, Kat's gig at the diner and all the shit we have to do on the farm, I've barely seen her this week.

And it's been a *strange* week.

After that chat with my parents where my mother dumped that shit about Dani all over Katherine, she's pulled back. It's subtle. Sometimes she looks like she wants to say something but doesn't. Or when she would usually reach for me or crawl into my lap, she doesn't. Almost like she's preparing herself for the worst case scenario.

Maybe that's the smart thing to do.

On top of that, I've been working all week, so we haven't had any one-on-one time since our fuckathon last weekend. And I walk around half-hard all the time from random X-rated thoughts of her.

I go through the motions and pierce the chick in my chair. When we're done, I thank her and head to the front register where hopefully being around the other guys will dissuade her from making any unwelcome offers.

Except that's wishful thinking because just before she's about to walk out the door, she grabs a pen, takes my hand and starts writing on my palm.

What the...

She gives me a little wink and tells me to call her. I look down and see the name Shana and her phone number.

"Dude, she wrote in a permanent marker!" one of the guys yells, laughing.

I head to the bathroom to wash it off, except it doesn't.

Mark, one of the owners, passes me on my way out. "If you don't want that number, feel free to post it on the fuck wall."

I turn my head to see where he's pointing in the break room. And sure enough, there's a wall of phone numbers.

"Think of it as the penny jar at the gas station," he says with a wide grin.

"The penny jar?"

"Yeah, you have a penny you don't want right now, but maybe one of the other guys needs a penny. So write her description and phone number on one of those notecards and post it on the fuck wall. Never know when you're going to need one of those girls yourself."

Jesus Christ. He's a fucking pig.

I should be grateful he gave me a job. Because I need it. Badly. But the dick bought a copy of that fucking photo of me and Dani and is planning to use it to advertise the shop. *It was really nice of Rudy to mention that goddamn photograph when Mark called my old job for a reference.*

I wait until Mark walks off to ignore him and head back to my station. The whole night, this bothers me. It bothers me that I feel the need to talk to Katherine about what I do. It bothers me that despite our limbo status, doing my job felt like cheating because I had to touch another woman. And it bothers me that these assholes treat girls like some kind of communal property.

When I get home, it's after two in the morning. We usually turn off all of the lights at night, but the light over the stove is on, and beneath it is a sandwich and a note. *Hope you had a good day at work. Figured you didn't eat. xo, Kat.*

This girl. I smile.

She's right. I haven't eaten.

I crack open the door to Izzy's bedroom and see her sleeping before I check in on Kat, who fell asleep reading her Kindle.

After I devour my food and take a quick shower, I collapse on the couch in the office and turn on the TV. I want to sleep with Kat, but I'm in a bad mood, so I settle for sleeping on the shitty couch. I decide to tell her what happened tonight because she should know this is part of what I do. It's not like I'm hiding anything from her.

Once I make that decision, I start to relax and doze off, but then a warm body slides over me and a sweet voice whispers in my ear. "Wanna snuggle?"

I clear my throat. "If snuggling is code for fucking, then yes."

She laughs. God, that laugh. It instantly erases my foul mood.

I wrap my arms around her. "I'm kidding. We don't have to have sex. But yes, I want to snuggle." Especially after the distance that's grown between us these last few days.

Her thighs come to rest on either side of my stomach, and she nuzzles against my neck. "We could call it a snuggle fuck." She giggles. "Where snuggling turns into sex. That's probably the best kind of cuddling."

My cock couldn't agree more. Especially when she presses herself against it.

"I missed you tonight," she whispers. "I miss you every night."

My hands still. Everything from work comes rushing back to me, and suddenly I need to tell her what happened before we get naked.

"What's wrong?" She swallows. She's quiet a long moment before she says, "You don't have to tell me you missed me too. That was probably a stupid thing to say."

I sit up but keep her on my lap. Her hair is wild around her shoulders, and it pains me that she thinks I didn't miss her.

Wrapping my hand behind her neck, I shake my head. "Of course I missed you. That's not why I got quiet." My thumb rubs against her soft cheek. "Something happened tonight. I don't know if it's going to bother you, but I thought I should mention it."

She sits up straighter and looks at me with so much vulnerability in her eyes, it breaks my heart a little.

"What happened?"

"Don't get freaked out. It's not a big deal. You know I do tattoos. Well, I also do piercings, and I just realized I had never mentioned that to you before. And tonight, a woman came in to get her nipples pierced, and I wasn't sure if that would bother you."

Kat's head tilts down, and with only the TV on, her face is shrouded in darkness. "Okay," she says hesitantly. "Is that all? You pierced her?"

"Yeah. That's it. Oh, and she grabbed a Sharpie and wrote her number on my hand. I was in shock or I would've pulled away."

I brush the hair out of Kat's face and then hold up my hand so she can see the writing.

Then she surprises me. "Why are you telling me this?"

If I didn't know better, I'd be tempted to think her blank expression means she doesn't care. Except Kat always cares. About everything. Even my dumb ass.

"I guess I wanted to know if that bothers you. If you were okay with me piercing people. Most of the time, it's piercing ears or some guy's nipple, but sometimes girls come in for more exotic things."

She nibbles her bottom lip. "Are you planning to call her?"

What the fuck? "No, of course not. Why would you think that?"

She shrugs, her expression sad. "Because I get that we're not really together, and you can do what you want, I guess."

My grip on her hip tightens, but before I can say anything, her shoulders slump. "Are we setting ourselves up for trouble?" She closes her eyes and takes a breath. "Are we too different?"

"What does that mean?" A heaviness settles on me, a sinking sensation I haven't felt in a while. Not since Kat and I started whatever this is. Her eyes travel over me, over my tattoos, and I get what she's trying to say before she even puts words to the sentiment.

She shakes her head. "You're leaving soon. And with what happened tonight... Am I keeping you from exploring other options?"

I scrub my face, not sure if I should be pissed or amused.

At least I'm not alone in this. Feeling this confused.

"Let's just clear up this shit right now. Number one, yes, I fucking missed you. Two, I would never go out with anyone or mess around with another woman while I'm with you, and three, we might as well call a spade a spade because God knows I'd fucking kill any man who laid a finger on you. So if it's okay with you, while we're doing this, we're monogamous. Cool?" Yeah, so basically two and three are the same thing. I wanted to tell her that fuck yes, we're in a relationship, but mid-rant I realized I couldn't because that would lead her on.

She just stares at me in that hypnotic way that makes me feel slightly dizzy.

I pull her closer. "I'm not really a casual sex kind of guy, Kat." Sure, I've had it, but I've always preferred being in a relationship. "What we have here, this is special to me." I want to say more, but I don't. I shouldn't.

Finally, she nods and bites that lip again, only this time it's to hide a smile. Then she whispers, "I have a way we can forget all about Shana Boobalicious."

And then she grabs my hand, the one with the phone number on it, lifts her shirt and places it on her breast as she arches into me.

I laugh, relieved that I didn't hurt her feelings, and put every ounce of emotion I can behind the kiss I give her. "Who the fuck is Shana?"

48

KATHERINE

THIS HAS BECOME MY FAVORITE THING, EAVESDROPPING ON BRADY while he puts Izzy to bed. Tonight, he's serenading her with *Baby, It's Cold Outside.* And he's terrible, like totally off key, but oh, my God, he's adorable.

I close my eyes as I imagine him bent over her crib, stroking her soft little tufts of hair. Sometimes he rocks her to sleep. He bought her a little night light, a turtle that projects stars on the sky, and he tells her stories about the constellations and Greek gods. She likes the one he tells her about beautiful Princess Andromeda.

When he closes out his off-key song, my heart flutters in my chest.

"Night night, sweet pea." His deep voice comes through the monitor, and then I hear the distinct sound of him kissing her, probably on her forehead.

I shouldn't do this to myself. I shouldn't focus on all of the things I love about him. I shouldn't focus on how much he adores his niece or how he slaves all day here at the farm before he works half the night at the tattoo shop. I shouldn't care this much. But I do.

When he comes out of the nursery, I hold out his hot chocolate, unable to hold in my grin.

He clears his throat. "Don't laugh. I know I can't sing." He watches me over the lip of his mug as he takes a sip.

"Izzy loves it when you *sing*." I put air quotes around the word, and he shakes his head. I don't grab him or wrap him in a hug the way I want to. I don't tell him how much I love seeing him and Izzy together or that I'd love to pack us a picnic and take her to the park this weekend. *Boundaries.*

His big palm rubs the stubble on his chin. Out of the blue, he says, "I hate leaving you guys."

My heart thuds wildly in my chest until I realize he's talking about heading off to work. *Not about returning to Boston. Duh.*

Forcing a smile, I whisper. "Gotta do what ya gotta do."

When he puts the mug on the counter behind me, he pauses to kiss my forehead. "I have a guy who wants double sleeves, and even though we're still finalizing his design, I'll probably work on him until late, so don't wait up."

I want to tell him that I won't. That despite our little chat about Shana Boobalicious a few nights ago, I'm trying really hard not to have any expectations. Which means I've been forcing myself to go to bed at a decent hour and not wait up for him. Because the word he used to describe us was 'monogamous.' *Not* 'in a relationship' or 'committed' or 'in love.' There's a difference, and Brady's a smart enough guy that I suspect he was very specific about his word choice.

I know I need to distance my heart. That phone call with his parents was the wake-up call I needed. Because a couple in a relationship would discuss the awkwardness that ensued after his mom brought up Dani. But we didn't discuss it. In fact, he's been uncomfortable around me all week.

Deep down, I realize I shouldn't have jumped his bones the

other night, but I missed him. Even now, even when he's standing two feet away, I miss him so much my heart hurts.

I shake my head. "Before I forget, Mrs. Mac is watching the baby tomorrow evening so I can do some holiday shopping." His head cants slightly, and I know what he's thinking. It deflates me more. "Don't worry. Santa's getting you a big lump of coal." He laughs nervously, and I motion toward the door. "You're gonna be late. Have a good night at work."

There's no sense in us talking about how we shouldn't buy each other anything, or if we do, how we shouldn't spend a lot of money. I really don't think I could handle that conversation right now. It's five days until Christmas, and judging by the expression on his face, I'm pretty sure he hasn't even thought about it.

That shouldn't slay me. But it does.

The next day has me feeling even more bummed out. The kittens are adopted, and Brady gets called into work early. I was hoping we could decorate the Christmas tree together, but end up doing it by myself.

The silver lining is I finally found what I hope is the perfect present for Brady.

Behind the counter, the old woman folds the fabric and smiles broadly. "Would you like this gift wrapped, dear?"

"Yes, please."

Her wrinkled hands tuck the fabric into a white box and then she lines it up on a large piece of textured red paper.

I stare at the impressive displays that line the walls. "Is this your shop?" I hoist the bag with gifts for my parents and sister a little higher.

"Yes, ma'am. Been doin' this for forty years."

"I can tell. Your designs are beautiful. They must be hard to part with."

She nods and a deep sigh leaves her. "It helps when the customer loves them like I do. And I can tell this is for someone special."

Suddenly, heat stings my eyes. "Yes. Very."

She pats my hand. "Well, that makes it easier."

I hope Brady and Izzy like it. The gift cost more than anything I own except my car, but I want to give them something meaningful, something that would remind them of their time here. So they'd know someone loves them. Because I do.

As I head to my car, which finally works thanks to Brady, I debate whether or not to call my parents. They're going to ask me to come home for Christmas, and while I'd love nothing more than to visit for a few days, I'm worried that things are too weird between me and Brady for me to leave.

That sucks to admit. But our vibe has been so off this week, I'm not totally sure where we stand. Maybe that's just insecurity talking. In some ways, life has gotten in the way. I've had to pick up more shifts this week because people keep calling in sick, and Brady's job at night has stolen the little time we usually have to hang out.

I tuck my packages in the trunk as I debate what to do. I don't need ESP to know my parents will flip if I simply mail home their gifts, but I'm not ready for the grand inquisition. And if leaving for a few days ends up straining whatever this is with Brady, I don't know if I want to risk it.

Which sounds so desperate, I want to slap myself. *Tontita.*

I'm sitting in traffic when I see a billboard for Saints & Sinners Tattoo Parlor and realize I'm just a few blocks from Brady's shop.

A few honks and one illegal turn later, I'm pulling up to a

brick building with huge glass windows that are all lit up and shine brightly in the night.

But that's not what why my mouth is hanging open.

That would be the enormous photo of Brady draped around a half-naked redhead that's hanging in the window.

My stomach is mid-free fall when I realize that must be the image his mother mentioned on that Skype call last weekend.

It's a stunning photo. All of the color has been stripped out except for her long, blood-red hair.

Wow. Dani is gorgeous.

And very, very topless.

Except you can't see her boobs because they're squished behind Brady's arms, which are wrapped tightly around her.

Mierda.

My stomach continues its descent.

He's standing behind her, looking sexy as hell, the ink on his arms and shoulders standing stark against her bare skin. And there's a *lot* of bare skin. His forearms are pressed against her breasts, giving her all kinds of crazy cleavage. Above them, it says, *Saints & Sinners Tattoo Parlor. Don't you wanna get inked?*

I stumble out of the car, unable to take my eyes off the photo. No wonder Brady didn't want to talk about this. Damn. Does this mean he still has feelings for this girl? She's so freaking beautiful.

I glance down at the jeans I bought at Goodwill last summer. Embarrassment flushes my cheeks. I've never really thought about Brady's life in Boston, but of course he dated hot girls. He did this glamorous photoshoot with Dani, and here I am with dirt under my nails, second-hand clothes, and a car that barely runs.

By the time I reach the front door, I'm wishing I had just gone home, but I don't have time to change my mind because some guy yanks the door open and waits for me to pass through so he can exit.

"What can I do for you, darlin'?" a burly man asks from behind the counter.

"I'm..." I clear my throat. "I'm here to see Brady."

He laughs and shakes his head. "There's an awful long line to get to him tonight." He motions behind me where three pretty college girls sit. "Those are just the walk-ins. He also has two other appointments."

I force a smile. "That's good for business, though, right?"

"Not complaining." He lifts his chin toward me. "What'd you want? Maybe one of the other guys can help you."

"Oh, um, I'm Brady's... friend. I was just popping in to say hi."

He leans toward me and lowers his voice. "I'd say go on back, but he's piercing some girl's big titties. Swear to God, we've never had so many nipple piercings as we've had these past couple of weeks."

I swallow down the lump in my throat. "No... no problem. Thank you. I'll stop by some other time."

Like never.

I shouldn't feel like death warmed over, but as I drive home, I blink back the tears in my eyes.

He told me about his job. He freaking told me that he does nipple piercings. I shouldn't be so upset. Heck, I shouldn't be upset at all. The man straight-up told me he's monogamous, and I believe him.

So then why does this all hurt so much?

Because you love him.

49
BRADY

Izzy's little howls on the monitor pull me from a dead sleep. Barely awake enough to walk upright, I stub my foot as I scramble to get to her room.

Working night shifts suck ass when you have to get up early, which is why I quit back in Boston.

"Hey, baby." I cuddle her to my chest as I collapse on the rocker. She wraps her arms around my shoulders and sticks her nose in the crook of my neck.

I pat her butt as we rock back and forth. The sun is up, so it must be later than I thought.

Fucking fuck, I'm tired. Too tired to even drag my ass to the kitchen and grab a cup of coffee.

When Kat texted me last night and said she had to work this morning, I straight-up wanted to cry, but I swore my job wouldn't interfere with her schedule at the diner, and I want to hold myself to that. She's bent over backwards to help me, and I know she needs the income.

"Bway Bway," Izzy whispers. Peeking through my heavy lids, I see Izzy staring back with that adorable grin. She grabs my face with both hands. "Hungwee."

Chuckling, I nod. "Okay, honey. Let's get you some breakfast."

After I change her diaper and snuggle her in something warm, we head to the kitchen. It's odd not having Kat here in the morning. It's honestly one of my favorite parts of the day, seeing her first thing.

But we haven't really had that kind of week. We can't seem to catch a break to hang out.

When I crawled in here at three this morning, I didn't want to wake her, so I crashed in the office. I'm starting to rethink that, though, because I fucking miss her.

From the back porch, I hear a familiar noise.

After I get Izzy situated with some cereal, I open the back door. Bandit stares back at me.

"Hey, asshole. What's up?"

The raccoon glances at the empty cardboard box, and I remember the kittens got adopted yesterday.

"Lost your buddies, huh?"

I peel the banana I was about to eat and break off a chunk. Leery he's going to bite me, I put it on the floor between us. He makes that snick, snick sound and sniffs it suspiciously.

"Where's the trust, man?"

He finally gobbles it, and I hold out another piece. He takes it from my hand this time and snarfs it down.

"See, if we could do this without you urinating on my belongings, we might find a way to get along."

I feel bad for him now that he's all alone.

Which reminds me how much Kat loved those kittens. I bet she's heartbroken over losing them.

It's the breakfast rush, though, so I shouldn't bother her now, but I make a mental note to call her later.

As I'm striding back into the kitchen, something in the living room catches my eye.

Holy shit.

A fully decorated Christmas tree sits in the corner. With little glass ornaments, twinkle lights, and shimmery little angels.

I blow out a breath. *Kat must've done this after I went to work yesterday.*

Pulling out my phone, I glance at the date.

Well, damn. Christmas is in two days.

I press my palms into my eyes as panic sets in. The holidays are honestly the last thing on my mind, but maybe I need to slow down and put a little effort into this for Izzy's sake. She might not remember opening gifts, but some day I can show her pictures, and maybe that will be meaningful for her.

This is the year she lost her parents, asshole. Of course it'll be meaningful.

As always, Katherine is ten steps ahead of me. I hardly know which way my sorry ass is headed, but she just gets what needs to be done and keeps me afloat.

I'm supposed to work tonight and tomorrow, but as I stare at the tree, I'm wondering if that's the right thing to do. Each night I miss Kat and Izzy like I left my fucking lungs at home.

I've been vacillating between wanting to give Kat a holiday bonus and buying her a present. She might need the money, but I have a sneaking suspicion she'll think I'm a dick if I hand her a check. I really want to buy her something nice, but I wonder if that would send the wrong message.

Fuck it.

I pick up the phone. For once, I'm not going to overthink this. I'm going to give her the gift. Because even if we're in this weird limbo place, I think of her as my friend. My best friend, actually. And I want her to know that she means something to me.

Ten minutes later, I'm feeling a little better about life. I sit next to Izzy, who mashes a banana all over her face.

"You know this is supposed to go *in* your mouth?"

"In yo mowth!" she giggles before she tosses her sippy cup onto the floor where the lid pops off and juice goes everywhere.

I stare at the juice puddle as it spreads.

Yeah, this parent stuff is definitely not as easy as my mom and dad made it seem growing up.

After I clean up the mess, I grab my phone to thank Kat for decorating the tree when an incoming call from my realtor makes me freeze.

Because I already know why he's calling. And it hits my gut like a boulder.

50

KATHERINE

JAYCEE NUDGES ME OUT OF THE WAY TO PIN SOME MISTLETOE OVER the doorway of the diner.

I poke her in the ribs. "You're gonna regret that if Old Man Johnson comes in here and tries to plant a wet one on you."

She makes a gagging sound and laughs. "Maybe, but I won't complain if those kisses come from the Walker twins."

"Perv," I tease.

She holds a hand over her heart and closes her eyes dramatically. "And damn proud of it."

Being at work, being busy and chatting with the girls, is making me feel better. I don't know why I was so emotional last night. I should've just waited until Brady was done with his customer to say hello. It's not like he was cheating on me, for God's sake.

Honestly? I took this shift today to get out of the house, to get some space and perspective. I was still feeling miffed last night and needed a reason to get away. Which I know is totally immature, but I didn't want to have to face him before I'd found a little balance.

We just need a night to hang out, and everything will be fine. The man is working himself to the bone. The least I can do is have some patience and stop feeling like a scorned girlfriend.

The cheery holiday music is helping me chill out. Everyone is so dang chipper around here today, it's contagious. Carol handed out Santa hats this morning, and we're all wearing red and white.

After refilling someone's coffee, I'm passing through when a guy in Jaycee's section opens his briefcase and papers spill all over the floor.

"Shoot," he mumbles.

"I got it." Leaning down, I pick up the fliers, which feature full-color photos of houses and properties. I apologize for the one I step on.

He gives me a wide smile. "Honestly, nothing could put me in a bad mood today."

"I think the holiday mood is rubbing off because I'm starting to feel the same way." I point at his stack of properties. "Are you a lawyer or a realtor?"

"Realtor." He laughs. "I hate lawyers."

Grinning, I motion toward his cup. "Want some coffee?"

"Absolutely."

I'm filling his mug when my eyes land on the paper in his hand. Which features a photo of a farm. Mel's farm.

"Whoa!" he yells, and I yank the coffee pot away.

"Oh, God. I'm so sorry." I've overfilled his cup, and coffee runs in rivulets across the table. I reach for the napkins in the dispenser and try to sop up the mess. "I feel terrible. Breakfast is on me."

He laughs and shakes his head. "Don't worry about it. I just landed the biggest deal of the year, and I don't think anything can ruin it for me."

A lump forms in my throat. "Yeah?" I motion toward his

stack of papers. *Please let it be a different property.* "Which"—I clear my throat—"which house?"

He waves his hand. "This little old farm is gonna buy my kids a pool for Christmas." I listen in shock as he says a buyer came out of nowhere and made an amazing offer. Doesn't want to haggle. Just wants to close. On our farm.

"That's... that's great." My voice comes out barely above a whisper.

"Seriously, hun, don't worry about the coffee."

I force my lips up into a smile. "Congrats on your deal. Your client must be ecstatic."

My heart crumbles as he taps the table and barks with a laugh, "He was absolutely speechless!"

51

KATHERINE

I'M NOT SURE HOW LONG I DRIVE ALONG THE WINDING BACKWOODS road, but by the time I get home, it's dark.

Home.

A maniacal laugh spills out of me. *Oh, God. Brady and Izzy are leaving. This won't be home for long.*

And this really has been home for me. Melissa made sure it was. When we were kids, we'd sit under the big oak and talk about boys, and she'd tell me about her crushes and first kiss. It's where she told me I'd fall in love some day with the perfect boy, someone who would love and cherish me. Because that's what she believed she'd find some day. And she did.

The driveway blurs behind my tears that I blink away. *Deep breaths.*

I pull up behind Brady's Harley, wishing I could get my emotions under control. I should let him tell me. He'll probably be all professional and distant. Well, more distant than he's been this week.

Maybe I'm jumping the gun. Just because someone made an offer doesn't necessarily mean he's going to take it, right?

The knot in my stomach tightens. The farm is a helluva lot of work. *And he hasn't even been through a harvest yet.*

I know I'm selfish for wanting him to stay. His life is in Boston. It's where he belongs. Not here in the middle of no man's land.

As much as I love working on the farm, it's not like I'll have a job here once Brady sells it.

The idea of heading back to Corpus looking like a failure, after all my parents sacrificed to help me get through college, makes me nauseous.

I think about Congressman Mitchell's offer last spring. He liked what I did for Eric's dad. Mitchell wanted me on his team.

But do I really want this? To head back to Austin? I don't even have clothes to wear if he calls to interview me. It's not like I can waltz into his office in torn Levis and cowboy boots.

Reaching into the back seat, I grab a beat-up box of tissues, conveniently tucked away from the last time I got my ass handed to me.

The slam of a car door makes me wipe my face quickly and look around. On the opposite side of the house, a figure walks toward my car. Squinting, I make out a dark polo and shiny watch.

Oh hell, no.

I jump out of the car. "What the hell are you doing here, Eric? You do realize stalking is illegal, right?"

My ex-boyfriend laughs. "Glad to see you've missed me, Katherine."

He studies me, and the surprise is written all over his face. *Yes, I work at a diner.*

I untie my apron that I forgot to take off before I left the restaurant and toss it on the porch. Of all the times for him to see me, I wish it weren't when I smelled like chicken-fried steak and grease, looking like I've been bawling my eyes out.

Of course, he looks like an Abercrombie model. Superbly styled. Not a hair out of place. Asshole.

"Baby, I've missed you. Come home."

I roll my eyes. "You *missed* me?"

"I've been trying to contact you for fucking months. Of course I missed you."

"Too little, too late, Romeo," I snark as I head for the front door. As I unlock the door, I turn back to glare because he's right on my heels. "What the hell do you think you're doing?"

He motions toward the house. "I figured you'd let me in, and we'd sit down and discuss this like two responsible adults."

"Responsible?" I laugh. "So you're responsible now?"

"Don't be like that. You knew I'd come around."

I open the front door and put my hand on his chest to keep him back. "Stay here. I'll be back in a few minutes." He smells like expensive cologne and leather. God, I used to love how he smelled. Now it reminds me that words are meaningless. What is it they say? That tough times reveal a man's true character? Well, Eric failed the test. Epically.

His eyebrow quirks up. "You're really not going to let me into the house?" He runs a hand through his blond hair, looking perplexed.

"I realize you're not accustomed to people denying you anything, but no, you're not coming in this house."

He snickers, and the sound makes me contemplate strangling him.

"What's so funny?"

"Get your cute self out here, and I'll tell you." He glances at his watch. "Hurry, though. I have a conference call in half an hour."

"Of course you do." How did I date this asshole for a year and a half? I grit my teeth and point to the porch. "Stay." Then I slam the door in his face.

Brady pokes his head out of the office as I storm into the kitchen, but I ignore him as I march toward the liquor cabinet and pour a tumbler of whiskey. My nerves are shot, and I seriously need to calm down to deal with Eric.

"Are you okay?" Brady's voice is raspy, like he's been sleeping.

A few gulps later, and I'm gasping from the fire shooting down my throat.

"I'm fine," I choke out.

Finally, I face him, and I might be on the brink of losing it, but I'm not so far gone that I don't notice how beautiful he looks standing shirtless in the middle of the kitchen with his jeans hanging low on his hips.

He scratches the stubble on his chin and lifts his eyebrows. "You don't look fine."

Blowing out a breath, I shrug. "I've had a bad day."

"Is that why you're home late? Guess it's good I cancelled my shift tonight."

"Oh, shit." I glance at the clock and realize he was supposed to head to Austin hours ago. "I'm so sorry. I... I..."

"Kat, don't worry about it. I wanted to hang out." He tucks his hands into his pockets, a deep frown forming on his handsome face. "Actually, there's something I need to talk to you about."

I close my eyes and brace myself to hear that he's leaving. Instead, I jump when a knock comes at the front door.

Brady looks toward the living room, and he starts to step toward the door, but I grab his arm. "Don't. That's for me." I let go of him and chug the rest of my drink. "It's my ex."

His whole body tenses. "What the fuck is he doing here?"

I hand him my empty glass. "Your guess is as good as mine." I look up at him, wishing I could wrap myself in his arms and close ourselves off from the world. "Can we talk in a little while? I need to deal with Eric first."

He nods, his jaw tight. "You going to be okay out there?"

"Yeah. He's a dick, but he'd never hurt me." More than he already has, anyway.

Brady leans back against the counter, his whole body tense, and looks me hard in the eyes. "I'll be here if you need anything."

"Thanks." I smile weakly and drag myself to the front door.

Three deep breaths later, I force myself outside. Eric looks out of place in his designer clothes, reclining on the dilapidated bench in front of the large front window. The drapes are closed behind him, but the Christmas tree lights twinkle through the small sliver that remains open.

Eric's presence is messing with my head. Everything about this place represents family and love and belonging while he only reminds me of what it's like to feel alone and left behind.

But it's a relief to realize how little I feel for him, which makes me wonder if I ever loved him at all. Because right now, I just want him gone.

Crossing my arms, I shake my head. "Why are you here?"

He flicks off an imaginary piece of lint from his khakis. "To end this nonsense. To bring you home for Christmas. To celebrate your birthday with you."

A deep well of sadness bubbles over. My birthday. I'd almost forgotten.

My lips flatten. "You're a bright guy. You really don't think there's something to salvage here, do you? I think I was pretty clear when I left Austin that we were over."

He chuckles. "You left everything I ever bought you on my front steps. A little dramatic, but given the circumstances, I understand why you were upset."

"You understand…" I sputter, almost apoplectic. "You *understand* why I was upset?"

"Baby, look, let's get out of here. We'll spend the next few days catching up at my place and then we'll head to Corpus to visit your parents. You know they're worried sick about you."

Seriously, I can feel the pulse in my neck. I'm so angry, I'm vibrating. "Why the hell are you talking to my parents?"

He lifts his hands dramatically. "Someone had to. You left them in the dark while you shacked up with some loser." A moment later, the emotion in his eyes dims. Just like that, he's cool and collected. "In all honesty, this was a little predictable. You ran off to prove something to me, and now you're slumming it. I get it. We all need to sow our wild oats. It's not like I haven't had a little fun these last few months. But the holidays aren't for hookups, they're for family."

I stare into his icy blue eyes, dumbfounded he thinks *that* will win me over. "You really are an asshole." But… how does he know I'm with Brady? Unless my parents made a few assumptions and mentioned those concerns to Eric. *God, this just gets worse.*

He bristles. "Language, Katherine. Have you forgotten all of the media prep work we did?"

I hate you.

I do. I hate him. I hate his misogynistic ideas about women and his need to control how I dress and speak. I hate his smug expression and that annoying laugh. And I fucking hate that he conned me into believing the lies his father told on that campaign. *Mentiroso.*

I'm about to unleash a tirade when he says the only thing that could give me pause in a moment like this.

"Katherine, think about your options. Your time has run out here. Besides"—he lifts a judgmental brow—"it's not like your guy here is going to turn down the offer he got for the farm."

Time stands still as I process those words.

"Ho—how do you know?" I stammer. "How do you know about that?"

His lip quirks up in an amused grin. "What do you think?"

My eyes narrow as I take in his confident posture on the bench. The wide spread of his legs. The way his arm is casually draped over the back.

"You're buying a lavender farm?" I can't help the surprise in my voice.

"Why not?" he whispers, clearly not wanting Brady to over-hear. "If this is what you want, yes, I'll buy it for you, and you can play Holly Hobby for a few months until you start working on Mitchell's campaign in the fall." His eyes travel over me in a way that I used to appreciate but that now skeeves me out. "You're lucky you're so cute." He winks, and I want to knee him in the balls. "Mitchell remembers you. I just spoke to him last week. He'll take you any time, but you have to be ready to go in September." He waves a lazy finger around in the air. "So maybe you can get this out of your system in the meanwhile."

"Did it ever occur to you that maybe I genuinely like it here? That I enjoy the day-to-day things I do on the farm enough to not want to go back to politics?"

He laughs so hard, it startles me. "Get serious."

"Do you just throw money at all of your problems? Was that what you were planning to do if I really had been pregnant? Just throw money at me until I did what you wanted?"

That smirk slides off his face. "I would've taken care of my responsibilities. Besides, I distinctly remember you telling me you *never* wanted kids. That is, until you thought you were pregnant."

"I didn't want a baby, but there was no way I was getting an abortion because we messed up. Because it was inconvenient," I hiss. *Because he didn't think it would look good for his father's campaign.*

"*We* messed up?"

"Yeah. *We*. Because *maybe* you could've mentioned the condom broke that last time we were together."

His nostrils flare. "You were supposed to be on the pill."

"I got food poisoning. I threw up for forty-eight hours straight. I was freaking delirious. Sorry if I forgot to take my pill or threw it up." Honestly, I don't even remember. It was hard when my face was planted on the cold bathroom tile.

What I do remember is being alone. That Eric was too busy to stop by to check on me even though I told him I thought I needed to go to the hospital. Eye-opener number one.

Eye-opener number two came a few weeks later when I realized I hadn't gotten my period, and my supposedly devoted boyfriend, who claimed he wanted to marry me, flew into a fit of rage and refused to talk to me.

So yes, I fucking left all the shit he got me on his front porch. And I underscored my animosity by quitting my job so I wouldn't have to see him again.

I was here with Mel and Cal when I started spotting.

My eyes well with tears. For my friends who took care of me. For the loss I felt when I realized the baby was gone.

Eric sighs deeply, like the memory of what happened inconveniences him, and then he motions behind him toward the house, "Well, looks like you got what you wanted anyway. And hey, you got the baby minus the stretch marks. Convenient."

I stare, not quite believing what he's suggesting.

Pendejo.

"I'd rather slum it with Brady than do anything with you," I bark. "You think you can just get everyone around you to do what you want. Well, guess what? I can't be bought." I lower my voice. "And if Brady decides to sell the farm, that's his business. You and I are still done."

"Look, Katherine, there's no need to be a bitch," he sneers as he leaps off the bench and stalks toward me.

The front door swings open with a bang. Our heads turn to find Brady glaring at Eric, who is frozen mid-stride. Brady has put on a snug black t-shirt, but with those tats decorating his arms and muscles bulging, he looks like a formidable opponent. He's bigger than Eric. Taller. Broader. There's no contest. If they face off, Brady will kill him.

"Kat, are you okay?" he asks, looking every bit the badass biker. I nod, not wanting him to get caught in the senator's crosshairs by fighting with my ex. Eric's not worth it.

Eric rolls his eyes. "She's fine, asshole. Go back to digging your ditches."

I'm so mortified right now.

Brady steps closer and brushes his thumb across my cheek. I automatically lean into his palm. And in that instant, all of the sadness I'm feeling, all of the heartache, dulls slightly, and I can breathe again.

A moment later, Brady turns toward Eric and leans close, towering over him. And then he lowers his voice. "Have your little chat, but if you touch one hair on her head or threaten her in any way, I will beat your ass until you are begging me to stop. I don't care who the fuck you are. Am I clear?"

Eric's nostrils flare, and he holds up his hands like he's giving up, but that mouth of his keeps going as he backs up and walks slowly down the front steps. "Katherine, you were the fucking valedictorian of your high school class and graduated salutatorian in college. You should put that to good use or you're letting your family down. Think about all of the sacrifices they made for you to get this opportunity. How can you throw that away to grow some pretty-smelling weeds? To date some tattoo artist? Besides, your father will never accept this guy."

He waves a dismissive hand toward Brady. "Think about what I can offer you. Think about Mitchell's campaign. That job won't stay on the table forever."

Eric presses the key fob to his Mercedes and opens the door. "I'll be at the governor's mansion over the holidays with my parents. Call me when you change your mind."

52

BRADY

IT'S HARD TO HOLD A BABY AND STILL BE PISSED, BUT I STILL CAN'T quite shake the tension from tonight.

Slamming the front door woke Izzy, so I've been trying to get her back to bed for the last hour even though I really need to talk to Kat.

Izzy shoves her pudgy hand into my eye as she nuzzles closer. My lips quirk up. This girl loves to snuggle. Maybe it's because of everything she's lost, but if she could sleep all night in my arms, she probably would.

I tuck the blanket around her little body and resume rocking and patting her rear.

I'm going crazy not being able to talk to Kat right now. I heard bits and pieces of that conversation. Like the part where she yelled she'd rather slum it with me.

I know what she was trying to say, but that still stung.

The front window was cracked open, and I could hear them yelling from the kitchen. I almost walked out there several times to make sure she was okay, but I get needing closure. At least... that's what I initially thought that conversation was about. Now, I'm not so sure.

My thoughts wander to what she said last weekend, when she asked if we were too different. If we were setting ourselves up for trouble.

Knowing now what she's giving up, I feel like shit. Not that I care about that douchebag. I mean the job offer, the real job she's giving up to stay here with me.

If my ongoing argument with Cal taught me anything, it's that making sacrifices has its consequences. Sometimes it makes you resentful. And the last thing I want is for Kat to resent me down the road for hindering her career. Not that she's that kind of person, but neither was I before I got saddled with my parents' languishing company. I'm not proud of that, but now that I've had some time away from Boston, I realize that's what I was feeling.

Every awful scenario runs through my head as I sit here in the dark.

It would kill me for Kat to hang around here until I'm hopelessly in love with her and then go back to that dickhead.

I've already had my heart broken once when Dani decided she'd rather date a guy who treated her like shit. What is it with girls who like to date assholes? Not that Kat is one of them. I mean, fuck, I hope not.

Valedictorian. Of course she was a brilliant student. I can see that now. How she marketed the hell out of our little farmers' event. How she rebranded all of our products. How she's amazing with people.

Our products.

I rub the back of my neck. Yeah, ours. I may own this farm, technically, but the soaps, the lotions—all of that stuff—that's her baby. Her inspiration. It was her drive that got Melissa to start that side business.

I'm kicking myself for shutting down that conversation last

weekend when she brought up her ex. At least I could've been a little more prepared for what went down tonight.

Was she really pregnant last May?

My gut aches when I think about that douche putting his hands on her. Touching her. Loving her. *I should have fucked him up.*

I close my eyes and rock the baby a little faster, needing to clear my mind. But it's hard. Especially when I got that offer on the farm this morning. My realtor said a company out of Dallas was looking to get into lavender and thought the farm would make a great addition to their land holdings. Now that I realize how precarious things are with Kat, I think I should consider it.

My first reaction was to turn down the offer. Crazy, right? Doesn't make sense.

But right now, nothing in my life makes sense.

53

KATHERINE

THE LONGER BRADY'S IN THE NURSERY, THE HARDER IT IS TO KEEP my emotions in check. It's almost midnight when I give up waiting for him and head into my bedroom. I change into a t-shirt and shorts and crawl into bed. Alone.

He's either really mad at me for all of the horrible things Eric said or he's planning to drop the bomb that he's leaving.

God, did he overhear me talking about being pregnant? And now he thinks I'm some girl who just jumps from one bed to another.

But if he heard that, does he know Eric is behind the offer on the farm?

A sinking feeling overwhelms me. Because worse than all of that is the thought that maybe he doesn't care enough to be upset by any of this.

Especially if he's leaving.

I'm blinking back the sting in my eyes when when the nursery door finally opens. I can't let Brady see me like this. Quickly, I take a deep breath and roll over to face the wall.

Whatever he does, whatever he chooses, shouldn't be because I'm some emotional basket case, and if we talk now, I don't know if I'll be able to keep my emotions in check. But no matter what, I won't manipulate him with tears. He's a good man. I don't want him to feel like he owes me anything. He already looks after his parents and Izzy. I won't be another burden for him.

A soft knock on my door makes my heart hammer.

"Kat, you awake?"

The door creaks open, and I pull up the blanket. "Yeah." I assume he's gonna come sit by me, but he doesn't. Just stands in the doorway.

That dread builds in my chest. *He must be leaving. That's why he's keeping his distance.* I take a deep breath and force my voice to sound even. "Think we can talk in the morning?"

He doesn't respond right away, and in that silence, I squeeze my eyes closed, not wanting him to see me so close to a breaking point. Because if he flips on the lights, I won't be able to talk without crying. Without telling him how much I love him and want him to stay.

"Um, sure." Then more silence. "You okay?"

Gulping down the lump in my throat, I will myself to stay calm. "Yeah."

Go away, Brady. Let me pull myself together.

He sighs, and mumbles something I can't quite make out before he closes the door.

I exhale in relief, but my heart is pounding. Because everything in me, *everything*, wants to yank open that door and run into his arms.

I've always known this moment was coming. Always known our time together would end.

And I told him I wouldn't fall in love.

I wonder if he knows I've broken my promise.

54

BRADY

THE MORNING LIGHT FILTERS THROUGH THE KITCHEN WINDOW AND catches the auburn highlights in Kat's dark hair. She's standing at the sink, staring out at the oak tree, looking like she's a million miles away. I'd give anything to know what's going through her mind right now.

I want to grab her and greet her like I have on so many other mornings. With a hug and a kiss. Maybe while I mumble some dirty joke against her skin. But the distance between us is cavernous.

Instead, I reach for the coffee pot and pour a cup. "Morning. Want to sit down for a minute?"

She flinches, like the sound of my voice scares her, but she grabs her coffee mug and turns to face me. Her eyes are a little puffy, and if the dark circles beneath them are any indication, she got as much sleep as I did. Worry creeps through my limbs.

Is she that upset over her ex? Does she regret being here? *Fuck.* Does she miss him?

But her expression is blank, emotionless, which is not like Kat. She's usually so emotive. So expressive.

So this, this gives me pause.

I feel like my feet are being held to the fire, forcing this decision. My parents' bills are mounting, my bank account is almost tapped, and I'm bleeding cash on repairs here. So I brace myself for this conversation.

We sit across from each other, and I'm dying to ask a thousand questions about last night, but I don't.

She takes a deep breath, and then she asks, "Are you gonna sell?" Before I can process what she's saying, she whispers, "Because I heard. About the offer."

Shit.

"How? How do you know" I wanted to be the one to break the news to her.

One shoulder rises up in a shrug. "At work. Your realtor came in. I saw one of his flyers."

"I was going to tell you when you got home last night, but then your ex showed up."

Again, her expression is blank.

Of all the times for her to be reserved. Jesus Christ. I'll never understand women. Because today, today I need a fucking hint. Does she want this, whatever this is between us?

I watch her over the rim of my mug as I take a sip. "It's a great offer. Way more than I expected."

It's now or never. I need to lay this all out on the table for her. I need to know.

"So Kat—" I clear my throat. "I want to know what your plans are." Because I don't plan to hang out in Texas if she's taking off. I realize it's early in our relationship to be deciding these things, but fuck. I need to know. Relationship? Yeah. We're in one. We've been in one. And this is where the shit hits the fan. Do I sell and head back to Boston or... what? Stay? I need her to give me some kind of indication of what she wants.

"*My* plans?" She looks confused.

"Yes, your plans. Are you—are you... hanging around? Or are you planning to take off?"

Her brow furrows. "Take off? Why do you think I'm the one leaving?"

Why does she look offended right now?

I scrub my face, hating everything I'm about to say. "Eric made some salient points last night."

"Salient points?" Okay, now she looks pissed.

"What I mean is you have a great job offer on the line, and I don't want you to feel like I'm holding you back. I know what it's like to have huge, life-altering decisions thrust upon you. To feel like you don't have a choice. And I want you to know you do. You do have a choice. If you want that job, you should take it. You don't... you don't owe me anything." I say the words I know I should, but I hate every one of them. Hate that she'd accept anything that's linked to her ex. But a job is a job. I don't want to stand in her way if that's what she wants.

Her jaw tightens before she clenches her eyes shut. "The only thing holding me back is everyone telling me they know what I should do. I've heard it my entire life, and I'm sick of it." She glares at me and pushes up her glasses. "I'm sick of people questioning my judgment. If I wanted to work on another campaign, don't you think I would be by now?"

This beautiful girl looks fierce with the sun streaming down behind her, making her glow. And it will surely kill me to let her go if that's what she wants, but I can't let her throw away her career. After everything she went through growing up. After how much her family struggled to make ends meet. I can't let her do this for me. For this decrepit farm. For promises I probably shouldn't make.

Clearing my throat, I force the words out. "Don't you think you should reconsider? That kind of career is a lot to give up."

There's a flash of emotion in her eyes, but then it's gone, and in its place is a cold detachment. For one long, brutal moment, she gives me that blank stare. "You know, Brady, maybe you should take that offer on the farm."

And then she scoots her chair back, dumps out her coffee in the sink, and heads to her room, leaving me gutted when she says she's packing.

Goddamn it.

My head hangs forward as I listen to her belongings thump around in the other room. *So this is how it ends.*

And it kills me.

Because I hadn't thought that her taking the job meant we were over exactly. I think some small part of me was hoping we might be able to work things out. Are these two mutually exclusive, her job offer and our relationship?

I think about my parents and the responsibilities I have back East. About needing to raise Izzy. About the million bills sitting on the counter over there. About my nearly empty bank account.

Do I want to drag her down with me? Because that's what this feels like right now. Like drowning. Because even with the farm's side business and bath products, we won't stay afloat, not with the bills I have coming in from Boston.

What do she and I have if I sell the farm?

As I mull over my choices, I know fighting for her when she has so much of her future on the line is selfish. And I won't be the prick who drags her down when I have nothing left to offer her.

55

KATHERINE

WHAT HAVE I DONE?

I close the door to my room and lean my head against the frame, wishing I could take back the last ten minutes of my life.

But would I say anything else? Would this moment be any different if I told him I loved him? If I told him this was killing me?

I didn't mean to tell him to sell the farm. The words rushed out of me before I could stop them. I was pissed and emotional and hurt, but when Brady didn't blink an eye at my words, I felt heartbroken.

Of course he wants to sell. Of course he wants to get back to his life in Boston. Who stays in a small Texas town because of a girl?

He must not have heard Eric last night. I know Brady well enough to know he'd never take that asshole's money.

As much as I want to tell Brady that Eric's behind the offer, I know that selling would help Brady and his family. Where the money comes from doesn't matter.

And Eric is crazy if he thinks I'm coming back here once this place is his.

Reaching for my duffel bag in the closet, I toss it on the floor before I reach for my clothes. I don't have much. Jeans and t-shirts. A few flannels. My boots. One pair of pumps.

One item remains on a hanger. That black dress. The only nice outfit I own.

My fingers run along the silky soft fabric.

I won't bring it, I decide. It reminds me of the funerals and that night with Brady.

Maybe I should have known all along that any relationship that starts steeped in death is doomed to fail.

I wipe my eyes, and before I can think too much more about what I'm doing, I grab my laptop and tuck it into my bag. Then I reach for my notebook and scribble out the note before I totally lose it.

As I head for the door, I toss the bag over my shoulder and grab my binder, the one with all of the recipes and scent combinations.

My heart is in my throat when I step into the kitchen. Brady's feeding Izzy, and her beautiful little face grins at me, sending the knife a little deeper.

How did I ever think I loved my ex? This. Brady and Izzy. These are the people I love.

I swallow. Hard. It's tough to keep my act together, but I will the tears back.

Leaning over, I stick my nose in her soft hair. "Love you, baby. So much." I touch her cheek, overwhelmed by loss. Of Cal and Melissa and my sweet, darling Izzy. I hope she remembers me. When she's in Boston and in bed at night and wondering what life must have been like with her parents, I hope she remembers that so many people love her.

I'm sorry, honey. I'm so sorry I let your parents down. Images from that night flash behind my eyes. The way the barn door banged open in the rain. The dark expanse of night, so dark, I couldn't see the stars. How I couldn't scream their names loud enough when I saw their truck underwater.

I bite the inside of my cheek to keep my emotions at bay.

"Kat."

I ignore him and place the binder on the table. My voice is thick, but I can't help it. "You're gonna need this. It has every recipe. Every combination of scents. It's alphabetized. The vials in my bedroom are all labeled too, so you should be able to figure it out."

"Kat—"

"If you have any trouble, email me, and I'll try to explain."

"*Katherine.*"

I shake my head and sniffle. "But please don't call. I don't think I can handle talking to you right now."

He suddenly stands and pulls me to him, and I bury my face in his chest.

I love you.

The words echo through me as I cling to his t-shirt, but I clench my jaw to prevent those words from slipping.

"Don't go," he whispers, making me tremble.

He doesn't mean it. He has to sell. His parents need him too. What's he going to do here? How can he afford to stay?

I back away and shrug my bag up my arm. He turns my chin and makes me look at him. A deep sigh leaves him as his eyes rove over my face. "Don't go. Stay for the holidays at least."

Glancing away, I try to get my bearings. When I look at him again, he seems just as anguished as I feel. In a moment of weakness, I ask the words I know I'll regret. "Can you give me a reason to stay?" My heart flaps wildly in my chest. "Tell me you're not going back to Boston. Tell me you're not leaving and I'll stay."

He squeezes his eyes shut like that's the last thing he wants to hear.

"That's what I thought," I say to myself.

He shakes his head. "I just... I can't make that promise." He releases me to press his palms into his eyes.

When he looks at me, I give him a sad smile. "I can't get any deeper knowing where this is headed. I'm in too deep as it is, you know?" The heat in my eyes burns, but I blink it back. "Good luck in Boston. I really wish you the best." Reaching behind his neck, I pull him down to me and kiss him. "I'll miss you. So much," I whisper against his lips before I turn away.

When I step back, he looks away. I know what that means. The word I couldn't say. *Goodbye.*

Thankfully, my car starts right up, and I tear down the driveway. I know I'm leaving behind half of my belongings, but nothing compares to the fact that my broken heart lies at his feet in that farm house.

It doesn't matter. It's where it belongs.

56

KATHERINE

WHEN I REACH THE MAIN ROAD, I REALIZE I CAN'T SEE THE ROAD through my tears, so I pull over to the rest stop by the highway, the one where my parents and I slept when I was a kid, and I cry harder.

I must fall asleep because the sun is starting to set when I pry open my eyes.

My head is throbbing, and I can't contain the groan that rumbles in my throat because I'm so sore from sleeping like a pretzel. It takes me a second to orient myself, and then I wish I hadn't.

I wait for the tears, but none come. Instead of heartache, I feel numb. And maybe that's a good thing. A defense mechanism. Internally, I thank biology for pulling the plug on my emotions.

Grabbing my phone, I realize it's dead. I dig in my bag but can't find my charger.

"Dumbass," I grumble, dreading my next move. But it's the only thing I can do.

I head home. To Corpus.

~

The air is cold and salty when I finally stumble out of my car and up my parents' driveway. Corpus Christi is on the Gulf of Mexico, so even though it's December, the ocean is only a stone's throw away, and I can smell it. Feel it in the wind that whips my hair into my face.

The driveway is lined with cars. It's Christmas Eve, so I'm not surprised, but dang. I'm not in the mood.

My hand freezes on the door handle. *Deep breaths.*

The first step into the hallway makes me pause. It smells like tamales and cinnamon and lemon Pine Sol, such a familiar scent that reminds me of family get-togethers. Like the year our whole family was so poor, we gave each other socks for Christmas. Everyone got really into it, and it became a game to see who could give the ugliest pair.

I poke my head into the kitchen. A dozen people are buzzing around. My dad is stirring some vat at the stove. Probably *menudo.* My mother is braiding my cousin's hair. Everyone is smiling and eating and hugging. Tori finally sees me.

"Holy shit. It's Katherine!"

Everyone turns to me, mouths open.

"Hey, guys." And goddamn it. I left their gifts under my bed at the farm.

I sigh and force a smile.

I'm not sure what I'm expecting. Yelling? Threats? A one-way ticket to a convent? But that's not what happens.

Instead, my dad yanks me off my feet into a bear hug.

"*Mija!*" My father twirls me around until I'm laughing.

He's wiping away tears that only make mine well up. Ugh. Can I go twenty-four hours without crying? This is ridiculous.

When my dad releases me, my mom rushes in for a hug. "*Gracias a Dios!* She's home!"

People hand me off like a rag doll to hug me and pet my hair. Yes, really. They pet me. And then they make me sit down and eat because they claim I'm too skinny.

It takes all of sixty seconds for Tori to saunter over and sit on my lap like she's five, not seventeen.

"Dude, get your bony ass off me." I try to shrug her away, but she clings to me like a koala bear.

"I missed you, sissy."

Aww. My heart melts a little. "Missed you too, Tor."

She grabs my face and whispers, "Did you bring your hot man toy?"

I shrug out of her hold and shake my head. "Don't call him that. And no."

She studies my face and then gasps, "You guys broke up?"

Again, everyone's attention is on me. "Yes, we broke up. Is everyone happy now? Brady's going back to Boston. And no, before you ask, I am not getting back with Eric. You may not know this, but he's an asshole."

My little cousins start laughing and my mother flutters around like I just declared that I like to pole-dance with pasties in my free time.

Two hours later, my parents kick everyone out so we can talk. They'll be back tomorrow for Christmas anyway, so it's not like I ruined anything.

My dad points to the couch. "*Siéntate.*" He sighs. "Explain everything. Like why you didn't come home this summer and why the senator's boy has been calling us."

"Dad, you might want to sit too." Because it's gonna be a long night.

LEX MARTIN

To their credit, they don't interrupt me, even when I tell them Eric got me pregnant.

Anyway, they must have suspected I was hiding something major to not come home all this time.

At hearing this news, my mom cries quietly while my father clenches his jaw and rubs her shoulder.

I explain how the asshole finally came around. *Two weeks later.* And by that time I realized he wasn't the kind of man I wanted to have a child with. Someone who cuts and runs at the first sign of trouble. And then I tell them I was with Mel when I miscarried a few weeks later.

"*Mija,*" my father chokes out, "I wish you had told us something. I never would've talked to that lowlife if you had."

My lower lip quivers. "I'm sorry, Dad. I didn't want to disappoint you."

He laughs and shakes his head before he pulls me into another hug. "How could that even be possible? My girl is the first person in the family to graduate from college. And from a damn good school. You worked for a senator. How could I be disappointed in you?"

I mumble into his shoulder. "I just feel like you guys had all your hopes pinned on me. You worked so hard to get me those opportunities. To get me to a place where I could get a job like that." Leaning back, I sniffle. "All those times you didn't get things you needed because I needed school books. Or how the electricity would get turned off but you'd still fill my meal card with money."

Seriously, my parents are amazing. I don't even bring up the years they spent as migrant farmers because I'll bawl.

He pats my back. "How did you know about the electricity?"

"Tori would call me."

"Traitor!" she screams from the other room.

My dad chuckles at my eavesdropping little sister.

But the words I've used to describe my ex linger in my mind. *Someone who cuts and runs.* And my stomach drops. *Is that what I just did to Brady?*

I back away from my dad, misery seeping into my bones.

My dad must notice my expression. "Did you get the flowers we sent for the funerals?"

I nod, not wanting to think about that day.

"We felt real bad about Mel and her husband." His voice is thick. "She was always such a good girl. Always treated everyone real good."

"I know, Daddy."

He's silent for a while, and then he sighs. "¿Y el otro? El hermano del Cal. Tell me about him."

A sad smile lifts my lips. That's easy. There's so much to say about Brady.

I tell my dad how wonderful he is. How hard he works on the farm to provide for his niece and parents. How well he took care of me when he arrived. How much he loves his niece.

"But I'm worried that maybe I gave up on him too soon." I clench my jaw to control the emotion that wells up in me. "I was scared. I didn't want to be left behind when he moves back East." The silence lingers between us. Finally, I whisper, "Because I love him. And shouldn't I put my money where my mouth is and fight for what I love?"

My dad grabs my hand and pulls me into another hug, not saying anything for a while. At last he sighs. "I'm glad you came home, *mija.* You deserve someone who will fight for *you.*"

57

BRADY

Izzy cried all afternoon and half the night. Hell, I felt emotional too. I could barely grumble Merry Christmas to my parents when they called a few hours ago.

The truth is, nothing is the same without Katherine.

Her scent is everywhere. On my clothes. On the sheets. In the house. I can't escape her. God, I don't even want to.

Breaking up, or whatever we just did, fucking sucks. And it sucks even worse when it happens during the holidays.

Because here I am sitting on the floor next to the Christmas tree she decorated, lamenting my life like an asshole, staring at this beautiful gift she left me. And I'm only talking about the box and the wrapping paper. Because of course Kat went all out and had it wrapped in some expensive red paper and a huge gold bow.

And it makes me feel worse.

Izzy whimpers in my arms. She fell asleep a little while ago after another crying fit. I lean back against the couch and pat her back. Her little face is still flushed.

"This sucks, Iz," I whisper. "I'm sorry. I'm fucking up everything."

Really, I want to drown at the bottom of the bottle of bourbon I have stashed in the office, but I can't exactly go on a bender with a baby in my arms. Plus, it'll probably only remind me of the last time I drank—with Kat.

I stare at the tree until the sun starts to set. When my arms go numb from holding Izzy, I drag myself off the floor and tuck her in bed. Her sleep schedule is totally off. Kat would tell me to keep her up right now so the baby can sleep later.

Kat. Kat. Kat.

I'm going insane.

Fuck it.

I stalk to the living room and grab the gift, ready to chuck it into a closet, when a note slips out.

It's just a folded piece of notebook paper.

Don't open it. Don't do it.

I open it. The handwriting is messy. She must have scrawled it out just before she left.

Dear Brady,

I can't pretend I'm not heartbroken because I am, but please know that I understand why you're leaving. I think you're an amazing man. Your family is so lucky to have you.

I wanted to give you something to keep you and Izzy warm back in Boston. Something to remind you of your time here. I hope you'll remember me. You'll always own a piece of my heart.

Love,

Kat

I don't think there's a part of this note that doesn't completely depress me. I give in and pour myself a shot before I continue, but I tuck away the bottle. I figure I can still change a baby on one shot.

The box is heavy on my lap, and my fingers sink into the sides as I grip it.

A minute later, I'm staring at a large quilt, the kind you inherit from a relative. With rich fabrics and tiny stitching. All in dark blues and burgundies. *This must have cost a small fortune.*

If I was depressed before, it's nothing compared to seeing the words sewed on the front. Above the image of a small farm house surrounded by wildflowers, it says, *Texas: Home is Where The Heart Is.*

Is that what I'm doing? Leaving my heart behind? Because it sure fucking feels like it.

If I ever wondered what it was like to get my heart jacked with a rusty crowbar, I now have the answer.

I've tried calling her a million times over the last week, but it goes straight to voice mail. At the very least, I want to know she made it home safely. I assume that's where she went, back to Corpus.

My cell buzzes in my pocket.

"Hey, Mom."

I slump into a chair, exhausted from feeding all the animals, feeding the baby and making ten thousand phone calls. How women everywhere do this, day in and day out, I'll never know. Men have it easy.

"Your father and I have talked. We think this is the right decision."

Emotion clogs my throat. "Mom, I'm not sure what to say."

"There's nothing to say. At the end of the day, you don't have a choice. This window of opportunity won't last forever." She gave me her whole spiel last night. I had no idea she felt this way. "Did you call Mrs. MacIntyre? Can she and her husband help?"

Groaning, I mumble, "She had some choice words for me, but yeah, they'll help."

My mom chuckles. I really don't know what about this situation is funny, but I table my complaint.

Sighing, I tell her I'll call and let her know how it went. She thinks this is a foregone conclusion, but really, this could all blow up in my face.

"Love you, son. Happy New Year! And please drive carefully. You know how everyone gets tonight."

"I will, Mom. Don't worry."

"And bundle up that baby! I don't want her catching a cold. Is she over that bout of constipation? You know, baby poops—"

"She's fine. Her poops are fine. Everything's fine. And yes, I'll drive safely."

At least I'm laughing when I get off the phone. And really, it's nice to know she's in my corner.

I hang up and get Izzy bundled up. Because we have an appointment. And it's something that will probably change our lives forever.

Izzy has been quiet the entire drive. Which freaks me out a little. I even stop to check on her. To make sure she didn't sneak a Cheerio and accidentally choke on it. Finally, I stop at Target and buy three baby mirrors so I can see her in my rear view mirror from every angle.

Not gonna lie. This whole thing makes me a little nauseous. The longer I drive, the more time I have to think about my plan. And all of the ways it could go wrong.

When I get out of the truck and poke my head in the back of the cab, Izzy grins. I smile back as I fix her little barrette, which is hanging off her forehead.

"Can't have you going in there looking like your uncle doesn't know how to dress you." I pull up both of her socks and fix her pants. "Iz, I know this has been a rough week, but do you think you could be extra good for me today?"

She nods solemnly. It probably helps that she has no clue what the hell I'm talking about.

Reaching down to her feet, I grab my duffel bag and make sure I brought everything. I mean, if I forgot something, I'm shit out of luck at this point, but looking through it calms my mind.

Before I get the baby out of her car seat, I pat my coat pocket to make sure I brought the most important item of all. And then it's time.

58

KATHERINE

Voices ebb and flow down the hall. The cheer in everyone's muffled voices makes me a little stabby.

I suspect my parents know I'm in a foul mood because they've left me alone. Either that or they've had their hands full with every relative in South Texas who has undoubtedly decided to visit. The front lawn is probably overflowing with cars.

But that's a nice distraction from the conversations I've been having with my parents. No wonder they want me to stay here "to get my bearings."

At least they seem to understand what I'm saying about my old job and why I don't want to go back to politics.

My parents even look moderately sympathetic when I talk about Brady.

I'm exhausted from last night. My mom made me whip up an ungodly number of tamales for the family visiting tonight. I finally doze off but a knock on my bedroom door jars me awake. I'm guessing my pity party is coming to an end because Tori rips off my comforter and jumps on my bed.

"What the hell?" I glare.

"You can't lie in bed all day, loser. It's New Year's Eve. Get the fuck up. We're going to par-tay like we're hoochies in a Prince video."

I smile pleasantly until she smiles back, and then I yank the comforter out of her grip and burrow deeper. "How do you even know who Prince is?"

"Mom's been watching old episodes of *I Love The 80s* on YouTube." She sits on me like the slug that she is.

"Tor, we need to establish boundaries," I grunt under her weight.

She snorts. "So does that mean you won't give me Brady's number? You know, if I wanted to call him and show him a good time?" Then my little sister starts grinding on me.

I whip the blanket off my head and shoot her the dirtiest look I can muster. She laughs harder.

She holds up her hands. "Kidding. God, you should see your face!" But then she stops laughing. "Your eyes are kind of puffy." She kisses my forehead and whispers, "I'm sorry you look like shit for the holidays."

"You were such a sweet baby. What happened?"

"You adore me. Admit it." Then she tucks herself under the blanket and spoons me.

We lie there and listen to the festivities in the other room.

"So you love this Brady guy, huh?"

I sigh. "Yes."

"Enough to have his babies and live on a farm and go all Laura Ingalls Wilder?"

"The chick from *Little House on the Prairie*?" I mull that over. "They didn't have running water. So I'd say yes, but I need indoor plumbing."

She snickers. "Please tell me Brady is hotter than Almanzo. He was kind of douchey."

"It was that awful haircut."

"Hmm. Yeah." She snuggles closer and sticks her cold nose

in my neck. "So if Brady were to show up on a horse, all white knight and shit, you'd forgive him for letting you go?"

Another deep sigh leaves me. "There's nothing to forgive."

"So you're not mad at him?"

"God, no. I just wish things were different. That he didn't have to go back to Boston. But I knew what I was getting into. He was always honest with me."

"It still sucks hairy balls, though."

"Yeah. It does."

We spoon in silence, and I have to admit it's nice having my sister comfort me. Makes the ache in my chest a little less acute. Less like I'm getting sliced repeatedly and more like I'm bleeding out from one gaping wound.

After a few minutes, she crawls out and declares that it's time to stop moping. "Mom says dinner is on at seven. You should shower too because you kinda stink."

When I don't move, she drags my comforter off my body. "Shower," she demands. "Now!"

As I drag my listless body out of bed, I mumble, "Geez, you're bossy."

The smile on her face is priceless. "Learned from the best, homie."

59

KATHERINE

I GLANCE DOWN AT MY JEANS AND FLANNEL AND THEN LOOK around. Everyone is dressed up today, and the house is packed. Someone must have brought some firecrackers because I don't remember the last time *this* many people came over.

"Why are y'all wearing ties?" I ask my uncles as I hug them one by one.

Tío Chuey glances at my mom and then back to me and shrugs. "Just came from Mass. You shoulda come too, my little heathen."

"You went to church for New Year's Eve service? I thought you only did Christmas?"

"Nah, I do all the major holidays. The cute ladies host a big potluck after." He waggles his eyebrows.

Ew.

I pat his big belly. "Looks like you've been indulging."

"You know it!"

I laugh and kiss his chubby cheek. I'm greeting the rest of my relatives when my uncle herds me toward the end of the extended dining room table and then calls out to my parents.

"Sit," my mom barks, pointing to me and then the place setting in front of me.

Tori saunters over and pulls out my chair. Leaning over to her, I whisper, "Is it my imagination or is everyone acting weird?"

"Our family *is* weird. You just never realized it." Then she pretends to fellate a celery stick, but nobody seems to notice that my sex-obsessed little sister is being a total pervert.

Slouching in the chair, I wait for the rest of the family to grab a seat and for my mom to give the go-ahead to pass around the casserole dishes that fill the table. Except everyone keeps standing. And staring. At me.

Why do I feel like I'm in the middle of a *Twilight Zone* episode?

My mom moves next to my dad, who clears his throat. "It's real good to have everyone here today. Margie and I are blessed y'all could make it."

What the?

This is *so* strange. "Tor, seriously. Why is Dad being so formal?" I whisper.

She winks at me and motions for me to pay attention.

My dad shifts uncomfortably, and I'm afraid he's gonna tell us he lost his job or has cancer. Mentally, I start calculating how much money I have in the bank to pay their rent.

"Margie and I are so grateful to have Katherine home with us." Everyone turns to stare at me again, and I give an awkward wave. "In a few hours, it'll be a new year, and we wanted to kick it off with something good."

He pulls out a big black bag and motions toward me. "I'm sure everyone knows that my daughter is an incredibly talented public relations and marketing... type person."

Poor Daddy. I smile. He's trying so hard.

He clears his throat. "But did you know she's also very

talented with perfumes and making bath soaps and lotions? What do they call that oil stuff, Margie?"

"Essential oils."

"Yes, essential oils. Katherine is real good with essential oils." *Where the hell is he going with this?*

Dad slowly unzips the bag. "In fact, she made all of these products." He pulls out some soap and lotion and bath gel.

From the farm.

My mouth drops open, but I can't speak.

He gives me a little smirk. "And I have enough for everyone to take home some of these beautiful... *productos.* It's a belated Christmas gift from a family friend."

"Dad, where did"—I swallow hard—"where did you get that?"

The chair next to me scrapes the floor and a familiar deep voice rumbles in my ear, "From me."

Chills break out on my arms, and I close my eyes.

You know that feeling you get when you're at the top of a roller coaster, about to take the plunge? That moment where you're not sure you'll survive if you move forward but certain you can't go back?

My heart is in my throat when I turn and see those black jeans.

I look up until I reach those intense green eyes and Brady's beautiful face. Izzy grins in his arms, and I launch out of my seat and into their embrace.

My family is aww-ing and ooh-ing and clapping behind me. I ignore them and bury my face in Brady's neck.

He's here.

Blinking back the heat in my eyes, I kiss Izzy, who claps and squeals.

"Missed you guys," I sniffle.

One of my aunts reaches for the baby, and the moment both of his arms are free, Brady lifts me into another hug.

"What are you doing here?" I whisper as I fight back the tears.

His hand sweeps through my hair, and he says the sweetest words I've ever heard. "Had to come get my girl."

As he sets me down on the floor, all of the reasons we couldn't be together come rushing back to me. "Aren't you leaving?" I ask, my voice wobbly with emotion. "Aren't you selling the farm? What about your family?"

For a moment, all I see is him. The sounds of my family fade in the background as he cradles my face in his calloused hand.

"I can't go, Kat. Not with you here. Because you're my family now too."

My knees go weak and I grip his shoulders. He smiles, dimple and all. "I love you, Kat. I love you so damn much, I can't breathe without you. I can't sleep. I can't eat. Hell, I can barely function. When you're with me, I love the farm and all the broken things I have to fix and those scary-ass chickens and that ridiculous raccoon."

A ripple of laughter sounds around us, but I'm riveted by the look in his eyes. He shrugs. "I don't have answers. I don't know how I'm going to help my parents or save the farm. Trust me when I say nothing makes sense in my life. Nothing but you. So no, I'm not leaving, not if you'll have me. And maybe you can help me figure out a way to keep the house for Izzy."

Tears are streaming down my face when my sister yells, "Would you kiss him already before he changes his mind?"

Everyone laughs, and I lean up on my toes and wrap my arms around his neck. "I love you too, Brady. But I kinda think I have for a while."

"Thank God." He chuckles, looking relieved. He brushes my

hair out of my face and leans closer to rub his nose against mine. "What do you say? Wanna help me make a go of it on the farm?"

I fight a smile. "Only if you promise me one thing."

"Whatever you want."

"You gotta give Texas football a chance."

He rolls his eyes with a laugh and nods. "Well, if my parents disown me, we know you're to blame."

And then he kisses me while my family hoots and hollers around us.

60

KATHERINE

THE NEXT AFTERNOON, I BOUNCE IZZY IN MY ARMS AS WE HUG MY family goodbye and load up Brady's truck. As it turns out, my sneaky parents hid Brady and the baby in their bedroom for an hour last night so they could surprise me.

Once we're on the road, I let out a big breath. While I've enjoyed seeing my family and introducing Brady to everyone, I'm really glad to finally be alone with him. After dinner and fireworks last night, he and Izzy slept in Tori's room, and my sister bunked with me. And then we had another big family breakfast this morning, so we really haven't had more than a few minutes alone since he arrived last night.

There's no use in trying to hide the huge smile on my face as I watch him drive. "I can't believe you drove all this way with Izzy."

He glances at her in the rearview mirror. "I told her we were coming for you, and it's the strangest thing—I swear she really understood."

Shifting in my seat, I turn back to her and grin. "Missed you, *mamacita*."

Izzy holds out her arms and yells my name.

"Sweetie, when we stop in a little while, I'll get you out of your car seat and hold you."

Brady shakes his head. "She missed you like crazy. I'm lucky she's even talking to me at this point. Swear she was pissed at me for days."

"Aww, Izzy, don't be mad at your uncle, but thanks for the solidarity, babe."

Izzy smiles back at me, and Brady shakes his head with a laugh.

I shift my attention back to him. "For real, though, I can't believe my whole family helped you. How did you do this? When?"

"Last few days. Since *someone* wasn't picking up the phone, I had to get crafty." He shoots me a dirty look.

"I'm sorry. I left my charger at the farm and was too depressed to motivate and buy another one. But how did you track me down?"

He gives me a big, stupid grin. "I sweet talked Mrs. Mac for your number in Corpus. But first she yelled at me for being a dumbass and not chasing after you sooner."

"That was sweet of her."

He laughs again.

Reaching over, I run my hand against his smooth jaw, still missing him so much even though he's sitting right next to me. "You shaved."

"I was meeting your parents. Damn right I shaved." A silly smirk tilts his lips. "I'm maybe even thinking I won them over a little."

"I'm shocked you softened them up so quickly, but I guess I shouldn't be. You are very charming." I swear my mom fluttered around him.

"Truthfully, I'm a little stunned your dad didn't try to put my balls in a nutcracker. He sounded like a scary dude on the phone when we talked a few days ago. But I like that he's protective of you, so I understand."

"I saw him pull you aside before we left. What did he say?"

"That it meant a lot to him that I cared enough to drive all that way. I mean, of course I made the drive. I'd do it all over in a heartbeat."

I love you. The emotion swells in my chest. "My dad really doesn't warm up to people that quickly. I'm so glad you guys hit it off."

I'm feeling dumb for thinking my parents wouldn't give him a chance. Although I do think our conversations over the last week have made them rethink how close-minded they've been.

And then I tell him what's been weighing on my heart since I left the farm. "I'm sorry for taking off like that."

"I didn't exactly make a convincing argument about why you should stay. Then you were gone." His voice drops to a whisper. "And it fucking wrecked me." He reaches over and threads his fingers through mine. "I love you, Kat. I should've told you before you left."

Everything in me feels jittery, pumped with elation and hope and a little fear. I blurt the words before I have time to censor myself. "Is this crazy? Is this too fast? You're turning your whole life upside down to stay here. Are we insane?"

He looks over with nothing but confidence and adoration in his eyes. "No, this isn't crazy." His thumb strokes my hand gently. "My brother said he loved Mel after knowing her for seven days, and I'm starting to see the wisdom behind the things he went after. You and I have been taking the slow route in comparison." He glances over again. "Cal and Mel were happy, right? And in love?"

"Madly in love."

"Which sums up how I'm feeling about you. So maybe this is unconventional, but it feels right, doesn't it?"

LEX MARTIN

My heart is a jet airplane taking off into the sunset. "Yes, it feels right."

"So there's our answer." A hint of concern etches his brow. "Look, let's see how we get along when we're not dealing with so much traumatic shit. You don't have to pledge your undying love and loyalty to me... yet." He glances over with a wink. "But I think we have something special."

Feeling a little choked up, I nod.

He leans over for a sweet kiss and smiles. "Our home isn't the same without you, babe."

Home.

No word has ever sounded so good.

61

BRADY

WHEN MY TIRES FINALLY HIT THE GRAVEL ON OUR DRIVEWAY, I couldn't be more relieved. It's been torture being around Kat and not be able to touch her. *Really touch her.*

My hand pats the pocket on my coat jacket. I brought her Christmas present with me just in case I had to go into full-scale grovel mode, but decided to wait until we got home to give it to her.

As we unload the truck, I watch her as she hugs Izzy, and my head goes a little fuzzy with emotion. Because I love my girls so damn much.

Kat's the light at the end of this dark tunnel, one I've been traveling since before my brother died. I hadn't realized it, but I wasn't happy. I wasn't complete. In fact, at the time I couldn't even tell you what I was missing.

When I unlock the front door, I kiss Kat's temple and take the baby from her arms so I can get Izzy ready for bed. Which can't come soon enough, because if I have to wait one more minute to be alone with Kat, I might lose my mind.

As I'm heading down the hall, I hear her gasp, and I turn to see her in the kitchen in front of several drawings I did of her.

LEX MARTIN

She's holding the image of her sleeping, curled up in bed with a sheet draped over her.

She looks at me with tears welling in her eyes. "They're beautiful."

"What can I say? I missed you. A lot. I even recycled while you were gone."

"Aww! Really?"

She grins up at me, and I kiss her forehead. I have to admit I appreciate how easy it is to please her.

Izzy yawns in my arms and rubs her eyes.

"Let me get this baby to bed, and I'll be out in a minute."

Izzy is wiped from the road trip, so it doesn't take long after I tuck her in before she's asleep. Once she's snoring softly, I head out of the nursery on a mission, because I'm dying to get my hands on Kat. I hear her using the sink in the bathroom, and when the door opens, I yank her into me, and she laughs.

"Shh. Don't wake the baby," I mumble against her lips.

"Mmm."

Her whole body melts into me, and although I'm desperate to connect with her in a very naked and horizontal way, I want to give her a Christmas gift.

With an arm around her shoulder, I maneuver her to the living room, next to the Christmas tree.

"I'm sorry for being an ass last week. For putting work first."

Pushing up onto her toes, she kisses my jaw as she winds her arms around my neck. "You don't have to apologize. We both made mistakes and withdrew. I guess I got afraid. I knew I had promised to keep this casual, and then suddenly nothing about what we had seemed casual. And, well, I've only been in two relationships, and only one was serious."

I can't help the surprise on my face. "Really?"

She nods, a shy smile on her lips. "Really."

As I sit on the couch, I tug her into my lap. Fuck, she smells

332

good. I breathe into her hair. "What else do I need to know?" All of a sudden, I'm nervous about what I want to ask. "Did you love him? Your ex?"

She takes a deep breath. "At the time I thought I did. But when I compare my feelings for him to what I feel for you, it's no contest. You're the World Series. He was Little League."

I bark out a laugh. "You're so perfect for me."

But she's not laughing. In fact, her eyebrows furrow. "So I need to tell you something, and you might get upset."

"Lay it on me." I like this no-holds-barred thing we have going on.

She takes a deep breath. "Eric's family was behind the offer on the farm. I just found out about it when he showed up on our doorstep last week."

My jaw tightens, and I scoot her off my lap.

"See, I knew you'd be upset. Which is why I didn't tell you about it. Because I know your family needs the money."

I let that sink in. It's a difficult pill to swallow.

She continues. "I'm tempted to say I hate him, but that suggests I feel *something* for him, some kind of emotion, but I don't. Honestly, I'm not sure what I saw in him. But what I do know is he and his family can afford some little farm. That expense means nothing to them. And if it meant helping you and your parents get out from this mountain of debt, then I thought it was worth swallowing my pride."

I blow out a breath. "You were going to let me take that money because you wanted to help my family?"

She nods, her lower lip trapped between her teeth.

"From someone you hate?"

Her whole body is tense, like she's afraid I'm going to yell at her.

"Yeah," she whispers. "Pretty much."

I laugh. "I'd be really pissed if I went through with it and found out later."

Her hands fidget in her lap. "If you sold the farm, I'd hoped you wouldn't find out. That you could go back to Boston and restart your life. Use that money to raise Izzy. To take care of your parents."

A silence stretches between us, and finally, I groan. "You're amazing. I don't even know what to say."

"You don't have to say anything. You're worth it."

"I'd say you're the one who's worth it."

Resting my forehead in the crook of her neck, I breathe her in. Her hands thread through my hair, and we stay like that for a long minute. When we part, I ask something I've been dying to know. "So what happened with him? Why'd you break up?"

"I realized the senator didn't mean half of his campaign promises, and Eric knew this and let me go along like an idiot." She rolls her eyes. "That's why the campaign hired someone right out of college. Someone who was dumb enough to believe the spin and sell it. Because I was passionate. Convincing. Especially when it came to fracking. Anyway, I overheard Eric and his dad talking one afternoon and found out his father had no plans to enact any reform. Of course, I was livid. Eric and I argued about it. I told him I was going to quit. Which he thought was insane since, hello, I worked for a senator. But I couldn't in good conscience continue to lie for the campaign."

"I'd be pissed too." I pull her back into my lap, and she rests her head on my shoulder. "Since we're having this big discussion, can I ask you something else? Because I heard parts of your conversation with Eric last week."

She stills, and I lace our fingers together, wanting to reassure her.

"You can ask me anything you want."

I tuck a strand of hair behind her ear. "Were you really pregnant last spring?"

A deep sigh leaves her. "Yeah." She's quiet for a moment. "Right after that argument, I got really bad food poisoning and threw up non-stop for two days. It compromised my birth control, and I was too sick to realize it. Then a few weeks later, my period was late."

I rub her back. "So what happened? Did you? You know..."

"Oh, God, no. I didn't get an abortion. I mean, I'm totally pro-choice, but I don't think I could've gone through with it. Eric was pissed I had gotten pregnant. Upset about how it would look for the campaign. You know"—she lowers her voice—"'son of a conservative senator knocks up girlfriend.' We weren't in a good place at the time—we had already been arguing about the campaign when this happened." She blows out an exasperated breath. "Anyway, then I came here." She takes a deep breath. "I had just arrived when I started spotting. The doctor said sometimes pregnancies terminate without rhyme or reason."

"Damn, that's heavy."

"Kinda."

"I'm sorry, babe. That's a lot to go through."

She nods against me.

"Mrs. Mac said you guys were engaged."

"No way. Before the pregnancy scare, he had brought up marriage. But I couldn't see that kind of future with him. I had never really wanted kids—I helped raise my sister. I didn't want to be saddled with children while he was traipsing around the state."

I clear my throat, wishing we'd had this conversation sooner. "Do you still feel that way? About kids?"

She laughs and turns to kiss me. "No. I want kids, silly. Just not with him. I mean, how could anyone be around Izzy and not want kids?"

Thank God. A wave of relief washes over me. "Cause, you know, I have a kid."

Kat laughs harder. "Really? I hadn't noticed."

I'm surprised by how right that seems. Yeah, Izzy is my kid. I'm tempted to feel guilt. To feel like I'm being proprietary for something, someone, who isn't mine. But Cal would want me to feel this way, I realize. Cal would want me to love Izzy like she's my own. And I do love her. With every fiber of my being.

Kat nudges me. "What about you? Have you had many relationships?"

"Not really. A couple of girlfriends in high school. A few in college. None of them serious." At least, none of them move-to-a-different-state serious.

She nibbles her bottom lip. "What about Dani?"

"No, we were just friends."

"How is that possible?" She clears her throat. "I saw that photo." Then she comes clean and admits she dropped by the tattoo parlor, but chickened out and took off.

"Mmm. My little stalker," I joke as she smacks me playfully.

"But you guys looked *close*." Two little lines form between Kat's brows.

"Dani was always clear she wasn't interested in me that way. I told her it was fine, but then I wanted more. It was really a one-sided crush." The expression on Kat's face tells me she needs a little more convincing. "Sweetheart, I've barely seen her since she and Jax started dating last winter. She says she's never been happier, and I'm glad for her. In fact, I'm starting to feel lousy I've been so down on their relationship."

Kat's whispers, "She's just so beautiful. And you two look really hot together."

"You know who's really hot? My girlfriend."

A laugh falls from her lips as I turn her so she's straddling me. I stare up at her, wanting to know just how much she means to me. Wanting her to realize that she's my orbit now.

Our kiss is lush and deep. I lick into her mouth and stroke against her tongue. Her breath comes out heavy, like a gasp, and I move her closer until our hips fit together. I'm pulsing against the zipper of my jeans, dying to strip her out of her clothes,

It only takes a minute to realize the Christmas gift will have to wait.

62

KATHERINE

Breaking away from his kiss, I take off my glasses, setting them down on the coffee table, and then reach down and strip off my t-shirt. Brady stares at my sheer white bra and starts to lean toward me.

I put a hand up to stop him, and he growls.

"Not so fast," I chuckle as I tug on his shirt.

He scoots me off his lap and reaches behind his head to yank it off. As I'm standing in front of him, admiring this stunning man, he unbuttons my jeans and slowly slides them down my hips.

Brushing his nose across my bikini line, he murmurs, "I like this white lace."

"Because it's virginal?"

"Because it's sheer," he deadpans.

I'd laugh, but I'm too distracted by his mouth that's nibbling a trail across my stomach. I run my fingers through his thick hair and shiver when his hands slide up the back of my thighs, so close to where I want them.

A second later, my jeans and shoes are gone, and he's pulling me down to straddle him again.

At first, he just holds me to him. "I missed you, baby. I love you. So damn much."

My heart swells, understanding how momentous it is to find someone who loves you. Someone who looks at you like you could put stars in the sky.

"Love you, too."

He leans up to kiss me. And it starts out gentle. Just a whisper of his lips against mine. Soft. Like he's trying to memorize what this feels like. How we fit.

Arching my head to the side, I sigh as he kisses up my neck and presses me closer until my breasts meet his solid chest.

How I've missed this. His warmth. These strong arms. His calloused touch.

Dipping my head down, our mouths meet as I rock against him. I'm aching to be closer. To feel his body slide against mine. To feel him move inside of me.

He threads his fingers through my hair, deepening the kiss, and I suck his tongue until he groans.

Pulling me down with him, he reclines on the couch where his touch becomes fervent. He lowers the cups of my bra and grabs both breasts, licking one nipple before nipping it with his teeth.

Those dark, green eyes watch me as I flush from his touch.

And then he gives me that look. The one that sends shivers down my back. "Scoot up," he rasps.

We're lying horizontally on the couch, and we take up the whole thing. Where does he want me to go?

He answers my question by lifting my hips and moving me over his shoulders, so that my knees rest on either side of his head. I stare down at him and I feel that wicked grin everywhere.

Those rough hands slide up and down my thighs.

"Take it off." His voice is low and gravelly as he tugs my panties down my legs.

Oh, God.

My nipples tighten painfully as he watches me wiggle out of my undies so they're dangling off one ankle.

I've never done this before. Yeah, Brady's gone down on me, but this is more intimate.

Way more intimate.

He bites the inside of my thigh, and every cell in me flares, like he's the match and I'm the kindling.

Reaching behind my back, I unclip my bra and let it slide down my arms. His eyes darken as he watches me.

"Hold on to the couch," he orders.

I nod, feeling out of breath and desperate for his touch.

He takes a deep breath. "My beautiful girl. I'm gonna make you come so hard."

Those rough fingers pull me closer until I feel his hot breath between my legs. He nibbles up my thigh. Drags his teeth on my skin. Licks one side of my mound.

My breath comes out in a rush.

He studies me there as he drags his finger through my crease.

"Is this for me?" he asks, his voice rough. "Do I make you this wet?"

"Ye... yes."

He's barely touching me, and I'm trembling.

That finger runs across me again, and my whole body quakes.

Damn.

Leaning up, he takes one agonizingly slow lick, leaving me gasping.

Then he takes another. And another.

My fingers dig into the side of the couch to stay upright. But then he slides two thick fingers into me, and I groan and lean back.

I can see everything. How his wet fingers thrust in and out of me. How he swirls his tongue on my skin, making the throbbing worse.

Reaching down, I part myself so he can get closer.

He stares back, his eyes feral. And then he really starts to lap at my skin.

God, the sound. His tongue against my wet skin. My gasps. His grunts of approval.

"That feels so good," I moan as I thrust against his welcoming mouth.

As I watch him, I'm filled with the need to pleasure him too. So I lean farther back and grip his erection through his jeans.

But it's not enough to touch him like this. Not enough to pleasure him the way he's pleasuring me. And suddenly I know exactly what I want to do even though I've never tried before.

"Stop," I whisper and start to get up.

"What's wrong?"

"Nothing is wrong." I thread my fingers through his thick hair. "I just need to reciprocate."

I flip around onto my stomach, keeping my knees just above his shoulders.

"Aw, fuck, Katherine." The appreciation in his voice makes me even more eager.

He grips my ass as I lean down and take him out of his jeans. He's so beautiful and thick and hard. He smells like warm male and soap. I rub my lips along his tip, and he hardens more in my palm. And then I open my mouth and take him in.

"Fuck, yes, baby. Suck on my cock."

The groan that rumbles beneath me makes me smile around him, but when he pulls me down onto his mouth and resumes his torturous licks, I can barely think. All I know is that I'm close. So close my thighs are quaking around him.

He pushes my knees wider, and then those talented fingers spread me.

I'm so hot. So hot, I'm burning. Trembling above him.

That wicked tongue flattens as it strokes more earnestly. Those thick fingers press into me. His rough hand grips my ass.

"Oh... God..."

I can barely focus on what I'm doing as he increases the pressure, so I give up trying and just suck gently on his tip while my hand strokes his erection in an erratic rhythm.

And just when I think it can't feel any better, when I can't get any higher, he twists his fingers inside of me, hitting me in just the right place, and I come apart, clenching my eyes shut as the rest of me tightens and throbs so hard, I have to hold onto his hips with both hands so I don't smother him. I'm still quivering when his hands skate up and down my thighs.

"C'mere, baby," he whispers. "Let me hold you."

Those words warm me. Because I love how he always wants to take care of me.

And I can't wait to show my appreciation.

63

BRADY

Jesus Christ. I could die right now and be a happy man.

Kat crawls over me and collapses. She's still gasping. I chuckle and run my hand through her silky soft hair.

"Good?"

She sighs, nuzzling into me. "Life-altering."

I kiss her neck. She's so warm as she molds herself to me. I close my eyes to appreciate this moment. Just being together.

I'm still throbbing between our bodies, but I like how sated she feels. How calm and relaxed. Like we could hide away forever. Even on this awful couch with the springs that want to bust a hole in my ass.

We lie entwined as she catches her breath.

A minute later, she pulls back, and I move her hair out of her face. A smile lifts her lips. "Love you," she whispers and leans down to kiss me.

"Mmm. Love you too, baby."

And then she nibbles on my neck. "I want you to come just as hard as I did."

I laugh. "Yeah?"

She pushes on my chest as she sits up and leans back to

shove my jeans lower. When she turns back to me, I'm so struck by her beauty, my mouth goes dry. Her hazel eyes are wide and vulnerable. Long, thick locks of dark hair tumble over her shoulder and dance just above her breasts.

She licks her lips, which are swollen and wet and completely tantalizing.

I grab her and knead her skin. Those slender legs slide on either side of my hips as she moves against me. She's slick and hot and feels so good, I want to pound into her.

But I don't.

Instead, I steady her hips and thrust against her.

Her eyes shudder closed, and I do it again and watch as my dick parts her folds.

"Brady," she moans, letting her head fall back.

I repeat the motion until her thighs tighten against my body and I know she's close again. I lift her up and position myself against her opening, holding her weight up as I slowly nudge in and out.

"Holy shit." She's shaking again.

Kat leans forward to grip my shoulders, her hips bucking against me. I know she wants to me to fill her. I'm dying to feel her too.

A little whimper leaves her mouth, and it breaks my resolve to go slow. She sinks down on me so fast I see stars.

"Fuck," I grunt as I take her ass in my hands and slide her up and down on my shaft. "You feel so fucking good."

Her gasps sound in my ear. "Yes," she moans on each thrust, encouraging me, so I go faster, until I can't fucking wait another minute.

I flip her onto her side against the back of the couch and hook her leg over my hip and pump into her. Hard and fast and furious.

Her nails dig into my back. She chants louder.

And when I reach a hand between us and rub that spot, she comes apart, quaking and rolling, squeezing my dick so hard that I follow with my release.

We're panting and sweaty when I wrap my arms around her and hold her close. She squeezes her thigh muscles, and I laugh from the intensity of still being inside her.

Which makes me realize I never grabbed a condom. After everything she just told me.

I lean up on one arm and gaze down at her. "Sweetheart, we okay just on your birth control?" Kind of an idiotic question to ask *after* the fact, but I should still ask.

She nods. "Yeah. We're good." I kiss her and collapse back down as her leg tightens around my hip. She whispers, "You're the only one."

"The only one for what?"

"To go bare."

It takes a moment for that to sink in.

"Even with your ex?"

She nods, and a primitive sort of pride fills me, the kind that makes me want to toss my girl over my shoulder and run off so no other asshole can appreciate her.

Kissing her lips, I grunt, "Good." And then it dawns on me. "You're a first for me too."

She's quiet as she runs her hand up and down my bicep. "Really?"

I can hear the happiness in her voice. "For a lot of things, Kat." And for many more things to come I hope.

Her hair tumbles over us, and I inhale her sweet scent. *Mine.* This girl is mine. For as long as she'll have me.

The barn is quiet the next morning when we feed our merry

band of random animals. A quiet contentment fills me as I watch Kat pet Sampson, who neighs and huffs against her palm.

"Who took care of these guys while we were gone?" she asks as she brushes out his mane.

"The MacIntyres."

Bandit pops out of nowhere and grips Kat's leg in a bear hug.

"Oh, wittle baby," she coos. "I missed you."

Kat picks up the raccoon and hugs the thing to her chest. He grins at me over her shoulder.

She's mine, asshole.

"He peed on my stuff again," I gripe.

She gasps, narrowing her eyes at him. "You're a very bad boy. I don't know what to do with you."

I take the raccoon out of her hands—holding him at arm's length, mind you—and set the little bastard on the ground where he scampers off to harass the goats.

Reaching for Katherine, I just hold her for a moment before I whisper, "I've been a bad boy too."

She laughs, and I squeeze her tighter.

We stroll back to the house hand-in-hand and head into the kitchen where Mrs. Mac is giving Izzy a snack. Our neighbor raises an eyebrow. "So are you two lovebirds official now or what?"

I laugh. "Yup. We're official."

"Thank goodness." She motions toward the other room in a less than covert way and chirps, "Well, I see you have things to do around here, so I'll be getting outta your hair."

As soon as the front door closes, Kat laughs. "What in the world was that about?"

"A surprise," I call out as I get a box out of the office. It jerks in my arms, and I steady it and hold the gift out to Kat, who grins.

She's reaching for the lid when it pops open, and a furry face meows at her.

"Valentine!" she squeals and grabs her favorite kitten. "You got him back for me?"

"Yeah. I felt bad about giving them away. I figured, what the hell? It's one kitten. Besides, Bandit needs a buddy."

She squishes me in a hug, and I laugh and wrap my arms around her, careful not to hurt the furball.

Once she's done smothering Valentine, I sit her at the table next to Izzy's high chair and take a deep breath before I hand her a jewelry box.

I rub my chin with the back of my knuckles. "I brought this with me to Corpus, but then decided to wait until we got home. And then I wanted to give it to you last night by the Christmas tree, but we got naked instead."

"Naked!" Izzy yells. "Naked, naked, naked."

Dammit.

"Brady Shepherd." Kat folds her arms. "You *are* a naughty boy."

I lean close and whisper into her ear. "I might need to be punished later."

She gives me a playful smack, and I laugh.

Motioning toward the square box, I tell her to open it.

Slowly, she pulls off the lid, and her face lights with a smile.

"A hummingbird! Brady, I love it." She leans over to kiss me and then holds out her arm. "Put it on me?"

I clasp the bracelet on her wrist where a little hummingbird dangles between two garnets. They're birthstones for her January birthday.

"It's beautiful. I love it." She pauses a moment. "Hey, um, did you open the gift I left you?" she asks, barely above a whisper.

I drag her chair closer and nuzzle against her neck. "I loved it so much, I didn't think I could survive one more fucking

347

minute without dragging your ass home." I nip her ear as I lace our fingers together. She looks a little dazed as she smiles up at me. I like knowing I make her just as crazy as she makes me. "By the way, tomorrow night, we're going out to celebrate your birthday."

Her grin widens. "How do you know about my birthday?"

"I learned a lot of things from your driver's license." Like the fact that her birthday is tomorrow.

"So... we're going out, out? Like on an actual date?"

"Like an actual date. Seeing how you are my actual girlfriend, I thought it might be nice."

She bounces in her seat. "Really?"

"Yes, really. I hear there's a great restaurant in the Tower of Americas in San Antonio. You can see the whole city from up there. I made reservations. Izzy is staying with the Macs, and we can take our time."

She jumps into my lap, wrapping me in a hug, and I push my nose into her hair.

"Love you, Brady."

"Love you, too, Kit Kat." And I plan to show her just how much.

EPILOGUE

KATHERINE
- Eight months later -

OH, DEAR LORD, I'M TIRED. WE HARVESTED THE LAST OF OUR lavender crop today. My hands are sore, my legs ache, and my feet feel like they might fall off, but I've never felt more satisfied. Seeing those wheelbarrows full of *our* first harvest—Brady's and mine—was amazing.

I'm ready to collapse into bed when two strong arms wrap around me.

"Hmm." I lean back against Brady. His damp chest fits against my back. "You smell good."

"Wish we could've taken that shower together," he growls in my ear.

I chuckle. As amazing as it's been to have my family in town to help with the lavender, it's definitely put a damper on our sexy times.

"It's better if my dad doesn't kill you," I tease.

Really, my dad loves Brady. He took one look at all of the

improvements Brady made on the farm this spring, and I swear he swooned a little. But we do go out of our way to not flaunt our living arrangement in his face.

Brady groans. "Why did we decide to have everyone over tonight?"

"Because my family is heading back to Corpus the day after tomorrow. What time are your parents coming over this evening?"

He pulls out his phone and glances at the time. "Half an hour. Mom said she's bringing that recipe you asked for."

"Oh, good." Turning around, I thread my fingers through his damp hair. "See how nice it is to have them close by?"

He grumbles because they call him every ten minutes, but I know deep down he likes being needed by them.

Turns out they sold their landscaping business to Jose, who had been running it in Brady's absence. And they realized that if they sold their house in Boston, they could get something much more affordable here. I *might* have sent them a few property listings. Anyway, they bought a small home two miles away from us and still had plenty left over in savings for their retirement.

I love his parents. Adore them. In fact, his mom was a big advocate of Brady staying here and fighting for our relationship. His dad supported it too, but his mom was the one who told him she'd kick Brady's ass if he let me go.

His parents aren't the only ones doing better financially. Brady's situation has turned around too. Fortunately, his roommate in Boston had his girlfriend move in, so Brady was off the hook for the lease.

Once we settled in here after the holidays, he offered me a partnership to help him run the farm, which I gladly accepted, and my first order of business was to expand our bath products. I didn't have to look that far because Frank, one of our customers at the farmers' fair, loved my lotions and soaps so much, his company bought the exclusive rights to sell our whole body line. And since Frank and I hit it off so well, he hired me as a part time consultant, which means I can work from home.

So for the first time in ages, the farm is doing really well. Now, Brady only works in Austin when he wants to.

He thought about quitting the parlor, but I know he loves having that creative outlet, so I encouraged him to continue. He works by appointment one or two nights a week, and that gives him time to draw and paint. I love that he's putting his MFA to good use. In fact, his artwork hangs all over our house, and I'm setting up an online Etsy store so he can sell his art directly to clients.

And I'm happy to say my ex finally got a clue and has left us alone. But Eric's also been pretty busy lately with that payoff scandal that landed him and his father in some hot water with the feds. Can't say I'm surprised. Or particularly heartbroken.

"My parents are watching Izzy tonight, right?" Brady murmurs in my ear.

I nod and fight a smile when I feel him harden against my belly. "Babe."

"What?" He laughs as his hands lower to my ass.

"Seriously. We can't. People will be here soon." But oh, God, I want to.

He groans and peels himself off me before he reaches down to adjust himself.

"Later," I promise, kissing his cheek. "We just have to be quiet."

Brady scrubs his face. "Fine." Then he grumbles, "Was it my imagination or did I hear we're supposed to dress up tonight?"

"Hmm. Yeah, I think our mothers are pretending we're the Brady Bunch. Heh. Get it? *Brady* Bunch?" I make a silly face, and he rolls his eyes, a smile ghosting his lips. "Speaking of getting ready, I need to get dressed, and I won't if you're here being all handsy, so scoot."

"You like when I'm handsy."

"I *love* when you're handsy, just not when I'm getting dressed."

Laughing, I push him out the door with instructions to change into something more appropriate and then try to entertain my parents. They've been staying in my old bedroom for a few nights while we harvest the lavender.

Neither Brady nor I could really deal with sleeping in Mel and Cal's bedroom, so we converted it into an office, and we turned the old office into our bedroom.

When I exit my room twenty minutes later, I'm glad I took the time to put on makeup. This dress is too pretty to have me looking like a haggard mess. My sister and I were out shopping last week, and she talked me into getting it. Of course her prompting is the only reason I'd be fool enough to get a white sundress. I'm sure Izzy will get her handprints all over it in five minutes.

When I step out into the living room, my dad wraps me in a big hug.

"*Mija*, you look beautiful."

"Thanks, Dad."

Then my mom, who I swear was wiping her eyes a second ago, gives me a hug. *What in the world?* Is this because she's happy I'm finally wearing a dress?

"Tori is setting the picnic table out back," my mom says, sniffling.

I swear she's going through menopause.

We head outside where we have a picnic table set up under the shade of the big oak tree. Brady's parents, my sister, and the Macs are already back here. My parents follow behind us with an armload of casseroles.

Izzy jumps out of Tori's arms and comes tearing across the yard toward us in a little red tutu and Boston Red Sox t-shirt. "Daddy! Daddy! Upsies! Upsies!" She lifts her hand to Brady, wanting him to pick her up.

He adopted her in late January. Watching how wonderful he is with her, how much he adores her, makes my heart feel like it's going to burst.

Brady's explained to Izzy that he's her uncle because he's afraid to take that away from Cal, but she insists on calling him daddy. Of course, he realizes she doesn't understand right now, but he doesn't want her to wake up one day and be shocked by something she could just know all along.

I tell her she has two daddies, and they both love her with all of their hearts.

Brady scoops her up and bounces her in his arms before whispering something in her ear that makes her giggle. She looks over to me, and he nods.

"Swing? Pweese?" she asks me with the sweetest expression on her face.

"Sure, darlin'." Here come the smudges, I laugh to myself.

I take her from Brady's arms, pausing to kiss his cheek. Then I go to put her on the swing when he stops me. "Why don't you put her on your lap, and I'll push the two of you?"

"Okay." I grin back at him.

Man, he looks so handsome this evening in a pair of dark jeans and a green polo that stretches across his broad shoulders.

I swallow the sudden lump in my throat when I see how he's looking at me. Like we're the only two people who exist.

His eyes travel down my face, over my bare shoulders and past the fitted white halter top before swinging back up again. A slow smile lifts his lips, and I shiver under his gaze.

I hear the words without him speaking. *I love you.*

An effervescent feeling that I can only describe as utter happiness rushes over me as I hug Izzy to my chest.

He stands there, watching us, a wide smile on his face.

I sit on the swing with Izzy, and Brady leans one arm on the chain of the swing.

"You look beautiful tonight," he whispers, brushing my hair back. "But then you always look beautiful."

Leaning back, I smile at him, my heart so full of love for this man.

I expect him to go behind us to push the swing. But instead —*ay Dios mío*—he gets down on one knee.

And then he takes out a little box.

Oh my God!

My mouth drops open, and I look around and realize everyone is taking pictures of us.

"Brady." I'm trembling from head to toe.

"I love you, Katherine. More than I ever thought was possible to love someone. Say yes. Be my wife. Be Izzy's mom. Let us love you forever."

I don't even have to think about my answer.

I'm nodding as Izzy and I go crashing into him. He catches us with a grunt and a laugh, barely keeping us upright when the baby and I squish him in a hug.

Hands reach down, and I realize Tori is scooping up Izzy. She gives me a wink and steps back with the baby in her arms.

My eyes cut back to Brady. "Yes, yes!" I laugh before kissing him again. In front of everyone.

Yes, I kiss him shamelessly. Because I love this man, and I want everyone to know it.

Our families start clapping behind us, and then finally my sister yells, "Get a room for the porno. I'm hungry."

My fiancé laughs, and we stand up and hug our parents. My

heart swells as I take a mental snapshot of our big, loud Texas family.

I don't know how this all happened. I don't know what I did to deserve such an amazing man or such a wonderful family. But if Cal and Mel taught me anything, it was to cherish every moment I have with them.

And I plan to. Each and every day for the rest of my life.

TO MY READERS

Thank you for reading SHAMELESS! I'd love to hear what you thought and hope you'll consider leaving a quick review on Goodreads and the vendor where you purchased it.

Tori's book is next! In RECKLESS, she's all grown up and trying to stay out of trouble. Keep flipping for a description of her book. You can read the first chapter of RECKLESS on my website where you can also subscribe to my monthly newsletter and get access to exclusive giveaways.

If Dani's story piqued your interest, be sure to check out her book, FINDING DANDELION, which is now available.

RECKLESS SYNOPSIS

Tori...

For the record, I'm not going to hook up with my boss.

I'm a lot of things—a screwup, a basket case, a flunky. But when I take a nanny job to be near my pregnant sister, I swear to myself I'll walk the straight and narrow, which means I cannot fall for my insanely hot boss.

I don't want to be tempted by that rugged rancher. By his chiseled muscles or southern charm or the way he snuggles his kids at bedtime. Ethan Carter won't get the key to my heart, no matter how much I want him.

Ethan...

Between us, she's the last thing I need as I finalize my hellish divorce.

What sane man trying to rebuild his life wants a hot nanny with long, sexy hair, curves for miles, and a smart mouth? A perfectly kissable, pouty mouth that I shouldn't notice.

My focus is on my kids and my ranch, not the insufferable siren who sleeps in the room next to mine. It doesn't matter that she wins over my kids in a heartbeat or runs my life better than I do. Tori Duran is the one woman I can't have and shouldn't want, no matter how much I crave her.

Reckless is a companion novel to *Shameless* and a complete standalone.

Head to www.lexmartinwrites.com to read the first chapter or purchase a copy.

FINDING DANDELION SYNOPSIS

When soccer all-star Jax Avery collides with Dani Hart on his twenty-first birthday, their connection is instantaneous and explosive. For the first time in years, Jax isn't interested in his usual hit-it and quit-it approach.

But Dani knows better. Allowing herself a night to be carefree and feel the intensity of their attraction won't change anything when it comes to dealing with a player. So when Jax doesn't recognize Dani the next time he sees her, it shouldn't be a total shock. The fact that he's her new roommate's brother? That's a shock.

Dani doesn't regret that night with Jax, just the need to lie about it. Since her roommate has made it clear what she thinks about her brother's "type" of girl, the last thing Dani wants is to admit what happened.

Jax knows he's walking a fine line on the soccer team. One more misstep and he's off the roster, his plans to go pro be damned. Except he can't seem to care. About anything... except for the one girl who keeps invading his dreams.

Despite Jax's fuzzy memory of his hot hookup with his sister's friend, he can't stay away from her, even if that means breaking his own rules. But there are bigger forces at work–realities that can end Dani's college career and lies that can tear them apart.

Jax realizes what he's losing if Dani walks away, but will he sacrifice his future to be with her? And will she let him if he does?

Finding Dandelion, the second book in the *Dearest* series, can be read a standalone novel. This new adult romance is recommended for readers 18+ due to mature content.

Head to www.lexmartinwrites.com to purchase a copy.

ACKNOWLEDGMENTS

This book made me miss my home state of Texas so much. If you're ever in the Hill Country, I hope you'll check out the lovely lavender farms and support that local industry.

I have several people to thank, and I need to start with my husband for all of the sweet things he's told our daughters over the years. I borrowed a few of his lines, but it's because he's so damn cute. Matt, I really appreciate your epic patience while I write and edit and freak out and do it all over again. Love you and our little home fries.

I got the theme for this book from something my grandmother always said to me. She's in so much of this story, and I wish I could tell her how much she's influenced me. I miss you, *abuelita*.

To my own big Texas family, and especially my parents, thanks for supporting me through this adventure.

Kimberly Brower, thank you for picking up my first release and seeing something special. You're the best agent ever.

To RJ Locksley for editing all of my books; Lauren Perry for these killer cover photos; Najla Qamber for this divine cover design; Amanda Maria for proofreading; Kylie, Beth and George at Give Me Books for handling my blitz and cover reveal; Jade Eby at Write Assistants for answering all of my Vellum questions and formatting my paperback; and Jena Camp at Indie Girl Blog Tours for helping me get organized with my release—you guys are worth your weight in gold.

Whitney Barbetti, you are my Magic 8 Ball. Whenever I get stuck in a draft, on an edit, in a layout, or in my life, you have an answer. I'm so grateful we met. Thanks for talking me off those ledges.

KL Grayson, Staci Hart, Stacy Kestwick, and Cole McCade, each of you kicked my ass with edits in the best possible way. Thanks for the tough love. I couldn't have written this book without you!

Alexis Durbin, Leslie McAdam, Becca Hensley Moore, Jenn Wood, Kristina Goff Brooks, Audra Adkins, Sarah Alban, and Jules Barnard, you're the best betas ever! Thank you for your precious feedback.

Jullie Anne Caparas and Doris Gray, what the hell would I do without you? I have no damn clue. Thanks for making me pretty swag and mugs and tshirts. *tackle hugs*

I have immense gratitude for Becca and Krista Ritchie, who always help me with any self-publishing crisis that come up.

Serena McDonald, thanks for your late night pep talks and for being an awesome friend. Candi Kane, I can't have a release without running everything by you—my cover photos, my blurb, my giveaway ideas. Thanks for always being there for me! Selena Lanovara Scott, thanks for your Harley expertise. You're a bad ass, babe. I finally found someone who loves Dunkin' Donuts more than I do.

To my Wildcats, you guys fucking rock my socks. *ass smacks* Kim Ber Lee, thanks for naming the diner!

Bloggers, there are so many of you to thank. Aestas Book Blog, The Dirty Laundry, The Literary Gossip, Three Girls and a

Book Obsession, Love Between the Sheets, Give Me Books, One Click Addicts, Smut Muffins, Schmexy Girl Book Blog, The Bookaholic Fairies, The Book Bellas, Smokin' Hot Book Blog, Rumpled Sheets, Sinfully Sexy Book Reviews, The Romance Vault, I Bookin' Love To Read, Smut Fanatics, Book Baristas, Literary Misfit, Owl Always Be Reading, and Teacups & Book Love are just a few of the bloggers who helped me out early on. A big hug to you and the many others who shared my books with their readers.

A huge thanks to Laurence, Joseph and Rob, the attorneys who helped me figure out the adoption process in Texas. I left out one detail, but I'm guessing you're not gonna read my romance, so we're good! haha.

To my friend who said you can indeed get pregnant while taking birth control pills and using condoms, thanks for sharing your real life experience with me. Your son is adorable, btw!

Lastly, to my readers. You have no idea what kind of impact you've made on my life by reading my books. Thank you from the bottom of my heart. I hope I give as much to you as you give to me.

Brady's story has been rattling around in my head for a few years, and I'm really grateful to share it with you. I know it's a darker story than my others. Last year was a dark year for me, and I suppose that seeped into the book. But I'm also a big believer in happy endings, so I hope that underscored Brady's journey with Kat.

If you enjoyed this story, let me know. Perhaps there'll be more to come with some of these characters.

xo,

Lex

ALSO BY LEX MARTIN

All of my books can be read as standalones. Each one features a different couple.

Reckless

The Dearest Series:

Dearest Clementine

Finding Dandelion

Kissing Madeline

All About the D

(cowritten with Leslie McAdam)

ABOUT THE AUTHOR

Lex Martin is the *USA Today* bestselling author of *Shameless*, the *Dearest* series, and *All About the D*, books she hopes her readers love but her parents avoid. To stay up-to-date with her releases, head to her website and subscribe to her newsletter, or join her Facebook group, Lex Martin's Wildcats.

www.lexmartinwrites.com